D1202638

"The Skaladeskas always know where you are."

Marina felt a nauseating shiver creep over her shoulders, but now she understood a whole lot more. "You're tracking me. A bug? A GPS? Where? Why?"

"Lev wants you. And so does Roman. They all do. They need you...or so they think."

"You don't." The words slipped out before Marina could take them back, and she immediately regretted the way they made her sound. As if she cared.

"Damn right. You," said Varden, his voice cool and bitter, "are a threat to me and my position among the tribe. If you return and take your place as Lev's granddaughter...well, let's just say that will adversely affect my influence on him as well as Roman."

"Fear not, Dr. Varden. There's no chance of that happening."

AMAZON ROULETTE

A MARINA ALEXANDER ADVENTURE

C.M. GLEASON

AVID PRESS

Amazon Roulette: A Marina Alexander Adventure

© 2015 Colleen Gleason, Inc.

Cover design: Kim Killion
Interior design: Dan Keilen

ISBN: 978-1-931419-84-0

To Gary March
For years of asking about those copper bugs.
Thank you for keeping me going!

PRELUDE

The Lake Superior Basin
100 Million Years Ago

The ground shook, and molten liquid struggled from beneath to erupt. At last, it burst free, spilling over the land—a searing, fiery red river that covered the earth.

Forceful magma eruptions such as these lasted twenty-five million years, pushing the strata of the earth into a massive divergence, leaving a sweeping, deep rift. Millions of years later, this massive basin would be known as Lake Superior.

The most widespread individual lava flow on earth, what is called the Greenstone Lava Flow, covered what became the Keweenaw Peninsula and stretched into Wisconsin, submerging rocky ground under its molten path. When the doming, rifting, and eruptions caused by the earth's molten core eased, it left sediment that would later form the greatest concentration of natural native copper on earth in Michigan's Upper Peninsula.

This profusion of copper-bearing rock settled in a swatch of area a mere three to six kilometers wide, and extended from the northernmost point of the Keweenaw to approximately 150 kilometers south.

Millions of years later, a long series of glacial advances and retreats scraped the land, gouging out the rest of the Great Lakes. Tall black spruce trees were buried under glacial sediment. Eons later, fine sand dropped by the flow of water overmulched the trees and smothered them. Some of the glacial movement caused erosion on the surface, exposing copper to the elements. Some chunks of copper were carried southward.

Once formed and flooded into the greatest freshwater surface in the world, Lake Superior became a catalyst that influenced weather, culture, and environment for the entire basin.

Great and violent thunderstorms erupting from the lake spawned hurricane-like gales, waterspouts, and tornados. Odd, eerie cloud formations with streaks of orange and blue colored the sky after these storms. During twilight, the colorful phenomenon known as the Northern Lights flared. Strange mirages formed due to shifts in air and temperature, leaving the impression of inverted landscape elements floating in midair, or shifting weirdly about.

It was no wonder early people considered that great lake a divinity in her own right.

Four thousand years ago, men who lived near this body of water attributed not only the wealth of fish and other sources of food, but also the soft bronze metal found in the ground, to the goodness of this great and divine lake. Mishi Bizi, the water panther, was thought to conduct the powers of the water and the underground, giving these gifts in exchange for worship and sacrifice.

Perhaps it was Mishi Bizi himself—or perhaps it was the scrape of a glacier—that long before had left the glint of metal exposed, catching the attention of an early miner. Once the usefulness of the metal was understood, it did not take him long to find other caches of copper.

Early man became adept at identifying places to mine the native metal by examining the terrain as well as rock and ground formations. He observed the hoarfrosts, and noted the areas where foliage did not turn white, and found copper there. He watched for long, continuous depressions in the soil, knowing the ground would be weaker above a soft vein. Spindly or stunted trees, odd-colored vegetation, and strange patterns of fungus also indicated the presence of the useful metal.

Men and women dug for centuries, hammering the soft metal and breaking off hunks of it to use for tools. Sometimes, they found tiny pebbles of the metal and made beads. Other places yielded sheets of the metal, and still others exposed large, boulder-like hunks.

There has never been another place on earth that yielded such a massive amount of copper.

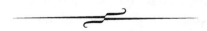

Then…more than three thousand years ago, a strange ship appeared across the great expanse of Lake Superior. Men of another place and language landed on the shores.

The local man traded his copper for the strangers' goods. There was an abundance of the metal, and the foreigners found the rust-colored material intriguing. The natives taught them about copper's healing properties, showed them how it could be twisted around a wrist or strung in beads on a leather line and worn to promote healing and protection.

The foreigners stayed, then left…then returned and took more copper with them.

For decades, they visited, filling their ships with the ore and disappearing into the vast expanse of the gray-blue shimmer of Lake Superior. The native man didn't know who they were or from where they came. But still they traded.

And when the foreigners visited and one of their numbers happened to die, instead of burying them in a mound as the Lake Superior natives did, they sought a hidden copse of trees, or a cavern in which to repose the body. They created odd formations with white stones—always white stones, all the same size—and piled them in a pointed hill above the body. This, they explained, marked the direction in which the body's soul would move in order to shift into the afterlife.

When the foreigners came for the last time, they had many dead on the ship upon their arrival. The few remaining found a deep cave and placed their leaders and friends far into its depths.

They piled the stones in an antechamber to the place where they were buried, taking days and weeks to make the hills just so. They measured the sky, plotted the ground, and determined the perfect position, using information from their homeland.

And when they were done, when they knew they would leave the beautiful lake with its bronze metal for the last time, they closed the entrance to the cave. Blocked off the sacred place so the souls of their companions would rise into the sky, or sink into the ground, and become one, immortal, with the earth.

Then, their monumental task complete, they left the country of copper.

PRELUDE II

June 30, 1908
Tunguska, Siberia

The sky had been glowing for days. Night reigned for mere moments, then gave way to a red glow filling the heavens. The weather had been unseasonably warm—even hot—for weeks. Cyclones of greater intensity than usual churned over the ground in Tunguska. Drought caused the grasses that fed the goats and reindeer cared for by the Skaladeska tribe to turn brown and dry, and even the brief but sparse thunderstorms could not save the plants.

A dull booming in the distance rose in intensity through the hours of the day.

The air began to shift. The environment changed.

All creatures living in this region felt the imminence of something, and they ran for shelter. Reindeer, hares, birds...all sought their dens, holes, the brush of their nests. Men of the local tribes, knowing that their death was coming, bathed, then changed into clean clothing to await their end.

A streak of red swept the sky, near the horizon.

The earth gave a great tremor, then stilled. It had threatened upheaval with smaller vibrations in the days before, but this one caused the trees to shake.

The wind picked up, stirring the leaves and clattering the branches in an eerie dance.

A second streak of orange-glowing fire blazed across the sky, flattened to a black saucer, and disappeared.

The wind gusted violently. The earth trembled.

A whistling sound rent the air, followed by the cutting, rock-strong wind. It pushed a man so heavily he fell into the trunk of a tree, then tripped into the glowing embers of his fire.

A hideous noise—indescribable, fierce and bone-shattering—filled the air. Everything moved, shook, trembled, clattered, crashed. Suddenly blazing trees fell with dull thuds, their burning branches crashing into each other, setting the moss and grass to burning.

A violent thunderbolt rolled and clapped, deafening the creatures that remained. The world was wrapped in thick, angry smoke, blanketing the air, smothering the land.

Suddenly bright lightning flashed over the hill, like another sun had suddenly risen, as more thunderclaps boomed in the air. The ground shook. Nothing could stand upright. More red and orange flashes blazed through the sky...

And then, at last, the sounds began to fade. The glow in the sky settled into a pink dust.

Miraculously, the wail of an infant filled the silence.

A babe lay in the midst of the destruction.

The morning of July 1, 1908, dawned.

It took nineteen years before a scientific expedition at last found its way to the devastation that had been wrought that day and night of June 30, 1908.

The expedition, led by Leonid Kulik, discovered 850 square miles of flattened trees. It found some charred remains of tree trunks, but other trees were still growing tall and strong and green. Few eyewitnesses remained to tell the tale, and many of their stories conflicted.

Over the decades that followed, various theories for the cause of the event were presented. Many scientists believed a meteorite had struck the earth...but no metal remains were found in the area.

Others presented the theory that the meteorite had exploded before striking the earth, four or five miles in the air...but again, there was not enough metallic evidence to prove this theory.

Still others suggested that a spaceship had exploded, or the volatile volcanoes of this Siberian region—some of the most destructive in the history of the earth—had caused the great devastation. Or that an earthquake had shifted the world in Tunguska. Or that aliens had landed, and then left...

Whatever the cause, life in this region was forever changed.

And the infant birthed during—or protected by—this event now thrived among the secretive tribe of the Skaladeskas.

His name was Lev.

Still the earth is bruised and broken
by the ones who still want more.

— Marty Haugen

PROLOGUE

October 1—Present Day
New York City

The executive conference room stretched long and silent, the midafternoon sun shining through silver-tinted windows. Through the smoky view one could see much of Midtown Manhattan, the architecture appearing no more than a hodgepodge of black, gray, cream, and brown building blocks. Yellow cabs mingled with trucks and other toy-sized vehicles twenty stories below.

In approximately three hours, the doors would open and the room would be filled with an elite group of some of the most powerful men and women in the world. Dressed in five-thousand-dollar suits and armed with top-of-the-line electronic tablets and smartphones, the members of the private group known as The Alliance would settle around the table for a convivial meal.

For by the time they entered the room, their off-the-record, ultra-private meeting with several powerful politicians would be over, the negotiations completed, and all that remained would be the opportunity to socialize over excellent food and libation. The Alliance members would congratulate each other on another year of being "overlooked" by the EPA, the legal system, and other regulatory agencies throughout the United States, Europe, and Asia.

Present would be the CEO of a major chemical company, currently being investigated by the US's EPA for dumping in the Ohio River.

And also the CEO of a well-known international electric corporation that had been violating clean-air and -water standards for years, both in the US and Europe, where its name was equally well known.

Also attending was the CEO of an energy company recently in the news for a massive spill of benzene into a medium-sized river in Nebraska. So far, no legal action seemed to have gained traction...thanks to the strength of The Alliance.

A mining company was also represented at the meeting. It was one of the more notorious ones in the world, known for continued, wide-ranging environmental destruction during their metal extraction processes. An electronics company in South Korea, a leather tanning corporation from Taiwan...and other manufacturing companies were represented.

And integral to the entire group: one of the most powerful lobbyist groups in the world.

But for now, the French doors swung open to the empty conference dining room, and three staff members from Le Beau-Joux Events hurried in. They pushed carts laden with silver, fine china, and chargers of gleaming red. Crystal goblets for water, different ones for white wine, and a third, broader style for a red vintage clinked delicately against each other as their cart rumbled alongside the mahogany conference table.

Fourteen place settings. First, the ruby chargers, fifteen inches in diameter. On top of them went sleek, square black plates, hand-painted specially for this event with a design of tiny red berries that rose like Braille dots on the edges. Then a translucent gold plate, hardly larger than a teacup saucer, was arranged in the center of each black square.

Next, the staffers arranged gold-plated silver utensils around each plate setting: eight pieces per guest. Three crystal goblets. A teacup and saucer. Then the staffers set to folding the napkins.

It took them ten minutes to fold fourteen black-and-white patterned napkins into an intricate lotus-flower shape. Each origami specimen was carefully settled onto the center of the gilt saucer, looking like an Escher version of a water flower on a golden lily pad.

The staffers had just finished assembling the centerpiece—a long, low monstrosity of exotic orchids in red, pink, and white arranged in a soft black leather vase that stretched nearly half the length of the table—when the door opened once more.

LaTrelle, the event supervisor from Le Beau-Joux, looked up. "May I help you?" he asked the newcomer.

"Yes. I have brought the special delicacies." The new arrival paused in the doorway and gestured with the silver tray he carried. On it was a rectangular container about the size of a shoebox. It was made from some sturdy black material lacquered into a shine, and there were elegant silver handles on each end, making it look like a miniature trunk. Two heavy silver ribbons had been fastened around the box, and they were held in place by red wax seals.

Sealing in the freshness, LaTrelle supposed, trying to make out the symbol on the seals. Whatever. But...

"Special delicacies?" He frowned, pulling out his work order to check the event menu while his colleagues continued their tasks, setting up crystal salt shakers and onyx pepper mills at regular intervals among the orchids. He flipped through the papers on his clipboard, scanning quickly. "You mean dessert? There's supposed to be flambé of pears with caramel custard finished with sea salt, and then a chocolate flan, but—"

"Ah, no," said the man. He had an accent LaTrelle couldn't place—but that was nothing new. Half the people in New York had accents. "Not dessert. A special delicacy, ordered by Mr. Wen-Ho. I have the purchase order here." Still carefully holding the tray, he plucked a folded paper from the inside pocket of his pristine white caterer's coat. A brass nametag gleamed over the handkerchief pocket, but LaTrelle was too far away to read it.

LaTrelle looked at the document and shook his head. Sure enough. Authorization for twenty "special delicacies" from a company called Gaia, Inc., billed to Mr. Wen-Ho's account on Le Beau-Joux letterhead, signed off by Missy Addington, his boss, yesterday. An additional note added: *Because of its highly perishable quality, Gaia, Inc., will deliver directly to site before four p.m. day of event.*

"Nice of Missy to tell me," he grumbled. She was usually much more organized than this, but he'd gotten a call four hours ago that she was sick. Really sick—sick enough to be on her way to the hospital due to an extreme allergic reaction. A nasty rash and fever. So he'd had to take over management of this major event, and that wasn't a problem at all, except for things like this. After all, LaTrelle intended to start his own catering company to do chi-chi events like this…just as soon as he saved up a little more money.

For now, he chalked up this pothole in the road of life to experience and learning how to turn on a dime. "Does it—they— need to be refrigerated—uh—sir?"

"No. But they are very fragile. I'll place it on the sideboard myself," the other man told him, moving to do just that. He set a box in the center of one of the black-and-white lily pad napkins, arranging it with precision.

"What's in it?" asked LaTrelle, looking at the shiny black box. "Some sort of special sushi or caviar?"

"Maybe it's chocolate-covered ants," suggested BeckyAnn, one of the servers who'd come to stand near him as he watched the man place his burden on the buffet. "Or grasshoppers. Don't they eat them over in China?"

"Sushi is Japanese," LaTrelle told her patiently. "Mr. Wen-Ho is from Korea. And I don't know if they eat chocolate-covered insects over there. Bird nests, yes."

"Maybe it's raw dog—literally," joked Yoyo, the other server. "They eat dog in Korea, I know that."

"Ugh." BeckyAnn made gagging sounds, but stopped when LaTrelle gave her a warning look, jerking his head toward the man from Gaia, Inc. He had settled the box carefully on a raised serving platter he'd brought, arranging it in the center of the credenza at the back of the conference room.

"I think we're all finished here for now," LaTrelle said, straightening a salad fork. "Is there anything else we can do for you?" he asked the newcomer.

"No, I think everything is just fine," he replied with a smile. "I'm confident the guests will enjoy their delicacies. It's one of our specialties. When it's time to serve, simply crack the wax seals and open the box."

"Great," said LaTrelle, already thinking about the lobster croquettes that needed to be finished in the next two hours. "Thanks very much for setting that up for us," he added. "What was your name again, sir?"

"Dannen. Dannen Fridkov," he said. Then, after giving a brief bow, he strode from the room.

ONE

Ten days earlier: September 21
Keweenaw Peninsula
Upper Michigan

Don't you think we ought to get back? The sun's getting pretty low," Kendra McElroy said to her companion. "Aren't there bears around here?"

The bottom of the orange ball of sun rested just where Lake Superior met the horizon, appearing many miles in the distance from the mountainous terrain over which they'd been hiking. Below, its blaze cut a matching path over the glistening expanse of water that stretched out past another small crop of mountains. The air was crisp and filled with the scent of pine, along with the screeches of crows and seagulls.

The last two days had been filled with furious thunderstorms, ragged lightning spearing into the forests, and torrents of rain—all of which caused the Sturgeon River to swell. But today, at last, had been a fine day for exploring the terrain where, for ages upon ages, massive amounts of copper had been mined. The Copper Country, as this northernmost jutting peninsula was called, had been the source of literally tons of its namesake metal extracted from the earth by man from prehistoric times through the mid-twentieth century.

"Don't you want to watch the sunset with me?" Matt Granger tightened his grip on her hand and wagged his eyebrows suggestively. "It'll be so romantic."

Kendra laughed. He was so cute! "You call black flies the size of bats romantic? And bears and wolves lurking about? Besides, it's getting cold." She paused to zip up her fleece vest and wished for a hat. What had started as a sunny Indian summer day had turned into downright cold.

"I'll keep you warm."

"That's what you said when we went skiing...and I nearly froze to death!" But she was still smiling, and, dropping his hand, he moved closer so he could slip an arm around her waist. "It is a beautiful sunset, I'll grant you that. Your Copper Country is something, even with the flies."

"Let's just climb over this little hill, and we can sit and watch the sun go down...then we'll head back. I promise I won't let any bears get you."

"I'm going to hold you to that."

They sat on a rocky outcropping with the rippling waves of pines and fiery-leaved trees spanning the distance between them and the water. A golden moon hung behind them, and Kendra could see more stars dotting the twilight sky than she saw during the darkest part of night back in Columbus.

"I'm glad the storms ended and we had the chance to come out here before we had to leave," she said, tipping her head to rest on his shoulder. She was cold, and getting hungry, but there was no one else she'd rather be with. "It would have been a bummer if I'd had to go back without seeing this."

"There's nothing like the fall colors up here. The colors are so intense...well, take a look." He pointed. "Do you see that big fallen tree over there? Looks like it was hit by lightning, probably during these last few days of storms. Hey...maybe it's that cave that guy was talking about. He said he was going to come back and look inside tomorrow." He hoisted to his feet. "I'm going to go take a gander. You never know what might be there."

Kendra watched Matt with an indulgent smile. That was her guy: an archeologist trapped in a computer programmer's life. He'd grown up here in the Upper Peninsula of Michigan, and they'd met at Ohio State two years ago. This was the first time he'd brought her home, but their sixteen-hour drive from Columbus to Houghton had been filled with tales of exploring copper mines and camping on Isle Royale, so she felt as if she'd been here many times.

He'd taken her on the five-hour ferry ride to Isle Royale, a wild, uninhabited island in Lake Superior, on their first full day in Houghton in order to show her the prehistoric copper mines. To Kendra, they looked like little more than deep holes; they weren't anything like the cave mines she'd expected to see. And the hammers that had been used to chip away at the copper veins were shaped like large eggs. Sure, they were four thousand years old, but how anyone had recognized them as tools used by the cave men, she had no idea. But because Matt, who fancied himself the Indiana Jones of Northern Michigan, found it interesting, she found it interesting.

Or, at least, she acted like she did. True love required sacrifice.

"Hey, Ken, come here!" he called. His voice was high-pitched with excitement. "It does! It looks like there *is* a cave behind here."

She pulled to her feet, glancing at the sun, which had dipped a third of the way below the lake. "Is it a mine?" she asked, interested in spite of her freezing ears. It would be cool to be the first to find an old mine, and Matt would be in raptures for days. She pulled her hair out of its ponytail and shook it out, hoping it would help keep her ears warm.

"I don't know. It's pretty far from the other areas copper's been found; probably not a mine. But maybe a home site or burial place. It looks like it's been hidden behind these rocks for years… see the black smudge there? That guy was right—lightning must have struck here and tumbled some of these rocks out of the way. And the trees were growing in front of it? When this one fell, it moved them out of the way." He was beginning to sound excited. "Ken, this could be something!"

"We can come back tomorrow before we leave," she offered, looking unappreciatively at the narrow sliver of black. "I'm getting cold."

"I've got a flashlight in my bag…come on, let's go in."

"What about bears?"

He grabbed her hand. "No bears in here, Ken…the entrance has been closed off for years. Centuries, probably—maybe even millennia! There could be prehistoric artifacts in there." His eyes were wild with excitement.

"Come on, hon. You're not going to find anything tonight."

"I just have a feeling about this place. What if there's something important in here? People have been arguing for years whether the cave men traded their copper with the Europeans, but there's not been one whit of evidence. What if there's something in there that proves it?" The words tumbled out of his mouth almost faster than he could form them.

Kendra tamped back her growing annoyance. Men needed to be taken firmly in hand and reminded of reality in a calm, logical manner. Even treasure hunters like Matt. Especially treasure hunters like Matt. "Honey, this is a cave. One of hundreds up in this never-ending forest. What makes you think it's any different from any other cave you've explored since you were ten? It's probably an old bear's den, in which case, I don't want to stick around and see if it comes back."

But Matt was already inside, and she saw the glow of his flashlight. Huffing angrily, she climbed over the broken tree trunk and stood in the doorway. "Come on, Matt!"

"Kendy, look at this!" He poked his head out of the entrance, and even in the lowering light, she could see his the whites of his eyes, they were open so wide. "I think I've found something!" He was a five-year-old on Christmas morning.

Sighing, she started forward and slipped into the damp darkness of the cave. At least in here, the steady wind from the lake wasn't blasting into her ears. The interior was tall enough that she could stand easily. "What?"

"Look at this!" He was pointing to a small triangular pile of stones. The only thing keeping him from jumping around was the fact that his head brushed the ceiling.

"It's a pile of stones."

"Don't you remember me telling you about that lake in Wisconsin? Where they found those pyramids on the bottom?"

She didn't. "Yeah, I guess." She rubbed her hands together and wished for a pair of gloves. "Can we go now? We can come back tomorrow."

"I've seen pictures—this looks like a miniature version of those pyramids. Archeologists don't know where they came from—they weren't made by the Native Americans. Some people think they think they might have been from the Phoenicians! Oh my God, if this is true, I—" He took a deep breath and stopped. "Let me start from the beginning."

"Can't you tell me on the way home? I'm really getting cold, and I'm hungry, Matt!"

But he was in lecture mode. Rapid-fire lecture mode—one that nearly left her in the dust with the rattling off of dates and theories and numbers. "There've been people trying for centuries to prove there were other people here—from Europe or Asia— who either mined or traded for the copper. There was tons of copper taken from the earth here—three thousand years ago, and we're not finding any remains of it. So where did it all go? Five hundred thousand tons of copper doesn't just disappear."

Kendra gave up and sat on a large boulder. "But you told me yourself, there's no evidence that much copper's missing—"

"But there's no proof that it *isn't*! No one knows how much copper was mined up here by the people with the stone hammers. I've done some of my own calculations, and I believe it's true— nearly five hundred thousand tons of copper taken out of those prehistoric mines."

"Honey, you told me, it's a legend! A myth! That there's no evidence any other culture lived here at that time—whenever it was—besides the natives. And you said yourself, all the experts say there's—"

"But what if it isn't? And what if this little stone pyramid was made by the same people who made the pyramids at the bottom of Rock Lake? What if there's another site in this area that's not underwater!" He looked at her in the dim glow of the flashlight, his eyes pleading and, at the same time, lit with an unholy flame. Was this how Howard Carter had talked to his wife while in search of Tutankhamen's tomb? (Had Howard Carter even been married? Poor woman.) "Just go in with me a little further, okay? It's warmer in here, isn't it?"

"Not really. But what if we get lost?"

"We won't. I've been exploring caves since I was ten; I know how to find my way out. Come on, sweetie, this could be really big! Just twenty minutes more, okay? If we don't find anything, we leave. I promise."

But it was only fifteen minutes later that Matt's dreams came true.

They rounded the corner of the tunnel they'd been walking through and found themselves in a chamber the size of half a football field.

"Oh my God…" he breathed. Kendra stopped behind him and felt her heart begin to race.

"Oh my God is an understatement," she said. "Wow!"

Two tall piles of smooth white rocks created neat pyramids, approximately ten feet tall, one at each end of the chamber.

"Mother Nature's amazing, but there's no way she did this."

Matt came unfrozen and started toward them, beaming his light around. "This is incredible, Kendy! There's no way the ancestors of the Ojibwa made these. No way. This has got to be from another culture."

"It's amazing, Matt! I can't believe it!" She really was excited, and had almost forgotten how cold she was. Almost. "Can we go now? We can come back tomorrow and spend more time looking around."

He hesitated, beaming the light around the room a little more. Then, "All right. Let's go. It looks like the flash is getting a little dimmer anyway." He grinned and put an arm around her. "I can't believe it, Kendy! Just call me Indiana Jones!"

She had been. He just didn't know it.

"Or maybe it should be Keweenaw Jones!" he said gleefully.

They walked out of the chamber and started back through the tunnel, hurrying now that they were on their way out. Kendra followed Matt when the area became too narrow for them to walk side by side, and she hurried along hardly paying any attention until she realized she was half crouching for the first time.

The ceiling was too low.

"Matt, I don't think we're going the right way."

"Yes we are. Just keep following me; I'll get us out of here."

"Matt, I'm bending over. I didn't have to bend at all on the way in!"

He stopped and she bumped into him. "Maybe you're right. I'm feeling funny, too. Kind of lightheaded."

"Let's turn around and go back this way." She tugged at his arm, realizing her head was starting to feel a bit muzzy too.

He pushed past her and she turned around to follow him. She noticed the flashlight beam, which had started off as a clean white light, was dirty now. A dingy yellow.

"Where are we?" she asked, panicked, ten minutes later when they had neither returned to the chamber nor found the tall, wide tunnel they'd come in through.

"I don't know, Kendra. Let's just go up around this corner, maybe the main tunnel is up here." But he didn't sound certain, and the note in his voice made her stomach squeeze painfully.

She was feeling dizzier now. Perhaps it was because she was hungry and tired…or perhaps it was because something bad was in the air.

When Matt rounded the corner, he tripped over a small stone and tumbled to the ground. As he fell, he slid against the side of the cave wall, and suddenly, stones and dirt and pebbles were raining down on them.

Kendra screamed his name, and more rubble fell in a loud rush, sending dust and pelting rocks onto her head and shoulders.

The light was gone; either he'd dropped it or it had broken. It was dark, evilly dark, like she'd been dropped into a bottle of ink.

"Matt!" she cried. Then something heavy slammed into the back of her head and the darkness swamped her consciousness.

TWO

September 21
Somewhere in Siberia

Looks like they've been gone a long damn while," said Gabe MacNeil. "But this is definitely the place."

He scanned what had once been the Command Central-like room in a compound tucked deeply into the Siberian mountains. More than five years ago, he and a civilian named Marina Alexander had been captured and nearly killed by the group of ecoterrorists who lived here. They'd escaped, but had no way of identifying their location or navigating their return after being swept away down a river, then on foot over rough terrain through miles of the infinite wilderness.

He ran his fingers over the empty slot where a hard drive once existed and noticed the shells of broken computer monitors. Glass and debris littered the floor and countertops, and the furnishings had been gnawed or made into burrows by the wild animals that had taken refuge. The high-tech, solar-powered hideout of the Skaladeskas had clearly been abandoned months, if not years, ago. Between political jockeying with Moscow to get assistance or even permission to look for the compound, and the vast expanse of Taymyria and its mountains—not to mention all the other terrorist leads the CIA and Homeland Security had to follow up on—it was no wonder it had taken so long to find what was left of the place.

At least there'd been no sight or sign of threats from the Skalas during the last five years. Gabe figured it was too much to hope they'd gone away for good, but he was an optimist at heart.

"They made certain there wasn't anything valuable left for us either." Gabe's commander, Colin Bergstrom, had been wandering around the room. "Did quite a number on the place."

Other members of the recovery team were present, sweeping for any possible evidence, and documentation as well. Considering the fact that some of the roofs and walls had been destroyed by what looked like small, local explosions, it didn't seem likely anything of importance had survived the elements.

Gabe was a member of Special Task Team G, the elite counterterrorism arm of the CIA that worked inside the homeland. Thus, he'd been surprised when Bergstrom insisted on accompanying him to remote Taymyria, located in Siberia. There'd been no obvious reason for Bergstrom to travel with his subordinate when he came to verify that the ruins had indeed been the stronghold of the Skaladeskas. Yet, from the very beginning, the discovery and investigation of Victor Alexander—Marina's father—his brother Roman, and their group of ecoterrorists seemed to be a personal concern for Gabe's commander.

"Want to show me what else you remember?" Bergstrom asked, adjusting his glasses. They always left little red marks on the sides of his nose, and he had a habit of shifting them out of place as if to relieve the discomfort. "The living quarters? And wasn't there a library of some sort? And a lab?"

Although it had been five years, and at the time Gabe had been weak from torture and lack of food and water, as well as a bullet through his arm, he remembered quite a bit of the layout.

Part of the reason the Skalas had remained hidden so successfully for so long, aside from the fact that they had equipment that blocked any external radar or sonar scans, was the way the compound had been camouflaged. Large solar panels and architecture were built into the side of the remote mountain, carefully designed to blend with their surroundings and provide their own source of energy. But once inside, the environment had been created to be sleek and simple, and yet state of the art.

"I wasn't ever in the living quarters," Gabe replied as they walked down a debris-strewn corridor. Was that stain from when he'd been shot, or just a bit of mildew that had spread near the floor? His arm ached at the memory, and not for the first time, he wondered how—or why—the man named Rue Varden had shot him in the bicep instead of in the chest or head when he was in point-blank range. "Marina was kept in much nicer accommodations than I was, being the only blood relation to the Skalas' heir apparent."

"They came after her father. Roman Alexander brought his brother back here. Think he'd come after her again, now?" asked Bergstrom. "Or be in some sort of contact with her. She's the heir to the group. Wouldn't he try and get her to join them?"

"She wouldn't go," Gabe replied. He realized with more than mild surprise that it had been more than ten months since he'd last seen Marina. Not for any particular reason other than the fact that they were both busy with the constant travel and odd hours their respective careers—and, in her case, volunteer work—demanded. For those reasons, their relationship was a casual, non-committed one—though he certainly enjoyed her company. "They nearly killed her, too, remember?"

Bergstrom looked at him with an odd, closed expression. "Stranger things have happened. Sometimes women do inexplicable things for a man."

Gabe frowned. That uneasy feeling he had about his superior and his connection to the Skaladeskas intensified. "What's going on, Colin?" he asked, stopping abruptly next to a sagging door. "Why did you come here?"

Bergstrom gave him an unreadable look as he smoothed a hand over the wisps of hair on his scalp. "I wanted to see the place where Roman Alexander hid for so long."

Gabe's suspicions crystallized. "That's it. You knew him, didn't you? In England, when he was at Oxford. When all of that stuff came down in the early seventies, and he was suspected of stealing those secrets from the astrophysics lab. He and that other scientist disappeared right afterward—and they were never found." His eyes narrowed. What was he missing? "But it was never proven they stole that data. And then in the eighties, his identical twin Victor showed up in Northern Michigan, and lived there for decades until Roman brought him back here. And now Victor's dead."

"That's right," Bergstrom said. His expression had turned faintly amused. "Chalk it up to a case of extreme curiosity."

They continued walking, but Gabe's thoughts didn't settle. Something was off. His boss had gone on a trip to Siberia simply due to curiosity? Not likely.

Just then, they came upon a massive metal door, reinforced by half-dollar-sized bolts. Gabe tucked his questions away for the time being, to be pulled out and mulled over later—probably on the plane back to Langley.

He examined the door, more than a little surprised it seemed to still be intact. For behind the impervious metal enclosure was a priceless library—or, at least, there'd been a library when he and Marina were here five years ago. He supposed they might have tried to pack it up and remove it, though that would have been difficult to do during the speedy evacuation that certainly had occurred.

But then again, Lev—the old man who was Marina's grandfather and also the patriarch of the Skaladeskas—had seemed to value the room's contents above all else. Including his or anyone's life.

The collection of books protected by this military-strength door had been given to Ivan the Terrible's grandfather by a Byzantine king, and contained scrolls, documents, and other pieces of writing from ancient civilizations. On his deathbed, Ivan had entrusted the library to one of Marina's ancestors, shipping it secretly out of Moscow to Siberia to keep it safe from his enemies. Here it had remained, hidden and protected by members of her family…a family that had turned to ecoterrorism in the last decade.

The Skaladeskas believed Gaia, Mother Earth, was a complete living and breathing entity. Distraught by the destruction of the planet's natural resources, the tribe had begun to act out in defense of the earth—including causing several earthquakes more than five years ago. That incident was what had put the group on the radar, so to speak, of the CIA and Homeland Security, and what had caused Marina Alexander and Gabe MacNeil to end up working together.

"Help me get this door open," Gabe said, adrenaline suddenly rushing through him. Was it possible they'd left the library here? Or at least some of the documents? Surely not…

Maybe they believed it would be protected until they could return and salvage it. According to Marina, the library was priceless and an incredible find. She compared it to the Library of Alexandria, or something that might be found in that crazy movie *National Treasure*—which Gabe had enjoyed in spite of himself.

"We're going to need something more than that," Bergstrom said, gesturing to the piece of iron pipe Gabe had picked up. He withdrew his weapon and aimed it at the metal lock. "Duck," he said, his face set, and fired.

Christ. Gabe hardly had a chance to move before the gun discharged, and the bullet pinged onto the metal, then ricocheted. *That was close.*

Which was why he hadn't done such a foolhardy thing. Something was definitely up with Colin Bergstrom.

The sounds of gunfire brought some of the recovery team running, their own weapons in hand. Once the situation was explained, they went to work on the door with other, safer tools—ones that wouldn't damage the people on one side and the artifacts on the other.

"MacNeil," someone called from down the corridor. "We found something."

Gabe turned from the activity at the metal door to see Sasha Tulling approaching. "Look at this," she said, holding out a small wad that looked like a used plastic sandwich bag.

Inside the dirty, crushed plastic was a small metal object. A computer jump drive.

"Sonofabitch. It looks intact." He turned it around in his fingers. Miraculously, there was no sign of rust or mildew or any result of exposure to the elements—thanks to the plastic bag's protection.

"I plugged the drive into my laptop," Sasha told him. "It works. There's a password and some other encryption, but there's data being read."

"Where did you find it?" Gabe asked as he heard a soft *ping* at the metal door. They were making progress; one of the iron bolts was now gone.

"In a corner with a bunch of debris like this. Good thing, because I think the plastic helped protect it."

"Damn good thing," Gabe replied, nodding, still examining the drive.

Just then, a grunt of satisfaction and the accompanying sounds of victory came from the two men working on the bolts. "Got it," one of them said, just in time for Gabe to see the door sag ajar.

He brushed past the others and slipped through the opening. And stopped.

What had once been a chamber filled with display cases and shelves, comfortable and lit like an old study, was now nothing but raw earth and stone. The walls, floor, ceiling…all had been removed or—

"They took the whole room away," Gabe breathed. "They drove it off. Like a damn railway car."

THREE

Northern Michigan

Something warm and wet brushed her face.

Kendra stirred, forcing her eyes open, and was aware of pain. Just pain.

After a moment, she realized she couldn't move.

A faint illumination eased the blackness into gray, and she found herself staring into two glowing amber eyes. The bear!

Something snaked out, something wet and warm again, and slopped over her nose and she tried to scream. But nothing came out but a tiny squeak. It was tasting her!

Cold sweat rushed over her, washing away the pain and replacing it with terror.

Then, miraculously, the bear turned and dashed away. And that was when Kendra noticed the light was moving. Sort of bobbing.

She heard a voice, something in the distance.

And then the skittering scattering of paws on the ground. And then the amber eyes again, but this time the light was stronger and she could see that it wasn't a bear…but a dog.

A dog.

From the graying darkness came a warm, welcome pool of moon-white light beaming from the head of a figure.

"Bruce!" the figure said into a handheld transmitter. "Boris made the find. I've got at least one of them; let me check it out and I'll let you know. Over." It was a woman, speaking in quick, assured tones, even as she hurried toward Kendra.

She set a large lantern on the floor, jammed the transmitter into something on her belt, and knelt next to Kendra.

"Can you hear me?" The light flashed into her face, but Kendra was so glad to see it, she barely blinked. She managed to nod.

"My name is Marina Alexander, and I'm here to help get you out of here. Are you hurt?"

Kendra didn't know how to answer that; she hurt everywhere, but she was still breathing. She formed Matt's name with her mouth instead.

"Matt Granger. Your companion. Was he with you when this happened?"

She managed a nod.

Marina Alexander responded with a nod of her own, and pulled the transmitter from her belt. "Bruce, get the team to checkpoint three. McElroy's here, and awake. She says Granger's with her. He's probably under this pile of rubble. I'll meet you there and we'll go from there. Over."

"Check. Over."

Marina squatted next to Kendra and reached out to touch her hand, the only part of her, she now realized, that wasn't covered with rocks. "We're going to get you two out of here. Just hang tight a bit longer." Her eyes were half hidden by the brim of her lighted hard hat, but Kendra could see the steady calm in them, and knew she was in good hands.

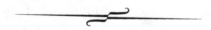

It took two hours to remove enough debris to extract Kendra McElroy without bringing the rest of the cave down around them, and then the team continued to dig until they located what was presumably Matt Granger's shoe.

As the underground controller for the mission, Marina supervised the search and rescue team inside the cave and was also stationed closest to the pile and its victims. Under Bruce's direction, the stone and silt that had fallen from the cave-in had been removed piece by piece, by hand, to free McElroy, then transported out of the area via human chain. Each piece had to be lifted carefully, in a vertical motion, to ensure that no other rock or chunk of earth was dislodged or moved, causing another avalanche or spill.

But before the search and rescue—SAR—team could begin to remove the rubble, they'd had to shore up the roof and sides of the narrow passage with titanium poles, timbers, and pieces of plywood. A whole chunk of the ceiling had fallen into this passageway, but the walls still appeared to be intact—for now.

Yet the team would take no chances. And other than shining headlamp and flashlight beams over the mound of debris, there was no sure way to determine how deep the cave-in was and how far they'd have to dig to get to the other side—if there was an other side. They didn't have that sort of sonar equipment with them, and the sheriff's department in this small, strapped county didn't either.

But when Bruce Denning, Marina's obstacle controller, stood on a crate and shined his light up along the ceiling, he was fairly certain he saw empty space beyond, indicating that the pile didn't extend too deeply. "Four hours, tops," he said.

If Granger was completely buried in the stone and dirt, then it was likely he'd smothered or been crushed. But there was a chance he had an air pocket in which to breathe, or had been separated from McElroy and was on the other side of the pile. Either way, despite the urgency of the situation, the extraction had to be slow and careful.

"Got a cell phone," Marina announced when she lifted a skull-sized rock and found the smashed device. She felt a spur of hope: the deeper they dug without finding Granger, the more optimistic she was that he'd be found on the other side. Of course, there was the danger that he was in a chamber with thin oxygen or trapped gases that could be poisoning him as they worked. Based on Mrs. Granger's timeline—she had reported her son missing—and what little they'd gleaned from a weak and dazed McElroy, the cave-in had occurred at least ten hours ago, at approximately eight p.m.

"Let me take a turn," Bruce said, moving closer to Marina. "You've been working on this nonstop for six hours, and I know you didn't eat lunch."

Marina was nothing if not practical—she'd be no good to anyone if she were weak or exhausted—and the sheriff's deputies were helping with the tedious removal of the debris, so she agreed and took the opportunity to follow the trail of glowsticks back out of the cave.

The sad thing was that McElroy and Granger hadn't been more than a quarter mile deep into the cave when they were blocked in. Marina had noticed the subtle turn in the passage they'd obviously followed, and knew if they hadn't missed that turn, they would've easily found their way out. Thus, this was one of the more simple and straightforward rescues in which she and her dog Boris had participated—it was straight in and straight out, with no narrow passages to squeeze through, no pits to cross or water to flood, and very little descent. The hardest part had been finding the actual cave, which wasn't on any of the county maps. That was where Boris had been his usual brilliant self.

"Alexander coming out," she said into her handheld, notifying the entrance controller she was exiting the cave. Low-frequency radios were the best way to communicate through miles of rock. "Denning is taking over as underground controller. Over."

When she emerged into fresh air and a dawning world, Boris was madly happy to see his mistress.

"Hey, buddy," she crooned, kneeling next to her canine partner. She was chilly and exhausted, but her German Shepherd was a priority. He was part of the reason she'd agreed to take a break. Loosening the strap that kept her helmet in place, Marina couldn't hold back a moan of pleasure. She swore she had permanent ridges in her skull from the countless hours she'd worn one over the last twelve years, not to mention the times it had been jammed or knocked against her skull from a falling rock or low ceiling.

As always, Boris was warm and eager for her embrace, and he swiped her dirty, sweaty jaw with his tongue. "You were so good today, big boy," she said in a praising tone that made his ears perk up into perfect triangles. "You found them so quickly, didn't you?"

His eyes, the color of toffee flecked with coffee, flashed to hers. She could see the intelligence burning in them, could fairly read his response: *I did good. I know I did. When can I do it again? Huh? When? When?*

"The work's all done, big boy," she said, using the same key phrase she always did, and fished a tennis ball out of one of the canvas bags of her kit. She'd already rewarded him immediately following the find, but there was no reason not to praise him again. "The work's done. So now we can play. Let's play!"

Her voice rose in excitement as she showed him the tennis ball, and Boris went on full alert. Even his happy, panting tongue retracted as he got serious again. He went still and stiff, yet fairly quivered beneath his fur.

"Ready?" she asked, and then whipped the ball into the trees.

Boris was off like a flash, streaking into the forest as Marina watched like a proud mother. She'd handled and helped train other dogs on search and rescue/recovery missions, but Boris was the first one she'd worked with herself from puppyhood. Not coincidentally, he was the best partner she'd ever had.

It was pure luck that Bruce and the rest of the Michigan-Ohio Search and Rescue Team had been up here with her and Boris in Northern Michigan, where she still occasionally vacationed, even though her father was dead. She, Bruce, and the rest of their team all been doing a training session for a local SAR group that wanted to obtain their Type II designation from FEMA.

When Granger and McElroy hadn't returned in time for dinner the night before, Mrs. Granger had begun trying to contact them, and then got the sheriff involved (as it turned out, he was her brother, so he could hardly say no even though the couple had only been out of contact for a few hours). Sheriff Tollefson was currently conferring with Danny, the communications manager, who was simultaneously talking with Bruce over the radios.

"How's she doing?" Marina asked one of the medics, gesturing to McElroy, who was on the other side of the small clearing that had become Command Central.

A portable solar light that was quickly becoming unnecessary in the dawn illuminated the collection of crates, plastic storage tubs, and tables. The sheriff was acting as incident manager, but since he didn't have much experience in cave rescue, he'd deferred to Marina and Bruce in most of the planning and execution.

"We're waiting for helo, eh," said the paramedic. He spoke in the familiar Upper Peninsula accents, with an emphasis on initial syllables. "She's got a fractured tibia and two ribs, and's little dehydrated with hypothermia. We made her as comfortable as possible, eh, but we've got no choice but to wait for air transport."

Marina nodded. There was no easy way to transport an injured woman with broken bones over these rugged hills and small mountains in the middle of nowhere. The closest road was one of those primitive, two-track paths, and it was three miles away. Aside from that, hopefully they'd need the medevac copter for Matt Granger as well. The alternative wasn't worth thinking about.

"There's been a delay them taking off from Marquette General or they'd've been here by now," added the paramedic. His th's sounded more like d's. "Some big blackout hearing about, coming up from St. Louis."

"St. Louis? That's hundreds of miles from here."

The medic shrugged. "Ya, I know it. But a big grid went down and it's causing havoc with air traffic control all over the country."

Marina picked up Boris's tennis ball and threw it again. "Do you mind if I talk to McElroy?" She wanted to see if the young woman had any sense as to how close her boyfriend had been standing to her when the rocks came down. If they were holding hands, for example, that was not going to be a promising bit of information.

"Knock yourself out, eh," he replied.

McElroy was lying on a stretcher that had been set up on a stand so the chill from the ground wouldn't seep through the pallet. Several blankets had been layered over her, and Marina knew at least one of them would have a built-in heat pack.

The woman opened her eyes when Marina pulled up a campstool to sit next to her. "Matt?"

Marina had to shake her head soberly. "We're still digging. They're waiting for air transport for you. How are you feeling?"

"Not so good." She pressed her lips together as if to collect her strength. "Thank you for finding me." Her words were slow and low, but audible. "Please find Matt."

"We'll find him," Marina told her. *Not sure what condition he'll be in, but we'll find him.* "Boris told me he's there, and it's just a matter of time. Boris is never wrong. Kendra, can you remember how near he was when the cave-in happened? Were you holding hands or touching at all?"

McElroy moved her head in what seemed to be negation. "No. He tripped over something…and when he fell, he bumped against the wall. And then…it all came down."

Marina's heart sank. If he'd triggered the avalanche, then it was likely he was buried beneath all of that rubble.

"I told him…I wanted to go back." McElroy rolled her head on the thin pillow again, her face filled with pain and misery. "But he found…the cave. A guy we met while hiking…told him about it. And Matt had to find it. He had to…look inside." Her lips formed a weak smile. "He thinks he's…Indiana Jones."

Marina nodded with understanding. "That's how I became interested in caving," she said, and reached for a bottle with a long straw. It contained warm herbal tea that would not only hydrate McElroy, but raise her temperature as well. "I've done archaeology in caves as part of my anthropology studies." In doing so, she'd traveled everywhere from Myanmar to Costa Rica to Spain…not to mention Siberia. Her insides tightened and she pushed away the reminder of the package sitting in her office at home.

That unexpected trip to Siberia had been five years ago, and hadn't been related to her studies. Firmly diverting her thoughts, she helped the young woman lift her head slightly to sip, and then lowered her back down. Then a distant rumbling caught her ears. "The medevac chopper," she said, gesturing to the sky.

But McElroy had more to say. "If something happens," she said, closing her fingers around Marina's wrist. "To…Matt…" Tears welled in her eyes, but her gaze remained fixed on Marina. "He's the one who found it. Make sure he…gets the credit."

"Credit?" Marina's interest was sparked. "What did he find?"

"Stones. White stones. Deep in the cave. It was a big room… we were going to come back tomorrow with…equipment. He said it was a big discovery. Proof that…" Her eyes became confused. "I don't remember. But he found it. Make sure," she said, the rumbling growing loud enough that the others had stopped talking and were rushing to where the helo was going to land. "Make sure he…gets the credit."

Marina nodded. "I will. I'll make certain of it."

The medics came over to prepare their patient for loading into the chopper, and Marina was more than ready to return to the interior of the cave. Finish the mission—which was hopefully still a rescue, and not a recovery—and then she'd take a look inside the cave to see what Matt Granger had found.

All of a sudden, she wasn't tired at all.

FOUR

Binger Blue stretched and rubbed the nape of his neck. Sitting in a Grand Prix for twelve hours didn't do a thing to help his messed-up back, but a PI did what a PI had to do to service his clients. He'd simply add the trip to his chiropractor onto the final bill.

Jerome Blankenship had been inside his lover's condo for well over five hours. By Binger's assessment, that covered more than a couple of humps and maybe a good meal or a movie. Or else the guy had a hell of a lot of stamina. Either way, and he'd lay money on it, the man ought to be leaving anytime now. It was after seven and Mrs. Blankenship was expecting her husband for dinner at eight.

And a status report—hopefully including the money shot—to be delivered by Binger Blue before ten.

He trained his long-lens camera on the shaded windows of the condo's backside, looking for signs of movement. The only reason he was able to get into this exclusive, gated golf community to stake out Blankenship was thanks to the widespread blackout that had wonked up the gate's mechanism. Even though the power was back on after three days, the mechanism hadn't been reset and it wasn't working right. He had a fake groundskeeper's ID that couldn't be scanned, but visually it looked legit. Plus, it was near the end of golf season in Chicago and they brought in extra help to keep up with the scads of leaves covering the course, or so Binger had learned.

He'd gone through all the trouble because the only time he had a chance to catch Blankenship in the act was when he was coming or going from the lady's condo. Cora Allegan's photo in one publication or another was a weekly occurrence, so they were very discreet lovers and never appeared in public together, even innocently. And that was the reason Mrs. Blankenship had finally had to hire True Blue Gumshoe to get photos.

Nothing yet. Damn. Was he gonna be here all night?

He lowered the camera, and as it settled onto the small bump of his belly, he returned to his book, *Harnessing the Energy Around You: Feng Shui & Chakra Secrets for Beginners*. If he sat in this vehicle much longer, he'd be forced to try his hand at *feng shui-ing* the stained bucket seats and paper-strewn dash. Hey, maybe the big honking chip in the windshield could count as a crystal. And his half-empty Big Gulp could be the water—though standing water wasn't supposed to be good. It had to be flowing or something.

He was just getting back into the paragraph about clogged chakras and how to get the wheels of energy spinning again when he heard the sounds of three car doors slamming in rapid succession.

Snatching up his camera, he looked out over the lengthening shadow from Ms. Allegan's neighbor's condo and straightened up in his seat. Curiouser and curiouser.

From his vantage point in a small turnoff near the golf course, Binger peered closer and saw two—no, three—figures detach themselves from the vehicle that had just parked on the street in front of the condo. The trio started up the front walk.

They were tall, dressed in loose white clothing, and seemed to be empty-handed. Tannish skin, blondish hair, three men maybe thirty or so in age.

Not a pizza delivery, that was sure. Probably not Jehovah's Witnesses. They looked too foreign in their strange clothing and weren't carrying Bibles or anything.

Not party attendees—not only weren't they dressed for merrymaking, but they showed no sign of joviality, looking neither to the right nor the left as they strode up the walk lined with red and white flowers limper than an octogenarian's dick. Apparently Ms. Allegan's sprinkler system hadn't been reactivated after the three-day blackout ended.

Binger watched through the lens, slumped down in his seat now, the prickling of the hair on the top of his bare foot telling him it was in his best interest not to be seen.

The visitors waited at the front door for a moment, two of them standing sentinel on either side of a porch the size of a card table, and the third apparently knocking. Binger scooched lower in his seat, his eyes barely seeing over the top of his dash, the camera's eyepiece digging into the tender skin under his eye.

The front door opened, and Binger caught a glimpse of Cora Allegan dressed in pink. Through the glasses he saw the puzzlement on her face, then the register of shock as one of the men spoke to her.

Her hands fluttered then spread in an indication of "so what?" or "what else can I say?" and then, before they had the chance to fall to her sides, she was standing out on the card-table porch. One man's arm was around her waist, and it was clearly not a friendly embrace.

Binger gave a moment's thought to the whereabouts of Jerome Blankenship, but when he did not appear and the door closed behind Cora Allegan and her visitors, he figured the married man was remaining hidden to protect himself from being caught in the act of bonking the CEO of Vision Screen Industries, who also happened to be the daughter of a US senator.

What the hell? He realized belatedly he was holding a camera, and began to click rapidly. Not the money shot Mrs. Blankenship was hoping for, but—

Suddenly, it didn't matter where the cowardly and adulterous Mr. Blankenship was—for suddenly Cora Allegan was slumped between her visitors and Binger was tossing his camera aside, ready to bolt from his vehicle. He opened the door, his hand on the Colt he'd been licensed to carry for ten years and had never had to use, watching as the three hurried down the twilit walk, dragging her between them.

He stepped out of the car, shouting to gain their attention, but before he could take two steps, something was lobbed through the air toward him. A small black item landed on the ground and, clutching the camera to his body, he dived out of the way and tumbled into a tall swath of cattails. He rolled down a gentle incline, landing in the dank, cold muck of a small swamp that was more commonly used to trap golf balls than for the habitat of frogs or turtles, and waited for the explosion.

Silence.

Nothing.

The low rumble of a vehicle motor came to his ears, and Binger slapped his hands in the organic muck to push himself up. Peering over the edge of the incline, he looked around. The black object remained where it landed, on the ground ten yards from his Grand Prix, spewing out dark smoke. Well? Was the mother-effer going to go off or just sit there like a smoldering firecracker?

He wasn't about to get his ass blown up, so he waited. The car that had parked at the end of Cora Allegan's walkway was gone, its taillights just disappearing around one of the gentle curves of the golf community street.

Binger hesitated another two minutes until the smoke disappeared, and when nothing else happened, he crawled up the incline, taking care to keep his profile low.

He tried to assimilate what he'd just witnessed: The abduction of Cora Allegan, CEO of one of the largest manufacturers of computer and television monitors in the US, illicit lover of Jerome Blankenship, president of Chicago's Nellworth Bank, and daughter of Missouri senator Ronald Allegan.

Right under Binger Blue's very blue eyes.

The door to Cora Allegan's condo opened, and a bewildered Jerome Blankenship stood there in his boxers and t-shirt. Guess he hadn't dressed for dinner yet. Blankenship stepped on the porch, looking about, and Binger seized the opportunity.

He yanked off the lens cap and snapped a few pics of the man standing in his boxers on his lover's front porch. At least Binger would close one case tonight.

Then he slipped the camera away and emerged from the mud and cattails just as Jerome Blankenship bent down to retrieve a flat white object that looked like an envelope.

It appeared that the abductors had left some sort of calling card.

Fenton, Michigan

"Right here," Mike Wiley said, trying not to dance with impatience as he directed the UPS driver through the back door of Wiley Amusements.

The man in the brown shirt wheeled a large, long wooden crate into the center of the crowded shop, narrowly missing a vintage *Pac-Man* machine. More often than not, Wiley trucked his own pieces home from auctions or wherever he'd acquired them, but this baby had come all the way from Brazil—or somewhere down there. Bagger, his contact in California, was the one who'd found it and shipped it in, and Wiley'd been expecting it for weeks.

He didn't even wince as the edge of the crate jolted the table where he'd laid out all the parts for his current project— the rebuild of a Williams *Dirty Harry* pinball machine. Besides replacing the Magnum pistol that moved around the playfield, he was going to put in a drop target just to spiff it up a little, maybe get a few more bucks for the machine. Collectors liked the vintage ones, but they also liked them if they had a little something more. The prototypes of *Dirty Harry* had originally had drop targets, but when Williams went into manufacturing it, they left them out even though the software supported it. So someone was going to get a tricked-out machine.

But that wasn't going to happen anytime soon, because Dirty Harry was going to go by the wayside faster than a cigarette butt out the car window now that Wiley's latest toy had arrived. He watched impatiently as the driver settled the crate, slid the metal tongues of the dolly out from under it, and then offered him an electronic screen on which to sign.

He scribbled his name with the stylus and flapped a hand toward the door, already searching for the crowbar that had been on his worktable the last time he looked. After a few choice cuss words, he finally found it under an old table version of *Galaga* he'd promised to reboot for the guys over at The Shark Club (he still called it that even though it was now a microbrewery) and began to work on the crate.

The nails screeched softly as he got the lid up and then tossed it aside, narrowly missing his favorite *Lord of the Rings* pinball machine. That one was his current favorite, but this sweet old machine by Bally might just replace the One Ring in his heart.

His first look at her—*Fathom*—got his heart to pounding and his palms going damp. No, she wasn't as rare as *Pinball Circus* by Midway (that one would have him on his knees, sweating and crying if he actually got his hands on one of the three in existence), but she was *sweet*.

The green, blue, aqua, and teal colors of the undersea theme were slightly faded and the top glass was shattered in a circle at the near left corner—probably someone slammed down a beer bottle in disgust after the ball slipped through the flippers. Had to've broken the bottle, too, hitting it that hard. And—holy shit—was that a bullet hole in the back glass?

Wiley couldn't pull the crate sides away fast enough, and finally he was standing next to the unencumbered machine, able to run his fingers over a spot that was most fucking definitely a bullet hole. Clean through the A in *Fathom*, right through the back of the display.

He looked at the machine with new admiration. Bagger'd told him it came from the estate of a drug lord down in Brazil or Peru—somewhere in the jungle. Guy named Rico got himself offed a while ago, and according to Bagger, they—whoever they were—were cleaning out the secluded mansion he'd been hiding away in.

"Guess you saw a little action down there, huh, baby," he said, smoothing his hand over the dirty glass, imagining how nifty she was going to be when he got her all fixed up. "Well, it's a lot less exciting here in Michigan than down there in the jungle, I can guarantee you that."

He fished the screwdriver from his pocket and began to remove the back so he could take a look at the electronics for the scoreboard. He whistled some old Robert Palmer as he pulled out the wires, noting the corrosion from the humid jungle air, testing connections as he went. Not too bad. She was definitely working.

Then, tucked down in the corner of the section, he saw something that had him freezing still and his insides plummeting. It looked like a black satin pouch, shoved down deep into the space.

His first thought was he'd come across a forgotten stash of coke or heroin. But there was no fucking way it could've gotten through customs, could it? Or could it?

Maybe it was weed or even something more valuable. Jewels? Diamonds?

He looked nervously around the cluttered shop as if to see the Feds—or the drug lord's rivals—bursting in. "Chill out," he told himself with a little laugh. "It's probably nothing."

He hesitated only another few seconds, then aimed his flashlight on the pouch. The silky black sack had a coppery glint in the light. It looked as if it would fit comfortably in his palm.

Wiley reached for it, intending to pluck it from its moorings. But when he touched the bag, it stuck to his fingers like some thick, black, gooey web.

"Ugh!" He pulled his hand away, and a piece of the sac came with it, tearing it open.

A swarm of bugs erupted.

Wiley jumped back, startled and disgusted as the fingernail-sized insects poured out, shooting into the air. The next thing he knew, they were in a frenzy in his little shop, flying like mad bees—or a slew of tiny pinball balls in a violent, four-dimensional multi-ball game.

A couple landed on his arms and flew into his face and he swatted them away, watching as some flew into the fly strips he had hanging from the ceiling. Others bumped into each other or the walls, ricocheting around the room in a crazy whirlwind. He picked up a newspaper and swung at the little bastards, flinging them into the walls and onto the floor.

After what seemed like forever, they were all gone—dead, smashed, or otherwise disappeared. Wiley noticed his fingers. They were black and sticky from where he'd touched the sac, and he wiped them on a rag. But some residue remained, and even after he washed his hand, the black essence stayed like some sort of permanent ink.

The bugs hadn't bit him; they'd just seemed crazed or incensed from being disturbed. But he couldn't help rubbing his arm and cheek where they'd slammed into his skin in their effort to escape. Psychosomatic itching, he knew, and forced himself to stop scratching.

He swept up the bugs and a variety of other dust and dirt from the floor and threw it away, took another look at *Fathom*, and decided to call it a day. A beer and some barbecue pork sliders up the block at The Laundry sounded about right. And, truth to tell, Wiley wasn't very keen on finding another black pouch under the machine's playfield.

He'd wait till tomorrow and tackle *Fathom* again. And this time, he'd be armed with Raid—or something stronger.

FIVE

Matt Granger's body was found shortly before ten a.m. on September 22nd, the morning after he was reported missing.

From the looks of it, he hadn't had a chance of survival. The massive contusion on the back of his head and lack of blood indicated he had died quickly, if not instantly—for which Marina was grateful. At least he hadn't suffered while waiting for rescue, only to expire before they could dig him out. An injured person buried beneath the rubble for hours, in pain, trying in vain to breathe dusty, gritty air through nostrils coated with dirt and sand was a nightmare Marina had encountered too often, and had once experienced herself.

But still she grieved for him, for the loss of a young, intelligent, earnest man she'd never even met, but whom she felt she'd come to know through all of the information the SAR team had gathered about him. A man who loved the outdoors, who'd taken his girlfriend on a walk through his favorite hiking area after showing off his hometown and family to her.

Now Marina was even more determined to assist Kendra McElroy to ensure that whatever "find" Granger had discovered would be appropriately attributed to him.

As they were moving the body onto the stretcher, Bruce felt a small box tucked into one of the pockets of Granger's cargo pants. It was a jewel case.

"Aw, hell," he said, flipping it open. Five headlamps beamed down on the diamond solitaire as it glittered like ice in the darkness, and the team grew even more sober.

The box closed with a sharp snap, the sound hard and final in the silence of the cave. Bruce caught Marina's gaze, his face dirty, weary, and tight with regret beneath his helmet. She shook her head soberly, and they all went silently about their tasks, arranging the body and gathering up whatever equipment could be removed at that time.

Dana had radioed the news to the com manager—that a recovery, not a rescue, had been made—and Sheriff Tollefson would break the news to Kendra McElroy, as well as his sister, Matt's mother.

There was little left for Marina and the team to do now, other than remove the braces that had propped the walls and ceiling in place, along with the rest of their gear. Silently, they trudged out of the cave into midmorning sunlight.

With Marina's permission, Boris went over to investigate the contents of the stretcher while she removed her helmet and gloves. When he recognized the scent to which he'd alerted earlier, he gave a soft, short bark of recognition, then turned to his handler.

"I know, Boris, I know," she said, kneeling next to him and sliding her arms around his neck. He'd done his job, finding the scent he'd been given, but he also understood something wasn't quite right about it. His intelligent eyes were sad, liquid gold, surprisingly cognizant. Marina was one of those people who believed dogs had something like souls, because she'd seen evidence of it over and over.

"You and that dog are amazing. It's almost as if you're one person."

The voice behind her had Marina's heart jolting off rhythm, then settling back into place.

She rose, turning to face Bruce. He'd removed his helmet, which resulted in an unobstructed view of his eyes. His dark blond hair was mussed, and he sported the same red marks on the side of his temple and jaw she knew she did. "*He's* amazing," she corrected him. "I'm just the handler. He knows what to do, and I just follow him."

"Yeah, that's just like you not to take any credit, even though you trained him. And you read him." Bruce's voice dipped into a low, rough rumble. "But you're just as amazing in your own way."

Marina's attention dropped to his left hand, which was not only holding his helmet, but had a gold band on the ring finger. One day, she suspected, that ring would be gone. It wouldn't be because of her—at least consciously. But it wasn't gone yet. And even if it were…Bruce was a good friend and trusted colleague. She didn't think about him in that way. At least, she tried not to, but there were times—like now—when she became sharply aware of him, of his physical presence, his bravery and intelligence—and his attraction to her.

"If someone needs you, you're there," he continued, his voice still low, his body too close to hers. "No matter who or what they are. Always."

"We make a good team," she said lightly, easing away. "All of us. And how fortunate that we were up here for the training session when this happened, otherwise I'd have been without my best team."

"Are you still seeing that guy, that spook?" Bruce asked, his voice casual except for a bite at the end.

Marina shrugged. "Yes, occasionally." *Occasionally* was an exaggeration, as she hadn't seen Gabe since they met up in Colorado for a skiing weekend several months ago. Wow. It had been about ten months, now that she came to think of it. Between their work schedules and the traveling they both did, it was hard to coordinate getting together. And much as she liked him and enjoyed his company—*all* aspects of it—Marina wasn't interested in getting into any serious type of relationship.

There were numerous reasons she'd never be wearing a gold band on her finger again, and only some of them had to do with the mark of the Skaladeskas, which was tattooed on the bottom of her heel.

"Occasionally?" Bruce repeated.

"Yes. You know how my schedule is," she said with a laugh. "I hardly have time to do my laundry." Then Boris nudged her, giving Marina an excuse to break eye contact with her colleague and crouch to see to her dog.

When she straightened up, she said, "I'm going back in the ground. I want to check something out." While the last thing she wanted to do was give Bruce any encouragement, she also was determined to investigate what Kendra had told her. And she was too experienced a caver to go inside without the proper equipment, and without at least one other person plus Boris.

"Just can't get enough of that damp, dark earth, can you?" he said with a grin, settling his helmet back in place. "That's all right, I'll cover you." That look was gone from his eyes, and Marina relaxed. There wasn't anyone else she'd rather have with her inside the earth than Bruce—and she knew he felt the same way.

That was, she supposed, part of the problem. They liked, respected, and relied on each other too much.

Normally, on an in-depth caving expedition, explorers traveled in groups of at least three so if a person got injured or stuck, someone could go for help and the other could stay with the injured party. But in this case, Marina knew they weren't going deep or far, and, based on what she knew of McElroy and Granger's trip, there weren't any small passages to get caught inside. She and Bruce were also savvy enough to know not to bump against a wall that might be fragile, and to move carefully and slowly while in the ground. Aside from that, they still had their shortwaves and could radio out for help if the worst happened.

Marina brought Boris too, and she and Bruce retraced their steps into the main passage, climbing through what was clearly a recently exposed entrance. But once a half-mile inside, she found the turnoff where the younger couple had gotten mixed up on their way out.

"This way," she said, noticing a place where the dirt had been scuffed by a hiking boot. Boris was such a good tracker he hadn't gone in that direction very far before turning around and catching the fresher scent, which ultimately led them to McElroy. But now, she followed that tunnel deeper into the ground.

As she led the way, Marina couldn't help but draw in a deep breath of the damp, chill cave air. Call her crazy, but she found it almost as comforting as sitting in her shaded backyard at home, breathing fresh-cut grass and summer flowers. Walking along, she took note of the widening passage and the rough sandstone and granite walls. They were stained a rust color from all the iron and copper here in the Keweenaw Peninsula. The ground angled down as they walked deeper into the earth, still able to move upright and with ease through the tunnel. Even the air remained easily breathable. It was no wonder Granger and McElroy had come so far: it was a simple, uneventful hike.

She ducked under a low chunk of rock and, when she came up, realized she'd stepped into a vast chamber. Marina stopped, putting her hand back in silent command to Boris, and stared.

"Whoa," her companion said as he came up behind her.

"Yeah," she murmured, looking around the space. Her heart was pounding with excitement and her mind leapt with boundless theories and possibilities as she took in the sight.

This was definitely a Find.

The space was massive, at least twenty meters high and perhaps forty meters long. The walls were smooth and rounded, if not man-made then at least altered by Homo sapiens. At each end of the oblong chamber was a pile of white stones—just as Kendra McElroy had said. Each stone was about the size of a cantaloupe, smooth and white, and they were piled up like pyramids. Each pyramid was roughly two meters square at the base, and just a bit taller than Marina's five foot, six inches.

"What is it?" Bruce asked. He eased closer, bumping her helmet's rim gently with his own and using the opportunity to steady her with a hand on her waist.

"I don't know," she said, moving gingerly into the chamber. Her silent command to Boris told him to stay, and he remained at the entrance, watching with sharp eyes and tongue out of sight, indicating his rapt attention. He was working now, and he knew it.

Easing along the wall, she smoothed her gloved hand over the stone, taking care not to put any significant pressure on it. The walls were dry without any damp rivulets, and the floor of the chamber was just as arid.

Other than the pyramids, the space was clear and empty of everything other than a few scattered animal bones and random piles of dirt. The pyramidal stones seemed to have some sort of plaster or binder holding them in place.

"It's got to be old," Bruce said, walking up next to her. "Really old. What do you think, professor?"

His use of the title wasn't just a nickname; Marina held a PhD from the University of Michigan in Historical Epigraphy, with a specialization in Asian Studies. But that didn't mean she wasn't educated about her home state. Her first several archaeological digs had been in the Upper Peninsula and the northern Lower Peninsula of Michigan. "Very old. I've never seen anything like this arrangement of stones. They aren't Native American as far as I can tell. Though they're similar to the cairns found in Scandinavia, they're too…uniform."

She crouched, thankful for her headlamp as well as the handheld flashlight she had with her, and looked closely at the stones making up the base. Inching her way around, observing each rock, she examined them as she spoke. "There are some pyramids or cones made from stones that were found in the bottom of a lake in Wisconsin," she said. "I'd have to look it up, but I think they were similar to this arrangement. Theories—most of which are not accepted by mainstream archaeologists—are that the pyramids were made by European or Mediterranean traders that came and began to trade for *copper*."

Marina paused as a little frisson of excitement zipped through her. For years, there'd been arguments between scholars and historians about whether prehistoric non-natives had come to North America for copper, and there was compelling evidence to support it—for there had clearly been vast amounts of the metal mined here, but little to no trace remaining in the area. And the amount of copper used across the Atlantic was greater than would have been available locally.

Something prickled over her skin when she realized there were images engraved on one of the stones. Her heart began to pound as she knelt more closely to look, angling the flashlight as she tried to brush away dirt without disturbing the carved stone.

"Looks like ogam," she muttered. "It can't be."

"Like what?" Bruce was standing over her, watching as she traced her finger ever so lightly over the images.

"An ogam. It's an alphabet—well, more of a text system. It's recognizable by this sort of straight line carved or drawn like this—see how they are perpendicular to that other long line?"

"It looks old."

"If it's what I think…it's ancient," Marina said in a hushed voice. She could hardly believe what she was seeing. Ogam text *here*, in the Americas?

Then, as she looked even more closely at the tall, angular images, her palms went damp and her face flushed beneath the heavy, hot helmet.

She'd seen this specific type of work before—this same rusty red color with the same angled lines—on a fragment of stone.

And that stone was sitting in a package in her office at home.

SIX

September 21
Meramec-Tate Power Generation Facility
St. Louis, Missouri

For Christ's sake, Akinowski, the whole damn High Plains region is in the goddamn dark!" Senator George Sheever's voice screamed from the desk phone speaker. "For two *days*! What the hell are you doing about it? I've got the goddamned president of Goerken-AgriBiz up my ass about the convention this week, not to mention the fucking Business Association bitching about the loss of revenue. But that's nothing compared to everyone else! No one's flying, no one's landing, no one can fucking *get gas*, send email, or watch the news without any goddamn electricity, and your damn plant is the one that brought everything down! What the hell are you doing to fix it?"

Charles Akinowski had stopped listening to the raving lunatic on the other end of the line. Sheever was an asshole every single day, but no doubt he was particularly bent because he couldn't get on a plane to fly back to Washington, far away from his constituents—and, more importantly, his wife.

As Sheever continued to scream and rant like a child, Ake, as he was known to his friends, turned the volume down and returned his attention to where it needed to be: what had caused the rolling, far-reaching blackout that had turned the Midwestern

United States from Kansas to Missouri and Kentucky, Illinois, Wisconsin, southwestern Michigan, Iowa, and most of the Plains states black as night.

He was the executive director of the facility that had been pinpointed as the origin of the failure that took down most of the grid in the regional transmission organization, or RTO, that provided electricity to much of the High Plains region. The blackout had halted or rerouted air traffic over the central United States, and Ake hadn't slept more than five hours in the last two days—let alone been home—since this all came down. Thank God Michael understood and was bringing him something to eat every day—cooked on the grill, because there wasn't any power anywhere to cook with, including here at the plant.

After the historic blackout throughout Ontario, Ohio, Michigan, and Pennsylvania in August 2003, there had been particular attention paid to the structure of electric grids. Studies done, tests made, and theories offered about whether and how a grid could be taken down by a terrorist attack, natural event, or some other incident. There was a school of thought that suggested one small fault could be the downfall of a massive grid, but a conflicting study seemed to prove otherwise.

In other words, no one really agreed how to keep such far-reaching outages from happening, and thus no one had done a whole lot of anything, including FERC—the entity that was responsible for regulating RTOs. Yes, there was talk about terrorists trying to attack by exploiting the weak point of a grid, but most experts agreed it would be difficult to predict how—or even *whether*—a blackout could occur even if an attack was attempted.

Here at Meramec-Tate, a series of unexpected, inexplicable voltage increases had caused the major transmission cables to fail, and caused the cascading fault that rolled through the entire RTO. Why more than one cable had experienced an unexpected surge in voltage was the mystery Ake was desperately trying to solve, even as his operating staff worked to replace the cables and get the operations software running properly again.

Any unexpected surge or lessening of power running along the lines would cause them to fail, which was why every power-generating plant had software that automatically juggled and disseminated the flow of electricity to keep it in an even range, diverting surges to other lines or wires when necessary. If the software failed for some reason—which was part of what had happened in 2003—then human operators were expected to manage it manually.

But when the unexpected increase in power had happened on six different major cables within a thirty-minute timespan, there was nowhere for the extra megawattage to go...and everything went down. And the resulting streams of power surges and interruptions caused the same failures in substations throughout other parts of the grid, radiating further afield before man or computer could stop them.

Ake looked at the phone, where Sheever still screamed, and noted that two other lines were blinking on hold. This was one of the few times he'd been alone in his office since all this happened, and he couldn't talk to anyone else right now. He had to concentrate on coming up with some sort of explanation for the FERC administrator, who was due for an update within the next hour.

No matter how many reports he looked at or crew members he talked to, Ake always came back to the same question: how in the hell had six different surges measuring more than five thousand megawatts happened in the same place in such a short time?

There hadn't been any bad weather to cause lightning strikes—let alone six of them.

And yes, it had been hot, and some of the fault might have been attributed to an increased use of air conditioners...but that was routine management, and no one on his staff was that incompetent.

A bomb could have caused that kind of damage, if you wanted to think along the terrorism path—which everyone tended to do initially anyway—but there was no evidence of that. No big explosion. No fallout. Nothing.

Nothing to explain the sudden changes in voltage.

All at once, his office door burst open. Andy Nabbins, one of the crew, rushed in. "Thought you might want to see this," he said.

Ake glanced at the phone, which was still squawking with an overabundance of F-words, and shrugged. He reached over and pushed the button to disconnect.

Silence. Blessed silence.

"What do you have?" he asked, trying not to sound too hopeful.

The young man, who happened to be one of the smarter, more proactive engineers on the crew, looked as weary and stressed as Ake knew he did himself. But Nabbins also had streaks of sweat and grime on his face and overalls from working out among the lines. He was holding something black in his glove, and the scent of electrical fire clung to it. Ake sniffed experimentally. It smelled like something else too.

Nabbins dumped the thing onto his desk, right in the middle of a pile of papers.

They both looked down. The irregular black mass was a bit smaller than a golf ball, and whatever it was, it was charred black, hard, and shiny.

"What is it?" said Ake, poking it with a pencil. It shifted and rolled a bit to one side, and little black flakes scattered on his desk. And then he looked closer. "Is that a bug?" He used the pen tip to poke at a piece of the mass. It did appear to be an insect of some sort, fused into whatever the rest of the mass was.

"That's what I think," said Nabbins. "And not just one—look more closely. It looks like a bunch of them, all sort of melted or burned together."

Well, damn, it sure did. As Ake looked more closely, he forgot about the pen and began to use his fingers to push and prod, pulling at the cluster. The whole damn thing appeared to be insects. They looked as if they'd melted together.

"We found a bunch of these wads in the yard," Nabbins explained, referring to the enclosed area over which the transmission lines traveled from the generator to beyond. "A dozen or so. And there are more, fused onto A5, B15, and B3."

A5, B15, and B3 were three of the lines that had failed.

That couldn't be a coincidence. "These bugs—could they have caused the surges?" Ake said, more to himself than to Nabbins. "Or…are they a result of the voltage surge? They flew into the wrong place at the wrong time and got zapped into crispy critters."

Either way, it was a random event—the bugs flew into the yard at the wrong time and got electrocuted. And at least now he had something to tell FERC.

Then he looked even more closely. "Are these real?" he asked, noticing a metallic glint on one of the wings. A little prickle of unease crept through him. The cluster smelled like fried metal, too.

Then he shook his head. He'd been reading too many Crichton books. Still…

"Why don't you and Berch collect all of the clusters you can. I'd like an entomologist to take a look if we can find a specimen or two. We might have to look into some pest control, if that's what caused this. I guess," he said, looking up at Nabbins, "if a seagull can fly into the engine of a plane and cause it to fail, forcing an emergency landing in the Hudson, a swarm of bees—or whatever these are—can fly into the transmission cables and cause a power surge."

But the more he thought about it, the more Ake realized… that didn't make sense.

At all.

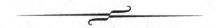

Fenton, Michigan

Mike Wiley stared at himself in the mirror. He was holding on to the bathroom sink, hardly able to keep himself upright.

He couldn't remember ever being this sick—not even the morning after he'd turned twenty-one. Or after his divorce was final.

At first he thought it was some sort of flu. Yesterday, he'd gotten the *Fathom*, and late last night, he'd come home from The Laundry more than a little hammered off a measly two beers. That should've been his first clue—the last time he'd been that out of it after two beers was when he was twelve.

And yeah, his skin kept itching where those bugs had flown into him, but he figured it was all in his head. Those things had creeped the hell out of him.

But now there were large, raised patches on his arms and cheek. He'd gotten his wife to pick up some hydrocortisone cream and Benadryl, but neither seemed to make any difference to the ugly rash. They looked like dark red lumps of cottage cheese and they were starting to spread—not only growing larger, but also popping up in other areas on his skin.

And he'd been weak and dizzy, cold and then clammy-hot all day yesterday. His wife was gone overnight last night at her dad's, so he'd muddled through a restless sleep, hoping it was a twenty-four-hour bug.

It was a bug, all right. He was sure of it.

Those damn jungle bugs hadn't even bit him and they'd given him some sort of something. He figured he'd better get himself to the doctor and get some antibiotics unless he wanted to be sick for another week.

The guys at Block Brewery were going to have to do without him for Trivia Night tonight, but Wiley figured he'd be back with a vengeance next week.

Somewhere in the Amazon jungle

Lev had not yet become accustomed to the damp heat and lush greenery of the rainforest. After more than a century living in the rugged mountains of Siberian Taymyria, he found the change of environment extreme, yet not unwelcome.

Not at all unwelcome. For Gaia was just as beautiful here as she was in his native land, where he'd been birthed, molded by the Earth Mother, and then released back into the world.

And here, in the midst of brilliant color and a melodic cacophony of birds, insects, breeze, and tumbling water, Lev saw no evidence of how ill and damaged the earth was. This place seemed untouched by the heavy hand of man, and when he closed his eyes and placed a hand on the ground, Lev felt Gaia's heartbeat. It resonated through him, deep in his belly, mingling with his own breath and heartbeat.

If he'd ever questioned that the very ground upon which he walked, the very trees that sheltered, the seas and wind that stirred energy all about were linked and growing and *living*, he need only press his hand to the earth and feel. He need only to close his eyes and listen, for when he quieted his mind, he could hear the trees growing, moving, sending their roots deeply into the earth.

Every creature on earth, from every blade of grass to every insect wing to the microscopic plankton and the pad of every mammal's footstep—the very rock and soil, the veins of water, the flake of shale and the glitter of gemstone and crystal—all of it lived and breathed, inhaled and exhaled, suffered and celebrated, in one great organism. *Gaia*.

His mother.

But Lev well knew how full she was, how bloated her body had become, stuffed with plastics and electronics and man-made waste. How violated she was, shaved and scalped, hectare after hectare, razed and plundered by turns with machinery thrusting into her depths or polluting her with poisoned breath. It went on and on as man devastated and took, causing this great living being to shudder and weaken.

The rape and violation must be stopped.

And Gaia must be healed.

As the midday sun pressed down upon the jungle, filtering through the tallest trees he'd ever seen, Lev sought a soft, quiet place to settle his old, frail bones. The compound in which the Skaladeskas now resided was enclosed and overgrown by vines, bushes, and trees—camouflaged from aerial view, and unnoticeable from the tiny capillary of the Amazon that flowed nearby. But the enclosed area—though safe from the threats of wild animals—offered no privacy, nowhere for him to commune with his Great Mother.

He'd always known Gaia had many facets to her terrain and personality, and leaving the harsh, determined Siberian mountains to spend the rest of his days in her moist, sensual warmth was a good decision. In his youth, Lev had been better equipped to tolerate the spare beauty and difficult surroundings of his Tunguska birthplace—of cold, stark, jutting earth and sparse greenery. But now, he knew it was fitting to be here, in the soft embrace of Gaia's crown jewel, as his life waned.

He had been brought to this place so he could help to heal Her, and until he did, Lev's work would not be finished.

More than a year ago, Roman and his woman Stegnora, along with Varden and Fridkov, had managed the logistics of the evacuation from the Siberian mountains with ease that indicated they'd long prepared for such an eventuality. Lev had chosen the location of their new home, for he'd been led here in a dream, to this very place—more than three decades ago. And Roman, his son, had listened.

Lev shook his head and closed his eyes, pushing away the disconcerting thoughts of his offspring as he drew in a long, deep breath of loamy air. The fragrance of many unnamed flowers accompanied it, and he paused to simply embrace and enjoy Gaia's many gifts. To offer up thanks to Her.

He settled beside the river—such a small vessel in comparison to its origin, the mighty Amazon—beneath a smooth-trunked tree he'd seen in his dream. It offered upthrusted roots that formed a chair-like space, as if it had waited for him.

Gaia was welcoming him to his new place.

Once comfortable, he reached for his drum and drew it into his lap. The instrument was made with the tight, stretched skin of an elk and an etching of that same creature had been forged onto it by his own hand. Lev wasn't an artist, but the morning after he awakened from his first shamanic vision, he'd drawn the animal as if guided by an unseen tutor.

The drum felt familiar and comfortable settling between his bent legs, and he closed his eyes. His hands floated to rest on the grass on either side of him.

Take care on the grass, for it is the hair of Gaia.

He'd warned his twin sons Roman and Viktor of that many times when they were young. And now Viktor was gone—possibly dead, or at least returned to the Out-World—while Roman was determined to bring the Out-World to its knees at any cost. Lev felt a pang of loss when he thought of his other progeny—the granddaughter he hadn't known existed for nearly thirty years. Mariska—Marina, as she was called in the Out-World.

Perhaps *she* would understand. Perhaps someday, she would be the one to clearly see what the family must do…and the value of the treasure they protected.

He would make certain of it. It was his legacy. Their legacy— one of two with which he'd been blessed and burdened.

A man was fortunate to have one legacy to which he could give his name…but Lev had been given extraordinary gifts. And with them came the responsibility of two.

Marina surely understood one of them…but she must be taught to comprehend and absorb the other. If she did not, if the Aleksandrov line died with her, then Lev would have lived in vain and the gift from Gaia would be wasted.

Lev closed his eyes and inhaled his mother's essence. Gaia must be protected; She must be healed. He could feel Her labored breaths beneath his palms. He sensed weakness rolling from deep within Her, uncertainty in the vibration of her being. And yet… there was strength shifting beneath the soil. In the depths. He felt it.

It wouldn't be long before he was with Her…sinking into the earth, turning from skin and bone and soul to dust and ash. But for now…

He closed his eyes, softly, rhythmically tapping his drum, thinking once more on the words of the Sacred, the words by which he'd strived to live his life…the words by which he would continue as long as he breathed and stepped upon the earth.

Gaia is one with us, and all living creatures are one with Her. And if there be a species of this earth that threatens the whole, then it shall be expelled.

SEVEN

September 22
Au Pointe, Michigan

Marina felt a variety of emotions as she walked through the overgrown patch of rubble. Anger. Confusion. Awe. Grief.

Until five years ago, her father had lived in a small, neat house on this bluff overlooking Lake Superior in the Upper Peninsula of Michigan.

What little was left of the house after an explosion that barely missed killing Marina and Gabe was decorated by spindly saplings, stubborn, wavy crabgrass, and, oddly enough, a few straggling blueberry bushes thrusting up from the foundation.

"You think you'll ever rebuild?" asked Bruce, reaching out to steady her elbow as she climbed over a large, loose chunk of concrete. "This is a nice piece of land. Lakefront and all that." He grinned, his eyes crinkling much too attractively behind dark sunglasses.

Marina kept a reasonable distance from the edge of the bluff. Lake Superior, cold and granite blue, thrashed against the shore twelve feet below. She had a healthy appreciation of the power of the lake—of any water—and her palms turned a little damp when she thought about being submerged, encompassed, and enveloped by the mighty element. It was a phobia she had battled for more than a decade, and one that had ultimately cost her father his life.

Or, at least, the man she'd believed was her father. As it turned out, Victor Alexander—also known as Viktor Aleksandrov—was not, in fact, her real parent. Why she'd been led to believe this for more than thirty years was a question she'd not yet answered.

"Lakefront—you could call it that, but it's not really suitable for sitting on the beach or building a dock," she replied as Bruce walked past her to gaze at the lake surging and churning below. "It does have a nice view."

"Yes…you can almost see Canada from here." His laugh rumbled low, and she smiled in response before sobering at the rush of memories.

She and Gabe MacNeil had been abducted not very far from here, and taken right across the lake into Canada by the Skaladeskas. But more importantly, the very bluff on which she and Bruce now stood had a hidden submarine launch her so-called father had used for his own escape.

He'd ended up in Siberia, in the hidden lair of the Skaladeskas, just as she and Gabe had done.

Marina wasn't certain why she'd been drawn to stop here today. The round trip to Au Pointe was nearly two hours out of the way down and around the Keweenaw Bay from where she, Bruce, and the others had found McElroy and Granger…but something had inspired her to make the trip.

She'd only been here once since the Skaladeskas took her to Siberia. Only once since she'd learned the truth about her family and her heritage.

After the events in Detroit, when she, Gabe, and FBI Special Agent Helen Darrow had managed to stop the Skaladeskas from carrying out their threat, the CIA had visited this site and combed through the rubble, looking for evidence and information about the Skalas. Marina knew she wasn't going to discover anything they hadn't taken, but the sight of that tall, angular script carved into the walls by the stone pyramids had shaken her…and, because of the unwanted package she'd stowed away in her office, the script reminded her she was inextricably entwined with the Skaladeska tribe.

Boris gave a happy woof, and Marina looked to see him halfheartedly chasing a rabbit through the scrubby grass and brush. Then she turned back to the rubble, searching for the stairs that led into the ground.

"What's this?" Bruce asked as she began to climb down the brush-strewn, overgrown spiral staircase. "Basement?"

"After a fashion." More like a secret hideaway, where Victor had kept information about the Skaladeskas, as well as his escape route out onto Lake Superior.

Marina didn't know what she expected to find, five years after the place had been destroyed and then searched through, but she was compelled to look. To make certain nothing was here.

Or perhaps to make certain nothing had changed.

She wore her helmet, and flipped on the headlamp when she got to the bottom. Bruce's own beam shone over her shoulder as she picked through the chunks of concrete, rotting wood, and tufts of old upholstery.

She'd taken all of two steps when she saw it: a crinkled brown paper sack, too clean and new to be very old. Probably some kids sneaked in with a six-pack…though this was such a remote location, why would they bother climbing down in here?

Maybe a squatter? Someone who needed a place to stay? But there were plenty of abandoned hunting camps this time of year…

Marina's heart was thudding as she reached for the bag. The paper crinkled in her hands, still dry and untouched by the damp, when she opened it.

Inside she found sandwich crusts, recent enough that the animals hadn't discovered them, and their crumpled paper wrappings.

She recognized the distinct sticker from Zingerman's Deli in Ann Arbor…the city where she lived.

A coincidence?

Hardly.

EIGHT

Dr. Brenda Hatcher looked grimly at the small plastic bag, then at the covered figure lying on the hospital bed.

Michael Wiley, aged forty-nine, had gone into cardiac arrest an hour ago. Though she and her team in the ER worked on him for over sixty minutes, there was nothing they could do to save him.

He'd expired less than two hours after being brought into the emergency room.

The patient had presented with what seemed to be a severe allergic reaction—quarter-sized, lumpy red lesion-like boils over his entire body. His face was so swollen he was hardly recognizable as the photo on his driver's license. His vitals were out of control. His eyes were unfocused and he had uncontrollable muscle tremors and some bleeding from his ears and nose.

The ambulance had brought him in after a 911 call, and he'd been incoherent since the paramedics found him collapsed on the floor of his living room, cell phone in one hand still showing the call to 911, plastic baggie in another. The only thing he'd been able to say was: "The bugs."

Over and over. *The bugs.*

Brenda looked down at the small plastic bag again—the one the patient had been clutching when Julio and Wayne found him. Inside were several specimens of a beetle-like insect still attached to a strip of sticky yellow flypaper. They glinted metallically under the bright hospital lights.

One would assume these were the bugs in question.

Brenda didn't know much about insects, except that in order to be classified as one, they had to have six legs. Or was it eight? No, that was arachnids. Though there were some poisonous species of insects, she knew all of the dangerous ones in Michigan, and these didn't resemble any that were on the list.

They didn't even look real, come to think of it. They looked as if they were made out of copper, and there was a black residue that smudged the inside of the baggie as if it had rubbed off from the creatures. She counted. Six legs. The insect looked like a beetle, with what appeared to be a hard, shell-like covering and minuscule hooks on the ends of the legs. Its head and thorax were much more slender than its oblong body.

They didn't look deadly. They looked like a normal garden variety of beetle, with a fancy copper shell.

But apparently, Michael Wiley thought otherwise.

Whether the medical examiner would as well remained to be seen.

Chicago
FBI Field Office

Special Agent Helen Darrow had been forced into the digital age six months ago. Her superior had presented her with a department-issued smartphone and an iPad—and told her to use them.

Gone were her small notepad and Day Runner calendar (she had been having trouble finding the inserts for it anyway now that everyone else had gone digital), and in their places were two heavier, more delicate contraptions that didn't fit into her slim, no-nonsense pocketbook. Plus, her fingernails—which really weren't very long anyway—got in the way of typing on the touchscreens. Nor could she answer her smartphone when she was wearing her favorite cashmere-lined leather gloves in the freezing Chicago winter, which was another pain in the rear, especially if she was driving. *And* the beastly things had to be plugged in and charged every night.

Which had made things a little difficult during the three-day blackout. But Helen, team player that she was, hadn't said a word to her boss. A few pointed looks, sure, but no snarky comments. At least out loud.

Now, however, as she looked at the man sitting across from her, Helen was grudgingly grateful for the digital tablet—and the end of the crippling power blackout. She'd used a rubber-tipped stylus to type *Binger Blue* into the search field, and was pulling up the information about the short, wiry man on the other side of the table even as she talked to him.

"You witnessed Cora Allegan's abduction?" she asked with one eye on Mr. Blue and the other on the screens as she scrolled through. *William (Binger) Blue, True Blue Gumshoe* (really?) *Private Detective Agency.* Hm. That could be interesting. Or he could turn into a pain in the ass if he decided he was qualified to work the case himself.

She smiled at him with particular warmth and noticed his automatic response: he sat up straight, pulled his eyes up from where they'd dropped to the area of her breasts (and she wasn't even wearing a low-cut blouse), and smoothed a hand over his wispy, thinning hair. He wore a copper bracelet around a slender wrist.

"I was on a stakeout," he told her. "It's confidential," he added quickly, as if to forestall a follow-up question. "My client doesn't want the information to get out at this time."

Helen nodded, scrolled, and scanned. *DOB 7/29/1966, current residence Des Plaines, IL. Divorced, 1997. No children. Northwestern University, 1990-1994. (No degree) Loss Prevention,*

Macy's, 1993-2005. Licensed private investigator, 2005. Registered firearm owner ID, 2003. Renewed 2008. No record. "Was your client pleased with your report?" she asked casually.

Binger Blue's fingers tightened briefly. "I'm not at liberty to say." But the expression on his face spoke otherwise. He was *dying* to tell her.

"Of course. I understand completely." She smiled again, nudging up the warmth in her expression. Honey worked better than vinegar, and all that. "Tell me what you saw."

"It was almost seven o'clock in the evening. I was about eighty feet away and saw a car pull into the driveway at Ms. Allegan's home. Three people got out of the vehicle, two men and a woman, and they walked to the front porch. They were all dressed in plain off-white clothing, like undyed linen. All the same style: loose pants and loose tunic shirts. I couldn't see their shoes."

Helen had picked up a pen and was scrawling notes, pleasantly surprised at the coherent report Binger Blue was giving her. "Any other identifying factors?"

"I was looking through the lens of my camera—it's a long-range lens—but they were facing away from me as they walked up the drive. They didn't seem to interact with each other at all, and they all had light-colored hair. I tried to take a few photos. They didn't turn out great because I was so surprised—well, you can see." He pulled a sheaf of photos from his inner pocket and shoved them at her.

A quick glance told Helen there was some hope of identifying the men, but Binger Blue hadn't been exaggerating when he said they hadn't turned out great. She nodded and collected the photos in her folder. "What happened next?"

"One of them must have knocked or rang the bell, because Ms. Allegan answered the door herself. They talked for a minute, then the next thing I knew, she was out on the porch with them and the door closed behind her. I thought maybe she didn't want anyone inside the house to hear the conversation. Then she sort of slumped between them, like she'd fainted or something, and they carried her off to the car. That's when I jumped out of my vehicle and shouted at them. One of them threw this at me, so I ducked behind some landscaping." He dropped a lump of something iron gray onto the desk.

Helen picked it up gingerly. Soot and ash stained her fingers and she could smell old smoke. The metal object resembled a grenade. "A smoke bomb?"

Binger Blue nodded. "Yes, but I didn't know it wasn't going to explode, so it was effective in keeping me from chasing them or even getting a good look at the license plate. The vehicle was a black 2003 Cadillac and the plate could have been Illinois, but I wasn't at the best angle to see."

She nodded and made a few more notes, pleased with his clarity and conciseness. He was probably a damn good PI. "Did you notice anyone else who might have witnessed any of this?" Helen tapped on the iPad screen to bring up the notes she'd received from the CPD, who'd been notified when Cora Allegan hadn't arrived at her office for work yesterday morning and hadn't been reachable. The Chicago cops weren't thrilled that the Feds were in on this, but when the daughter of a senator goes missing, it becomes everyone's problem.

Now Binger Blue seemed surprised. "Do you mean no one else has come forward?"

She looked up from the iPad. "Someone else was there? Do you know who it was?"

He swallowed and began to play with his copper bracelet. "There was a person in the house. He came out onto the porch after they took Ms. Allegan away."

Helen waited. She didn't look anywhere but at Binger Blue.

His eyes skittered around the room, but she knew there was nothing to look at. Gray walls, gray floor, dirty white ceiling, colorless table. No windows.

She waited, her expression impassive. Her body remained completely still although her mind was racing.

Binger Blue drew in a long, deep breath then spewed it out. He pursed his lips, curling them in unattractively, then flattening them. "Jerome Blankenship."

Helen sat back unable to keep her expression blank. "Of Nellworth Bank?"

He swallowed and nodded. "That's the one."

"And you're telling me he was *there*? And he did nothing?" She snatched up the iPad and began to tap on the touchscreen. *Jerome Blankenship. DOB 11/05/1963. CEO Nellworth Bank, Chicago, IL.*

Married, Lucinda Fennel, 6/3/1998.

Oh. She looked up at Binger Blue, True Blue Gumshoe. "Caught him in the act, did you?" she said, a wry smile twitching the corner of her mouth. "Presumably you've already made your report to Mrs. Blankenship?"

He nodded again. "But she doesn't want it to be made public until she has her divorce lawyer engaged. She doesn't even want Blankenship to know she's got the money shot until she gets her ducks in a row."

Helen noticed he didn't look as miserable as he should have, after spilling his "confidential" information.

"This is the abduction of the daughter of a US senator," Helen reminded him. "Not to mention the CEO of a Fortune 500 company. It's *all* going to be public. You'd better get your fee from Mrs. Blankenship, *stat.*"

Binger grimaced. "I was afraid you were going to say that. I suppose there's no chance you could wait a day or so to pull him in…?"

She shook her head. "Like I said, you'd better get your fee *today.* So, what exactly did he see of the abduction?"

"I don't know what *he* saw," Binger said carefully. "For all I know, he was watching from a window. But I didn't see Blankenship until after they took Allegan away. He came out on the porch about two minutes later, as if he was looking for her. I saw him pick up a piece of paper or something white from the porch. I assumed," he said with a little cough, "he'd already been in touch with the authorities and had told you about it. Now he's going to know Mrs. B knows. Damn. How much longer are you going to need me? I need to get that check." He stood, gathering up his briefcase and cell phone, and hesitated—clearly waiting for her to dismiss him.

Helen nodded. "Good luck. Hope you get your fee. Thank you, Mr. Blue. I'll need a copy of that picture. The money shot."

He groaned, but she merely smiled. "You did your civic duty, Mr. Blue, and I thank you. So does, I'm sure, Ms. Allegan."

As Binger Blue swept out of her office, Helen was already mentally in the process of moving her accounts from Nellworth Bank to somewhere else. Anywhere else. To a bank where the adulterous CEO might actually make a report if his lover—presumably a woman he cared about—had gone missing while he was on the premises. *Douchebag.* He was damned lucky there'd been a witness basically proving he'd had nothing to do with the abduction.

A cool smile curled her mouth. She couldn't wait to drag him in and pose a few questions to the jerk. Let him squirm and sweat.

NINE

I don't understand what I'm doing here. Do you realize I've been sitting in this room for over an hour? I was on my way to a very important meeting when I was intercepted by your associate. You're wasting my time and yours, Agent…Darrow."

Though it was rare for Helen to dislike someone unless she knew them well enough to form a logical opinion, Jerome Blankenship had never had a chance to end up in her positive column.

Thanks to the report from Binger Blue (True Blue Gumshoe), she already intensely disliked Blankenship, even before she sat down across from him. Therefore, she hadn't been particularly warm in her greeting, nor had she been apologetic about his wait or even forthcoming about the reason he'd been brought into the field office. And though she certainly could have gone to him, catching him at his office or elsewhere more convenient for him, she'd made him come to her, having her team snag him as he left an early afternoon workout at the gym. To add insult to injury—she hoped—Helen had had him seated in the most bland, uncomfortable of interrogation rooms (and where the Wi-Fi only showed one bar—on a good day), and most definitely hadn't offered him any coffee.

Which was why she had a surge of satisfaction when she noticed his attention settle hungrily on her Starbucks cup. Not that it was coffee anyway—a chai latte was her preference—but clearly he didn't know that.

Helen smiled at him, pulled out her electronic tablet along with a trusty pad of paper and a pen, and took her time sizing him up. Early fifties, with the not-very-well-obscured evidence of hair plugs, steel-gray eyes, a thin, flat mouth, and shiny, buffed fingernails. Helen subdued a shudder. Manicured hands on a man were a definite, one-hundred-percent turnoff for her. He was wearing workout clothes, which made him appear less like an executive and more like the perfect male gym teacher for an all-girls school: frumpy and disheveled.

Important meeting, indeed.

She lifted her drink and sipped, pretending to skim through the notes on her tablet, but was really checking out the headlines on the *Chicago Tribune*. Then, just as he opened his mouth to speak again, she looked up. "Mr. Blankenship, I do appreciate you coming in this morning. I realize what an inconvenience it must be for someone in your position." She smiled again, allowing a little bit of apology to drift into her eyes as he responded in the manner she expected: by nodding peremptorily, as if granting her permission to grovel. Then she went right in for the kill. "But then again, I suspect Cora Allegan is even more inconvenienced at the moment. I understand you were with her on the evening she disappeared."

This had a most gratifying effect on the man across from her. His face leeched into gray, his shoulders snapped up tight, nearly to his ears, and his eyes went wide…then immediately narrowed.

"I have no idea what you're talking about." He stood. "I'm finished here."

"I have a witness who saw you come out of Cora Allegan's home moments after she was abducted."

"Whoever this witness is, he or she is mistaken."

Helen merely turned her tablet around so he could see the photo Binger Blue had taken of him standing on the porch of Allegan's condo. "Nice boxers."

Blankenship's face drained of what little color was left. Muttering a filthy word, he sank back down into his chair, bumping the table with his inattention. "Is there any chance of keeping that"—he gestured at the image with distaste, his voice thick—"confidential?"

"Your lover has been abducted and all you care about is whether word gets out that you've been unfaithful to your wife?" Helen didn't bother to keep her own disgust hidden. She shook her head, reminding herself she was neither judge nor jury—but then again, having been in a similar position as Mrs. Blankenship clearly was, it was difficult not to have at least a little flicker of empathy for the woman. Nevertheless, she drew in a slow, deep breath. Keeping her personal prejudices out of her professional life was one of her personal credos, and she'd done an excellent job for the decade she'd been with the Bureau. That was why she had been promoted to special agent in charge after only three years with the Feds.

Thus, she merely gave the man across from her a level look. "I have no intention of making this information public, Mr. Blankenship. At least, not purposely. I have no reason to do so. However, since you have been placed at the scene of an abduction, and you didn't come forward with any information about it, I can only hope no one would consider you an accessory…"

"What?" He bolted from his seat. "An accessory? Are you out of your damned mind? How dare you accuse me of such a thing!" Spittle flew and his eyes flashed. "Who do you think you are? I want to speak to your director!"

Helen merely watched him, her disgust growing. She lifted one brow, waited until he finished his tirade, then said, "Please take a seat, Mr. Blankenship. No one is accusing you of anything. However, I do find it curious that you made no move to come forward after Ms. Allegan disappeared. And I may not be the only person to do so. So perhaps if you give me a statement about the—er—extenuating circumstances that prevented you from doing your civic duty, we can nip any future issues in the bud."

He plumped into his chair like a belligerent child being put in a time-out and, folding his hands on the table, fixed her with a glare she assumed was his CEO look: meant to intimidate and seize control. "What do you want?"

"Please tell me what happened the afternoon and evening of September 21. You were at Cora Allegan's residence. Was anyone else there besides you and Ms. Allegan?"

His expression turned even more glacial. "No."

"What time did you arrive?"

"Two thirty."

"Did Ms. Allegan appear to be upset or distracted? Was there anything she did or said that might have indicated fear or concern for her safety?"

He shifted in his seat. "We didn't talk much." His smile oozed bravado.

"So she gave no indication she was in jeopardy or afraid, or that anything that might have portended her abduction was on her mind?"

"No. She was—well, she did mention a letter she'd received a few weeks ago. Said it was from those tree-huggers—one of those environmental groups. They were complaining about something." He shrugged. "Didn't really seem to bother her; she gets that sort of correspondence all the time."

"Did she give you any detail about who the letter was from— the name of the group? Whether there were any threats in it? Whether she'd received mail from them previously?"

"No. Not really. Like I said, we didn't spend much time talking."

Helen resisted the urge to roll her eyes. "Very well. So, if you please, can you give me some detail about what happened when her presumed abductors came to the door?" He opened his mouth to speak, but she interrupted. "There is a witness who saw what happened."

"If there's a witness, why the hell isn't *he* here, getting grilled? If you already know what happened, why am I here, wasting my time?"

Helen waited. He shuffled his hands around, shifted in his chair, and still she waited. Finally, he spoke. "We were—well, the doorbell rang."

"Approximately what time, would you say? You arrived at two thirty, so this was when?"

"Close to seven. I was—I needed to leave soon, and we were…finished." At this, the man at least had the grace to look slightly uncomfortable. "The doorbell rang around seven o'clock. She went to answer it."

"Could you hear or see anything? Any part of the conversation?"

"No. Not really. I was at the back of the house. Then I heard the door close, and when she didn't come back, I called out for her. Thought she might have gone to the kitchen to get some coffee. She didn't answer, but I wasn't concerned. Sometimes you can't hear from the kitchen. I mean, why would I be worried? Why would it even occur to me this had happened?" For the first time, Blankenship exhibited bewilderment and concern.

"And when she didn't respond, when did you realize something was wrong?"

"Not long. I was coming out of the back room anyway—I needed to leave—so I went into the kitchen and she wasn't there. I called again, looked around, then I did start to get worried. Then I thought maybe she was just talking to a neighbor on the front porch, and so I went out to look. No one was there. I checked the garage—her car was still in there. Her cell phone and purse were on the front table."

"So she disappeared, and it didn't occur to you that you should report her missing?"

"Doesn't someone have to be missing for more than twenty-four hours before a missing person report can be made?" Blankenship's snarkiness was back.

Helen set her jaw and made a few notes, biting her tongue. She declined to educate Mr. Blankenship that the twenty-four-hour rule was, in fact, a myth. When she felt she could be pleasant again, she looked back up at him. "Did you find anything that might give a clue to what happened—who came, how they took her—anything?"

He sighed, slumped back in his seat. "Your *witness* probably told you I picked up a piece of paper on the front porch."

"What was it?"

"Well, it wasn't a damned pizza delivery flyer, that's for sure, but it's not any more relevant than one. Just a piece of paper with a kid's drawing on it. Looked like a secret club symbol or something of that nature. I threw it away."

"It was lying on the porch and the only thing on it was a hand-drawn symbol? What did the symbol look like?" She tore a piece of paper from her notebook and slid it across to him. Presumably an important executive would have his own writing implement.

He frowned, pulled out a pen from his briefcase, and looked blankly at the paper. "I don't know. I only saw it for a minute. It looked a little like the Soviet Union symbol—the scythe. But not really; there was more to it than that. Like a G that had been stylized…"

Blankenship grumbled some more, but to Helen's satisfaction, his pen hand began to move over the paper. When he was done, he shoved it back across the table. "Something sort of like this."

Helen stared at it, and her heart skipped a beat. No way. She began to tap and scroll rapidly through her tablet until she got to the image she wanted. "Did it look like this?"

"Yes, it looked just like that," Blankenship said. "What is it?"

Now it was Helen's turn to settle back in her seat. She barely resisted the urge to lower her face into her hands. Of all the luck.

Now she was going to have to call Gabe.

Crap.

September 23
Napo, Ecuador
Near Inchiyacu

Leandro Córdoba slugged back a long drink from his water bottle. Despite the fact that he was traveling along a tributary of the Río Napo, gliding through thick, shaded jungles of the Amazon basin, the heat was heavy and potent. He'd been here for more than six weeks of his three-month volunteer mission and only once had forgotten to fill up his trio of water bottles before leaving the main health clinic.

It was the first and last time he'd done that.

"Is the village near?" he asked his companion, Dr. Rafael Saenzdiviteri.

They'd left the main camp three hours earlier, after loading medicines and equipment onto the flat-bottomed motorized canoe, along with enough food and water for three days. You never knew when a sudden rainstorm would unleash itself on the jungle, and if they were forced to beach and wait it out, it could be hours or even days. Lee was inclined to avoid such a predicament. He preferred the safety of the permanent housing back at their camp, which was much better protection from a hungry jaguar than a hammock suspended between a couple of trees.

Doc Rafe conferred in Quichua with their guide, the man navigating their boat down the unnamed tributary—at least, it was unnamed in Spanish. Surely it had a name in the local language. Lee had begun to pick up a bit of Quichua, but had to rely on his native Spanish for most of his communication with the nurses, physicians, aides, and other volunteers that worked out of the medical clinic near Inchiyacu. Only the locals spoke the language fluently.

"He says after another two bends in the river," Doc told him, swiping a thick, dark arm over his forehead. "And we will see the village on the east side. Look for the solar panel."

That was one of the oddest things Lee had experienced since arriving in the rainforest: the occasional solar panel in or near a primitive-looking village. There were rarely more than one or two in any given area, and because of the heavy growth of the top layers of trees, the power generated by the panels was feeble at best.

The first time he'd seen one, he felt as if he'd traveled into some fourth dimension or science fiction world. Even at home, in a civilized suburb of Barcelona, there weren't as many solar panels as one might think. But it was the best and most logical way to generate energy in such a remote area, and he'd become used to the anachronistic sight.

Lee ducked just in time to avoid being struck by a low-hanging branch. One of the other med student volunteers sponsored by Voluntarios/Aventurados: España had been knocked into the river on their first day and shocked by an eel. She was still limping. The water might look inviting, but there were plenty of snakes, black alligators, and of course piranha lurking beneath the surface.

Their guide made a sudden sound of alert and pointed to a shaded area near the riverbank. It wasn't until they were nearly upon it that Lee saw the capybara, soaking in the water. Only the nostrils of the guinea-pig-like rodent showed, which was surprising, as the animal was nearly fifty kilograms and the size of a large dog. The water must be deep near the shore.

Doc stood at the helm of the boat, his white hair ruffling in a welcome breeze. Lee had grown to like and respect the man, who'd devoted his entire medical career to caring for the people in this remote area. The older man was comforting and empathetic, inspiring trust and calm in his patients—just like Lee aspired to be once he finished his medical training.

Doc had asked Lee to join him on what was to be a single day's journey. There'd been reports of illness coming from one of the villages that had been established in a newly cleared area of the jungle. That, Lee had learned, was one of the problems with agriculture in the rainforest, and what caused the people to continually colonize: the land became infertile after too many years of farming, and so they spread out further into the jungle. Of course, the effect from the small number of indigenous people who lived here was minor compared to that of the lumber industry.

Saving the rainforest had been a common primary school fundraising activity, and Lee had heard the stories of deforestation ravaging the place. But one would never know it, here in the lush green jungle. The sounds of water lapping and surging against the boat and shoreline, the *ca-ca-ca* or *cooo-ee-ya* calls of the hundreds of species of birds, and the rustle of brush being disturbed…all of it made the world of twenty-first-century man seem light years away.

Although he hadn't been on Facebook or plugged in his iPod to charge in more than three weeks, Lee didn't miss the technology. For a young man who'd lived his entire life in and near a cosmopolitan city, and who'd done minimal hiking and camping, this mission to the most dangerous, remote place on earth had been an incredible eye-opener. He didn't need his iPod, his streaming movies. There was a different sort of music here, unending natural entertainment. He was never bored enough that he had to log in somewhere and check in with someone, manufacturing something to say. Of course, his mamá didn't like the idea of him being without his mobile or access to email, but Lee got to an Internet cafe once a week to send her a message.

A glint on the shore drew his attention, and as they passed two small, battered solar panels, Lee heard voices in the distance. The boat trundled along under the skillful navigation of their guide, and moments later, the vessel beached at a clearing. A group of young boys played football as their mothers watched and gossiped while working on their weaving.

Carrying a bulky medical case, Lee followed Doc up crude wooden and sand-packed steps from the shore as the boys watched. Several houses sat on a small hill that would protect them from a flooding river. The structures, made with planed lumber slats aligned vertically, were on stilts rising several meters above the ground. They had high-pitched roofs of thatched gray reeds that looked like unkempt hair.

"Do you want to go with me?" Doc asked.

Lee shook his head. It would be more efficient for them to separate, and if there was something he didn't know how to treat, then he could ask Doc Rafe. The fact that Lee spoke hardly any Quichua was a small factor; there was much that could be communicated with sign language. It was unlikely that many in the village spoke Spanish.

One of the women detached herself from her companions and approached them. After a brief conversation with Doc Rafe, she gestured to Lee to follow her, and she led him to the house in the center of the group. A crude staircase led to the main entrance, and he had to duck when stepping through the doorway.

Lee had been in a variety of homes since arriving in Ecuador, each slightly different, some more crude than others. This was a single large room, rather dark except for the pair of light bulbs strung across one wall and the bit of sunlight that filtered through cracks between the wood. The home was neat, although slightly cluttered with aspects of daily living, and it was much warmer inside than out. But, to his dismay, Lee noticed the irregular streaks of black and white on the inside of the walls, and suspected he knew what he'd find.

In the corner lay a young boy on a hammock, and Lee made his way immediately to the patient. The first thing he saw was the huge swelling above the eye, misshaping the brow and causing red discoloration in the skin around it. Near the boy's mouth was a black boil-like lesion, and other smaller red marks that looked like deep insect bites.

Definitely Chagas disease. And it had evolved into a chronic case, for which there was little he could do. The child likely wouldn't die—although he might need a heart transplant in the future—but it would be an uncomfortable existence.

Grimly, Lee began to dig in his bag for the Benznidazole and an anti-diarrheal medication. The boy was clearly suffering from both the disease and the dehydration that came along with it. The woman next to him was using a mix of crude Spanish, Quichua, and hand gestures to tell him her son had been sick for four weeks.

Damn shame they hadn't sent to the clinic back then, or the disease from the kissing bug could have been cured. And this also meant Lee would need to examine the others in the household to see if any of them were also infected by the parasitic insect.

The bug lived in the cracks of the walls, or up in the thatched roof, and came out at night, feeding on its human host. They usually attached themselves near the mouth, hence the name "kissing bug." The streaks of black and white on the wood were clear signs of its presence—being the same fecal matter and waste that caused the infection in humans and animals. It wasn't a bite or sting that caused the disease, it was the bacteria that clung to the beetle's legs that was the culprit.

Lee knew he'd have to talk to Doc Rafe about continuing treatment for the boy, but at least he could begin to make him more comfortable. He'd just finished dosing him with Benznidazole when there was a great commotion outside.

The boy's mother hurried from the hut as voices grew louder and more insistent, and Lee, his heart beginning to pound, rose to his feet. Something was definitely wrong.

He emerged from the building at the same time as Doc poked his head out the door of a neighboring hut. "What is it?" Lee called to him.

Descending from the houses, they reached the group of villagers simultaneously. Apparently, Doc gleaned a bit of what was happening, for he said, "Follow them," as a trio of agitated young women gestured toward the jungle. By now, Lee understood: they'd found something terrible.

Fifteen minutes later, they'd followed the women's weak trail back into the lush greenery. As the resident medical expert, Doc had been invited to come along, and despite his hypervigilance when it came to the unfamiliar dangers in the jungle, Lee accompanied him.

When they got to their destination, the young women pointed to a dark cloud of flies swarming over something in the brush. They weren't going to look, but Lee followed his mentor and several other villagers over to see.

It was a man—or what was left of him.

Doc Rafe knelt next to the body, which had not only been torn apart by some animal but was being feasted upon by an array of insects. The victim's exposed clavicle gleamed dully in the sun-dappled space, and his blood had long congealed, drying dark and thick as oil. He hadn't been there for more than half a day, or there wouldn't be this much left of him.

Two arms and a leg were missing, likely carried off by whatever had attacked. Lee suspected the villagers would be able to tell whether it was a jaguar or some other carnivore, but he didn't particularly care to ask about those details.

Despite the gruesome scene, the most striking thing about the victim was his attire—or what was left of it. Although his torso had been lacerated, mauled, and nibbled upon, it was still evident he had been wearing a business suit. And on his remaining foot was a mud-caked, scuffed leather loafer. Italian, and expensive.

The man, whose skin tone and straight ink-black hair seemed to indicate an Oriental heritage, looked as if he'd just stepped out of a business conference.

"Mother of God," Doc Rafe muttered, kneeling next to the corpse. He gingerly poked around the pockets of the suit coat and trousers as the villagers observed.

Lee watched as Doc produced a high-end mobile phone, a leather wallet-like case, and a money clip of colorful bills.

And absolutely nothing practical for travel in the Amazon basin. Not even a book of matches or a water bottle.

Crouching next to Doc Rafe, Lee picked up the money clip and thumbed through the purplish-reddish bills with a 2000 mark on them, along with Chinese characters. Yuan? Yuan in the middle of Ecuador?

The screen on the mobile was shattered, and moisture had gathered, surely rendering it useless.

But it was the small bifold leather case that yielded the most shocking and pertinent information. Inside were bilingual business cards and identification that established the man as Lo Ing-wen. Leandro knew enough English to read the reverse side of the business card.

"Lo Ing-wen, president of Oh Yeh Industries," he read aloud, then looked at Doc.

How had a Chinese executive turned up in the middle of the jungle?

TEN

Marina trudged up the walk to her red shake-shingled bungalow. She lived in a tree-lined neighborhood with winding streets southwest of campus. The area was mostly populated by tenured professors from the University of Michigan, separated from the student housing by both distance and price.

It was after seven p.m. and she'd just flown in from the Keweenaw Peninsula, landing her little Piper at Ann Arbor Muni Airport. Marina was exhausted from the rescue and heartbroken over Matt Granger's death—and more than a little unsettled that someone had been at her father's place—but even that unhappy knowledge couldn't completely squelch her burgeoning excitement.

Though she knew it would be opening her own private version of Pandora's box, Marina couldn't wait to compare the pictures she'd taken in Matt Granger's cave with the contents of the package she'd tucked away in her office. Despite its implications, she could no longer ignore the package...as well as the unsettling sense that the Skaladeskas had returned to her life once more.

But first, she was going to dump her stuff on the floor, feed Boris, and then fall onto her bed for a minimum of twelve hours. Then she'd order Cottage Inn pizza, open a bottle of Malbec, look at the pictures, compare the scripts, and decide what to do. She could almost hear her bed calling her. Even a shower could wait.

"Inside," she told Boris as she unlocked the door and flung her duffel bag onto the floor. She reached in to turn on the light, for the sun was low and the trees crowding her property kept the house dim even during the day.

The German Shepherd stepped across the threshold, just as glad to be home as she—and immediately stiffened.

A ruff of hair lifted along the back of his neck and spine. His ears went forward and then to attention. His nose was up and he was clearly scenting something. He gave a low yip of warning and looked up at his mistress.

By now, Marina had stopped in the entrance, her fingers curled around the doorknob. Her heart pounded and she wasn't sure if she should go in or turn and run.

Boris hadn't moved. He seemed to be waiting for her permission or direction. She knew his every mood and stance, and he didn't appear agitated as much as on alert, although the curl of his lip indicated concern. Something was wrong, but he didn't sense an imminent threat.

"Go," she said, making the hand gesture that sent him off.

His nails skittering on the tile, he bolted away, leaving the woven rug she'd brought home from Thailand in a crumpled heap in the foyer.

Marina waited at the front door, half in and half out, wondering if she ought to finally purchase the handgun she swore she'd never buy. Gabe had suggested it more than once, even since things had ended with the Skaladeskas. It was as if he expected something else to happen—and he didn't even know about the package sitting in her office. But though Marina had actually had to use a gun during their escape from them in Siberia, she was adamantly opposed to having one on hand.

Maybe that was one tendency she'd inherited from her father. Her real father.

Boris came pattering back from the depths of the house, his head up and eyes bright. He alerted as he would have done on a

SAR mission, sitting directly in front of her with one paw raised. Hm.

"All right, then," she said, more to herself than to him, and released Boris. "Show me."

He took off through the living room toward the kitchen and office. Despite the promise of security from her dog's teeth and claws, Marina pulled out the pepper spray she'd taken to keeping in a drawer by the front door and hurried off Boris's wake, following him to her office.

When she came into the shadowy room, she found her dog standing at attention, his eyes fixed on the sofa, one ear straight up and the other cocked toward the door, listening for her. He wasn't growling so much as sneering at the figure draped over the piece of furniture.

Marina's heart surged into her throat and then dropped well below her belly as she saw a person—a man—in her office. Sleeping...or something else.

Pepper spray at the ready, she turned on the light, flooding the room with white light from environmentally correct bulbs. It wasn't, as she'd immediately suspected, Gabe MacNeil who was sprawled on her sofa. Although the man's face was half shielded by a throw pillow, she could see he had close-cropped dark blond hair—so unless Gabe had cut and bleached his dark locks, it was definitely not him. Aside from that, if he wanted to sleep, he'd be waiting in bed, not here on the office couch.

It was a stranger...a stranger who, she saw with rising concern, had dark splotches of blood staining the shirt over his torso and arm, and by extension, the upholstery on her sofa.

Heart pounding, Marina slipped the pepper spray into her pocket and started toward him, ignoring a warning yip from Boris. Her dog moved with her, as if to block her from getting too close, but a firm hand gesture had him stopping and staying.

She gave her canine boy a quick pat of thanks and love on the head and, leaving the dog watching her with full attention, bent over the man. He was warm, still breathing—whew—and as she touched his throat to feel for a pulse, he jolted and shifted.

A low, deep groan that was clearly pain-filled accompanied his slow, jerky movements, and he turned just enough that his head lifted from behind the pillow and she saw his face.

Marina couldn't control a gasp of shock and she bolted upright, stumbling away from him. Boris was too well trained to move, but he gave a soft, concerned whine, his eyes going from his mistress to the man on the couch and back again.

Her hands had gone clammy and her insides were abruptly filled with butterflies. It couldn't be him. She had to be wrong.

She probably was. She'd only seen a glimpse of his face. But it was a face she'd never forget on a dangerous man for whom she had an unwanted, unwarranted attraction.

Pulling the pepper spray back out of her pocket, just in case—for the last time she'd seen Varden, he'd shot Gabe in the arm—she crept forward again. Her palms were clammy, and as she looked down at him once more, his eyelids fluttered.

They opened, and she swallowed another sound of apprehension. It was definitely Rue Varden's jade-green eyes that looked up at her, unfocused and filled with pain.

Marina stared down at him, fighting the gut-check warning that he was dangerous. Then, biting her lip, she tucked the pepper spray away once more. He was clearly injured and in no condition to hurt her, and she couldn't just let him lie there, bleeding all over her couch.

But first…she groped gingerly around the waist and pockets of his jeans, and then up under the denim around his muscular calves and finally under the arm on which he lay. The limb that was bloody she didn't touch until she was certain he didn't have any weapons tucked away. When she lifted his arm, he stiffened and groaned, and she saw that his thumb was swollen to the size of a pickle. A break or bad sprain, but no other injury. The blood must be from somewhere—or someone—else.

His eyes fluttered again, and as she looked down at him, Varden's vision sharpened. "You," he muttered, as if seeing her for the first time.

Marina, who had EMS training as part of her SAR background, looked down at him. "Whom did you expect?" She wanted to demand what he was doing here—here in Michigan, here in her house, and *here* in the place he must know was the presence of an enemy—but she didn't.

"Need help," he said, and struggled to pull himself up.

"I can see that," she replied, mostly holding back on the sarcasm. This was the man who'd helped lock her in a chamber in the mountains of Siberia, who'd taunted her when Gabe was being tortured by Roman and the other Skaladeskas, who'd sneered at her just before putting a bullet into Gabe's arm.

Yet…either by accident or design, Varden had also given her information. Information that had ultimately helped her to avert a major disaster in Detroit, and information that had helped her and Gabe escape.

"Need stitches." His accent was thicker than before, clouded with pain and effort.

Ignoring Boris's high-pitched yip of warning, she helped Varden come to an upright position. "Thanks for ruining my sofa," she muttered, looking at the stain. Then she turned her attention back to him. "Let me see what you've got here."

The words were barely out of her mouth when she realized the blood wasn't coming from his torso or arm, but from the back of his head, which had been pressed into the back of the sofa. It had soaked into the upholstery and all down the back of his shirt.

"What the—" she whispered, pulling a bloody hand away from the back of his scalp.

"I said…" he breathed, his eyes beginning to roll back into his head again. "Stitch me…up." She felt him shudder and sway against her, and steadied him against the back of the sofa. He was solid and muscular—a burden for someone of her size to lift, even though she was in excellent shape.

"You need to go to a hospital," she said.

He gave a violent jerk and forced his eyes open. "No." They were sharp and angry and cold. "Stitch me. You."

"Look, I'm an EMT, but I'm not equipped to do minor surgery here," she began, even as her mind was racing. She had a big enough needle in her survival kit, and she could use the same heavy thread she had on hand to repair tears in the tarps, but—

"You. Damn it." He lifted a wavering hand, and she saw, for the first time, the tattoo on the underside of his wrist. The mark of the Skaladeskas. The same image that was on the heel of her foot, the one her father had imposed upon her when she was a child.

The mark that branded her one of them, even though she hadn't even known the Skaladeskas still existed until five years ago.

She understood Varden's position. If he sought treatment in public, they'd see the mark. And since the earthquakes they'd engineered five years ago, the Skaladeskas were no longer running below the radar of Homeland Security, et al. The mark was an identifier, and Rue Varden did not want to be identified.

But why had he come *here*? To her?

Why would he imagine she'd help him, her enemy? He was the right-hand man of Roman Aleksandrov—the leader and brains of the ecoterrorist group…and her biological father.

"Wipe it away," he said, feebly gesturing to the back of his head.

Marina realized she didn't have time to question or to argue. He was obviously weak and quickly losing blood. His pulse was too faint, and the cast of his skin ugly. Of course she had to help him.

And then she could call the authorities.

"All right," she said. "You'll need to lie down."

He made a grimace, but allowed her to help him shift prone so the back of his head faced her. That was when she saw the congealed mass of blood clinging to his hair, right at the back of his skull.

"I need to sterilize and—"

"Just…stitch the blood…dy thing…*up*." He pushed the words from his lungs as if it were his last breath, his face muffled by the back of the couch. "Wasting…time."

She ignored him and ran back to the front hall to grab her duffel bag. As she hurried back to the office, she unzipped it and pulled out her first-aid kit. It was woefully inadequate for this situation, but at least she could pull out a few bandages and pour some alcohol on his wound. Find a pair of gloves, even.

"I have to ask this," she said, digging for something to wipe away the blood. "Do you have any history of Hepatitis C or AIDS?"

He made a sound that was something between a laugh and groan and a curse.

"No, really," she said. "I need to know. You're a doctor, you know that." She pulled a clean tank top from her duffel and wiped at the wound. A gelatinous mass of blood clots came with it, and a moment later, something wet shot her in the face. "Shit. You've got a damned pumper," she muttered, ignoring the blood coursing down her own cheek. She'd only seen something like this once before, but that was what the ER doc had called it. So much for medical terminology.

Another geyser from the arterial bleed squirted out, splashing her again, and she understood why Varden was so insistent for her to get the job done. The congealing blood had slowed it to an ooze, but now that she'd wiped it clean, it was going to surge crazily with each beat of his heart until she sewed it up.

She pushed a hand against the wound and used her other to wipe away the last of the clot so she could see the gash. Too late for gloves.

The injury was three inches long, and she suspected if there wasn't so much blood still pumping out, she'd even see a bit of skull. Shit. Damn. This was way out of her league.

And then she noticed a needle dangling from a piece of string off to one side of the cut. "What the hell?" she asked, pulling the skin together, pushing on it to stop the pressure. She could feel the surge of blood pulsing beneath her slippery palm. "Did you run the doctor off in the middle of stitching you up?"

"Couldn't...do it myself," he said, and shifted with the arm that was wet with blood.

"You were trying to stitch *yourself* up?" she said, and noticed his swollen thumb again. Broken or sprained or something. Oh, that explained it. She looked at the two sutures he'd managed. "Not bad for being handicapped and unable to see anything," she muttered, pulling the skin together. "But I'd better sterilize this."

"No," he said from between unmoving jaws. "Just...finish. Now."

The needle was slippery with blood, but there was enough red-stained fishing line—fishing line?—attached that she'd be able to finish closing the gash.

"Tight," he breathed. "Pull hard...and close. Go."

"You didn't answer my question," she said, gritting her teeth, trying not to think about all the blood. It streamed over her hand, covered the back of his head, and now soaked through her shirt and dripped down her face. She was a damned caver, not a freaking surgeon. She'd seen blood before, lots of it, many times, but she'd never been swimming in it like this. "Hep C? AIDS?"

He muttered something she didn't understand then said, "I'm clean."

Well, that was good, because she'd already been doused in his bodily fluids and any damage would have been done by now.

She made the sutures as tight as she could, pulling the skin together with fingers that ended up cramped from the stress and tension of holding it hard and close. Occasionally, she felt him wince, or a hitch in his rough breathing. But by the time she was done, his eyes had closed and his breathing had eased into something regular. He'd passed out.

She had to grab scissors from her desk to snip the fishing line after she tied it up. Then she looked down at her bloody hands and clothes—not to mention the floor, sofa, and her patient—and swore under her breath.

It looked like a crime scene.

Despite her antipathy for Varden, she wasn't going to let him lie there encrusted in blood. So she went off to get a bowl of hot water and a clean rag. He hadn't wanted her to take the time to sterilize the wound, but at least she could wash him up a bit.

Despite his current weakness and vulnerability, this man was a member of an ecoterrorist cell. He was dangerous and wanted by the CIA and probably a variety of other law enforcement agencies. He'd *shot* a CIA operative. At close range.

But he hadn't killed him. *He hadn't killed him.*

Why not?

She'd asked herself that many times since then.

"Why did you come here?" she said, more to herself than to him, as she soaked away the blood from his hair.

His breathing changed and he made a soft sound, almost as if he'd heard her and wanted to respond…then he relaxed again and his breathing slowed.

Five years ago, Gabe and his boss, Colin Bergstrom, had shown up out of the blue and told Marina about the Skaladeskas. They were looking for her father, Victor Alexander, from whom she was estranged. That was when she learned his real name was Viktor Aleksandrov. Marina had done her best to blow them off, but they were CIA and not quite as easy to blow off as Bruce and his inappropriate attentions.

Still, Marina hadn't truly believed what Gabe and Bergstrom were telling her until a man broke into the house and tried to abduct her. Dannen Fridkov had been following Roman Aleksandrov's orders to bring Marina—the last "Out-World" member of the Skaladeska tribe—back to them. She'd narrowly escaped him by climbing out the upstairs window and clambering off through the high branches of close, leafy trees.

Was that why Rue Varden had come here now? Or did it have to do with the package she'd received four months ago?

Marina couldn't help but glance toward what her Pandora's box—the package that sat on the top of her tall bookshelf. After opening it, she'd kept it out of reach, away from temptation, until now—until Matt Granger's discovery.

"I'm not going back," she said, unbuttoning Varden's blood-soaked shirt and carefully pulling it from beneath his torso. His muscular arms and chest were bruised and scraped, and there was a long, shallow gash down one side of his torso past the hip.

That cut had stopped bleeding and didn't need much attention, although she wiped it clean with an alcohol pad.

Then, her nose filled with the smell of too much blood, her clothes soaked with it, and remnants still under her fingernails, beginning to dry on her hands, Marina stood. She needed a shower and she needed to call Gabe.

ELEVEN

Marina woke slowly, her brain mushy and groggy, and pulled herself upright. Boris lunged to his feet from where he'd been sleeping on the floor next to her bed.

There was something…something she had to do.

Then, as she peeled away the scattered pieces of memory, she remembered stepping into the shower, washing away the blood… sitting down on the edge of the bed, closing her eyes for just a minute, just *one* minute…and then nothing.

Varden.

She leapt off the bed and felt the towel she still had around her loosen and slip to the floor. Boris was prancing about in response to her agitation, but a glance at the clock told Marina she'd only been asleep for a little more than an hour.

Her hair was still damp, and swung in choppy strands around her face, clinging to her neck as she yanked on a tank top and loose shorts in a scramble to get downstairs and check on her patient. Before getting in the shower, she'd texted Gabe to call her ASAP, but with no further details. She didn't want to put specifics in a text in case…well, in case someone was monitoring her.

Even though she'd been a sort of unofficial civilian consultant the last time they dealt with the Skaladeskas, she was unsure of protocol with other law enforcement agencies—did the Feds get involved if a terrorist was here, or was it the local police she should call? She knew Gabe and Bergstrom would want to get their hands on Varden anyway, but who should take him into custody?

And how fast could Gabe even *get* here?

Boris galloped down the stairs in front of her and led the way to the office, but when Marina walked in, she saw an empty, bloodstained sofa.

"No!" she exclaimed, spinning in a circle, hoping in vain to spy Varden hiding in a corner.

She ran out of the room and searched the house, to no avail. He was gone. And not only was he somehow, impossibly gone, but he'd taken a loaf of bread and a jar of peanut butter with him—as evidenced by the dirty knife in the sink, a few crumbs on the counter, and the disappearance of both items. The only bit of real food she'd had in the house.

"Damn," she muttered, unable to believe he'd had the ability to even stand, let alone walk out of the house so soon.

She went back to her office just to see if she'd been hallucinating. Unfortunately, she hadn't been. But this time she noticed blood streaks and splotches by the window, on the window frame, and in a clear trail to the sofa. He'd come in that way, and, she thought grimly, likely gone out that way as well.

As she stared at the empty couch in dismay, Marina noticed a scrap of paper wedged between the bloodstained cushions of the sofa. Because there was a red stain on it, she picked it up. It was a receipt from a drugstore in Naperville, Illinois. That was near Chicago. And it was from yesterday.

A little shiver rushed over the back of her shoulders. So Rue Varden had been in Chicago yesterday—four hours from here by car, five by train, one by commercial plane.

And now he was gone.

Damn.

Marina retrieved her cell phone and found Gabe's return text: *Need to talk to you anyway. On way to MI. ETA 20:30. Soon enough?*

She checked the time. That would be anytime now. A little tingle of anticipation fluttered in her belly. It had been months since she'd seen Gabe, and she'd missed him. Hopefully he'd be able to stay for a day or two. Or at least overnight.

Marina automatically glanced at the front door as if expecting to see him walk through, then went over and locked it. The last thing she needed was a lecture from him about leaving her doors open. Not that it mattered; obviously, Varden had found a way in through the window while she was gone.

He'd have probably died if she hadn't returned today, Marina realized with a start. She'd have come home and found a corpse on her sofa instead of a patient. Now all she had was the knowledge that she'd aided and abetted a terrorist (maybe she shouldn't mention the incident to Gabe after all) and a ruined couch.

Realizing how hungry she was, and forcing away the exhaustion that hadn't been alleviated by her brief nap, Marina called for pizza and paced the kitchen, waiting.

After five minutes of that, she gave in to the curiosity that had been niggling at her since she walked into Matt Granger's cave. She took her cell phone back into the office in case Gabe tried to contact her again. Varden's blood had dried into dark brown splotches on her dark brown sofa, and was hardly noticeable except on the rug, and a smear by the windowsill. She cleaned it up as well as possible, but even so, she could still smell the underlying scent of it in the room. She opened the window.

Boris collapsed on the floor with a soft groan, obviously off duty and disgruntled that his sleep had been disturbed. He'd alert as soon as Gabe pulled in the driveway, so Marina knew she had a few minutes to look at the photos before he arrived. But when she sat down to turn on her laptop so she could upload the images from Matt's cave, she realized her computer was already on…just sleeping.

A prickle lifted the hair on the back of her neck. She'd been gone for a week. She hadn't left her laptop powered on. When she nudged the computer awake, it showed her Skype account…up and running. Marina used the online videoconferencing program regularly in order to speak with her academic colleagues, who often lived in different time zones and even on different continents.

But she hadn't left the program open. She knew that for certain.

And she knew she didn't have a contact named Dr. Herb Grace...but now one was showing in her account. And another one she didn't recognize. *Gaias_Son*.

The prickle turned to a chill and Marina turned to look around the room, almost expecting to see Rue Varden standing there. For surely it had been he who'd used her Skype program to connect with Gaia's Son...

She was still alone. Boris perked up, looking at her with interest when she rose from the desk, stepping away from the laptop to look down at it, but putting space between her and the machine nevertheless. As if it was poisonous.

Gaia's Son. Son of Gaia, of the earth.

She knew who he had to be.

Her palms became damp as her mind reeled. Varden had been talking to Lev. Her grandfather. Or...

Marina glanced up at the package she'd tried to ignore. It was shoved away on the top of her bookshelf and hardly visible from below.

Varden wouldn't have left the program running unless he wanted her to know about it—either that he'd been there or that he'd contacted Lev via video chat. He was too smart to make such a mistake.

Which meant he wanted her to know. Or *Lev* wanted her to know.

He wanted her to know how to contact him.

The prickling turned chilly when she heard the distinct sound from her computer, announcing the arrival of one of her Skype contacts. She held her breath and looked.

Gaia's Son was online...

And now he was calling her.

Her stomach pitched at the tinny sound of the ring emitting from the laptop's speakers. Answer? Decline?

That was the other thing Varden had done, Marina realized. He'd changed her settings...so when she went online, Gaia's Son knew it and was notified.

And now he was calling her.

She slammed the laptop closed, heart pounding, and scrubbed her palms on her shorts.

Not now.

Never.

All at once, Boris leapt to his feet, startling Marina. She spun from the desk, looking around once more. Her companion gave a short bark of warning, then rushed out of the office to wait in the foyer. It had to be Gabe.

She relaxed, a flash of anticipation rushing her along in Boris's path. The doorbell rang just as she passed through the living room, and she had a moment of gratitude that her dog was so sensitive to the comings and goings of the neighborhood. True, sometimes he was a little too sensitive—when the squirrels were mating and scampering through the trees or when a rabbit bounded across the front yard—but most of the time, she had no complaints. She motioned for him to down-stay and Boris slumped down obediently, but kept his head and ears up and alert.

A brief glance at the mirror over her table in the foyer told Marina that her dark hair had nearly dried in its choppy, wash-and-wear style, and that she still had a faint sleep mark on her cheek.

She opened the door and there was Gabe MacNeil...along with Colin Bergstrom and Special Agent Helen Darrow.

"Oh," she said, and stepped back to allow them entrance. *Damn.* "Come in." An uncomfortable tension tightened her stomach and she drew in a deep breath. Clearly, this was not going to be good news. Good grief. Could they have already traced the Skype connection from her house to Lev and the Skalas?

Gabe's dark eyes swept over her and their gazes met briefly. She saw a flash of warmth there followed by a nod of apology. "Marina," he said, stepping past her. "I hope you got my text."

"Yes, of course. I just didn't expect the entire cavalry," she murmured, and then extended her hand to greet Colin Bergstrom.

She hadn't seen the man in a few years, but he looked the same. His hair was still wispy and his glasses were still too heavy, leaving imprints on the bridge of his nose. Despite the August heat, he wore a suit coat and tie that was almost successful in hiding the small paunch he carried low in his abdomen. She put his age at close to seventy, though he looked spry enough to be in his sixties.

"Dr. Alexander, it's good to see you again," Bergstrom said. She'd always liked the man, for he was intelligent and empathetic as well as determined. And even when he was threatening to revoke one's passport, he did it with such skill that one almost didn't care. Almost. "I'm sorry to arrive so unexpectedly."

She held back a wry smile. This was nothing compared to the surprise in her office from earlier today. Her stomach gave a nervous flip when she thought of Varden and his quick escape. "It's the nature of the beast," she said. "Meaning your job. I just got home myself a couple hours ago, hence the duffel bag on the floor. Hi, Helen. Good to see you again as well." She extended her hand and received a firm handshake in return. "The living room is this way; have a seat."

Special Agent Helen Darrow was from the FBI office in Chicago and had been instrumental in stopping the Skaladeska terrorist attack in Detroit. Marina had only met her once, in the debrief after she and Gabe escaped from Siberia, but she'd talked to her on the phone several times. The other woman was close to her in age, but other than their shared gender, they were quite different in appearance.

Helen was dressed in the type of sleek, professional suit Marina hadn't owned since her days of job interviews. She wore heels that were at least three inches tall, and her shoes were a croco-skin design that made even Marina look twice. The SA's hair was just past shoulder length, honey-blond, and pulled back in an understated silver barrette. She kept her practical nails French manicured and neat, and she was actually wearing lipstick—even at nine o'clock on a Wednesday night after traveling from...

Chicago.

Marina faltered and a shiver rushed over her bare arms. Surely it wasn't a coincidence Rue Varden had shown up today, lately come from Chicago...and here was Helen Darrow. Who had also lately come from Chicago.

"Marina." Gabe caught her eye, and she paused in the foyer as the others went on. The moment his boss and colleague were out of sight, he moved toward her, kicking the duffel bag out of the way. The next thing she knew, he had her backed up against the front door and his mouth descended for a quick, thorough kiss with lots of soft lip and sweeping tongue.

He stepped back too soon and looked down, smiling a little as her hand settled on his chest. "It's been too damn long," he said, a touch of West Virginia in a voice that had become thick. "Sorry about the tag-alongs."

Marina had gone all soft and warm as soon as he touched her, and now she looked up at him, her pulse thudding along at a nice pace. She felt his heart pounding beneath her palm as well. "I'm sure you'll find an expedient way to get rid of them before the night's over."

"That's the plan. Uh..." He paused and looked down at her. "I think you look great, but did you want to grab a robe? I'm not sure Colin can handle this much of you."

She followed his gaze and realized she was leaving little to the imagination in the bra-less tank and loose boxer shorts she'd yanked on after waking abruptly. Someone as put-together as Helen Darrow might have blushed with embarrassment, answering the door in such a state—or then again, maybe not. But after years of primitive camping in foreign countries and doing archaeological digs in rustic places, not to mention the lack of accommodations on SAR missions, Marina had long stopped being modest about her appearance.

Nevertheless, she said, "I'll be right back."

While Marina went upstairs to change, Gabe joined the others in the living room. Helen glanced up as he walked in, her elegant brows rising knowingly as she crossed her long, very fine legs. Settled in an armchair, she'd removed her jacket and appeared relaxed in a sleeveless cobalt silk blouse and with her shoes kicked off.

"So you're certain she hasn't been in touch with the Skaladeskas," Helen said. "It seems to me that someone like Marina Alexander would be hard pressed to stay away from them if they're the guardians of an ancient library."

Gabe followed her gaze as it scanned the room. He'd only been here a few times, but the place was familiar to him. The vintage Hitchcock movie posters shared wall space with framed, matted, and shadow-boxed items that ranged from old parchments to simple wood carvings to scraps of woven fabric that looked hundreds of years old. Marina still had a bowl of crystals on the low coffee table in front of two weathered leather sofas. The stones looked like small chunks of glacier: clear, pale blue, iced pink, and one dark, blood-red one.

"As much as she'd love to get her hands on the contents of that library," he told Helen, "she wouldn't risk it."

"Wouldn't risk what?"

They turned as one to look at their hostess. To Gabe's mixture of relief and disappointment, she'd changed into yoga pants and a tight workout top that showed toned, tanned arms. Her thick, razor-cut hair was flipped every which way around her jaw line and neck, and her brown eyes scanned them all with wary interest. A Russian heritage was evident in the exotic set of her eyes, high cheekbones, and the olive cast to her skin.

"Your life," Gabe said. "Going after the Skalas' library."

Her eyes flashed to his and he saw annoyance and surprise. Before she could say anything, he spoke. "Marina, we've got some things to tell you—"

Boris leapt to his feet and began to bark, rushing to the front door. "Pizza," Marina told them, and walked out to attend to the delivery.

It smelled heavenly, and Gabe couldn't help but eye the large box as she placed it on the table. "You ordered the whole thing for yourself?" he asked hopefully.

"I was hungry," she said with a smile that, though strained, encompassed all of them. "But help yourself. This is classic Ann Arbor—Cottage Inn Pizza. I'll grab more plates, and then you can tell me what the hell is going on in Chicago."

"It's not just Chicago," Colin said as Gabe reached for a piece of pizza. "We were just in Taymyria and found the ruins of the Skaladeska compound there. Much of it was burned out."

"The place has been deserted for at least a couple years. My guess is they left pretty quickly after we got away," Gabe interjected. The pizza, with its thick, sesame-seeded crust, looked damn good. "Flew the coop before we could bring anyone in."

Marina's face had gone still and stark, and she dropped her pizza onto a plate. "Who the hell burned it out? Did we? Did *you*?" She turned to Helen, her voice sharp and strident, her eyes flashing. "I knew this was going to happen. Do you have any idea what we've *lost*?"

"We couldn't even find the place until now. It wasn't the CIA or the Feds—or even the Kremlin who did the burning," Gabe told Marina before Helen could fire the snappy retort he knew was coming. "It was the Skalas themselves. But don't worry. They took the library."

"What do you mean, they took the library? It would be impossible to package up and move all of those artifacts that quickly." Her expression was still tense and angry, but she'd sat down and picked up the pizza again. "They'd need special cases, and—"

"They drove it away, Marina. It was like a mobile library—the whole damn room was like a—a railroad car, or a semi-trailer. There's nothing there but a gap in the mountain. As far as I can tell, the library is safe."

Her brown eyes were chill when she looked at him. "I hope you're right. There were texts from Atlantis in that collection."

Atlantis? Seriously?

"Dr. Alexander," Helen interrupted. She had her own cool gaze focused on Marina. "Have you been in touch with the Skaladeskas? Have they contacted you or have you contacted them?"

"Why would I be in touch with the bastards who tried to kill hundreds of innocent people in Detroit?" Marina's voice was even, and she met Helen's eyes calmly. "You know what Gabe and I went through to get away—and to help you stop them."

"They've fallen off the radar, so to speak," said Colin in his easy, placating way. He generally played good cop to Gabe's bad cop. "We're looking for anything that might help us find them."

"Why now? Why all of a sudden? What's happened?" Marina looked around at all of them. "Of course something's happened, or you all wouldn't be here, trying to connect me to a group of ecoterrorists. Again." She was pissed.

"We're just looking for information," Helen said.

"The last time the CIA came looking for information," Marina replied evenly, "I was kidnapped, ended up in Siberia, and nearly got killed. More than once."

"You're our only connection to the Skalas," Gabe said, remembering how she'd dived into a deep, rough lake to save Viktor Aleksandrov despite her deathly fear of water. Weak and bleeding from the gunshot plus the torture he'd endured, Gabe had no choice but to wait on the boat while trying to stay in touch with Helen Darrow by satellite phone, back in Detroit. Those had been long, dark moments.

I will always go back. For anyone, Marina had told him.

Gabe pulled his thoughts back to the present. "And it appears that after more than five years of silence, the Skalas have decided to re-emerge. Cora Allegan—do you know who that is?"

"The senator's daughter. From Missouri," Marina answered, her eyes going sharper. "And the CEO of Vision Screen Industries. Weren't they just in the news for EPA violations? They owe millions in fines."

Helen nodded. "Yes. Did you also hear that she disappeared?"

"I've been out of the news loop; was on an SAR mission up north. All I know is there was a blackout. Is it related?"

"The blackout originated in St. Louis, and so far the word is there's no cause to suspect it was deliberate," Helen told her. "But in regards to Cora Allegan, we have an eyewitness who saw three people escort her unwillingly off her front porch. They left behind—deliberately or accidentally, we don't know—a piece of paper with the Skaladeska mark on it."

Marina settled back in her seat, mouth full of pizza. She seemed to take a long time to chew and swallow it. "There's been no news from her? How long ago was this?"

"Two days ago. No news," Helen said. She was watching their hostess closely.

"Rue Varden was here," Marina said abruptly. "Today."

Gabe nearly lost his pizza. "*What?*"

Helen sat up straight and pulled an iPad from her briefcase. As she began touchscreening on it with a fancy stylus, she glanced at Marina. "Care to elaborate?"

"He was here when I got home today, bleeding all over my office. I—uh—stitched him up and after he passed out, I went upstairs to change. But he sneaked off." She looked at Gabe. "That's why I texted you."

He swore under his breath. "Why the hell did he come *here*? You stitched him up?"

"I wasn't going to let him *die*." She leveled a look at him.

Helen's phone rang, and the high, shrill noise drew everyone's attention. "I haven't figured out how to change the ring tone," she said, fishing it from her discarded suit jacket pocket.

"The sooner the better," Gabe commented. But he was still eyeing Marina with irritation. She claimed she hadn't been in touch with the Skaladeskas, but Rue Varden had showed up here. Injured. Only days after the Skalas were in Chicago.

What had made Varden think he'd get help from Marina?

Helen finished her low, terse conversation then put the phone down. "We've got a dead body at Northwestern Memorial Hospital. In Chicago. With the Skaladeska mark on him."

Gabe sighed mentally. There went his hopes for a visit with Marina.

TWELVE

As an ER physician, Brenda Hatcher counted it a good day when no one died, and a bad day when she was so busy she didn't have enough time to do her job the way she wanted to.

Yesterday's shift—which finally ended at eight a.m. today—had been a particularly bad day. Mind-numbingly busy, plus she'd lost not only the forty-nine-year-old man with the bugs, but also an eighty-year-old woman who'd had an intracranial bleed with a golf-ball-sized hematoma. Of course, she could judge the ten-hour shift by how many lives she'd saved—four—or how many excellent diagnoses she'd made because of her instincts and training, but it was the days when she lost someone that really sucked.

Which was why Brenda was aimlessly perusing Facebook, a mug of hot cocoa in hand, on her evening off. She drank hot chocolate year round—even in Michigan when it often got into the upper nineties during the summer—because it was a better option than the bottled margaritas to which she'd once been addicted.

That was also why she was alone on this humid September night, with the sliding door to her apartment open to let in a breeze, and no one to talk to or to touch. Since Sly left two years ago, Brenda had been running solo and just trying to keep it together so her mom didn't worry. She couldn't even have a pet because of the hours she worked. Even if she was scheduled off at a certain time, she couldn't just walk out the hospital door if she had a patient, or if a big rush came in. So often a scheduled eight-hour shift turned into ten or twelve hours. She worked midnights and afternoons, and an occasional day shift—the variety of which screwed up not only her sleep schedule but her personal life.

Which was, again, why on her night off she had nothing to do and no one to spend it with but her friends online or her TV remote. But the pickings there were slim because she'd eschewed the cable bill in favor of her student loan payments once her ex-fiancé moved out, and generally resorted to DVDs or whatever she could legally stream for free off the Internet.

Fortunately, Brenda had several friends who had just as little of a life as she did: friends from med school and residency who kept odd hours and didn't have the money or the time to be social either. They'd set up a private online hangout through one of the free services, and it was here she and her friends sought solace—as well as the opportunity to brush it off and put the bad days behind.

"You have to learn to move on," they reminded each other when it got tough. "Put it out of your mind."

The truth was, if Brenda hadn't gotten pretty good at compartmentalizing, she'd have never made it out of residency. But there was no denying some days really sucked big donkey balls.

Like having to tell Mike Wiley's wife that her husband had died early this morning *while at the emergency room*—which some people found impossible to believe; especially if they presented with something seemingly as innocuous as a rash—and then leave the tearful, disbelieving, shell-shocked Mrs. Wiley and immediately walk into a different room where a big, burly man lit into her because she hadn't been in to see his son with an earache soon enough.

"We've been waiting three hours," he yelled, his round face reddening into purple. "Don't you people have any respect for us, making us stick around here all day long? You think we got nothing else to do?" The son started crying, holding his ear, and it was all Brenda could do to keep from crying herself.

Or from telling the father to do something anatomically impossible.

His kid had an earache. Mrs. Wiley's life, on the other hand, had been irreparably and horribly altered.

Brenda was glad to see that one of her favorite people had already logged in to—was just hanging out in—their virtual videoconference room. Hyram always had great stories, most of them about a crotchety old doc he worked with in his own emergency room. The tales were usually good for a laugh or a roll of the eyes in commiseration.

"Had one of those days we don't like to talk about, Hy," she said once they were connected and she had her headset on. "So I need a distraction. Got any new Doc Westin stories?"

"Sorry to hear that. How bad was it?" His face was only half onscreen because of the position of his laptop; he looked like he was doing something on the table in front of him.

"Two. One from a bug bite." A spot on her hand itched in empathy, and Brenda scratched at it, remembering how awful Mike Wiley's skin had presented, covered with that oozing, cottage-cheese-like rash.

"Ouch."

"Yeah."

"Okay, here's one to get your mind off things. Just happened yesterday, in fact. Westin's got this girl, twenty-three or so, waiting for him. They triaged her and she's complaining of fever, being too hot, sweating profusely. He walks in and she's sitting there in the gown, open in the front, and, man…he says it's a sight to behold. Her breasts are showing—and according to Westin, they're a very nice set, full and high and damn near perfect, and she's wearing this pale purple, lacy triangle of panties—and nothing else. Of course, even though the old guy can't get it up on his own, he can't help but notice, you know, and then he looks all the way up and sees the gal's face. She's all made up like she's going out—lipstick, eye shadow, hair's done, everything…but she's got a full beard and mustache."

Brenda almost spewed her hot chocolate at the computer screen, but managed to salvage it at the last minute. "Oh no," she managed to gasp.

"Right. So Westin looks at the chart, looks at the girl—or guy; obviously he's in the process of changing over—and says, 'You feeling a little hot? A fever—or maybe like you're getting hot flashes?' Patient nods, looking surprised. Doc says, 'Let me guess…you stopped taking your estrogen shots.' The woman—guy—whatever—looks at him like, 'Wow. How'd you know?'"

Brenda snorted a laugh and absently rubbed another itchy spot on her arm. "Westin always seems to get the unusual ones. I have to meet this guy some day."

"Next time you get to Chicago, you just come on by and I'll make sure you meet the old bastard." He flashed a smile, his face coming into full view for an instant before he turned away to shove a bite of pizza into his mouth.

"Will do."

"I've got another one," he said as he finished chewing. "You'll love this one. This old Italian lady—eighty-seven—comes in. She's complaining she's got snakes in her belly."

"Gastric upset? Too much garlic in her Alfredo sauce?"

"No, literally snakes. And she's got the damned x-rays to prove it." Hyram was grinning, his face grainy on the video chat.

"Okay…"

"Yeah. So she's been hospital-hopping, trying to get someone to get these snakes out of her stomach. She's got the films and she brings them when she comes in, and she shows Westin, shows him the snakes. And…the snakes she's pointing to, what's got her all freaked out? It's her intestines."

"Awww…no way." Brenda felt a flash of pity for the old woman.

"Yeah. She sees them in the films, you know, and she will not believe these aren't snakes. She can see them and she wants them *out*. And she's not going to take no for an answer."

"She really thinks her small intestine is a snake?" Her empathy strained even more. How terrible and terrifying it must have been for the poor woman to truly believe she had snakes growing in her belly.

"Yep. Poor thing. But she's determined. And Westin— probably the only one in Chicago to give her the time of day— talked to her for thirty minutes, trying to explain to her that they weren't snakes. But she's pointing at the picture, showing him, insisting there are snakes in her belly, and she's really getting agitated. He leaves, comes back a little while later, tries again because the old lady won't leave. She's determined that someone's got to get the snakes out of her stomach."

"Geesh." Brenda put her empty mug down and wished for her own pizza. But the phone number was on the fridge, and she was comfortable here on the couch. "What'd he do?"

"Well, he finally convinced her it wasn't snakes. He's got her settled down, and she understands there are no snakes in her stomach. So—true story, Bren, I swear it—he goes for the door, and she stops him and she says, 'Could it be a squid?'"

"Noo…!" She was half laughing, half appalled, and collapsed back on her sofa.

"Right. So Doc goes turns around and goes back to her and says—straight face and all—'Impossible. Squids are saltwater creatures, and there's no saltwater around here. You been to the ocean recently, Mrs. Whatever Her Name Was?' 'No,' she says. 'Then there you go. There's no way a squid could get inside you then.'"

By now Brenda was half hysterical on the couch—partly from exhaustion, partly from disbelief, and partly because she simply couldn't imagine having a conversation like that with a patient… but, in fact, she could. She had. There were all kinds that came into the ER. "Thanks, Hy. You made me feel a lot better."

"Glad to hear it. When you going to come here and visit me? It's only five or six hours, right?"

"Soon, I hope. When I get a weekend off. Maybe in a couple months."

"So about this bug bite—you don't have poisonous bugs in Michigan, do you? What kind of bug was it?"

"I'm not really sure it was a bug that caused it. The guy wasn't lucid and he was waving around a plastic baggie with a couple of beetles in it. I kept it, just in case, and I let the ME know about it." She looked down at her hand, which had continued to itch, and saw that it was getting red in patches. Huh. Must be that new laundry detergent she'd tried. So much for buying the cheap stuff. "But he was in a bad way—just covered with boils and an ugly rash. Spiked a fever of 104, heart rate accelerated. I'd've thought it was a drug reaction. Like that underground Russian drug."

"You mean Krokodile? That shit's bad stuff, but we don't see that here in the US. At least, not yet," he added.

"I know. But I just saw that write-up from the CDC about keeping an eye out for signs that it's come over here—especially after the Olympics in Sochi. Did you see it?" Hy nodded and snatched up another piece of pizza as she continued, "Sounds ugly. Maybe it was just on my mind; anyway, I'll wait to see what the ME says. He did go into cardiac arrest, so it might have been unrelated to the rash or the bug bite."

"Let me know, Bren. And let me know when you're going to come and visit. I'll show you a good time."

"I know you will." After a few more minutes of chatting, she disconnected. Her hand was really itching now, and she noticed her other arm was feeling prickly and itchy too.

Brenda frowned, glancing at the kitchen counter, where she'd left the plastic baggie with Mike Wiley's bugs in it.

No. That was silly. The bugs were long dead—there was no way she could have been bitten by them. She'd poked at one in the bag with her finger and got some of that black stuff on her, but that was just dirt, and she'd washed it off anyway.

It had to be that new laundry detergent.

Or maybe she was getting a strawberry allergy like her mom.

Brenda shook her head. Talk about psychosomatic hypochondria.

It was time to order pizza.

THIRTEEN

September 24
St. Louis

S o what do you think?" Charles Akinowski leaned on the counter, impatiently watching the man across from him.

"I think," said Dr. Wendell Svirishna, looking up from the
lump of charred insects, "that I've never seen an insect like this in
my life. Even burned to a crisp as it is."

Ake exchanged glances with his partner, Michael, who'd
introduced him to Svirishna, then looked back at the other man.
The scientist was an entomologist on staff at the St. Louis Zoo
and had gone to the University of Illinois with Michael. He'd
agreed to look at the insect on an unofficial basis because Ake was
still not willing to believe a swarm of random bugs had caused a
mega-state blackout—but Michael, who'd been hearing about it
day and night, had made an executive decision and called his old
friend.

"So, do you think it's possible it caused the blackout?" Michael
asked.

Dr. Svirishna was using his hands, encased in skintight purple
gloves, to gently separate some of the insects from each other.
Flakes of black fell onto the absorbent white paper on the lab
table. He picked up a magnifying glass and peered through it,
eyeing the residue.

Michael squeezed Ake's hand in warning when he would have pressed further. Ake glowered back. Didn't any of them realize what sort of pressure he was under to find out what had happened? Practically everyone on Capitol Hill, not to mention in Jeff City, was crawling up his ass, demanding answers. And the only thing he had was this charred lump of rust-tinted coal. He kept his mouth shut, but gave Michael a look that told him he was going to need a very big glass of Pinot Noir tonight—not to mention something spectacular to eat—as soon as they got home.

"Definitely Coleoptera, maybe family Meloidae...but any more, I can't tell from this specimen. Not very much to work with. But it's not native to this area," Svirishna said, moving the crumbling black pieces around in a large flat-bottomed glass dish. He peered, poked, hummed, and even used a small pair of forceps with needlelike tips to conduct minor surgery while Ake waited impatiently, his grimace telling Michael this was a waste of time.

Then, with sudden, excited movements, Svirishna took a small flake of black and put it in a smaller dish, then shoved it under a nearby microscope. Peering through the lenses, he shifted the dish around, used the forceps to move it, tipped it over, moved the fiberoptic light wand, and then popped his head up. "Copper. On the wing," he said, faint red rings around his eyes. "Copper is very conductive of electricity," he mused. "Hmm."

"Erm...yes," Ake replied. "It does have a coppery look to it. Are you suggesting that copper was transferred to the bug—"

"Insect," Michael murmured.

"*Insect*," Ake said from between clenched teeth. "You think copper got on the insect when it flew into the wires? No chance of that."

"Well, there seems to be a residue of copper on the insect itself. If not from the wires, then I don't know from where. I'm not a metallurgist, but that's what it looks like to me."

"Isn't it possible if the insects had some of that metal on them, they might have caused a surge of electrical power when they flew into the wires?" Michael said. He looked at Ake from behind round glasses, his eyes owlishly hopeful.

"No way," Ake replied, more sharply than he probably should have. "It's not possible that scant amount of copper dust would cause a power surge of that magnitude. And besides, what would cause a swarm of bugs—*insects*—to collect like that and fly in an organized swarm into a bunch of wires?" He was shaking his head even as he stared down at the burned-out mess. Yet...the same uncomfortable feeling he'd had when Nabbins first brought him the bugs was back, churning his stomach. It really wasn't possible.

Was it?

"If you could find me another specimen," Svirishna said from behind the microscope lens. "Preferably one that wasn't burned to a crisp."

"I'll get my guys on it right away," Ake said, trying and failing to keep the sarcasm from his voice.

Michael glared at him and lifted his chin in a manner that indicated Ake might have lost the chance for that spectacular dinner he needed.

At least he'd get the glass of Pinot. He could open the bottle himself.

"Even if you can just find more parts," said the entomologist, seeming not to have noticed Ake's irritation. "We can use them to identify the insect. It's obvious they aren't native." He pulled back suddenly from the microscope, as if he'd just had an idea. "I have a friend who might be interested in looking at this. Eli Sanchez. This is right up his alley—he's one of the best coleopterists in the world. Just won an ESA award, in fact, for his work on atypical insect metamorphosis."

"Coleopterist?" Ake repeated. And what the hell was atypical insect metamorphosis? And someone won an *award* for it?

"A beetle specialist."

"I don't really think this is worth bothering an internationally recognized coleopterist," Ake said, trying to imagine a man who spent his entire professional life studying nothing but beetles. "I'm sure he's very busy."

Svirishna waved off his protests. "Not at all. This is right up Eli's alley. He loves things like this, and the more offbeat, the better. I'll give him a call. He just returned from somewhere in the Amazon, and if I know Eli, he'll be looking for some new project to occupy his time. He's at the University of Illinois at Champaign, about three hours from here."

"I appreciate it," Ake said. He couldn't justify taking off in the middle of this crisis—could he? "I'll talk to him by phone first before I drive up there. Then we can decide what to do."

In an unknown location

"Who are you? What do you want?" Cora Allegan tried to keep her voice steady, but she was quickly losing that battle. She'd gone from shocked and terrified to exhausted, confused, and angry.

As the daughter of a US senator unbound by term limits, she'd been aware of the risks of being abducted—for ransom, for political gain, to make a statement—since she was sixteen. And being the CEO of a Fortune 500 company that designed and manufactured cutting-edge electronics, she was also aware of the same risks to herself from a corporate perspective.

Although she'd been frightened at first, the stark helplessness had eased into anger when she realized if her abductors had merely wanted to kill—or even hurt—her, that would have happened by now. Instead, she'd been drugged and transported to...somewhere.

"My name is Roman Aleksandrov," said the man to whom she'd spoken.

Cora focused on him, trying to keep her mind clear and steady. She'd demanded the same information from every person she came in contact with since opening her eyes and finding herself in the custody of strangers, but this was the first person to respond.

Clearly, he was in control.

He was a handsome man, completely bald and by all evidence intentionally so. She guessed him to be in his late sixties—maybe close to seventy—but he was fit and his eyes were sharp and clear, yet filled with an unsettling lack of emotion. His fair skin was lined with more than an occasional wrinkle, but it didn't sag even at his jaw. Unlike every other person she'd seen since her abduction, he didn't wear the loose pants and tunic made from natural-looking linen. That alone should have been her first clue this man was someone different. He was dressed in dark brown linen trousers and an untucked, crisp white shirt whose open top buttons proved he didn't lack for hair anywhere but on his head. Leather sandals graced elegant feet.

"Who are you working for?" she asked again, rubbing her raw, reddened wrists. They'd been duct-taped together in front of her for most of the time, but at the moment she was unbound and otherwise unfettered. She'd been left in this small room several hours ago and had been alone until he opened the door and walked in, unannounced. He sat down in a chair and looked at her as her gaze went from him to the door and back again.

She could have made a run for it, but Cora was too intelligent to think she'd get very far.

Although she'd examined the windowless room and listened carefully for any sounds that might indicate her location, she was unable to determine where she was being held. The only thing she knew was that it was hot and humid and there was an eerie lack of mechanical sounds beyond the walls.

"You are the CEO of Vision Screen Industries," said Roman Aleksandrov. He spoke in precise tones that indicated English wasn't his first language.

"Yes, and I'm the daughter of Senator Ronald Allegan. The US government doesn't take kindly to having its citizens abducted, particularly ones attached to high-level, visible officials. I don't know what you think you'll gain by doing this, but you won't succeed. The sooner you release me, the easier it'll be for you." She sat up straight, trying her best to appear confident and unafraid, despite the fact that she was still wearing the pink sweatpants and shelf-bra tank top she'd pulled on after sliding from Jerry's arms and out of bed to answer the door. No real bra, no underthings. Not even a pair of shoes.

Roman's face eased into a complacent smile. "I'm fully aware of how the US government treats its citizens—at every level of the political and financial spectrum. As well as its other resources. And you needn't worry. I'll be releasing you very soon."

Cora's heart began to thud. Those words, though spoken in a benign voice, nevertheless sounded ominous. "What do you want? A ransom? My father will pay it, but that doesn't mean you'll walk away with the money."

"What I want," Roman said, sitting back in his chair and steepling his hands, "cannot be bought."

Before she could respond, he stood and continued to speak. "Your company manufactures OLED monitors. It's grown exponentially in the last year, despite the high cost of those types of computer screens. They're a new technology, and quite expensive to produce. Currently."

Cora nodded. So this wasn't about her father. She tried to keep her mind focused as Roman Aleksandrov walked idly about the space as if he were a professor giving a lecture.

"The growth is amazing, and it's partly been due to the unprecedented trade-in program Vision Screen Industries has offered to new direct customers. Your organization has accepted hundreds of thousands of CRT and LCD monitors in exchange for deeply discounted prices on the new, cutting-edge monitors. But all of those old screens…hundreds of thousands of them, taken in by your corporation on a…what did you call it? The Recycle-Win-Buy program?"

She couldn't keep her brows from drawing together in utter confusion. "What is this about?" she demanded, her heart beginning to pound. "What does kidnapping me have to do with a trade-in program?"

"You, the CEO, personally put the plan together as a way to radically increase the sales and value of your company in a short time. Perhaps you mean to inflate the stock price and then sell, or perhaps you simply desire to grab market share."

"As would any other executive of a for-profit organization," she retorted. "I have a duty to my stockholders. Do you have some sort of religious or cultural problem with capitalism? Is that what this is about?" Her insides churned with renewed concern. If he was a radical from an anti-Western, anti-capitalist terrorist group, she could be in more danger than she'd anticipated.

Roman Aleksandrov steepled his fingers together again and gave her another cool, humorless smile. "Not at all. I have no problem with capitalism or making profits. I do it on a regular basis, in fact. Quite satisfactorily. However," he said, his face turning hard, "when the CEO of an organization takes in hundreds of thousands of cathode ray monitors, as well as LEDs and other hardware under the guise of recycling them…and then pays for them to be secretly tossed into landfills—"

"What are you talking about?" Cora replied. Now her body was flushing with heat and her hands were shaking. Was he a greenie from one of those damned environmental groups? How had they found out? She'd been so careful. So careful that only two other people knew the truth. And neither of them would have betrayed her. Even the EPA, who'd caught VSI dumping waste, didn't know about the monitors.

"All of that lead. All of that cadmium and mercury and hexavalent chromium, slipping into the ground. Polluting the water. Seeping into our land and poisoning our earth and her resources. All the while your father was in Washington, promoting his own environmental bills and holding up your corporation as an example of one doing it correctly. What did he call it? 'A baby-sized carbon footprint for a giant of a company'?"

"You have no idea what you're talking about," she said. "That's an absurd accusation."

"You know it isn't. You know how many places in the world you've had those filthy things shoved into the helpless skin and organs of Gaia."

"Gaia?"

"Gaia. The earth. Our earth." He stood in front of her, and she was overcome with the desire to shove violently at him, push him away and run from the room and fight her way out of here. He smiled, as if reading her mind. "Our beloved, irreplaceable earth. Gaia is in our care, and you've caused her great hardship."

"Burying some monitors is nothing in the grand scheme of things," she said. "Look at the Gulf Oil Spill, and all of the other—"

"I'm fully aware of the other pollutants in the world, and what the Out-Worlders have done and continue to do to our beautiful Gaia. They too will pay—and, in fact, some of them already have done so. And a good many more of them will do so...in only a few days' time." He smiled benignly. "But today is *your* day for recompense, Ms. Cora Allegan. After inflicting such pain and destruction on our helpless earth, it's your time to experience the same."

"What are you talking about? I'm the CEO of a company! I didn't *put* those things in the ground. But someone obviously screwed up. I'll pay the fines," she added quickly. "The EPA will slap more fines on the company and we'll pay them and I'll fix the recycling program, and we'll be square. You can't hold *me* responsible for what my company did—for an error the corporation made."

The man gave a short laugh. "You said it yourself. You are the CEO. The company is under your management and guidance. You and a select few others are going to be made into...what do you call them? Poster childs—poster children? Poster children for this kind of willful destruction of our earth."

Cora was aware of a definite numbness filtering over her body, up through her limbs and through her chest. "I'll pay the fines, I'll even pay to have everything excavated, brought back—"

"I said earlier that what I want cannot be bought," he replied flatly. His voice became low and tight, laced with fury. "What I want is my earth back, unravaged and unraped by your selfish actions. I want the groundwater empty of the poisons. The fish and the birds and animals who died from the lead and mercury your actions have or will inflict on them—I want them healthy and alive. I want the earth, the dirt, the stones and plants that draw from the ground—I want them pure and clean. But you cannot give me that, Cora Allegan. It's too late. There's no turning back the clock."

"But—I don't understand," she said. An ugly chill had settled over her, as if she'd been submerged in an icy lake during the winter. "What do you want?"

"I want you to experience what Gaia has experienced at your hands. Just as she was helpless against the pain and poison *you* inflicted upon her, so will you experience being helpless in *her* presence. So will you attempt to thrive and survive when faced with her strength and power, unarmed and unprotected against whatever she chooses to inflict upon you."

Cora was shaking her head, utterly confused and at the same time terrified by the cold, steady words. He must be crazy. Yet he sounded much too sane…and that was what frightened her the most.

"What exactly are you talking about?" she asked.

"I told you I would release you. I will indeed. You'll be released into the arms of Gaia. If you survive, so be it. If you do not, I consider it nothing more than our earth exacting her revenge upon you."

FOURTEEN

Ann Arbor

Marina slipped from bed, casting a regretful look at Gabe's messy dark hair and a broad, tanned shoulder, half covered by a tangle of sheets. She fairly purred at the memory of last night's activity. *I definitely needed that.*

Hell, she could use even more of that particular form of exercise and relaxation, but it was morning, and Boris needed to go out...and she had other pressing matters to attend to before she and Gabe left. Hopefully before he awoke.

Last night when Helen Darrow insisted she come back to Chicago with them in order to assist in the investigation, Marina agreed—but only under her terms. Which first included a good night's sleep in her own bed. Having Gabe in it as well had just been icing on the cake. Helen clearly hadn't cared for the idea, and Marina wasn't certain whether it was because the special agent didn't like to be derailed from her plans, or because Gabe was staying with Marina. There was some sort of history between him and Helen.

Marina didn't know the details—only that they'd had something going on eight years ago, before Helen was transferred from Washington, DC to Chicago. Though she'd witnessed Gabe and Helen being nothing but professional and easy with each other, Marina sensed there might still be some unfinished business between them. The thought didn't particularly bother her anyway; much as she enjoyed Gabe MacNeil, on many levels, she had no claim on him—nor did he on her.

Helen's sensitivities aside, it was logical for Gabe to remain in Ann Arbor to ensure Marina's safety before escorting her to Chicago. And although there had been obvious benefits to that, it gave Marina very little time and privacy to see to the other issue on her mind.

She let Boris out and stood on the damp lawn in bare feet while he did his business. Marina closed her eyes, feeling the cool, smooth prickle of grass amid her toes. The morning smelled fresh and damp, with a little bit of summer still clinging to the air. Curling her toes into the soil, feeling the dirt and plants, she imagined herself taking root…becoming grounded, melding into the earth. Becoming part of it. Breathing with her.

It was as if Marina could feel the heartbeat of the great organism called earth—or, as her grandfather thought of it, Gaia—beneath her bare soles. The energy, the pulse of its life, thrummed through her as she drew in a deep breath of warm morning air, smelled the fresh grass, the scent of crushed leaves, the aroma of oak bark—soon to turn chill as autumn swept in.

Marina understood this part, at least, of her Skaladeska heritage. This melding with the earth, the appreciation and sense of oneness with it. Perhaps that was why she was attracted to caves, why she felt at home traveling into the bowels of the planet, deep into the womb of the mother.

Boris dropped the tennis ball on her bare foot, bringing her back from a moment of meditation. She scooped it up and fired it across the small yard and into her neighbor's lot so Boris would have a good distance to travel.

Marina's backyard was shady, filled with several large trees— trees that had been instrumental in her escape from an attempted abduction when a man named Dannen Fridkov tried to bring her forcibly to the Skaladeskas just after she met Gabe. But since that incident and the attacks in Detroit had been aborted, the last five years had been quiet and uneventful…at least, relatively speaking.

Being a caver with SAR training meant life was never quiet and uneventful.

Boris chased his tennis ball while Marina poked around the outside of her office window, looking for signs of Varden's presence. A few drips of blood on shriveled tulip leaves she hadn't cut away and a crushed begonia confirmed he'd come or gone or both via the entry, but there were no handy receipts or other clues that might have given further information.

She was about to call Boris to go in when the back door opened and Gabe came out. He was wearing a pair of loose shorts and nothing else, and he looked delicious. Smiling lazily at him from across the lawn, Marina took a moment to admire the sleek musculature of his shoulders and torso.

"Good morning." Gabe appeared just as rested and complacent as she felt. He bent to scoop up the tennis ball Boris had just returned, and threw it even further than Marina had done. His eyes turned serious and his tone businesslike when he turned to her. "Is he coming with us, or did you find someone to take him?"

A gentle nudge, meant to get her on the road. But Marina had one thing to do first, and she wasn't leaving until she did it. "I have to make that phone call, but I'm pretty sure my normal dog sitter will take him. Why don't you shower and I'll take care of that and pack up?"

"You don't want to join me?" His eyes crinkled at the corners as his lids drooped in invitation.

"Do you think that's a good idea?" she replied, seriously considering it. She could easily go another round. After all, she'd had a long, dry spell. And he had pretty amazing shoulders… among other attributes.

Gabe looked over at Boris, then sighed. "Much as I'd like to… it's probably better for us to get on the road. Helen texted and wanted to know our ETA. As one would imagine, the senator's on her ass to find his daughter—and she doesn't have much to tell him."

"I'm not sure what she thinks I can do." Marina picked up the tennis ball and gave Boris the command to precede her into the house. "But I'll do what I can."

When the CIA first approached her about the Skaladeskas after her father's disappearance, she'd initially rejected their request for assistance. But after what happened afterward, she no longer had that luxury—nor, in truth, the desire to decline—and she'd ended up working with the FBI as well, via Helen. She'd continue to do so, as long as she felt as if she had something to contribute.

As soon as Gabe went upstairs to shower, Marina slipped into the office. She didn't have much time, but hers was an older house. She'd hear the water turn off and know when he was done. He generally took his time, and would probably shave, so she would have a good twenty minutes. For just a moment, she was tempted to join him…but curiosity won out. This would be her only chance to look at the package for at least a day or two, if she was stuck in Chicago.

A niggle of guilt bothered her about keeping the packet secret from Gabe, but based on the events of yesterday, she didn't think there was any need to tell him about it. He already knew the Skaladeskas had been in touch with her through Varden. Telling him about the package would open another Pandora's box, and she was too much of a scholar to take the risk of losing what could be a huge find.

She sent a couple quick texts, then turned to her laptop. She hesitated only a moment when she opened it, but as soon as the computer woke up, she closed Skype. She'd deal with that later.

Or maybe she'd never open Skype again.

But she didn't, she acknowledged, delete the new contacts that had been added to her account. Not yet.

It only took a minute to connect her camera to the laptop, then another few moments to print off the pictures she'd taken in the cave Matt Granger discovered.

But it wasn't the photos she didn't want Gabe to see. It was the package shoved away on the top of her bookshelf.

Marina was only five foot six, so she had to stand on a stool to reach the package—which was why she'd put it up there in the first place. Out of sight, out of reach, out of mind. Or so she'd intended.

The box was small and flat, roughly the size of a ream of paper, and constructed of balsam wood. Because of its contents, the container was heavier than its appearance would suggest, and she lifted it down carefully. Her name was hand-printed on the outside of the wrapping. Twine had originally tied the packaging closed, but she'd tucked it inside the box in a neat coil.

There was no return address, no postmark, no stamps. But the single other mark on the outside wrappings had clearly indicated the sender: it was stamped with the mark of the Skaladeskas.

For a moment, Marina's thoughts took her back to the secret mountain hideaway in Siberia where she'd first met Lev, the frail patriarch who was also her grandfather.

She shook her head and pushed away the memory of her grandfather's weary face, trying to ignore the little pang of curiosity and sympathy. He'd been kind to her and had even shown her affection, but he was a terrorist. A cold-blooded killer. Just as Roman, Varden, and the others were. She could have no soft thoughts for him.

But Lev knew her weakness. He and Roman both did. And here before her was the evidence.

She looked down at the package. It had been hand-delivered to her home, left on her porch one day while she was away. But that wasn't nearly as unsettling to Marina as its contents, not to mention the message—both clear and implicit—that was inside.

Because of the marking on it, she'd had no concerns the box was an explosive—although in retrospect, perhaps she'd been a fool not to. But these men, these members of her family, didn't want to harm her. No, they wanted her alive and well.

Her ear half cocked, listening for the running shower to be turned off, Marina removed the box's lid and set it aside. Then she carefully pulled away the thick, soft cloth swaddling.

The top item was a piece of parchment, yellowed and worn. It was no larger than her hand, its ragged edges indicating it had been torn from some other specimen. With great care, she used a pair of forceps to gently lift it from its nest to set it on the desk. The paper seemed surprisingly sturdy, yet she wasn't about to take any chances with a piece from a Byzantine codex.

The distinctive style of minuscule Greek script identified it as likely being from the early ninth century, and, based on the *nomina sancta*, it was probably a Christian text. She believed the work had been a religious writing due to the way the author had abbreviated sacred names by placing a line over the initial letters. The grapevine imagery around the fancy majuscule of the title also implied early Christian, for those writers had taken up the Byzantine tradition of using organic symbols. Adriatic medieval wasn't Marina's specialty by any stretch, but she'd be a fool not to have done the research to identify the text's origins.

Yes, she certainly had done the research. And hated—and loved—every minute of it.

She didn't have time to gaze at it now, and pulled her attention from the scrap of Byzantine writing. The second item in the box was wrapped individually in a soft, unfamiliar fabric. Stretchy and colorless, the fabric was woven from some natural fiber that had a shiny element similar to plastic—a type of fabric she'd only seen in Taymyria, where the Skaladeskas had lived.

Beneath its covering cocoon was the fragment of a thin sheet of sandstone, etched with a curling, curving text more familiar to Marina: a circular Tamil Vatteluthu script. Likely early fourth century, probably from Sri Lanka.

She didn't know whether this particular piece had been selected because of her background in Pan-Asian studies or whether it was accidental. She suspected it was the former, for neither Roman nor Lev seemed the type to leave anything to chance. Either man would use any tool available to him.

Bribery. Blackmail. Abduction. Torture. Even death.

She shook her head, staring down at the pieces in wonder and disbelief.

Treasures. These pieces were *treasures.* Not just to her as a scholar, but for all of humanity—for she knew they were from the lost library of Ivan the Terrible. And, if Gabe was correct, and that library, which her family had been charged by the czar himself to protect, was still intact somewhere, there were many more left to be studied. Her heart pounded and she became nauseated with hope and fear at the thought of what it could mean to have those pieces at her disposal.

But it wasn't these artifacts that had prompted her to reopen the Pandora's box of temptation. It was the third piece, lying flat on the bottom, nestled in a soft woolen wrap.

Pulling the cloth away, she exposed a fragment of stone. Her heart tripped as she looked at the writings painted into the rock: elongated, rust-colored shapes. Faded after centuries—possibly millennia—but still visible.

She didn't even have to look at the photos she'd just printed to know the images from Matt Granger's cave were similar to the ones on the stone. Similar enough that her heart began to race faster and her palms grew damp.

But she picked up the photo and rested it next to the stone, just to be certain.

Very nearly identical.

Her heart pounding, she stared for a moment. There must be closer study, but her suspicions were enough to give her an adrenaline rush. For the drawings painted on the stone Lev had sent her were likely from the Mediterranean in the Bronze Age, possibly Phoenician...and the ones she'd found in the Upper Peninsula of Michigan would seem to be from the same people. If she was correct, this discovery could confirm what some outlying archeologists believed: that the tons of copper missing from Northern Michigan had been taken by Europeans. This could *prove* the Europeans had been in Northern Michigan during the time the copper disappeared—as far back as the Bronze Age.

The only question was *where.* Where had all those tons of mined copper gone? There was no trace of it in Europe. Not enough, at least.

Boris gave a sharp bark and Marina jolted. The water was no longer running upstairs and she quickly but carefully replaced the items in the balsam wood box.

She'd just finished shoving it onto the top of the bookshelf when she heard Gabe thudding down the stairs.

"Ready to go?" he said, poking his head in the office as she powered off her laptop.

Sliding it into its case, she glanced up. "I need about fifteen minutes. Tasha will be here in about five to get Boris—can you turn him over to her while I wash up and grab some things? She knows where everything is."

Gabe nodded, his attention sliding over her appreciatively. "You are the most low-maintenance woman I've ever met."

She grinned cheekily as she slipped past him into the hall. "I don't think you had that same opinion the first time you tried to interrogate me."

"Well, now, that's true," he replied in his West Virginia drawl. "As I recall, you demanded a hot shower, steak, eggs—and a glass of wine. At five o'clock in the morning."

"I'd had a long night." Marina dashed upstairs, his rumbly chuckle following her.

True to her word, in fifteen minutes she'd showered, stuffed a few necessities back into her duffel bag, and bounded down the stairs. Her phone dinged with a text from her mechanic at Ann Arbor Municipal. "Plane's fueled up and ready."

"I assumed we'd drive. It's only four hours by highway."

"And only one by air. Afraid to fly with me again?" The one and only time she'd flown Gabe had been a hectic, erratic flight in an effort to escape from two abductors intent on getting her to the Skaladeskas.

His only response was to roll his eyes. "Let's go. Once you get us up in the air I'll call Helen and get an update."

"I'm surprised you haven't already received one," Marina replied as they walked out to the car.

He glanced at her, his expression studiously blank. "I think she assumed I—uh—didn't want to be disturbed. Unless it was urgent."

"That was considerate of her." Marina hid a smile.

But they were on their way to the local airport when Gabe's phone rang. "Helen," he said. "I was just about to call you. Any news?"

He wasn't on the phone long, but he didn't do much talking either. Clearly there was news, and Helen was giving it to him.

He disconnected the call just as Marina pulled into the airport parking lot. "They thought the Skala died from an injury that appeared to be a knife wound, but that isn't the case. He had some sort of violent rash that bubbled up all over his skin—lumpy red boils, she said—that turned out to be the impetus for the cause of death. Sudden cardiac arrest, made his whole body shut down. Because the Skalas are a recognized terrorist group, the concern is the inflammation was from some sort of biological or chemical agent meant for an attack that's gone wrong. Either way, they want you under protective custody, so to speak, and us in Chicago ASAP. They're searching for the vehicle he was driving—he had a rental agreement in his pocket under the name Sazma Marcko— in hopes of finding something helpful in a sweep."

"Then let's get in the air," Marina said, leading the way to her P210.

FIFTEEN

Roman walked briskly into the chamber. He nodded at its occupants as he made his way to the far end of the conference table, where a crystal orb glowed softly. The ten people seated at the elongated triangular table were members of the *Naslegi*, the advisory council of the Skaladeskas. But it was Hedron's eyes Roman felt most heavily on him. The other man's gaze was weighty and filled with antipathy.

In a blatant show of disregard, Roman smiled coolly at his wife's brother. Then, as was appropriate, he turned his attention to the glowing sphere positioned at the apex of the triangular table. He bowed to it, making the familiar gesture with his right fingers: the first two, brushing down briefly between his brows then off the bridge of his nose in a reverent salute.

Gaia, Holy One, I am committed to Your life.

The Sphere of Gaia was large and heavy enough that a man could cup it in his two palms, but would be unable to close his fingers around it. And if he did hold it so, the heat that emanated from the orb would be evident. The smooth crystal glowed and swirled as if alive, its color constantly morphing from azure to aqua to cerulean to emerald. The sphere sat on a clear glass column that enthroned it at chest height, giving it the illusion of hovering in midair.

"Well? What have you to report, Sama Roman?" Hedron demanded.

Such a demand and in such tones was not only a breech of conduct, but a clear disregard for authority from a council member, no matter how high-ranking. There was a bit of shuffling around the table, and a barely audible gasp of surprise from an unidentified member of the *Naslegi*. Probably Clarista.

Roman scanned the chamber, unwilling to allow his rival—for of course that was how Hedron saw himself—to unsettle him. As if Hedron, who hadn't a drop of Romanovna or Aleksandrov blood in his veins, could ever aspire to be *sama*. Roman recognized a variety of emotions in the gazes of his comrades: shock and affront, curiosity, and, in a couple, the subtle layer of challenge. He took his time to scan the table, looking each person in the eye and noting who was with him and who was questionable.

As long as Lev lived, as long as the blood of the Aleksandrovs persisted, Roman had nothing to fear. There was only one true variable in the equation, and he had already begun to take the steps necessary to change that variability to certainty.

In that one goal, at least, his determination and Lev's were fully aligned.

"Thank you, Hedron, for your patience," Roman said when he finished his deliberate scan of the table's occupants. His voice was easy, dripping with the same sweetness as the honey he slathered over a slice of toast for breakfast. "Not being familiar of the way things work in the Out-World surely makes one feel out of touch, and out of control." He made no effort to hide the pity or condescension in his smile. Along with the lack of a Skaladeska bloodline, Hedron's biggest liability was his ignorance of what truly went on beyond the cloistering walls of their compound.

Roman, who'd gone to Oxford University and spent nearly two decades of his younger years living Out-World, easily wielded the power of his knowledge of the rest of civilization. It was he—with support from Nora and Rue Varden—who'd arranged for the hidden compounds in several locales throughout the world to be available to his tribe. The Skaladeska evacuation from Siberia more than four years ago had been smooth and efficient, thanks to their foresight and planning.

However, what Hedron lacked for in genetics and knowledge, he made up for in ambition and conniving. And since one of his sons had been apprehended by the Canadian authorities during a botched attempt to abduct Mariska Alexander, then conveniently died in prison before the Americans could get hold of him, Hedron had been even more subversive and belligerent. It was as if he believed his son's failure reflected upon him.

Thus, Roman wasn't foolish enough to wholly dismiss the man's determination to unseat him. Which was why the most important part of his current initiative was focused on the one element unknown even to the *Naslegi*: to bring the Heir of Gaia back to the fold.

"Proceed, then, Roman," said his rival. Pale eyes flashed belligerently. "We've waited long enough for your update."

Thus the seesaw of power shifted: demand and belligerence tipping against control and knowledge.

Roman inclined his head. "As you of the *Naslegi* are aware, we have a two-pronged approach for our current initiative. The first strategy is one that has been in the works for years, and its commencement was disrupted by our evacuation to this location several years ago. As of today, I'm pleased to report the third candidate for what we've termed our 'Amazon Roulette' has been apprehended and advised of her position. Ms. Cora Allegan, who is guilty of injecting an unforgivable amount of chemical poison into the earth, will be released into the arms of Gaia within the next twenty-four hours. Nora is tracking her and will report on her status as needed. It will be up to Gaia and Ms. Allegan's own abilities as to whether she survives."

"Have we reports on the others? The other two?" asked Ballio. He was one of Roman's allies on the board.

"Of course. Mr. Eustace Pernweiler and, more recently, Mr. Lo Ing-wen have both succumbed to their demise in the game of survival. Apparently Gaia saw no reason to protect them, and their chance at the roulette table of nature turned up to be a loss." Roman shook his head sadly. "Perhaps if they'd been more tolerant and sympathetic toward our earth, She would have better protected them."

"I ask yet again, Roman, the question you seem unwilling to answer: how do these events assist our overall initiative—to gain the attention of the Out-World?" Hedron's question was a barely civil demand. "Sending CEOs and corporate gurus into the jungle to see if they survive is hardly a stunning blow to the ways of the Out-World."

"As always, brother, your assessment of the situation is both simplistic and shortsighted," Roman replied.

There were low murmurs of assent and support, and Roman smothered a complacent smile. More often than not, Hedron's challenges backfired on him when he came across as shortsighted and narrow-minded.

Roman continued his explanation. "Of course the roulette initiative isn't meant to be a stunning blow to the Out-World at all, but more of a niggling, irritating, yet powerful reminder that we do exist, and that we will protect Gaia at any cost. We have, after all, been nearly silent for the last five years during our relocation and realignment. They've forgotten about us. But it's time to remind the Out-World who we are and what we mean to do as we prepare to launch the more powerful second prong—which will be executed on the first of October. Only eight days from now. That initiative will send a violent and far-reaching message that cannot be ignored. And, finally, Hedron, I must remind you... just as Gaia herself metamorphoses in small ways that eventually culminate in a large effect, so do we. One cannot always charge in with proverbial guns blazing and earth-shattering events."

Once again he scanned the occupants of the chamber in an emphasis of his words. He understood the desire to create havoc that would turn the Out-World's collective face firmly to them, to have the full attention of the murderers of Gaia. And it would happen, in due time. When he was assured they were fully prepared.

"In regards to the second, more—shall we say, *flashy*—prong of our initiative," Roman continued, "I have little to report at this time. We expect word from Bellhane, Marcko, and Fridkov shortly on their progress with the *Cuprobeus* project. If all has gone well, we can engage in this more flashy, attention-getting event—one that even my friend Hedron will appreciate." His smile was benign, for the rest of them were unaware of the third element of the initiative. "I am quite—"

Roman looked up as the chamber door opened. He frowned when Vera, one of the women who worked in the lab with Nora, peered around the opening. What was she doing here? No one would dare interrupt a meeting of the *Naslegi* except Lev. Hiding his surprise, Roman nodded for her to enter.

Vera's eyes were wide and her face set as she entered the chamber, walking briskly to where he stood at the head of the table. She handed him a small piece of paper with Nora's writing scrawled on it.

He glanced down at it, reading the words. His world shifted and a dark shadow swept over his vision.

Damn.

Sazma Marcko was dead. In an American hospital.

September 25
FBI Field Office, Chicago

Gabe's smartphone buzzed and he glanced down. Langley. Good. Maybe he'd get some news.

"MacNeil," he snapped into the mouthpiece as he settled onto the chair in an office he'd borrowed from one of Helen Darrow's colleagues.

"Gabe, it's Inez." Inez Macready was one of the computer geeks, and if she was on the line, she had news.

"It's about time you called," he said, only half teasing. "I thought you'd forgotten about me. Someone else must've come in with something sexier than a crusty jump drive. An Al-Qaeda laptop, maybe? An *Aum Shinrikyo* smartphone?" Inez had had the thumb drive they found in the Siberian ruins for more than a week, but he hadn't been holding his breath for any good news. Who knew how long it had sat there, and in what condition.

"Sexier than your stuff? Never," she purred. "I'd've been back to you sooner, but we had a hell of a time trying to make sure we didn't set off an internal worm that would've corrupted the drive. There were three of them. Someone wanted to make sure the drive was secure, which means it must be valuable. Then it took time to dig through the encryption, plus some of the external parts of the drive were corroded. Wanted to make sure we didn't do any more damage when we were pulling out the usable part of the hardware. It was a beast getting into the data—there was a lot of stuff on there, and we've only been able to get to the most recent layer. Which, by the way, had been deleted at one point."

"So basically, the drive was protected by worms and passwords but it didn't have any data on it? Any current data, anyway?" His spark of hope faded.

"That about sums it up. Lots of security for nothing…but it's a damn good thing I'm a brilliant forensic investigator. I was able to recover the most recent cache of data, which, like I said, had been deleted anyway."

"And?" Gabe felt his heart rate kick up a little. Deleted data could be good. Whatever people tried to get rid of was usually more interesting than that which they didn't.

"It's a list of names. I'm emailing it to you right now so you have it, but I figured I'd better call and let you know it's coming."

"Oh, you just wanted to hear my Southern," he teased, already opening his email. "Be honest."

"Yeah, right," she replied, her own drawl even more pronounced than usual. "Because I have no idea what a West Virginian sounds like."

He chuckled into the phone. "You might have a point. Anything else?"

"You're gonna love me."

"Really?" His voice dropped with interest. "I should've known you wouldn't lead with the good stuff. What?"

"Fingerprints. Got a few partials off the drive itself, and some others on the plastic it was wrapped in…" Inez's voice trailed off temptingly.

"You got a hit."

"Well, *I* didn't, but the lab did. Two of the partials were matched to one Dr. Reuben Aleksandr—the Russian spelling—Varden. No record, though. I'm sending you his abbreviated stats along with the list of names we found on the drive. I'll let you know if we find anything else. But for now, I hope this gives you something to chew on."

"Damn straight," he muttered into the phone. "Thanks, Inez. You're the best."

"I know." She disconnected the call just as Gabe's email downloaded the new message.

He clicked on Varden's info first. "Doctor? Hmm. What kind of doctor?" he muttered, scanning the details. Born 1975, Moscow. Really? Not Siberia? Hmm. Unmarried. No children. Pre-med at Oxford. Graduated from USC med school. Residency in Boston. General surgery. Hell, the man got around. And had credentials.

Gabe narrowed his eyes. "Sure you're the same guy?" he asked himself, clicking on the photo. The file image was probably a decade old, but still, clearly, it was the same Rue Varden who'd plugged him with a bullet at close range five years ago. It was those piercing green eyes and Slavic features that confirmed it.

"What the hell happened to 'first do no harm,' asshole?" he asked the sober-faced image, then read further. "No current residence listed. New Orleans a few years, left in '03…Haiti? Hmm. That was after the hurricane. What was he doing there? Then wha—the University of Michigan Hospital, *Ann Arbor*?" He sucked in his breath and looked again.

Yep. Dates of employment were a span of six years, off and on as a relief physician. He'd finished up just about a year ago. Off and on. Coming and going. Sonofabitch, the man had been underfoot for *years*. Within ten miles from Marina, working in her backyard—so to speak. Could not be a coincidence.

The question was…had she known?

Mouth in a flat, grim line, he reached for his phone to call her, then stopped. "Better look at the other stuff too," he told himself, clicking on the other attachment to Inez's message.

The list of names she'd culled from the flash drive he found in Siberia showed up in document format. Fifteen people and their respective corporations. Though he didn't know them all, from their names it was clear this was an international collection. Then, halfway down, he saw it: *Cora Allegan/Vision Screen Industries.*

Oh boy.

He reached for the phone again.

SIXTEEN

September 25
University of Illinois
Champaign, Illinois

I've never seen anything like it." Eli Sanchez's voice held a note of glee. "Suborder…possibly… No, it can't be… Archostemata? But…no, no freaking way. Unbelievable," he murmured, his eye sockets firmly planted on the microscope.

Ake glanced at Michael, who was sitting on a chair in the lab doing something on his smartphone. Hopefully getting a reservation for dinner somewhere in the area. They weren't actually in Chicago, but there had to be some good restaurants in Champaign…

"What do you mean?" Ake asked, returning his attention to the man who was one of the most prominent beetle experts in the world. He'd expected a fifty-something-year-old man with threading gray hair and beetle-like bug eyes, a small paunch, and maybe a goatee.

The only part he'd been right about was the goatee. Dr. Sanchez couldn't be more than forty and looked more like he belonged in a reggae band than in an insect lab. Of obvious Hispanic descent, he had shoulder-length dreadlocks, a single gold hoop in his right earlobe, and a dark brown goatee. The dreads were tied back, showing the small tattoo of a Chinese symbol on the side of his neck just above a faded red t-shirt. He was tall and lanky, and wore an open lab coat with the sleeves rolled up to bare muscular forearms. Jeans and Birkenstocks completed the look.

He was, Ake admitted freely, quite a package. Straight, too. Damned waste. He glanced at Michael, who, thankfully, seemed immune, and felt a tug of affection for his longtime partner. But then he turned his attention back to the entomologist and enjoyed the view.

Sanchez pushed back from the microscope, the wheels of his chair as enthusiastic as the excitement lighting his dark eyes. "Where did you say you found this specimen?"

Ake explained again, then said, "I just want to know what kind of bug—er, beetle it is. And if it could possibly have caused some sort of electrical malfunction in our power grid. I know it's a long shot, but there doesn't seem to be any other explanation."

"Unfortunately, what I have here—these charred pieces of elytra and tarsus, and a hint of thoraces—just isn't enough to allow me to fully categorize the type of Coleoptera, although it's possible it's an Archostemat…but that would be highly improbable."

He grinned at Ake's blank look, a wide flash of straight white teeth. "Sorry. Basically, of what you've given me, I'm only able to salvage parts of the hard outer wings of the insect, and a few small pieces of leg and thorax—the torso. There are over four hundred thousand species of coleops—"

"Coleops?" Ake couldn't quite keep the frustration from his voice.

"Right. Beetles. There are over four hundred thousand species of *beetles* in the world, and except for very basic categorization, it's often impossible to classify them without an intact specimen that can be dissected and examined internally. However," he continued, his voice filling with excitement again, "there's one thing I can tell you about this particular beetle. Its elytra—the hard covering, which is like an outer wing that protects the under, or hindwing—is amazing. I've never seen anything like it."

"The copper color?" Ake asked dubiously. This was a wasted trip. And they were too far away to make a detour to Chicago for a show, either. "I've seen lots of bugs—er, beetles—with copper wings like that. The Japanese beetles that infest my raspberries are almost that color." He frowned, reminded he was going to have to empty the traps he'd set for the pests when they returned.

Sanchez was nodding vehemently. "Yes, exactly. There are many species of beetles that have a metallic reflective color to the elytra. Blue, copper, green. But this one...I'm going to have to send it to a lab to be certain, but I suspect this beetle's wing is actually *made* of copper."

"Meaning...?" Ake pressed.

"Meaning I believe there is actual elemental copper in the *makeup* of the beetle. Lots of it."

Ake blinked. A feeling of something dark and unpleasant settled over him...as if he were just about to learn something he didn't want to know. "Are you saying this is a mechanized insect? Not a real bu—er—insect?"

Good grief. Had someone released a swarm of tiny mechanical creatures that sabotaged his plant? Terrorists with minuscule, robotic insects. His insides began to swish with nausea.

"No, it's a real insect," Dr. Sanchez told him earnestly. "It was a living creature at one time. That I'm fairly certain of...but if I could just get more pieces of the specimen, I could tell you more. There's hardly enough here for me to look at."

"I have my crew searching for more, but so far all they've found are those burned-out clumps of them."

Burned out and melted together...like metal. Not like living entities, but more like a mechanical—or what did they call them? That new trendy fashion and mechanical style—steampunk. That was it. Could they be like steampunk insects?

But the beetle guy believed it was a real bug.

Impossible. Unbelievable. But at the same time, it felt creepily *right.*

"If you find any more, get them to me. I'll be able to tell you more. I'll also tell you this, Mr. Akinowski: from what I can tell, there's nothing like this species of beetle anywhere in North America."

An unknown location

Cora looked up as the door to her room opened. Her stomach lurched and went into turmoil, but she kept her expression calm and neutral as she stood and moved to the center of the space—the same way she did on the day she learned she wouldn't be ousted as CEO of Vision Screen Industries.

Roman Aleksandrov, the man who'd threatened her earlier, entered—but this time he wasn't alone. Accompanying him was an elderly man who walked under his own steam, but slowly and carefully.

He was so old, Cora wasn't certain of his age—but she wouldn't have been surprised if he was into three digits. He wore the same type of clothing as her other captors with the exception of Roman: the simple undyed linen tunic over matching loose trousers. His stark white feet were bare.

"I am Lev," he said, fixing her with bright and intelligent but watery blue eyes. "Son of Gaia."

Son of Gaia? Was that like Son of Adam, or something more esoteric—at least in his mind?

She remained silent as he trudged across the wooden floor, hardly lifting his feet. For a wild moment, she considered launching herself toward him and taking the weakling captive, using him as a bartering tool for her escape, but Roman gave her a cold warning look that told her she wouldn't have a chance.

He would probably be right.

Despite his frailty, the old man exuded confidence and charisma, as well as something indefinable…almost otherworldly.

Something that made Cora reconsider her impression that he was fragile. Something that made the hair on her arms stand on end.

Lev eased himself into the chair she'd vacated, leaving Cora to tower over him. "You have committed crimes against our Mother Earth," said the elderly man. His voice did not match his body. It was strong and purposeful, yet low and rich at the same time. "Against my mother. You will have the opportunity to pay her recompense, and if she is merciful, you might survive."

By now it was clear this man was the one with the true power; that he could overrule Roman Aleksandrov and anyone else in this strange compound. Cora knew he was her best chance to change the tide, and she spoke earnestly. "I feel great remorse for what happened with my organization, and the misunderstandings and miscommunications that caused such terrible things to happen. I have already offered to pay whatever—"

"Be silent." Lev's voice lashed out, and, surprised by its vehemence and overt disgust, she obeyed. Power radiated from him even more strongly now as his eyes narrowed coldly on her. "The only reason you feel remorse, Cora Allegan, is because you are here. There were no misunderstandings, no miscommunications in your organization. You were solely responsible for the decision to ravage our earth. To violate our mother. To put capitalism and greed ahead of the greater good."

She swallowed hard, suddenly lightheaded and breathless. How could he know this? *How?* Colton Krawchuk had been dead for more than two years, and he was the only one who knew she'd made the decision to dump the monitors and pay whatever fines they might incur. *Might* being the operative word, for Cora had made a lot of friends at the EPA.

"I…I'm sorry," she whispered. Her hands were ice cold and she felt her insides loosening and shifting with terror.

"As am I." Lev glanced at Roman, who stepped forward and spoke.

"As I said in our prior meeting, you cannot return to us what has been taken from our earth. You cannot fix it, just as any violation of any living being cannot be undone. We Skaladeskas pass judgment upon you for your transgressions, but we do not sentence you. Your fate is for Gaia to decide."

He smiled and moved closer to her. "Good luck, Cora Allegan. I hereby release you into the arms of Gaia. If you survive, so be it. If you do not, 'tis nothing more than our earth exacting Her revenge upon you."

He was holding something slender and silvery. Before she could react, he grabbed her from behind and jammed the needle into her shoulder.

The room shimmered and her knees buckled. She hardly had time to draw in a breath before everything went dark.

SEVENTEEN

September 25
Chicago

Helen looked up from the tablet as Gabe walked into her office.

As always, he moved with that long, sleek stride, and, as usual, he had a fiery, intense expression in his eyes. He filled the room with his presence: broad shoulders, dark, mismanaged hair, confident movements, and he wore his nondescript CIA suit well enough to attract notice from all the females in the office. So much so that the admins had fairly fought over who would give up her desk for him to use.

She managed to submerge her own bump of attraction, the little surge of memory that nudged her on the rare occasion she saw Gabe, and gave him little more than an inquisitive look. "You've got something."

He settled into the chair across from her, and instead of lounging in it as he sometimes did, he sat straight up and shoved his own iPad across the desk at her. "We found a flash drive in the remains of the Skaladeska compound in Siberia. Tech managed to pull this data off it."

She took the tablet and saw he'd pulled up a list of names. "Cora Allegan. Holy shit."

"I've already got someone working on the rest of the list." Gabe leaned over to thunk a finger onto the screen. "This guy, Lo Ing-wen from Oh Yeh Industries—that's a mega furniture manufacturer in China—he disappeared two weeks ago. So far that's the only hit, but…"

Helen pressed her lips together instead of saying the vulgar word that came to mind. Some of the names on the list were familiar to her—Fortune 500 companies or mega-international ones. Others she didn't recognize. There were fifteen names; it would take some time to find out what they needed to know about each of them. She looked back up at Gabe, but before she could speak, her desk phone rang.

"Agent Darrow."

"Hyram Puttesca is here for you."

Perfect timing. "Put him in Room 3." She replaced the phone and rose, smoothing her ice-white suit. "With me, MacNeil. You'll want to hear this, I think."

Helen was aware of the way Gabe's eyes slid over her as she came around the edge of the desk, navigating in impractical silvery-gray heels she had no business wearing in the office…but had pulled out of her closet because he was here today and she knew they made her butt and legs look great.

Eat your heart out, hot stuff.

Eight years ago, they'd been a lot more than friends and well past merely lovers…but when she was promoted to special agent in charge and sent to Chicago, things fizzled. Distance, travel, and work schedules, confidentiality issues between their respective jobs—and, if she were going to be completely honest, a bit of insecurity on her part—had combined to cause the demise of their relationship. No hard feelings, no drama—it just ended.

"I've got Dr. Hyram Puttesca in consult," she told Gabe as he followed her down the corridor. "He was the attending physician for Sazma Marcko in the ER. He's the one who noticed the Skaladeska mark on his arm, and was smart enough to look it up—then notified us. Sharp guy."

"Did they find anything in Marcko's personal effects?"

"There was a car rental agreement. I'll send you the specs. I was just reviewing the report when you came in." She brandished her tablet, which housed the information she'd been perusing, and opened the door to her interview.

Dr. Puttesca was younger than she expected. He looked as if he was hardly out of med school, let alone residency. But he had a calm demeanor Helen suspected would be soothing in emergent situations, and his weary hazel eyes nevertheless gleamed with intelligence.

"Thank you for coming in, Dr. Puttesca. You mentioned on the phone you had something to show me."

"Yes." He shifted in his seat. "Thank you for seeing me. I… well, let me begin at the beginning. One of my colleagues—a friend, Brenda Hatcher, who I knew from my residency, is—was—working as an ER physician in Michigan. Near…uhm…Flint, I think it was. She had a patient less than a week ago who expired while in her care. It was sudden cardiac arrest, very unusual for an otherwise healthy man, and she was, understandably, upset. He was only fifty. The man presented with a severe lesion-like rash, his vitals were shutting down, and he was delirious."

Helen felt Gabe's impatience fairly emanating from the leg that almost brushed against hers, but she kept her expression smooth and encouraging. "And your patient here in Chicago, Sazma Marcko, died from sudden cardiac arrest, *not* from the knife wound in his torso. Could the SCA have been due to the wound?"

"Not likely. The wound was serious, but not life-threatening." Puttesca's expression became earnest. "But he also presented with a severe lesion-like rash, his vitals were tanking, and he was unresponsive."

"You think he had the same condition as your colleague's patient?" Helen's interest lasered in on the young physician. *Now we're getting somewhere.*

"And, it seems, so did my colleague herself." Puttesca's expression turned sober. "She passed away three days ago, and she appears to have suffered from the same evolution of conditions.

I'm here because I believe she was exposed to the same entity that caused her patient's death. I had talked to her on the—online the day of her patient's death."

"What is it?" Gabe asked. "A virus? She caught it from her patient? How?"

Puttesca's expression turned slightly sheepish. "Brenda— actually, her patient—believed it was a bug. Or several bugs." He dug into his rumpled suit coat pocket and withdrew a plastic bag. He hesitated, then shoved it across the table. "I suggest you don't open it, and definitely don't touch the contents without protection. I retrieved it when I drove to Michigan yesterday to pay my respects. She told me she had it, and I…well."

Helen slid the bag closer, positioning it so Gabe could look at its contents as well. Inside was a strip of sticky yellow flypaper, and attached to it were several insects. Some flies, but the greater number were beetle-like creatures, oblong and slender, with coppery wings and awkward heads and bodies.

"You and your colleague think these insects caused…what? The cardiac arrest? From a bite?" Helen asked, turning the possibility over in her mind and not certain how she felt about it. The bug certainly didn't look dangerous, and its mouth was tiny. Beetles didn't have stingers, so how would something like this *bite* someone in such a way they'd die?

"I know it sounds far-fetched, but…well, 'if you see something, say something.' Right? The presenting symptoms and resulting sudden cardiac arrest *are* unique," Puttesca told her. "Also, there are no other instances reported, so far, other than at Brenda's hospital…and now mine. Nor on any CDC report. So it doesn't appear to be a mere virus, and it seems isolated."

"So this bug that was in Michigan was also here in Chicago?" Gabe asked. "And bit these people? I suppose there could be a connection, but so what—"

Helen bolted upright in her chair, interrupting Gabe, and began to fumble for her iPad. "Wait." With quick fingers, she pulled up the report she'd previously been reviewing, flicking through the notes and photos with her fingertip. "*Wait*. Here."

She set the tablet on the table and jabbed her finger at the picture showing there. "This was found in the cuff of Marcko's pants, caught up in the fold."

She and Gabe, as well as Hyram Puttesca, looked from the plastic baggie to the photo of the remains of an insect and back again.

"They're the same."

Oh, yes they were. Gabe and Helen looked at each other.

They didn't know what it meant, but it had to mean something.

"Eli Sanchez." Helen pushed the honey-blond hair out of her eyes and looked up from her computer. "He's the entomologist we used for the Bertonshire case last year," she said as she scribbled a phone number on a sticky note.

Gabe wasn't familiar with the Bertonshire case, but all he needed was the name of the person who could help identify the bug they'd found. "It's a long shot, but I'll go see the guy."

They'd already showed the baggie and its contents around the office, as well as at a local gardening shop, to see if anyone recognized the type of insect. No one had seen anything like it, and a quick Internet search hadn't helped either.

"If the beetle isn't native to the area, and they both were exposed to it, it could help trace Marcko's movements—possibly even his origination, and where the Skalas are hiding out nowadays. I've got someone checking on the recent whereabouts of that first patient who died—Michael Wiley is his name—back in Michigan. I'm also sending people out to comb the area by Cora Allegan's house in case there are any matching beetle parts there, though that's a real long shot with sprinkler systems and that rain we had." Helen picked up her smartphone and glanced at a new text, then set it back down when she realized he wasn't leaving. "Anything else?"

Gabe sat on the edge of her desk. He hesitated, then plunged in. "Can you do something for me? Something just between you and me?"

Her attention flashed to him then flickered away, and he swore her cheeks turned slightly pink. "Depends what it is." But before he could make his request, she said, "By the way, I hope it wasn't a problem about the two hotel rooms."

It took him a moment to understand, then, unaccountably, his own face warmed. "Not at all."

"I didn't want to make any assumptions, although it's pretty clear you—er—well." She fixed him with steady gray-blue eyes. "Dr. Alexander seems like a good fit for you. She's smart and attractive and…well, worthy. But it would have been a tad messy to explain why we only needed one hotel room for you and the civilian consultant." And damned if she didn't give him a cheeky smile that almost made him feel like a lech.

"No problem. Really. We…uh…well, anyway." Gabe gathered his thoughts. He was wholly comfortable when it came to interrogating a suspect, debriefing an operative, interviewing a witness, or making a verbal case to his superiors…but it was a hell of a lot more difficult to discuss one's current relationship with one's former lover, who was also a colleague.

"All right, MacNeil. What's just between you and me?" Her tone was smooth and professional, her expression impersonal…so why did he feel a little breathless all of a sudden?

He regrouped. "I need information about Colin Bergstrom's history. His college years in particular—at Oxford. I need to know if he ever… Helen, he was at Oxford at the same time Viktor Aleksandrov—Marina's father—was. You need to dig deep." Gabe met her gaze steadily and saw the immediate dawn of comprehension.

"I see. And you obviously can't have anyone on your end look into it. Red flags would shoot up all over the place."

"I can't have *anyone* look into it—except you. Someone I know I can trust, someone I know won't let anyone else get wind of the poking around."

She nodded. "All right. I agree—we need to know anything and everything about the Skalas, and about anyone who might have a connection to them. Including your girlfriend. Gabe, I like and respect Marina Alexander—she's kind of a badass with that search and rescue caving thing going on, not to mention the flying aspect—but my gut tells me she's hiding something."

He gritted his teeth. Damned if he hadn't wondered the same thing—and damned if he was going to admit it to Helen. "She told us Varden showed up at her house. She contacted me. She's not hiding anything."

"And he was conveniently gone by the time you got there—only two, three hours later. Look, MacNeil, like it or not, she's inextricably entwined with the Skalas. And they have something priceless, something that could make her career. Something people in her shoes have killed for—"

"Helen, don't be—"

"I'm not saying she's there, and I'm not suggesting she ever would be, but you've got to look at the facts. You do know about her husband, right? Why they got divorced? It was over something like this, some artifact." Gabe must have managed to hide his surprise, for Helen continued, "If this library is real, this collection that seems to rival that of the lost Library of Alexandria, then it's something she'd probably do pretty much anything to protect, to have, to study. To get credit for the find. You saw her reaction when she thought the scrolls might have been destroyed."

"You're not saying anything I haven't already thought, Helen," he cut in. "Give me a little credit."

She shook her head. "This isn't me being catty, Gabe. This is me being careful, and smart, and looking at all angles. And I hope to hell you are too, because I'd hate to see Marina Alexander finish off what Sophie Ratachoux didn't."

How had she heard about Sophie? And how long had she known? All that had taken place more than five years ago…just before everything happened with Marina and the Skaladeskas. In fact, he'd been recovering from that incident when Bergstrom first sent him after Viktor Aleksandrov.

Damn. He gave a mental head shake. It was a good thing Helen Darrow was on his side, because she seemed to know everything.

Helen's lashes swept down over her expressive hazel eyes, hiding whatever was there. "You're a good spook, Gabe. I'd hate you to lose it all. Especially over a woman."

EIGHTEEN

Cora awoke in the jungle.

At first, she couldn't assimilate her surroundings: the soft, moist patch of knee-high grass, the tall trees arching over her and blocking out all but the smallest bit of light, the dull roar of bird calls and melodies, distant rustling, and the other chattering, clicking, swishing, and sloshing of nature.

And weaving in and around and over it all…the *stillness*.

The solitude.

Reality set in, and with a cry of shock, she scrambled to her feet, looking wildly about. Where was everyone? Where was she?

Then she remembered. Her sentence had been imposed:

You'll be released into the arms of Gaia. If you survive, so be it. If you do not, I consider it nothing more than our earth exacting her revenge upon you.

Cora smothered another cry, this one of disbelief and terror, as she realized she really was alone. And on her own.

At the thought, her insides loosened alarmingly. Her bladder emptied of its own volition, streaming warm liquid down her legs. Her insides jolted sickeningly.

Cora spun slowly around in the small patch of nowhere. Tall, ominous shadows rose in every direction, of every shape, size, texture, and shade of green. Vines and branches swayed and trembled. The scents of dark, peaty earth and damp moss filled her nostrils, along with sweet floral essence and a sharp, pungent, bitter smell.

Then she noticed the knife and the bottle of water. They'd been left sitting on the ground near her. And a gun: a handgun.

Her protection. Her only chance of survival.

Or a simple, controlled way out.

She fumbled with the pistol—which looked like it belonged in a Western sideshow—and looked inside the chamber.

One bullet. One damned bullet.

She laughed, more hysterical than terrified now, and picked up the blade. A puny shield against the snakes and spiders and canine-sized rodents and the wild cats and all the other dangers that crowded the jungle. Weren't there poisonous ants too?

Cora stifled a sob, realizing belatedly she also wore shoes, which were now wet from her own urine.

Shoes. Track pants. A tank bra. A knife. A bottle of water.

One bullet.

Holding the gun, she sank onto the ground beneath the expanse of a large, smooth tree and tried to think.

At least I'm still alive. At least I have a chance.

Dad's looking for me. He's turning the world upside down.

I am the CEO of a mega-corporation. I can do this. I can live.

Forget those bastards.

I'll find my way out on my own.

And they will pay.

Cora tried to focus, to rack her brain. She'd read that book—or parts of it, anyway—that really popular coffee table or bathroom book from a while ago. Something about "the worst-case scenario" guidebook.

It talked about what to do when a bear chased you, or when your car went into a lake…but what did one do when one was stuck in the jungle?

Climb a tree? No. She shuddered. There were snakes in trees. And cats could climb trees, which meant she could come face to face with a…whatever kind of wild cat lived in this place.

Wherever she was.

Find water.

That made sense. She had water in her bottle, but she would need more. And water often led somewhere…a river or stream she could follow, and it might lead her to a town or village or some vestige of civilization.

It was so quiet. Not a sound that didn't belong to nature. Not a plane flying overhead, nor the sizzle of a telephone wire, or the distant rumble of machinery.

Where am I?

Cora tried to keep her thoughts and feet alike steady as she clambered through the wilderness, searching for some source of water. She became aware of her belly's emptiness, and the way terror made her numb and clumsy.

There had to be someone to help her *somewhere.*

She tripped and fell, landing *splat* on her palms on the soft, moist, moss-covered ground. When she looked up, she found herself face to face with two dark, glinting eyes, glaring at her from the shadows.

Cora screamed and scrambled to her feet, whirling away to bolt blindly into the depths of the jungle. She ran and ran, scraping against rough tree trunks, through dangling vines and over small bushes, stumbling over uneven ground and stirring up a small flock of birds. She kicked a small dirt hill, and a swarm of crawling things erupted as she tore past, slapping umbrella-sized leaves and fernlike branches out of her way.

She didn't know how long or how far she ran, in which direction or even whether she'd gone in circles…she just knew, that after running and falling and resting…and then running and stumbling about again, that finally the sunlight had dimmed and a lot of time had passed as she staggered and tripped her way through the rainforest…and she had no more energy. She could go no further.

She slumped to the ground, heaving and gasping, sweating, bloody, dirty, and shaking. Tears poured from her eyes, her nose was running, and she was scraped and cut from the mad dash.

I'm going to die.

Then she looked up and saw something that made her catch her breath.

A stone wall, half hidden by jungle growth.

A village? Shelter? Something.

Something man-made had to be a good sign.

Cora pulled to her feet, heart pounding, a surge of hope rushing over her. Something on the wall glinted, catching the dappled light that managed to filter through the top-heavy rainforest trees.

Greenish metalwork laid in the stone wall formed a rectangular shape. It looked as if it framed an entrance or a doorway, but there seemed to be no way to open it. Set into the ground in front of it were bricklike metal pavers, and the same bricks, the same sea-green metallic sheen and overgrown with moss and dirt, were set in the stone wall in a random pattern. What kind of metal—oh, copper. Oxidized copper.

Heart pounding, she shoved at what must be the entrance, heaving against it with her shoulder. The rough stone and metal scraped her bare skin, but she pushed and prodded until, once more out of breath, she sagged to the ground.

It was only then she noticed the small lever, camouflaged behind a stone and cluster of natural growth.

Cora reached for it, and needed the strength of both arms to tug the lever…bit…by…bit…

A soft, grinding, groan-like sound told her she'd succeeded in her endeavor, just before the wall began to move.

"Hello?" she called, poking her head into the darkness. She wasn't afraid it was an animal's lair, for how would one find its way inside?

But maybe someone was in here. Or at least she could use it for a hiding place until she figured out what to do.

The door opened further, and as she took a step inside, she saw the interior walls, briefly illuminated by the daylight.

Bright green. More copper. They were made of pure copper. She'd never seen anything like this.

Cora hesitated, then walked further inside. If this place was a temple, perhaps there were people who came to worship here. Perhaps she could find help.

A small shaft of light beamed down from above, and she realized after a moment of shock that it was a skylight, high in the ceiling. Many yards out of reach, the illumination was hardly larger than a salad plate, but at least it gave off some cloudy light in the dark space.

Cora looked around. The walls, ceiling, and floor were the color of the Statue of Liberty—ornate and decorative, weathered— but the area was empty of everything else. No rubble, no animal remains, nothing.

It looked as if no one had been here for centuries. Maybe millennia.

What had she found?

Then she noticed an outline at the other end of the space. A door? Maybe she was in the antechamber to something bigger—a temple?—and that far door led into the actual worship space.

On either side of the door were two piles of round white stones. They were the only things in the chamber not made from copper. They had been arranged in tall, cone-like piles, as if to flank the door like guards.

Cora felt around the edges of the second door, searching for another lever or some other way to open it. Her fingers were stiff and cold from fear and desperation, and the scent of stale urine filled her nostrils, fighting with the damp and musty inside of the space.

A sob—her own—caught her by surprise as she examined the door in vain. Nothing. There seemed to be no way to open it, yet she continued to dig at it, as if somehow this would be her saving grace. As if somehow opening that door would save her— no matter how absurd it seemed.

When her fingers were sore and bleeding, Cora sank onto the ground, hugging her knees to her chest. She sobbed, rocking back and forth as she thought about her life, the choices she'd made, and whether she'd ever see her father again. And Jerry.

With a cry of frustration, she tipped her head sharply back against the wall, slamming into the coppery covering. There was a soft *ping* and the wall behind her groaned. Then began to move.

Cora leapt unsteadily to her feet. A small black crevice had been revealed, unmistakable but hardly wide enough for a finger. With a cry of triumph, she pulled and pushed, and the door inched open a little further.

No sooner had the soft spill of light cascaded into the chamber beyond than Cora heard a curious, ominous sound. Tiny, infinite scuttling legs…then the soft buzz of countless wings filled her ears.

She stepped back as a swarm of *something* poured from the dark chamber, surrounding her and the area, buzzing, darting, diving, and thudding into her and the walls.

Stifling a scream, she whirled and staggered into one of the stone pyramids. It fell, collapsing against her. Cora tumbled to the ground as the stones and the insects pelted her in turn.

NINETEEN

September 26
University of Illinois—Champaign

"This is the most fascinating specimen I've ever seen," said Eli Sanchez, the beetle expert. His shoulder-length dreadlocks were pulled into a messy club at the nape of his neck, exposing the Chinese symbol for peace inked just behind his left ear. A pristine white lab coat was open to reveal a vintage-style Beatles t-shirt.

Marina suspected his choice of attire wasn't a coincidence.

He was also gloved and masked, as were Marina and Gabe, on Dr. Hyram Puttesca's advice. They weren't sure what about the beetles—if anything—was causing the deaths, but no one was taking any chances.

Currently, Sanchez's face was pressed onto the eyepieces of the serious-looking microscope with *WILD Heerbrugg* printed on its base. He made a sound of interest then disbelief as he moved the dial of the fiberoptic light-control box, turning up the illumination on the specimens. His mask puffed in and out like an elevated heartbeat.

"...Reticulate...elytral window punctures...quite conspicuous... Hindwings...definite, strong venation...*cuticle scales!*... My God, this is unbelievable," he murmured to himself in snatches that meant nothing to Marina. Then he froze, his tall, lanky body going rigid. "*Three* ocelli?" he exclaimed, fairly dancing at the microscope even while peering down into it. "It can't be. But, by God... Do you have any idea what this means?"

"If I knew what ocelli were, I might...but probably not," Gabe muttered.

Sanchez's long-fingered hand gestured excitedly, like a surgeon expecting someone to hand him an instrument, all the while remaining in position over the microscope. Then he fumbled blindly on the table for a small pair of forceps. "Three ocelli," he said again, his voice filled with glee. "*And* scales! Where did you say you found this?" He popped away from the microscope, his dark eyes wide and sparkling with excitement.

"In a man's pants cuff," Gabe said. Marina could almost read his mind: if the guy was so excited about three whatever ocelli were, he'd be really stoked if he knew it might have something to do with a group of terrorists. "But what can you tell us about the beetle? Where it's from, if it's dangerous to humans...anything?" Now his voice had a bit of impatience. "In English, please. I can tell you we think it's related to a terrorist group."

"A terrorist group." Sanchez's brows rose, but he made no further comment. Instead, he gestured with the forceps. "Well. The specimen is Coleoptera, of course—a beetle, suborder Archostemata. That's one of the four major subgroups of Coleoptera, and the smallest of them, with the fewest species. There are Archostemats on every continent except Antarctica— that we know of, anyway. They're quite rare, and most specimens from this suborder have previously been found in eastern Asia. Siberia, that area."

Gabe looked at Marina, and she was aware of her heart ramming harder in her throat. *Siberia.* That couldn't be a coincidence.

"Are they dangerous?" she asked.

"Beetles aren't dangerous—at least in the way you might think of them as being dangerous. They don't bite or carry venom. They can be devastating to crops, of course, and yards, like Japanese beetles, and problematic in other ways—infestations in houses at times, sometimes in food—in fact, Spanish Fly is actually a species of beetle. But regarding Archostemata…we actually don't know a lot about that suborder simply because there aren't very many living specimens, and many of what we have to study are fossils. They're all very primitive species. But I…" He turned back to his work, pulling out the dish from beneath the microscope. "I can't believe…and the elytra…they seem—"

"Elytra?" Marina prodded.

"The forewings. The most easily identifiable characteristic of a Coleopteran—beetle—is its hard, protective front wings. They aren't used for flying, but to protect the hindwings, which are the more gossamer-like fragile ones beneath—and what they actually fly with. And even the hindwings on this one," he murmured, looking back at the specimen which was now sitting on the counter in full view, "they're amazing. They appear to be… *copper*…but they can't…it's impossible…"

Still muttering to himself, he lifted the insect delicately with the very fine-pointed forceps and placed it on a small block. Then he inserted a tiny needle through the side of the body. Holding the pin with a slightly larger forceps, he pushed it into a tiny cube of cork, which he then impaled firmly on a long black pin with a gold head. He placed the entire thing, now on a piece of white foam board, under the microscope again, and adjusted the light. He pushed a few keys on a keyboard, and leaned back, looking at a large video monitor above the lab bench. The beetle was there, in all its glory, much larger than life. He moved the light wands around a bit, and repositioned the beetle.

Marina caught her breath, getting this incredible magnified view of the beetle for the first time. There was a scale indicator on the video screen, showing the beetle to be about eight millimeters, and now that it was blown up to the size of a big-screen television, all she could think was what a primitive-looking creature it was. Its body was separated from the head with what looked like a short, ball-like neck, but surely had some specific entomological name. The critter looked as if a child had assembled it from mismatched parts. As she and Gabe watched the screen, they could see as Sanchez used the forceps to carefully open one of the outer wings. A moment later, he sliced it off with a small glass blade, and placed it into yet another glass dish.

"Will you look at that," he murmured like a man to his lover as he slid the wing under another microscope. "I'll be damned."

Then, with a strangled sound of excitement, Sanchez whipped away from the eyepiece. He looked even wilder than before, his intense eyes nearly popping from their deep sockets. "Wait a sec…" Giving his chair a good, solid shove, he went careening across the room, still in his seat. In a whirl of white lab coat and a bounce of dreadlocks, he dug open a small cabinet and withdrew a small wooden box. "It can't be…too much of a coincidence…" he muttered, extracting another dish. Another shove and he zoomed back across the floor, returning to the microscope bench. "But maybe…"

Marina peered over his shoulder at this new addition and saw a small jumble of what looked like melted metal before he slipped the dish in place under yet another impressive-looking microscope. Her interest spiked when she saw a glint of copper and something that looked like a thick hair…or an insect leg. "What is that?"

"Another specimen someone brought me a few days ago." Sanchez sounded supremely distracted as he traded positions between the two viewers, sliding back and forth on his chair, clearly comparing the different material. "Damn right. It could be. It could very well be. I think it's the same…or damned close." His voice dropped low and smooth again. More keypunching, and then two more video monitors were showing magnified bits of beetle.

"Another specimen?" Gabe moved for the first time, pushing himself away from where he'd been leaning against the wall. He glanced at Marina, then demanded, "From where? Are you certain?"

"As certain as I can be with it in this condition—melted all to hell and fried into a crispy critter." Sanchez gestured vaguely to the ashy black ball.

"Where did it come from?"

The tone of Gabe's voice seemed to penetrate Sanchez's train of thought, for the entomologist actually stopped moving and turned to face him. He yanked the mask down to expose the rest of his face, including a square jaw and expressive, sensual mouth underscored by a neat goatee. "A friend referred someone to me. They found this mass of fried copper and beetle parts over in St. Louis, where that blackout started. Right at the power plant that caused the blackout. Since the insect isn't indigenous to North America, they brought it to me to ID."

Gabe made a sound and, eyes wide, yanked out his phone. He tore off his purple lab glove and began to type on the screen with sharp, fierce stabs as Sanchez replaced his mask and turned back to work.

So this bug—insect—had been found near the source of the blackout? Marina felt a little shiver of inevitability, followed by a nudge of nausea. Surely it wasn't a coincidence.

Sanchez concentrated once again on the intact specimen Gabe and Marina had provided, poking it with a pair of forceps as it floated on its pin anchor. She watched the video monitor in fascination as he used the tool to ease one of the hindwings open.

The underwing glowed coppery in the strong white light of the light wand, and she moved closer to look at the delicate webbing of the wing. It looked like the most delicate of metal sculptures, translucent and rust-colored.

But this was a real insect, not a mechanized one. Wasn't it?

"What about that black stuff on its legs? It looks a little like dust, but it keeps smudging off on things. Is that normal for a beetle? I know bees sometimes have pollen that clings to their legs—do beetles have that sort of thing?" she asked. "And where would it come from? Can that help identify the origin of the bu—insect?"

By now Sanchez had removed the hindwing as well, and the impaled beetle sat, half denuded, on its specimen block. "It's not a normal trait of coleops, but there are some species of insects commonly called assassin bugs that carry bacteria on their mid-

or hind-legs. That, in fact, is how Chagas disease is spread. You might have heard of it. The kissing disease? Fairly rampant in the Amazon jungle." He continued to lecture as he pressed his eyes to the microscope, glancing up only briefly to fumble for a tiny metal pick. "But that's the family Reduvidae, order Hemiptera—and those would be real bugs." He said dryly, his eyes crinkling above the corners of his mask. "In the case of Chagas disease, the insect does bite its victim. But it carries bacteria from its own waste on its legs. The waste is pretty much liquid, as the coleop's diet is liquid—blood, to be exact. When it settles to feed, often near the mouth of the victim, it deposits the bacteria. The bacteria are on the skin. The bite itches, the person scratches, and the bacteria get into the body. That bacteria is actually what causes the illness—not the bite. In fact, some people think Charles Darwin died of Chagas disease."

"Lovely thought," Marina replied dryly, resisting the urge to rub the corner of her mouth behind her mask. She glanced at Gabe, who was having a quiet, intense conversation on his phone.

But Sanchez wasn't paying attention. He pulled the specimen out from under the microscope and pinned it into a small white box with a shiny bottom. "Something else I wanted to check," he muttered, taking the box over to another complicated device consisting of a large Nikon microscope with what appeared to be a very expensive digital camera on top, attached to a computer monitor. A keyboard sat in front of it, and several other boxes were attached by various cables and cords. He clicked a few buttons, turned a knob on one of the boxes, tapped the keyboard...then suddenly an image popped up on the computer screen.

It was an enlarged version of the beetle's head, and whatever he saw made Sanchez's breath catch. "Definitely three ocelli. I can't believe it. That's just—seriously, you must tell me exactly where you found this specimen. Get me security clearance or whatever—I've done work for the FBI. Helen Darrow can vouch for me. But I *have* to know..." He looked back and forth between them, his dark brown eyes sparkling with delight and filled with pleading.

"What's an ocelli? And why are three of them a big deal?" Marina asked when Gabe, still on the phone, shook his head mutely at the entomologist's plea.

"The ocelli are eye spots, which are the simplest form of an eye we find in nature—it doesn't have a cornea or a lens. It doesn't really see anything other than light or the lack thereof. Jellyfish have them, snails, many other creatures. Coleops can have them too...but all known beetles have only two ocelli...except for a very primitive, rare family called Jurodidae. And we've only ever found one living, non-fossil Jurodid. In eastern Siberia, like I said earlier. Here. Let me pull up an image."

Clearly unaware of the implications of his information, Sanchez sent his chair gliding over to another desktop computer, which was attached to a tower of several large external hard drives. His fingers tapped efficiently over the keys and he clicked the mouse a few times. Propping his masked chin on a gloved hand, he peered at the image that came up on the screen. It was of a beetle that looked exactly like the one Marina and Gabe had brought him.

But he was shaking his head. "Look at this. Not even close." That tone of excitement was stronger now. "See this? They're not the same damn beetle. The pronotum is narrower, the angle of the hind-coxae..." He tsked, but with glee. "Definitely not the same. Jurodidae for sure, but not at all *Sikhotealinia*. The variegation on the elytra, the mandibles...it's obvious they aren't—and that's without even a dissection!"

You could've fooled me. Marina figured this must be how some people felt when she was discoursing on the differences between cuneiform and ogam.

"And so...?" Gabe was still on his phone, but he spoke to Sanchez. His face displayed tension, but his eyes remained sharp.

"So that means you've brought me a specimen from a completely new species of beetle—one from the most primitive genus." Sanchez had pulled his mask away again, revealing a brilliant white smile. His dark eyes were bright with excitement and fascination. "I have *got* to write a paper about this."

"Great," said Gabe, pulling away from the lab table. "So you can't tell us anything about it? Where it's from?"

"Oh, I can tell you plenty about it—especially after a complete dissection. It might not be details you want, but once I'm finished, I can likely tell you where it came from and what its habitat is, what it eats—"

"And how about this—can you tell us how it's killing people?" Gabe asked. "Because we've got three deaths already, and who knows how many more to come."

The thrill died from Sanchez's expression. "Killing people. So that's it. I'll have to do some lab tests. It'll take time. Give me a day."

"How about five hours," Gabe said. It wasn't a request.

TWENTY

Chicago, Near the FBI Field Office

Marina hesitated briefly, then lifted the lid of her laptop. She pressed the power button, then, while the sleek silver device booted up, she walked over to draw the hotel room curtains closed. It was after four in the afternoon and this was the first chance since arriving in Chicago she'd had to be alone and to work on her own projects.

After arriving in Chicago, she'd spent all of the last two days, and into the evening, at the FBI field office with Gabe, Bergstrom, and Helen Darrow until being released to a Marriott less than a mile from the field office at ten o'clock at night. Early this morning, Gabe had showed up and taken her with him to meet with Eli Sanchez, then back to the office—doing his job keeping her in protective custody. Or so they claimed.

By four o'clock, she was done with hanging around the field office trying to manage some of her work on the iffy Wi-Fi in the conference rooms, and finally insisted on returning to her hotel.

Marina wasn't the least bit disappointed with the two-room arrangement for her and Gabe at the hotel. It had nothing to do with him and everything to do with herself needing space and privacy. She appreciated Helen's consideration—if that was what it had been.

Besides, there was nothing to keep them from sharing a room if they so chose—although she didn't expect to get a visitor. Gabe had escorted her here last night, then returned to the FBI field office with Helen and Colin Bergstrom until who knew how much later. When he picked her up for the visit to the entomologist, he looked as if he'd hardly slept.

The laptop was booted up by the time she returned to the awkward hotel desk, settling into the chair. She found it much easier to do work from a field site—in tents or even on the ground beneath a tree—than in a hotel room. The furnishings were so uncomfortable, and always seemed to be designed for a person taller and bigger than she.

When she checked her email, she found a response she'd been waiting for from a colleague in Amsterdam.

Where did you find this? Leif wrote. *Agree w your assessm't—it could definitely be Celtiberian. Note the lengthened characters in the sample you sent me, compared to attached sample I've reviewed. And appendages to limbs—hardly noticeable on confirmed sample, but more evident in yours. Completely different medium, too, of course. But if I had to conjecture, I'd say definite influence if not mere stylistic difference because of the medium. Did you say this was in North America? What a find!*

Yeah, that she knew. But there was even more Leif didn't know...couldn't know, yet.

Marina clicked on the attached image and peered at the enlarged picture her friend had sent, which, thanks to the high-res screen on her computer, was nearly as clear as real life. Now that she had a sample to compare it to, she saw her colleague's points. Close enough to be influenced by Bronze Age writings, but not identical.

Still, it was a vowelless ogam text. No other civilization or culture was using that style and combination of long, straight lines, with others angled or perpendicular to them. The writing was distinctive to the Celts in Bronze Age Ireland and Britain— which was also influenced by the great Phoenician empire, whose trade routes clearly extended to the Iberian Peninsula.

She hesitated, then pulled out the carved-stone sample she'd received from Roman, or Lev—or whoever from the Skaladeskas had sent the Pandora's box of priceless artifacts. Yes, she'd taken a chance by bringing it, but there was no way in hell she was going to let this opportunity lapse while Gabe and Helen had her caught up in this investigation. What else was she going to do, stuck in a hotel room or a small, windowless FBI office?

She still didn't know what they wanted from her, why it was necessary that she be uprooted and brought to Chicago. Surely they didn't expect Varden to return. And so what if there was a dead Skaladeska in the morgue...how did bringing her to Chicago help them? Did Darrow think Marina might be able to identify the guy?

Marina placed the fragment of stone once more next to the picture she'd taken of the Northern Michigan cave images and compared both to the image from Leif van Hoest.

Three samples: one from Northern Michigan, one sent to her from the Skaladeskas (presumably from the library of Ivan the Terrible, but its origin unknown), and a third one, sent from Leif as a sample of writings from the Iberian Peninsula during the Bronze Age...

Her heart pounded and her palms became slick—for right away she saw all the similarities. But she forced herself to take her time, to look closely, carefully, even though she already knew they matched.

And they did.

They *did*.

A chill rushed over her, followed by a shock of heat and a sudden thudding of her heart. The style and type of text in the three were the same...or very nearly so.

Her breath turned shallow and quick as the implications set in.

There had long been fringe theories that Europeans had been in North America as early as 500 BC; that they had traded with the primitive copper miners and taken much of the copper back home with them.

The Phoenician empire had stretched far beyond the Mediterranean Sea to the Iberian Peninsula and, possibly, to North America, something only few, very few, anthropologists and historians—generally on the periphery of well-respected scholars—believed. There'd never been proof, but Marina suspected she could very well be holding something like that right here.

There were other instances, too, of findings that were odd or out of place. Findings and discoveries that were unexplained.

She turned to her computer, fingers flying. *Stone pyramids lake Wisconsin*, she typed.

The search results came up: "Rock Lake Wisconsin stone pyramids" was on top, and there was a picture—

Marina caught her breath as she looked at images that had been taken underwater—at the bottom of Rock Lake in Wisconsin—of a large stone pyramid...a stone pyramid that was the same style and shape, though much larger than the ones Matt Granger had discovered in the Upper Peninsula of Michigan.

Her palms were damp and sweaty as she began to mentally connect the dots: the same stone pyramid in a Wisconsin lake as one on a smaller scale in Michigan, near the copper mines. Writings on the wall with the Michigan pyramids that bore more than a strong resemblance to the type of cuneiform characters used by Celt-Iberians, who likely had been influenced by the Phoenicians.

She tapped on the computer again, trying to remember what she'd heard about an ancient cuneiform tablet found with an American tribe. There had been a Native American leader or chief who'd had one among his effects.

Who was it? She typed in the search bar, scanned the results... Right. Ah yes. Chief Joseph. She read further, fascinated, and learned the Nez Perce leader had carried a piece of cuneiform in his medicine pouch with an inscription from around *2042 BC...* and he claimed it had been passed down from his white ancestors.

Fascinating...and almost eerily unbelievable. And what if—

A knock on the hotel door had her spinning from the computer. Gabe already? Marina felt a little nudge of guilt as she closed the laptop and went to answer the knock.

Her hand was on the knob, just about to turn it, when she looked through the peephole.

It wasn't Gabe.

Marina stepped back from the door, her heart pounding. The man standing on the other side was holding a large tray covered by a white napkin. A metal warming dish was on top of it.

The only problem was, she hadn't ordered any food.

He knocked again, this time announcing, "Room service."

Silently, Marina moved from the door and snatched her cell phone from the desk. The only person who might have sent something up was Gabe…and surely he would have warned her. Plus, he wasn't really the type of guy to do that sort of thing.

Maybe she was being a little paranoid, but she wasn't about to take chances.

She was sending Gabe a text when the knock came again. After a pause, she heard the distinctive sound of a keycard fumbling at the door.

Her adrenaline went into overdrive as the options barreled through her mind.

She was across the room—too far away to slam the security bolt closed, and if she made the move and didn't succeed, he would know someone was in the room. Her best hope was for whoever it was to think the place was empty.

As the door vibrated, Marina looked around for a weapon, a hiding place, an escape. Damned windows in a hotel room never opened more than a crack. She could hide in the bathroom, behind the shower curtain. Or lock herself inside the bathroom and call for help on her cell.

The door clicked and the knob turned as Marina ducked into the closet. She crunched herself into the darkest corner, leaving the door half open in hopes the intruder would only give the space a cursory look.

Just as the door opened, she heard a man's voice.

"What the hell are you doing, Bellhane? She's not in there. I just saw her walking through the parking lot."

Marina drew in a sharp, silent breath. She recognized that voice. That accent. That *tone*.

The other man, presumably the one who was trying to break into her room, responded, but her heart was pounding too loudly in her ears, and he was speaking indistinctly, so she couldn't understand what he said—nor the response from his companion.

The door closed with a dull clunk and rattle, obliterating any further conversation, and Marina tipped her head back against the wall in relief.

She waited a moment, then stood and made her way out of the closet.

Rue Varden was standing in the middle of her room.

TWENTY-ONE

Marina stared at Varden.

He stood there, tall and rangy in worn jeans and a leather jacket, looking as nonchalant as if he'd walked into his own room. He wore scuffed boots and was holding coffee in a to-go cup, his swollen thumb still bruised. Though his face seemed drawn and pale. Not a surprise, considering the last time she'd seen him—about seventy-two hours ago—he'd been fairly bleeding to death on her couch. But he still gave off an unmistakable aura of confidence and strength…along with a healthy dose of the arrogance that set her teeth on edge.

"This is becoming an unwelcome habit, you letting yourself into my private spaces," she said coolly.

"I just did you a bloody favor." He didn't seem at all surprised that she'd emerged from a hiding place in the closet. Nor was he inclined to comment about it. Instead, he walked over to the closed laptop she'd left on the desk and set down the cup, then picked up not only the photos, but the delicate text sample that matched. She could see the wound she'd stitched at the back of his head, and it appeared to have begun to heal. Someone had even trimmed a little more of the hair away.

"Sorry if I'm not kissing your feet with gratitude. What the hell are you doing here?" she said.

He must have noticed she'd scooped the cell phone back into her hand, for he held up a palm of his own to stop her. "Just hold off before you start calling in the cavalry. You just missed being snatched up by one of your uncle's thugs and taken at gunpoint."

"I thought guns were banned from use by the Skaladeskas."

Varden's mouth thinned into a humorless smile. "Only when your uncle is around. Roman is the one who abhors—and fears—them."

So Varden didn't know Roman was her *father*, not her uncle. Interesting. That raised the question whether Roman himself knew...or if that information was something Victor had told only Marina before he died. "I don't see any blood pouring from your body, so you're obviously not here for my surgical skills. What do you want?"

Something flickered in his eyes as they met hers, and Marina felt an unexpected bolt of attraction stab her in the belly. She had to resist the urge to take a step back.

"I told you," he said, his voice subtly lower. "I did you a favor by intervening in what would have been your second—or is it third?—capture by the Skaladeskas. One would have thought you'd learned to be more careful by now."

Marina's cell phone dinged with a text message alert before she could reply. She glanced down to see Gabe's response: *No I did not order room service for you! Don't open door.* Then her phone began to ring—Gabe, of course.

"If I don't answer this—"

"Go ahead." Varden's voice and stance clearly challenged her to take the call and report him.

"Marina," Gabe said the minute she answered. His voice was tight. "Are you all right?"

She didn't know why she responded the way she did. Or maybe she did—maybe it was a combination of curiosity and bravado. "I'm fine. Everything's fine; sorry to worry you. It was a mistake—they had the wrong room. But the steak sure smelled good!" She laughed and noticed a little of the tension eased from Varden.

"You're sure? If you're in trouble, tell me you're going to order a hamburger."

Marina kept her gaze averted from Varden as she replied, "I'm not hungry right now, but I'll probably order room service later. Pizza, or the salmon looks good."

"All right." There was obvious relief in his voice. "Good. Look, I'm going to be tied up here for a while longer. I'm due to talk to Sanchez in the next couple of hours, and there's some other avenues we're looking into.

"I'm getting lots of work done. I've got a big project on, so— no worries."

"All right. Gotta go. Maybe I'll stop by later tonight…?" His voice dropped low, implying someone was in earshot. Helen Darrow, perhaps?

"Sure." Marina couldn't help giving Varden a side-glance. She suspected he could hear much of both sides of the conversation. He gave her a knowing look that confirmed it, and she merely lifted a brow. "I'll be here." Tucking the phone back into the waistband of her yoga pants for easy access, she fixed her attention on her unwanted guest. "How did you know I was here? And be careful with that, *please*," she added when he gestured with the delicate stone carving. "It's several thousand years old."

"And I can only guess how it came to you. As for your question…the Skalas always know where you are."

Marina felt a nauseating shiver creep over her shoulders, but now she understood a whole lot more. "You're *tracking* me. A bug? A GPS? Where? Why?"

"Lev wants you. And so does Roman. They all do. They need you…or so they think."

"You don't." The words slipped out before Marina could take them back, and she immediately regretted the way they made her sound. As if she cared.

"Damn right. You," he said, his voice cool and bitter, "are a threat to me and my position among the tribe. If you return and take your place as Lev's granddaughter…well, let's just say that will adversely affect my influence on him as well as Roman."

"Fear not, Dr. Varden. There's no chance of that happening."

"That's precisely why I'm here. If I hadn't intervened just now, you'd be in the back of a car and on your way to the Amaz—to the Skaladeskas, whether you wanted to be or not. Lev is not well; he grows more frail by the day. And he is determined to see you."

"Is that why you added him—and yourself—to my Skype accounts? So I could communicate, or vice versa, if I chose?"

"I'm devastated you haven't attempted to connect with Dr. Herb Grace." His voice was dry. "Obviously you knew it was me."

"Oh yes, so clever of you. All I had to do was a search on Google for 'herb grace' and the plant rue came up. A bitter herb, unpleasant and toxic." She gave him a bright smile. "Needless to say, I made the connection instantly."

His lips twitched into something that might have been a smile, but was quickly gone. "I did that under orders from your grandfather. He does want to speak with you. In fact, he's quite desperate to do so, so he wants several channels of communication open for you."

"He sent me the package—and it contained that splinter of stone you're manhandling. I can only assume you delivered the box?"

Varden looked down at it, and Marina noticed he didn't seem to have a trace of the reverence she felt when touching something that old, potentially filled with so many anthropological secrets. It was the rare person who did, which was why it was so important she advocate for these lost treasures. "Yes," Varden replied. "He figures he'll tempt you into returning to the fold by showing you some of the treasures therein."

"Returning to the fold? I was never in the fold to begin with. I didn't even know the Skaladeskas still existed until my father disappeared five years ago."

"If I'd had my way—and a few others in the fold do feel the same as I do—that wouldn't have changed. I don't want you there. In that, at least, we are on the same side."

Marina stifled a snort. "Right. I still don't know why you are here. In my room. You want me to believe you intercepted a kidnapping attempt—which I'll accept, I suppose, since the guy was breaking in—but why are you still here?"

"I intercepted Bellhane then sent him off to follow you, telling him you were on your way somewhere in a cab—I'd heard you ask for one at the front desk. Or at least, that's what he believes. His job is to find you and take you to Lev—willingly or not. I'm here to warn you, so we can avoid having that happen."

"So you've done that. Thanks. See you later." She gestured to the door.

"Where's your father?"

"Victor?"

He looked at her closely, his startling green eyes sharp and suspicious. "You sound as if you aren't certain."

Marina kept her expression blank. "He's dead."

Varden shook his head. "You saved his life. Pulled him from the lake during your escape. You dove into the water and swam after him. Or so it was reported."

Discomfort tightened her middle as he studied her. It was almost as if he knew about her fear, about how incredibly impossible it had been for her to force herself to dive into the lake and try to save the man for whom she felt little but antipathy. A man she hardly knew. "Yes. But he died not long after. He wasn't well to begin with."

"You were trying to escape, and he'd done nothing to help you while you were being held captive—in fact, he even interfered… yet you risked your life to save him by diving into a frigid lake." Oh yes, Rue Varden definitely knew of her fear. And a lot more about her than she'd realized.

"If you've learned anything about me, you know that's what I do. I'd do it for anyone."

He held her gaze with his for a moment longer, then gave a barely perceptible nod. "Which is why I came to you." He gestured to the wound at the back of his head. "Although that didn't keep you from contacting your spook friend."

She gave him a cool smile. "Of course not." Then it was her turn to narrow her eyes on him. "How did you come to have need of my dubious skills, anyway? A tangle with Homeland Security while you were attempting one of your terror plots?"

The expression that flitted across his face surprised her. Fury was the only way to describe it, but the look was gone in an instant, and his eyes turned from hot to cool. "That was courtesy of Sazma Marcko. He took exception to one of my suggestions, and we got into a…tangle, I believe you called it. A disagreement."

"He's dead."

"Not by my hand."

"So someone else stabbed him." She lifted a brow.

"Marcko didn't die from a stab wound."

She couldn't deny that, and apparently, neither could he. "The beetles. You must know about them."

Varden lifted a brow. "Beetles?"

She gritted her teeth. "Don't play the innocent. We both know how Marcko died—though you certainly helped him along the way. And speaking of your predilection for violence…you shot Gabe MacNeil when we were in Siberia. But not enough to kill. Why?"

Varden shrugged. "Maybe I missed."

"At that close range?"

"'First, do no harm.' Despite my predilection for violence, as you put it, I'm a doctor, remember?" He turned to replace the stone splinter on the desk.

"But you're also a Skaladeska. You've got plenty of blood on your hands. What's a little more?"

He turned back to face her. "I've never killed anyone."

"Maybe not by your own hands—though I find that impossible to believe—but association is everything. The Skalas are going about their mission the wrong way. How many more innocent people will die while they try to…do whatever they're trying to do?"

"No one is listening, Marina. The governments give lip service, the corporations don't bloody care, and the earth is raped and ravaged without boundary. If something doesn't change, there will be countless more innocent people killed—or worse, they'll live on a planet that cannot support them, and they'll have a tortuous, painful existence. They'll die anyway—in droves, and much more unpleasantly."

"People are listening. Change *is* happening. But it takes time." Even as she spoke the words, Marina was aware of a sense of dread settling over her. She might not like him, she might not agree with his position and the violence his tribe propagated, but he was right.

Varden's expression turned bleak as he moved toward the door. "We have less than a decade to turn things around if we don't want the earth to be irreparably damaged and the downward slide to begin. The honeybees—surely you know of annihilation of their colonies?—and some of the most basic building blocks of our earth are being steadily destroyed. The rain forests, the Arctic Circle, the bees…all of these things are instrumental to the give and take of the earth, to her very being. They seem like small matters—a decrease in honeybees is no problem; the keepers just ship them from place to place to do their work, then move on to the next crop. California, Mississippi, Texas, wherever. Package them up in crates and truck them out. But once they're gone—or nearly gone—then begins the point of no return. You might deny the impact, but I know you are enough Skaladeska to recognize the change, to *feel* it. We are inextricably tied to the earth. And we'll do whatever it takes to save it."

Marina realized her heart was thudding, hard and deep, as the sincerity of his words sank in. She *could* feel it. He was right.

"There has to be another way." She sounded desperate even to her own ears.

He shook his head, his hand on the doorknob. "There isn't. Not with the time we have left. No one is listening. And so, we—at least those of us brave enough to do so—must take extreme measures. Make sacrifices and difficult decisions. For the ultimate good."

The heavy door clicked behind him with finality.

TWENTY-TWO

Gabe was on his cell phone when Marina answered the door to his knock.

He came in and strode across the room, giving her hardly more than a glance as he nodded in greeting while *mmhmm*ing into the phone.

"Right," he murmured, scrabbling around the desk for the requisite pad of paper and pen hotels always provided. Then, the tiny mobile phone tucked between his ear and shoulder, he bent to scrawl some notes. "And that's the entire list? All right. Let me know what else you find. Great work, Inez. Thanks."

He disconnected the call, then jotted a few more words on the paper. As he straightened, his attention skimmed over the coffee to-go cup on her desk...the one Varden had brought. And—oh boy—left behind.

"What's the news?" Marina asked.

"A few things. What have you been up to all day?" His eyes were rimmed with exhaustion, but his gaze fixed sharply on her.

"Working. I ordered room service and had that steak, though." She'd already decided not to mention Varden's visit. Not just yet, anyway. "You look beat, Gabe. Should I order something for you? Or would you rather just rest?"

"I ate something at the office." He sank into an armchair in the corner, tipping his head back. "I'd like nothing more than a hot shower and a few hours of sleep, but I'm expecting to hear from Sanchez before the night's over."

Marina eased behind the chair to rub his strong—and tense—shoulders. "I hate to tell you, but the night *is* over. It's nearly one in the morning."

"No wonder I feel like the walking dead." He managed a short laugh. Then, "Damn. I can't believe he didn't get back to me."

"He did say he needed a day," Marina reminded him.

"We don't *have* a day." He sounded irritated, and the muscles beneath her hands grew more taut. "Now that the beetle is connected to the Skalas, and the same beetle caused the St. Louis blackout, we know something is in the works. Plus Cora Allegan's abduction somehow has to be wrapped up in this too. She's on that list—I told you about it—the one on the flash drive we found in Siberia?"

"Right. Any more news on that?"

"Right away, we thought it seemed like a list of targets or potential targets, but who knows how long it's been there in the caves of Siberia."

"Conveniently wrapped in a plastic baggie," Marina added.

"Right. So the question is whether it was meant to be found and be a red herring, or whether it was valuable enough to be protected—but nevertheless, somehow left behind."

"Well, if Cora Allegan is on the list and she has now been abducted by the Skalas, it would seem legit."

"Exactly my thoughts—and that call I was on was Inez, back in VA. There are two other people on the list who have disappeared recently—Mr. Lo Ing-wen, president of Oh Yeh Industries in China, and Mr. Eustace Pernweiler, CEO of some leather manufacturing company in the UK. In the case of Pernweiler, there was a calling card—so to speak—left by the Skalas. No one realized it was important until our people got in touch with Scotland Yard and they, in turn, spoke to Pernweiler's admin, who'd tossed it in the trash."

"Same as before? Just a piece of paper with the Skala symbol on it?"

"Right. So far, nothing's been found at Oh Yeh, but that doesn't mean there wasn't one. As for the others on the list…well, three of them are dead—we're looking into those deaths, but one was definitely after a long bout of cancer—and three others are no longer employed by the companies they're listed with. They've moved on to bigger and better positions. And one has retired and spends his time on his yacht, sailing from New York to the Caribbean and south."

"What a life."

"You're telling me. Obviously the list is a little outdated, or was a preliminary group that has since changed. Allegan, Pernweiler, and Ing-wen have all been with their corporations for more than five years. The question is whether the targets are the actual people or the corporations, regardless of who is in charge." Gabe's attention strayed to Varden's to-go cup again, and Marina couldn't quell a nudge of guilt. "Regardless, the others on the list are being notified as we speak, and protection has been arranged."

"Of course."

"We keep coming back to what the blackout has to do with any of this."

Marina perched on the edge of her bed. "You must have a theory."

He scrubbed his forehead and brows with long, tense fingers that left red marks on his tanned skin. "Several. None of them quite click. The blackout might have been a test to see if the bugs—beetles—could cause a power outage, and that knowledge would be utilized for a future attack. How bugs could cause an outage, I don't know—but if a damned goose can fly into a plane engine and cause it to go haywire, I suppose it's possible beetles could. Hell, I don't know. Either way, the power disruption didn't cause enough upset or—thank God—any deaths that would make the event relevant, or at least relevant enough to the Skalas. It might not have been an attack after all."

"What about financial or economic disruption? There was some due to the blackout, but doesn't seem like there was enough to matter."

"Exactly. Yes, there certainly was significant inconvenience and some lost revenue, and there was a group that was coming in to St. Louis for a convention—some agricultural association—and the meeting had to be cancelled…hm."

Their eyes met and Marina said, "Modern agricultural practices aren't very earth-friendly, at least on the enterprise side. Maybe St. Louis *was* some sort of test, but I'll bet the location wasn't selected by chance."

Gabe perked up a little. "I wonder if there was any particular speaker or big revelation that was to be announced at the convention. It's worth looking into."

"None of the people on the list were there? Or related to any organization attending the conference?"

"Nothing jumped out at me on first pass, but I'll have Inez dig deeper…especially since the list is obviously outdated." His demeanor changed and he focused on her. "So…you must have had a visitor today—unless you suddenly started drinking coffee."

"Right. I did. A colleague came by earlier." Her expression must have warned him not to probe further.

He rose, weariness in every movement, his eyes wary. "All right, then. Good night, Marina. I expect to get an early start tomorrow. Do you want to stay here or go in to the office with me?"

"I have a choice? Well then, I'd rather stay here…unless you're going to visit Dr. Sanchez and try to shake some more info about the beetle out of him. Then I'd go with you."

"Be ready by seven, then. We'll pay a visit to Sanchez, whether he's ready for us or not. I don't have any damned time to waste. If it weren't so late, I'd storm his lab now."

Marina walked him to the door of her room. To her surprise, he paused with his hand on the knob and turned to look down at her. "I don't know what you're hiding from me, or what's going on…I don't know if it has to do with us or with the Skalas, or neither."

Her heart skipped a little beat. "Us?"

"Hell, is there an 'us'?" He leaned against the doorjamb, propped by a muscular arm.

"It depends what you mean." Marina put her hand on his chest. This was probably not the best time or place to talk about their relationship—whatever it was. Gabe was exhausted, stressed, and suspicious, and she was...distracted. To say the least.

"I just want to know where we stand. Are we together, or are we just friends—colleagues—who enjoy each other's company—on every level?"

"Friends with bene—"

He put a hand over her mouth. His eyes were dark. "I hate that phrase." Then his lips shifted into a halfhearted smile. "This isn't the right time to have this conversation, I know, but..."

"You can stay, Gabe," she said softly.

His gaze settled on her long enough that her temperature actually began to rise, along with her heart rate. "Regretfully, I need a solid night's sleep," he said at last. "And I doubt I'll get that here. Good night."

TWENTY-THREE

September 28

"If you had told me you were coming to the lab, I'd have waited there for you." Eli Sanchez didn't sound the least bit irritated or inconvenienced.

Marina couldn't say the same for Gabe, who didn't appear to have gotten his good night's sleep after all.

They were sitting in Helen Darrow's office and it was pushing nine o'clock—much later than the seven-thirty time at which they'd arrived at Sanchez's lab...and missed him, because he'd already been on his way to the FBI field office.

"I expected a call from you yesterday," Gabe reminded him. He sat in one of the corner chairs, but tension had him bolt upright with his phone in his hands and his shoes planted flat on the floor. He appeared ready to lunge to his feet at any moment, and the fact that his tie was slightly off center and he was on his third cup of coffee didn't help.

"You demanded a call from me, but I didn't promise one." Eli shrugged, easy and relaxed in demeanor as well as in attire. He didn't look like he belonged in a lab, with his switchback cargo pants and low hiking boots. The t-shirt (which announced "CARPE INSECTVM"—seize the insects?) beneath an open plaid shirt hinted at muscular pectorals and a flat belly. His short dreads were unconfined today and just brushed his shoulders.

Marina had the sudden urge to touch them, curious about their texture.

"The specimens are delicate," Eli continued. "I could've rushed the project and taken the chance of ruining the data, or I could've taken my time and been able to give you something I know is accurate. I chose the latter, and I'm guessing you would too."

Before Gabe could respond, Helen took over. "So tell us what you've found, Dr. Sanchez."

"I'm fairly certain the beetle's habitat is the Ecuadorean jungle, likely near the Inchiyacu region or perhaps somewhat south of there. It's a primitive specimen, as I mentioned yesterday, from a rare suborder. But these particular samples are both from the same unique species—one never before identified. Until yesterday." Sanchez was in lecture mode, but even so, some boyish excitement leaked into his tones.

"So how does that help us? What makes this bu—insect so dangerous?" Gabe's voice was only slightly less taut than his expression. "We need answers, Sanchez. We need reasons and causes and—"

"I can only give you my observations. You'll have to come up with the reasons and causes. What I've found is, the beetle has an inordinate amount of copper in it. And that's—ah, hold on." Sanchez pulled out his buzzing phone and, ignoring the black expression growing on Gabe's face, answered it. "Yes. I'm already here. Helen Darrow." He cupped his hand over the phone and spoke to the special agent: "Can you tell security to let Paul Labine in? You're going to want to hear what he says."

Helen set down her coffee and picked up the office phone, scooping a thick lock of hair behind an ear. She was dressed in a tailored pantsuit of powder blue with a silvery-blue shell and a chunky silver necklace that settled just below the hollow of her throat. Her slender three-inch heels were impractical from Marina's perspective, but she couldn't deny they suited both the ensemble and its wearer.

Marina, on the other hand, was dressed like someone who not only rarely entered an office, but who'd had little time to pack before being whisked off to Chicago: low-slung cargo pants, a scoop-necked black tee with cap sleeves, and sturdy sandals. She didn't feel the least bit underdressed in the company of so many suits, but the blasting air conditioning threatened to make her teeth chatter. She already had goosebumps on her bare arms. Probably why Helen wore slacks and long sleeves even in the summer.

Eli rose, waited at the office door, and finally came back in. The gentleman with him was short and stout, with wispy white hair and a set of sharp hazel eyes. He wore a suit and tie. Marina put him at around sixty, and shook his hand when Sanchez introduced them.

"Paul is a geo-metallurgist," he said, then perched on the edge of Helen's desk. "He can fill you in on his credentials later. I was just beginning to tell everyone what I told you last night, Paul—that I believe there is an unnatural amount of elemental copper in the genetic makeup of this particular beetle, which is why I called you over."

"Right." Paul Labine's voice was gritty but strong. "I took the specimens and tested them as you asked—and you're correct. There is a significant amount of elemental copper in the beetle's physicality. By that I mean in its actual cells."

Marina's attention sharpened. "How is that possible?"

"And that," said Eli with a smile, "is why Paul's here."

"Copper is a funny metal," said the older man. "Not only does it have antimicrobial properties—in fact, they're beginning to use copper in places like hospitals for that reason. They're putting a veneer of copper on door handles, for example, to help decrease the spread of germs. Let me clarify further, too, that in order to be antimicrobial, the copper has to be dry. And dry copper is almost miraculous in its ability to kill bacteria and germs on contact. But wet copper has no antimicrobial properties.

"Also, and more relevant to your situation, copper doesn't break down in the environment. This means we often find traces of it—and sometimes more than a trace—in the flora and fauna in an area with lots of copper in the soil. We hear of copper poisoning in sheep, for example, for many plants and animals can't survive when there's too high a level of it in the ground. But there are some animals that use the copper in their bodies to transport oxygen in their systems—similar to the way the human body uses iron to do so. That's why it's not at all surprising to me to find living beetles with massive amounts of copper in their bodies."

"So…these insects must have evolved, and be living and breeding, somewhere where there's a lot of copper in the ground. Somewhere in the Amazon jungle, in Ecuador…that has copper? Is there copper in Ecuador?"

Marina heard Gabe's question, but her mind was already spiking like a seismograph. It was all about copper. Everything happening was somehow all about copper. But how could that be anything more than a coincidence? Copper beetles connected to the Skaladeskas, being used to cause the blackout. And some deaths. Were they purposeful deaths, or were they accidental?

And then there was the whole question regarding the massive amount of the copper that was supposedly—possibly—mined from the Upper Peninsula five millennia ago, and was no longer accounted for.

And the Phoenician-style writings she'd found in the same area of the copper mines.

Plus a copper-infused beetle—an unknown species—existing in the Amazon jungle.

How could they be connected? How could it be more than coincidence?

And…Marina closed her eyes to collect her stream of thoughts. Roman had sent her a copy of the Phoenician writing…that was similar to—well, heck, fairly identical to—writing found in the cave Matt Granger had discovered.

That *had* to be coincidental.

Didn't it?

She opened her eyes to find Sanchez looking around: at Gabe, then Helen, then finally at Marina. His dark eyes were filled with enthusiasm and intelligence. "You asked for causes and reasons. I can give you some facts, and a few theories to go with them. These coleops have heavy amounts of elemental copper in them, which means they not only conduct electricity extremely well...but they also have an antimicrobial element. They can't bite or sting, but as I mentioned yesterday, some species of beetle spread germs and bacteria because it clings to their tarsi—their legs."

"The black residue," muttered Gabe. "I bet it's a carrier of some sort of super bacteria or virus."

Eli smiled and nodded. "That would be my theory."

"Sending out a sample for testing now," said Helen, looking up from where she was tapping on her tablet. "Especially if there is a significant amount copper wherever these beetles live and breed...maybe they've used the microbial properties of the copper in their bodies to build up resistance to this bacteria."

"It makes sense on so many levels. But there are countless unidentified, undiscovered organisms and bacteria living in the rain forest. If these beetles are existing and breeding in a highly-charged-with-copper area in Ecuador, most likely whatever is on their legs is going to be something we haven't seen before." Eli's eyes sparkled with wild desperation. "I *need* to get my hands on a live specimen."

"I don't think you'd want to do that," Gabe said, giving a wry laugh. "If these beetles are as dangerous as they seem to be. Stay suited up around them."

Marina got the distinct impression Sanchez not only didn't care about the risk, but would happily *bathe* in the beetles if he had the opportunity. She smothered a grin, then her levity faded. Not much different than how she felt about the ancient library maintained by her grandfather.

"Dr. Sanchez also told me about how he came to have two specimens, and that one of them was found at the site of the center of the St. Louis blackout," Paul Labine said in his rusty voice. "Let me rephrase. That a *cluster* of them, burned out and melted together, was found at the site."

"Tell them your theory about that," Eli said, settling against the edge of Helen's desk. He was still burning with excitement, and Marina could feel the energy rolling off him. She bet the University of Illinois had a higher than usual number of female students in the entomology department.

"Because copper conducts electricity so extremely well," Paul continued, "it seems possible to me that a swarm of these bugs—er, insects," he added with a nod at Eli—who shook his head in mock exasperation, "might have flown into the cables at the electric transformer plant. If they were caught up in the lines, their extremely high levels of the metal could have caused a surge of electricity to blow through the lines. It's even possible they carry an electric charge on their own—like electric eels. We won't know until we get a live specimen.

"Anyway, if there were several who flew into the lines all at once, causing the insects to zap and fry together in those big clumps, it could have caused several massive surges simultaneously. If the swarms were on different lines at the power plant, that could have caused the plant's automatic load-balancing system to go haywire. The load-balancing system is equipped to handle random ebbs and flows of electricity, but if it were hit with several strong ones all at once, in the same location, that could blow the system and cause the blackout."

Eli's brows were high and his eyes sparkled. He nodded all during the speech, as if to punctuate his agreement with Paul Labine's theory. Helen had ceased tapping on her tablet, and pursed her lips as she considered this new information.

Even Gabe seemed to buy into it. He exchanged glances with Helen, then said, "If that's what happened—which sounds reasonable to me—then the question becomes: were the beetles released in the area for that reason, and if so, to what end…and if not, how did they get there if they're native to the Amazon jungle and nowhere else? And are we going to find other casualties—

deaths from cardiac arrest caused by that bacteria—from exposure to those insects?"

"That," said Eli, crossing his arms, "is your problem. But I'm happy to help if you get any more beetle specimens. And if you have to go to the Amazon to find them, or want to send a team down to study them, sign me up. I just got back from a field trip in Nicaragua, but I'd leave again in a heartbeat. I speak Spanish and Portuguese fluently, as well as—"

"Got it. We'll let you know." Gabe had pulled out his cell and was texting something as Helen picked up her desk phone to call one of the admins.

Marina glanced at Eli, who seemed a more than a little disappointed he wasn't having a flight booked at that very moment, and she felt a little nudge of sympathy. After all, he had made the identification of a unique insect, an unknown one— and one implicated in an unusual death and possible terrorist attack. This had to be the most exciting development in the field of entomology in possibly ever.

Just as she would be—was, in fact—determined to follow through on the copper mystery and her newly forming theories about Phoenicians in North America, surely Eli Sanchez must feel the same way. He would want to be the one to work on the project, to see it through, to use his expertise to assist, to claim the credit for the discovery, and, most importantly, to write the paper. He needed grants for his lab at the university just like every other researcher did.

Speaking of discoveries… "I'd like to head back to the hotel," Marina said. "I've got work to do there, and some things to follow up on. Mind if I take your car, Gabe?"

The copper mystery awaited, and she wanted to dig back into the details of what she'd learned about Chief Joseph—he was the Native American leader who'd had the ancient tablet with Phoenician writing on it—and the small cuneiform slab. Along with what she'd found, or, rather, what Matt Granger had found, that could be the clincher…

Gabe's expression was odd—wary and a little suspicious. Marina felt a niggle of disloyalty, and sharply brushed it away. The conversation she'd had with Rue Varden in her hotel room was between the two of them, and Varden was no more a threat to her than Gabe was—at least, as long as she stayed way from the Skaladeskas. He'd made that clear. In fact, he had most likely saved her from being abducted. Without him, she wouldn't even be here now.

"I'll need the car. But I could take you back in a few hours," said Gabe.

"I'll see if I can arrange a cab," said Helen, looking between the two of them. "Give me a few."

"Which hotel?" asked Eli. "I can drop you off." He slid off the desk, clearly realizing his presence was no longer needed. "It's no problem."

Gabe started to say something, then stopped. "Appreciate that, Sanchez. Marina, if I could have a minute before you go." He gestured to the exit, and Marina led the way out into the hall.

He closed the door behind them, then got right to the point. "Rue Varden has been in and out of Ann Arbor for the last five to six years. Right in your backyard, Marina. If you have something going on with him, you're better off telling—"

Marina was as stunned as if she'd been blindsided with a two-by-four. "Five years? I didn't know. Believe me, Gabe, *I had no idea*. Until he showed up bleeding all over the place, I hadn't seen or heard from him—or any of the Skaladeskas—since we left Siberia."

Almost true. But the package from Roman or Lev wasn't really relevant.

Gabe's blue eyes were focused steadily, almost uncomfortably on her, and that moment reminded Marina how dangerous a man Gabe MacNeil was. A lethally trained CIA agent. God knew what he'd done with those hands.

After a moment, he nodded. "I just wanted you to know… Rue Varden's been around. Maybe watching you. Probably watching you."

Varden had nearly admitted the same thing to her yesterday, so that part didn't surprise her quite as much. Still. "Thanks."

"Maybe you want to reconsider and start carrying a firearm," Gabe added. "I can—"

"Not gonna happen. I've got Boris, and that's enough."

He drew in a breath then exhaled slowly. He looked as if he wanted to say more, but then thought better of it. "All right. I don't know how late I'll be here tonight, but—"

"I'm going back to Ann Arbor. Probably not till tomorrow, though. There's no reason for me to stay here. I've got work to do, some things to follow up on, and if you need me in person, you know it's only a matter of hours before I can get here."

"Right. All right. Wait till tomorrow, just in case something breaks with all this new information about the bugs. There was a car rental agreement on the body of the Skala—his name was Marcko—who died at the hospital, and we're following that trail. The car isn't at the hospital lot, so someone must have dropped him off. Maybe even knew he was going to die. So if you happen to see a dark blue Taurus with a Kentucky plate, let me know," he added with a short laugh.

Marina smiled at his attempt at humor. "Will do. See you later."

Neither made a move to kiss or even embrace the other, and she felt as if something had shifted in their relationship, such as it was. Of course, she was only going back to the hotel and would see him later tonight. Yet something had changed.

TWENTY-FOUR

Eli Sanchez drove a dark green Jeep Cherokee that had seen better days. Though the interior was clean—except for a collection of drive-thru coffee cups and a stack of plastic baggies containing what looked like beetle specimens—one of the bumpers was hanging on by a bungee cord. There was also a patch of rust on the corner of the passenger door, and a small dent near the front headlight. There was a bumper sticker on the back that said: "A spider did not bite you."

"Meet Juanita," he said with a grin as Marina climbed in. "She's been around a while, but, as they say, she runs good."

"What's up with the bumper sticker?" she asked as he closed the door after her.

Sanchez laughed. "About the spider bite? Yeah—no one gets bitten by a spider. The poor darlings are completely misunderstood. Maybe four percent of reported spider bites are actually spider bites. It's sort of an inside joke among us entomologists." He slid into the driver seat. "Where to?"

She told him, and settled back in the seat...then curled her fingers surreptitiously around the door handle when Eli roared out of the parking lot, taking a corner a lot more quickly than she would have.

"So tell me," he said, belatedly shoving on a pair of sunglasses, "how does a search and rescue caver and—what is it? an epigraphic historian?—end up working on a terrorist case like the Skaladeskas?"

"Nothing like getting right to the point." Marina couldn't hold back a smile. "And I simply say 'an historian, with a competence in epigraphy,' if you want to get technical."

"I do—want to get technical." He flashed a grin. "And I like to get to the point. It's the only way to go. Speaking of getting to the point—are you and MacNeil involved or not?"

Marina blinked at the random question. Right. "We're good friends. We've been through a lot together."

"Good friends? All right. That works for me." Eli flashed her a warm smile, then careened around another corner. He punched the accelerator as he passed a slower vehicle, then eased back into the right lane. As she clung to the grip, Marina felt a wave of sympathy for Gabe during the time she'd taken a small plane through an acrobatic routine in order to disrupt their Skaladeska kidnappers. Gabe had been more than a little green around the gills after that—but he, at least, had been in better shape than their kidnappers.

"Sorry," Eli added when he slammed on the brakes just before cutting off another vehicle. He gave a cheery wave when the other driver honked angrily, and the Jeep leapt forward again. "So?" he prompted. "You're not CIA, and you're not a Fed—you're not any law enforcement as far as I can tell...so how the hell did you manage to get onto the team as a civilian consultant? What the hell does an historian have to do with a terrorist group?"

"You just want to go to the Amazon." She smiled.

"Damn right I do. Hell if I'm going to let someone else study that sweet little coleop. So how does one get in on the big boys club—including Helen Darrow, by the way. She's got her own pair of testes, and far as I can tell, holds her own with the big guys." He glanced at Marina, a grin twitching his lips. "And, quite clearly, so do you, Dr. Alexander."

"Thanks. I think." She found it impossible to be offended by Eli Sanchez, and actually found him more than a little intriguing—and a lot attractive. Though he was a few years older than she, he had the quicksilver mind and mentality of a much younger man. If only he were a little less enthusiastic with his driving… "So you spent a little time on Google last night, I take it."

He nodded, that smile still playing around his mouth. "Hell yes. And I've got other resources besides Google, anyway. With all the international travel I do—well, suffice to say I'm not about to walk into anything without being prepared. Why do you think I wasn't waiting for MacNeil at my lab like a good boy?" Then he sobered. "Look, Dr. Alexander, I'm not trying to make light of this situation. It's damned serious. And that's why Homeland Security needs an expert on the team if they're going to work with that coleop—find it, categorize it, study it. I've already begun the process anyway. I think I've taken about five hundred megs of pictures of it already. And if even half the theories we talked about today are true—"

"I'm thinking they were pretty spot on. Knowing…knowing what I know."

"So what put you smack in the middle of the case? You were involved back in '07 when all those fake earthquakes were happening and the Skaladeskas were first IDed as a terrorist group."

"You *are* thorough."

"Oh, very." His voice dropped, and he flashed her a look. Then he ruined it by zooming through an intersection just as the light turned red, and slipping into the hotel parking lot with the roar of a muffler on its last legs. "You hungry? How about we grab a bite—it's not too early for lunch—and you can tell me about how you got on the team."

"Lunch? It's barely ten thirty," she protested, then her eyes widened. She flung out a hand and it smacked into his chest. "Stop. Stop!"

He obliged, slamming on the brakes. She was out of the Jeep in an instant, hurrying over to a blue Taurus with Kentucky plates. It was parked right there in her hotel parking lot.

Eli was on her heels. "What? What is it?"

Marina looked around. There was no one in the vicinity, and the car—fortunately—was empty. "The guy who died in the hospital from the bug, from the rash from the bacteria—we think anyway—had a rental agreement for a blue Taurus with—"

"Let me guess. Kentucky plates," he finished. Eli peered into the window on the driver's side, and she looked on the passenger side. The car was empty. "What the hell is he—or was he—doing here? In the same place you're staying? That can't be good."

Marina was afraid she knew the answer to that question, and had a sneaking suspicion Eli was only asking it rhetorically.

Either Varden or whoever it was he'd intercepted outside her room yesterday had driven the vehicle here. *If* it was the same one on the rental agreement. But really—what were the chances? She memorized the license plate as Eli tried the door handle.

To her surprise, it opened, and she pulled open the one on the other side. They both crawled in from either side, she in back, he in front, looking around.

"Nothing," he said, and they closed the doors. "Obvious, anyway. The sweepers would probably find something, but…" He walked around to the back of the car and unlatched the trunk.

It popped open to reveal an empty space. Except…they both spotted it at the same time: the small wisp of black silk tucked deep inside the trunk.

Sanchez reached for it first, employing his longer arms, and grasped the fabric. Then his expression changed and he swore, spinning from the trunk as three small insects erupted from the depths of the trunk. They shot out like infuriated bees, and Marina ducked instinctively even as Sanchez grabbed at them. The beetles missed her and easily evaded him, zooming off into the air. Their wings and bodies glinted like shiny new pennies in the sunlight.

"Damn!" Eli stared off after the insects, looking as if he'd just found coal in his stocking on Christmas morning. "Almost had them! Un-*freaking*-believable!" He looked as if he wanted to cry.

Then Marina noticed something, and her heart nearly stopped. "Dr. Sanchez, your hand!"

He looked down, then said something in Spanish.

His fingers were covered with black cobweb-like smudges.

TWENTY-FIVE

I think you'd better stand back."

Marina glanced over to make sure Eli was out of the way, then opened the door to her hotel room with care. When nothing happened—no bugs flying in her face, no hand grabbing for her—she gave it a hard shove, ducking to the side just in case.

Everything was still and silent except when the heavy hotel door swung back and slammed with a thud that echoed down the hall.

"What was that all about?" asked her companion. He'd thrust his hands deep into his pants pockets in an effort to keep from touching anyone or anything with his contaminated fingers.

"Wanted to make sure no one was in there waiting, or anything." She opened the door again and ushered him in. "Have a seat."

"I think I'll wash my hands first." His voice was grim. "Can't hurt."

"Don't touch anything. Let me turn on the water."

By the time Eli came out of the bathroom, vigorously drying his hands, Marina had her laptop open and was booting it up. Housekeeping had come in while she was gone, and the room was neat and clean—hard to tell if anyone else had been inside during her absence. Who had brought the car? Was it Varden? Or was the man named Bellhane lurking about somewhere?

"You said you had an idea." For someone who'd most likely just infected himself with untreatable bacteria, Eli Sanchez seemed relatively calm. He looked around, then, apparently deeming the armchair by the window the safest location, he sat.

"Yes. All right." Marina drew in a deep breath. "I suppose I'd better tell you what the options are before I do anything irreparable."

"Go on."

"The way I see it, there are two options. One is you seek medical treatment here from people who aren't familiar with whatever is contaminating those beetles—and quite possibly end up in the same condition as the others who've been infected. Or…" She hesitated. "Or I contact the Skaladeskas and tell them you need to be treated."

She had to give him credit; the guy hardly seemed surprised. He did lift his chin, giving her a skeptical look.

"So you know how to contact them? And you think this terrorist group is going to jump to help me?" He flexed his fingers as if to ensure they were still working properly.

"They will if I tell them we're both infected." Marina glanced at her laptop. Skype was open, and it would only be a matter of time before Lev—or Varden—tried to connect with her. "But before you agree, I'd better tell you a little more."

"Good plan."

She spoke rapidly, giving him the barest details about her relationship to the Skaladeskas and the sketchiest of information about why she was connected to the investigation. "My grandfather wants me to come to him," she finished. "So far I've refused, but of course we have to get you treated. They must have an antidote or antibiotic that can combat the bacteria. And if my grandfather believes I've been infected, he'll move heaven and earth to make sure I'm saved. And you by default."

"Are you sure you want to do this? Sounds dangerous. And what happens when they find out you aren't infected? I'm confident I'll get excellent medical treatment here in the States, especially now that we know what to look for; you don't have to negotiate with these terrorists for my sake alone."

"If he believes *I* believe I'm infected, Lev isn't going to deny me even if it turns out I'm not. He won't take the risk. And if you want to take your chances here in the US, then I don't blame you. If we follow through on this, I have a feeling we're going to end up in the Amazon jungle." Marina hadn't forgotten Varden's slip yesterday when he cut himself off from telling her she would be taken to the Amazon by Roman's thugs. That's where Lev was, and going there might be the only way to save Eli. But it would also be an opportunity for her to find out where the Skalas were hiding, what they had planned, and, hopefully, put an end to their ecoterrorism.

"You're saying we could end up where the beetle is?" Now Eli looked excited. "I'm in. I'll take my chances on that. If I don't, I'm probably going to die. If I do, I might die anyway—but then again, I might make the discovery of my career and not die."

Marina nodded. "I thought you might say that. But you should know, Dr. Sanchez—they might not let us leave. There's a chance we'll be their hostages—or worse. But Agent MacNeil and Special Agent Darrow—they'll do whatever they can to get us out. And I'll do whatever I can to keep you out of danger. I do have quite a bit of leverage."

She'd bargain with Lev, do whatever it took to make sure Eli wasn't imprisoned as Gabe had been. Now that she knew how badly they wanted her, she knew she had the upper hand. "Whatever we decide, we have to act quickly. The others died from sudden cardiac arrest less than seventy-two hours after exposure."

The sound of a telephone rang from her laptop. Marina turned to see *Dr. Herb Grace* trying to make a connection. With a finger to her lips to keep Eli from speaking, she accepted the call without video.

"Dr. Alexander." Varden's tone was smooth and businesslike. "I can only assume this is the Skype equivalent of a butt dial."

"Is there a cure if someone is exposed to the beetles?"

A beat of silence. Then, "Yes."

"I need it. Immediately."

Another pause. "I regret to say…it's impossible at the moment."

"I know you'd celebrate my demise, Dr. Varden, but if my grandfather learned you were the cause, how long do you believe you'd remain in his good graces? Aside from that, what happened to 'first do no harm'?"

"You expect me to believe you've been infected."

"I opened the trunk of a blue Taurus parked in the lot at my hotel. It was a rental car, with Kentucky plates—sound familiar?—and inside was a black silk web that had beetles in it. The black fungus is all over my hands. Surely you have the antidote."

Silence, followed by a muttered curse. "I don't have access to any at the moment. It would take me—" He swore again. "Bloody damned hell, Marina, do you have any idea what this means?"

"Unfortunately, I do."

Varden said something else, but the sound of a keycard in the door had Marina spinning from the laptop. She fairly leapt across the room, but both she and Eli were too late—the door was opening.

It wasn't Gabe. She already knew that, for he would have knocked.

However, she recognized one of the three men standing there as Roman's right-hand man, Dannen Fridkov. The one who'd tried to break into her home in Ann Arbor five years ago, and then went on to attempt to blow up half of Detroit. He was holding a gun, and though it wasn't pointing at her, it was nevertheless a not-so-subtle threat.

"Fridkov. And one of your companions is Bellhane, I presume," she said, pitching her voice loud enough so, hopefully, Varden would hear. "You can put your weapons away. I need you to take me—both of us, in fact—to my grandfather. Don't look so surprised. Isn't that why you're here?"

"You'd better be one hundred percent sure about this, Helen." Gabe rubbed his eyes vigorously as he spoke into his phone.

"Do you think I'd be telling you if I wasn't?" She sounded almost gentle, rather than peeved that he was questioning her. "I know what this means. What it could mean. But there are photos. Colin Bergstrom and Roman Aleksandrov—none other than Marina Alexander's uncle—attended Oxford University at the same time."

"Yes, I knew that much. Bergstrom told me that when he first put me on the Skaladeskas five years ago."

"All right, but there's more. Are you sitting down?"

"No, I'm in the damned elevator at the Marriott. I've been trying to reach Marina for two hours, and I—well, she's probably lost in her work or at the fitness center, but since I was out I thought—anyway, go on. What else do you have?"

"After she graduated, Bergstrom's wife, Stegnora, née Silkovsy, was in the physics program with Aleksandrov. He was a few years older than her. They worked together. And…"

The elevator swooshed to a halt, but that wasn't the only reason Gabe's insides dropped. "Don't tell me what I think you're going to tell me." *Dammit. Dammit to* hell.

"Do you want to know?"

He stalked out into the corridor, then stopped for a minute to remind himself of Marina's room number and then which direction to turn. *Sonofabitch.* "I can guess. Mrs. Bergstrom hasn't been around for a long time—longer than I've known him, much longer than a decade. He doesn't talk about what happened to her. I didn't know whether she was dead or they divorced or what. I never asked."

"They had an affair at Oxford—Nora and Roman Aleksandrov. Interestingly enough, Viktor was in England too, at the same time, but not enrolled at Oxford that I can find. In about 1974, Nora and Bergstrom came back to the US, and everything seemed fine. They had a son together, the Bergstroms—in '75. You've probably seen the picture on Colin's desk. Then, about thirty years ago, Nora seems to have disappeared."

Nora. Dammit, there'd been a Nora in Siberia, a Nora who was mentioned often and with respect. A Nora who'd been in the inner circle, a trusted confidante of that bastard Roman Aleksandrov.

"No wonder Bergstrom wants blood from the Skaladeskas," Gabe muttered as he knocked on Marina's door. "Anything else you want to add to the pot, Helen?"

"Isn't that enough. Is Marina all right?"

She wasn't answering the door. Maybe she was on a call. Or working out. "I'll get back to you." Gabe shoved the phone in his pocket and knocked again as he fished out his copy of her room key.

Just before he opened the door, his instincts prickled and he reached for the handgun beneath his jacket. Firearm in a firm grip, he slid the key card in and opened the door, all senses on high alert.

"Marina?"

Silence. Stillness. Yet something was off. He sensed something or someone. Adrenaline surged through him and, raising the weapon, he scanned the room with it, steady and wide. No sign of Marina, of anything out of place...

Gabe didn't see him until he stepped inside and allowed the door to close with its dull hotel-room clunk. Positioned in the corner, sitting in a chair, was the man who'd put a bullet in his arm in the mountains of Siberia.

"Dr. Varden." He kept the weapon trained on the man, who appeared to have no desire to save himself from owning his own bullet-in-a-limb.

"Agent MacNeil. It's been some time since our paths have crossed. I wish it were under better circumstances." Rue Varden spoke clearly and precisely, as if he'd spent a lot of time in England. He was a solid, well-built man near forty with startling green eyes, dirty blond hair, and high, Slavic cheekbones. Even in this unfavorable situation, he still acted as if his shit didn't stink.

Gabe gave him a humorless smile. "Considering the fact that I still bear a scar from our last encounter, and I'm the one holding a grudge as well as the gun this time, I can't help but agree with you. Your circumstances could be far better."

Varden inclined his head. "Yet you don't appear to have any lingering effects from our encounter. They still allow you to carry a weapon. I can only chalk that up to my excellent aim. Right through the fleshy part of the bicep, wasn't it? Painful, debilitating, but no permanent damage."

Arrogant bastard. "Where's Marina? Or were you expecting her to come through the door?"

"I regret that Dr. Alexander is on her way to the Amazon jungle, in the company of two men by the name of Bellhane and Guthrie…as well as, apparently, a colleague of hers by the name of Dr. Sanchez."

Gabe stopped breathing. "And how did you arrange that?"

Varden rose, apparently not bothered by the gun pointed at him. He shook his head. "I didn't. In fact, I arrived here as quickly as I could in hopes of stopping it. As it happened, Dr. Alexander and I were on a call when this occurred. And since I arrived here too late, I decided the next best course of action was to tell you what I know. Otherwise you could be blundering around for weeks trying to follow the trail."

Gabe's finger tightened on the trigger. *Varden and Marina were on a phone call?* "Excellent idea. And as a terror suspect in custody, you might be able to get some lenience if you come clean—"

Varden's green eyes hardened. "You will not be putting me into custody. And if you want my cooperation, and the invaluable information I'm about to share with you in a timely manner, you'll put that piece away and we'll have a civil conversation."

"Not an option. You walked away in Ann Arbor four days ago. I'm not about to let you do it again."

Varden shrugged. Arrogance rolled off him, and Gabe gritted his teeth. "Your choice," said the man in his formal accent. "You can attempt to take me into custody. And you can attempt to interrogate me. But since Dr. Alexander and Dr. Sanchez have both been infected by the extremely volatile cuprobeus bacteria, you're not going to want to waste time playing games. As I'm certain you're aware, the bacteria works very rapidly…and no one in the States has even heard of it, let alone knows how to treat it—or has the antibiotic to do so."

"Except for you."

"Precisely." Now it was Varden's turn to give a cold smile. "But be assured, Agent MacNeil. There is one thing in which your goals and mine are exactly aligned: neither of us want Dr. Alexander in the custody of Roman Aleksandrov and the Skaladeskas."

Gabe held the other man's gaze long enough to express his disgust and fury, along with a silent promise of revenge, then lowered his gun. "What do you know? And, more importantly, why the hell are you willing to tell me?"

"Your weapon and your mobile phone—put them on the desk there. I don't want you attempting to use either of them." When Gabe hesitated, Varden added, "If I had my own weapon, wouldn't I have had it in hand when you arrived? I had the advantage."

That wasn't the way Gabe would have played it had he been in Varden's shoes, but there was no point in belaboring the point. Varden was right: time was of the essence. He did as requested, then positioned himself close enough to the desk that he could snatch either firearm or phone in an instant. "Now. Talk."

TWENTY-SIX

Somewhere in South America

Although she'd traveled down a section of the Amazon in the past, Marina had never been in this part of the rainforest in South America. She wasn't certain of their exact location—for their would-be abductor, Bellhane, had confiscated both hers and Eli's cell phones, and in the interest of her companion's well-being, she'd agreed to leave them in her hotel room—but as far as she could tell, they were somewhere in the northwest quadrant of the continent. In the vicinity of the Ecuador and Peru border.

Dannen Fridkov had stayed behind in Chicago, which left Marina wondering what he was up to. She'd heard the phrases "New York" and "the first" in his conversation with Bellhane and Guthrie, the third Skaladeska, but that could mean anything.

What was of even more concern to Marina was how smoothly Bellhane and Guthrie had taken her and Sanchez and traveled from Chicago to a tiny town outside Quito, Ecuador, using a custom-built plane. The trip had taken fewer than fifteen hours.

The aircraft was an anomaly itself. The fiberglass Van's RV-5 had extended gas tanks—also made of fiberglass—which left the plane unable to be detected by radar. This meant they could fly untracked and unnoticed, and Marina found it more than a little terrifying to realize the extent of the Skaladeskas' resources and the ease with which they crossed borders in this post-9/11 age.

Yet she was relieved their travels had been so uneventful, for fifteen hours ago, Eli had grabbed the black silk webbing of the copper beetles. He was just beginning to show signs of the skin irritation they suspected would evolve into the deadly infection. She didn't know how much longer it would be until he began to experience other symptoms.

"How much further?" she demanded of Bellhane. What little sunlight filtered through the heavy canopy of trees seemed to be waning, giving Marina the impression it was near sundown.

Their last leg of the journey, after refueling the aircraft, had taken them over low mountains Marina doubted they would actually clear in this humid air—and she wasn't sure whether she was relieved or disappointed she hadn't been asked to pilot the craft. Perhaps the Skaladeskas had learned their lesson the last time they forced her to fly a plane for them.

A half-hour ago, they'd landed in a small clearing in the middle of nowhere. Since then, the party of four had been hiking through the jungle on a somewhat recognizable path.

Bellhane didn't deign to reply to her question, and Marina didn't press. Knowing her father and grandfather were eager to see her again, and that neither of their guides would dare hurt or otherwise upset the situation, she had taken the attitude of being on equal footing with Bellhane and Guthrie during their journey, rather than a captive. Clearly, neither of them cared for this turn of events, for they'd hardly communicated with her since leaving Chicago.

After traveling on foot for nearly thirty minutes—during which time Marina kept watch for any landmarks she might need in the future, as well as the position of the sun insofar as she could see it above the thick canopy of trees—a gate suddenly appeared. Festooned with ropey vines and buried in thick clumps of trees, bushes, and tall grasses, the metal nevertheless gleamed darkly through the greenery.

The gate was attached to a stone wall that disappeared into the thick jungle both to the right and left. The barrier was twelve feet tall and spiked with dark metal points, also decorated with greenery. Marina considered it curiously as Guthrie approached the gate, wondering how effective a wall it was with so many trees and vines growing close to it.

She exchanged glances with Eli, whose face was shiny with perspiration. His eyes had glazed a little, and though he'd donned gloves in an effort to keep from spreading the bacteria, she saw the angry, welt-like patches that had begun to form on his arms just above the wrists. "Anything I can do for you?" she asked.

He shook his head. "I sure as hell hope you're right about this."

"They'll help us. I have no doubt."

"I meant about the beetles." He gave an unsteady grin.

The gates swung open, and Guthrie stepped away from a small box on the left side of the entrance.

Marina didn't wait for an invitation; after all, this was her family's home, and time was of the essence for Eli. She took his shirt-sleeved arm and led him through the gate, leaving Bellhane and Guthrie to follow.

As the metal doors clanged shut behind them, Marina examined what could only be the Skaladeskas' new compound. At first glance, the hideaway resembled an abandoned ruin. It couldn't have been more different than the one they'd left in Siberia—which had been built into a mountain and camouflaged by solar panels, and was all sleek glass, silver, and white.

It was a low, sprawling structure, cloaked by the thick jungle. Made from cream-colored brick dingy with age, with few windows and a metal roof, the building was only one story tall. The low-pitched roof made deep overhangs to protect from heavy rain, and the place was simply buried among trees and grass and vines. Marina couldn't see the extent of the architecture, for, like its enclosing wall, it disappeared into the shadowy foliage, which rose up behind it like an impenetrable screen of every shade of green. Within the stone wall, most of the area had been cleared of trees and brush, leaving a yard of grass that ranged from ankle height to waist high.

Marina and Eli approached the only door in sight—although she was certain there must be several other entrances and exits—and it opened on its own.

A lone man stepped out, and Marina's breath caught in spite of herself.

Roman Aleksandrov. Her father.

He was handsome for his age and stood without stooping, with power and confidence, in loose linen trousers and a dark brown shirt that buttoned down the center. His shaved head was smooth and well shaped. He'd grown a neatly trimmed beard and mustache in the Van Dyke style, and though it was more gray than dark, it made him appear younger than his seven decades.

This was the first time she'd seen him in five years.

The first time she'd seen him since she learned he was her true father.

She wondered again whether he knew the truth.

He stood there, waiting silently, expectantly, openly—like a parent welcoming home the prodigal child. Their eyes met, and though she felt a shock of connection, and a jolt of apprehension mixed with anticipation, she didn't allow herself to show any emotion. Her stride remained smooth and purposeful as she helped Eli along.

When she was close enough to be heard, she spoke. "Roman, I need your help. We've been exposed to the cuprobeus bacteria and need treatment. You can see that my friend is already showing the ill effects."

Her father showed no surprise at her words. "You, however, are not." There was challenge and perhaps a bit of relief in his voice.

She didn't acknowledge his truth. Instead, she reached for Eli's glove and yanked it off. Then, ignoring Roman's swift, shocked intake of breath, she curled the fingers of both hands around the beginnings of the rash on Eli's strong, sturdy one, weaving their digits together before he could pull away, and looked at her father. "But I will soon."

"*Marina*," Eli hissed, yanking his hand from hers. He staggered a little with the force of his movement, a testament to his growing weakness combined with the exertion of their journey.

The leap of horror in Roman's eyes had faded. Yet his reaction had already confirmed what Marina suspected—and feared. That the infection could be spread from person to person merely by skin contact. "Come inside, then, Mariska. And bring your companion as well."

The interior of the building was just as acutely different from its exterior as the interior of the cold, sleek mountain hideaway had been. Though Marina had expected nothing less, she could not completely hide her amazement as she took in the details of her surroundings.

Once inside the entrance, she found herself on a wide ledge that overlooked a submerged chamber that could only be a laboratory. The ledge, which had a sturdy Plexiglas railing, ran around a circular space in eight chunks. Each chunk, or side, had at least one door on it. At the joints of the two ledges at ten o'clock and two o'clock, corridors led away from the octagonal hub of the building. At four o'clock and eight o'clock, a flight of metal stairs led down into the lab, which was outfitted with stainless steel tables, cabinets, a bank of computers and monitors, large video screens, and an array of tools and electronics. She saw a microscope that rivaled Sanchez's, as well as several other unfamiliar devices.

Five people wearing the loose linen trousers of the regular Skaladeska uniform, but topped with white tunics instead of undyed ones, were working in the lab below. None of them seemed to notice the new arrivals as they went about their business.

Marina felt Eli sway against her, and she turned toward him in alarm. In the last twenty minutes, he'd become much weaker. Now he looked even paler under his brown skin, and sweatier, and his breathing had become shallow and quick. She spun to Roman, and found him standing just behind her. "He needs help *now*."

To her relief, her father didn't argue. "Nora," Roman called down. "They've arrived."

So apparently none of this was a surprise to him. Marina wondered who'd communicated their imminent arrival and its purpose—Varden, Fridkov, or Bellhane. Not that it mattered... but perhaps it did.

Roman had edged nearer, as if he wanted to be as close to her as possible, then gestured to the nearest stairway.

"Take my arm," she told Eli when he tried to navigate on his own.

"I'm...all right," he muttered—then ruined it all by stumbling as he took the first step.

"Stubborn. Stick with me, and I'll make sure you get to see a whole slew of live bu—beetles," she corrected herself. He laughed weakly, then began to cough so hard, he almost toppled off the next step.

She took his arm as he grabbed the handrail, and they began their descent. Roman followed, and Marina heard him murmuring behind her. She glanced back and saw he was speaking into an electronic wristband, but she couldn't hear what he was saying.

When they were halfway to the bottom, Nora appeared at the base of the stairs. An attractive woman in her late sixties, she was slender and quick, with cropped corn-silk hair and intelligent brown eyes. She moved efficiently to assist Marina.

"You can save him," she said to the older woman. "There is a cure. Varden told me."

"He's progressed quite far," Nora said as they reached the bottom and she looked at Eli with a critical eye. Marina noticed she was wearing gloves and that a surgical face mask rested around her throat, ready to be pulled up and into place.

"Mariska, if you would come with me." Roman gestured with a graceful hand as Nora began to lead Eli toward a walkway beneath the balcony. The center of the lab gave way to a row of rooms on one wall, a corridor on another, and a large, glassed-in chamber on a third.

"No." Marina was firm, and she slid her arm around Eli's waist. "I'm staying with him."

"That's not necessary—"

She paused and turned to glare at her father. "The last time I came to you, you nearly had my companion murdered. You separated us and kept me prisoner and tortured him. That will not happen this time." And although she didn't say it, the unspoken words rested between them: *And if you want my cooperation, if you want me, you will agree.*

There was a pause. Then, "Very well." Roman gave a brief nod to Nora, and she began to walk again.

"You didn't mention anything…about torture," muttered Eli as he staggered against Marina. "Think I'll need…something else…to make up…for that. Sweeten…the pot. MacNeil…be… damned."

She flashed a look up at him, and saw he was grimacing in a sort of smile. Thank goodness he still had his sense of humor, even though his face was damp and drawn. "We can negotiate on that later, Sanchez. I'm not sure I want to get any closer unless I'm wearing a hazmat suit."

He laughed and it turned into a harsh, racking cough that necessitated them to pause while he tried to retain his balance. When the attack subsided, it was time for Nora to be the recipient of Marina's dark look. "How much further? He needs treatment now."

"Here," said the older woman, pushing open a door.

The place was outfitted like a hospital room, with one glassed-in wall, and immediately Marina felt slightly more optimistic. Eli was deteriorating before her eyes, jokes notwithstanding, and if he went into sudden cardiac arrest, she didn't know whether they could save him. When would it be too late, past the point of no return?

But this room appeared ready for any medical needs, and she was relieved to find a white-coated person, capped and masked, working at a sleek stainless steel station. Marina saw syringes, test tubes, and a small device that looked like a spray bottle attached to a large canister.

As they came into the clinic, the capped and masked person—doctor, nurse, tech; Marina had no idea what the man's role was—moved into action. He and Nora exchanged few words as they eased Eli onto the bed. Masks were yanked up over faces, and Marina and Roman were each given gowns, masks, and gloves.

Roman spoke to Nora, brief and low, and they both looked at Marina, who was in the process of snapping on her gloves.

"Wait for that," Nora told her. "You've been exposed as well? Sit here."

After that, everything moved quickly. Two other personnel came into the chamber, also gowned, masked, and gloved, and a flurry of activity—controlled, efficient, and smooth—filled the space. Marina didn't see much of what was happening to Eli, for no sooner had she taken a seat than Nora was examining her hands with her own gloved ones.

She turned away, still blocking Marina's view of Eli and the techs working with him. She heard something that sounded like a spray of water, then a hiss, just before Nora turned back. She was holding a syringe with dark red fluid in it.

It was at that moment Marina realized how much blind trust, how much leverage she assumed from her relationship with her father and grandfather. She tensed, ready to push the needle away, and Nora stopped and stepped back. She murmured something to Roman, who looked at Marina, then back at Nora. Then, stiff and reluctant, he turned and strode from the chamber.

The door closed behind him with a dull thud, and moments later Marina saw him appear on the other side of the glass wall, in an adjoining room. He stripped off his gloves, mask, and gown.

"You do not trust me. Yet you came here, to us." Nora looked at Marina steadily. "I've done you no harm in the past, and will do none now. You have my word, on the sacred life of Gaia. Now please…allow me to treat you. Your grandfather is coming and he wishes to see you."

Their gazes held. Marina looked into those brown eyes and saw earnestness as well as frightening intelligence. The only other time she and Nora had been alone was when the older woman visited her in the room where she'd been held captive in Siberia. Then, Nora had given her information she hadn't needed to give—information that ultimately assisted Marina and Gabe escape, and helped Marina to better understand Roman.

She had no real reason to trust Nora, and yet she had no reason to distrust her.

"Very well." Marina held out her arm for the needle.

As the slender cannula slid into her skin, another, more unpleasant realization struck her. Marina might have no reason to fear for her own life...but the same could not be said for Eli Sanchez.

For all she knew, the Skaladeskas could kill him—or allow him to die—and blame it on the bacteria.

And she would never know the truth.

TWENTY-SEVEN

"So Marina Alexander went off with the Skaladeskas." Helen's voice was carefully neutral. "After calling Rue Varden. And she took Eli Sanchez with her. And you let Varden walk."

Gabe shot her a dark look. He had no response that wouldn't sound weak or desperate. Or furious. Which was what he was. Maybe a little confused, too. But mostly furious. "At the very least, we must be concerned with Sanchez's safe return."

Helen lifted a brow. "Is that it? You'd let her go?"

"Not…necessarily." Gabe resisted the urge to get up and pace her small office. The door was closed, of course, and there wasn't enough room to take more than five steps in either direction.

There was, however, a crystal paperweight on Helen's desk that might make a satisfying crash if he flung it…somewhere.

Eyeing him warily, Helen picked up the paperweight and slid it into one of the desk drawers. "If you had been exposed to the bacteria—they're calling it the cuprobeus bacteria, do I have that right?—what would you do? If you knew you were going to die without treatment, what would you do? Would you go where you knew there was a way to be treated, or would you take your chances here, waiting for the CDC to fumble around? Maybe she had a valid reason—at least in her mind."

"Why are you defending her all of a sudden? For days you've been trying to convince me Marina is in bed with the Skalas, and now that we have clear evidence of it, you're being…"

"Reasonable?" She settled back in her seat and folded her hands over the button of her teal jacket. A wide gold band glinted on one of her thumbs, but not, he had noticed, on a ring finger. "Tell me something, MacNeil. How much of this is personal? Are you that much in love with her that you can't discern reality?"

He glared at her. "That's inappropriate."

She lifted her eyebrow again, but remained irritatingly silent as she watched him.

"All right then, hell yes, it's a little personal," he said from between gritted teeth. "Personal enough that it pisses me off she's been lying to me about being in touch with the Skaladeskas and Rue Varden."

"Understandable. I'm in your camp there. But we're going to check her cell phone records, and her laptop—both of which she conveniently left behind, which is interesting in and of itself—and see what sort of communication has been going on. I have to be honest, MacNeil," she said, sitting upright again, elbows on her desk. "If I were in her shoes, and I knew how to get a cure for me—and don't forget, for Dr. Sanchez too; and I suspect *that* would be the driving factor for her—I wouldn't hesitate. I'd be gone. I'd do what needed to be done to save his life."

Hell. That was what Marina always said, wasn't it? *I always go back. If someone needs me, I always go back.*

This was the ultimate definition of going back—back to her roots, back to her terrorist family, back to the place from which she'd barely escaped.

The first time he met her, she'd come out of a cave rescue after nearly dying because of that very credo. And when they were escaping from the Skaladeska hideout, across the cold Siberian lake, she went back to save her drowning father...even though Marina was—still was—terrified of drowning herself.

"Right. All right." He nodded. He felt slightly better, as if the arguments he'd made privately to himself were now validated by someone else. "But she could have contacted me first."

Helen quirked that damn brow again. "And you would have said, 'All right, be off with you, go with God'?" Her expression was saying, *MacNeil, you're smarter than this. You* know *better than this.*

But she didn't actually say it, for which he was immensely grateful. For the first time, Gabe felt sympathy for Colin Bergstrom and his personal ties to the Skaladeska mess. It was hell trying to keep personal baggage from influencing your professional life—especially when they were entwined.

"Now that we've got that out of the way," Helen said briskly, "let's get our strategy in line. Fortunately for you, you and I are the only ones who know you had a terrorist in your custody and allowed him to walk—"

"Suspected terrorist," he growled. "And as Varden pointed out, we have no valid charges to bring against him personally."

Helen's lips flattened. "Give me a chance. I'll find some."

"He doesn't want Marina with the Skalas any more than we do."

"Don't you find that curious?"

"Of course I do. But I believe him. And that means we're on the same side in that, at least. I also believe he did what he could to make sure we escaped from Siberia five years ago. He could have killed me, but he didn't. And Marina believes he gave her certain information that made it easier for us to get away."

"So what did Varden tell you that will actually help us?" Helen said. "Anything? It sounds to me as if he is merely protecting himself, while playing both sides."

"He wouldn't tell me—claimed he couldn't, didn't know for certain—where they were going."

Helen's expression spoke for itself, and Gabe rushed to defend his decision. "Look, he made it clear that if I didn't release him, take what information he chose to give me, then Marina—and the rest of us—would be in more danger. If the Skalas learned he was detained, they'll cut him off. But with him being free to communicate with his home base, he could do more to help Marina and Sanchez. He wants both of them out of there as soon as possible. I believe that. And I didn't have any other reason to hold him, Helen. There was nothing—"

"You could have put him in a cell and let him stew for a bit. I'd've liked a chance at him, too."

"We're on a time crunch for Marina and Sanchez to get treatment. I didn't want to do anything to jeopardize that. And don't forget, Varden's a doctor. He knows how to treat the cuprobeus bacteria. But he needs to have access to the antibiotic... which is not here."

"And if he was going to get it, he is going to need access to the Skaladeskas." Helen seemed to contemplate this then accept it. "All right, I guess what's done is done. Can't say I'd have made the same choices, MacNeil, but you generally know what you're doing."

"Generally?"

"Unless you're sleeping with the woman involved." She gave him a level look. Outraged, he opened his mouth to argue, but she cut him off. "Sophie Ratachoux."

He shut up. She had him there.

And, damn. Between Sophie—who'd been one of his colleagues—and Marina, well, maybe he wasn't as balls-out clearheaded as he should be. And maybe that was why Bergstrom had ended up in a desk job inside; he didn't trust himself out in the field anymore. Thoroughly irritated, Gabe fixed Helen with a look. It was his turn to ruffle someone's feathers. "Not when I was sleeping with you."

She lifted her chin, but he saw the faint wash of pink on her cheeks. "Yes, you were amazingly clearheaded during our affair. That tells me everything I need to know."

By the time Gabe caught up to how his comment had backfired—and "affair" was such a superficial word for what they'd had—Helen had changed the subject. "So we have a blackout caused by a bunch of copper bugs, a deadly bacteria that keeps cropping up and could potentially go wide, an infected civilian consultant and entomologist who are in the custody of the terrorists responsible for it, a missing CEO...where do we go from here? The CDC is already working on an antidote to the bacteria—I sent them everything we have, and so far we've been able to keep it out of the news."

Gabe nodded. "Right. Inez is working on the jump drive we found in Siberia, cross-referencing the data and list of names on there with every event, meeting, consortium, election, whatever, to see if there's any place a number of those people will be at the same time. There's got to be something else in the works besides that power outage. It wasn't enough damage to anyone or any industry."

"I concur. The Skalas are silent for five years, then all of a sudden they start abducting CEOs and bringing down power grids. Surely that's not the extent of things."

"Definitely not. If we only knew where to look." Now it was his turn to settle back in his chair and give Helen an arch look. "By the way, did I mention I put a GPS tracker on Varden before he walked?"

Helen sat bolt upright. Her eyes went wide and her mouth curved wryly. "Slick, MacNeil. Real slick. Way to play the hand."

Gabe gave a nod of acknowledgment. He knew she was referring not only to his interaction with Varden, but also the way he'd played her. "He'll find it, probably sooner rather than later, but it was my only option. It's tiny, and it's in his pocket. I made sure we had a little bit of a scuffle before he left so I could get close enough."

"Are you tracking him now?" She gestured to his iPad.

"Yes. He's on the road. Heading east on Interstate 94. He could be going back to Ann Arbor. But for all we know, he might have found the tracker already and put it on a semi..."

Helen grimaced. "True. Well, the only thing we can do is keep an eye on it and see if his location matches up with any of ours."

She scrolled through notes on her tablet with an agile finger. "So, the last time the Skalas had something big planned, we had communication from Roman Aleksandrov about it—a tease. First the random, small-scale earthquakes, then the video message from him taking responsibility for them and promising something more. So the power-grid outage would be the small-scale event, and we should be looking and watching for a bigger one to follow. Another outage, maybe? A bigger one, with greater economic consequences?"

"If they follow pattern," Gabe said, "that would make sense."

Before he could continue on that path, someone knocked on Helen's door. She gestured the new arrival to come in, and Gabe looked up to see one of the techs.

"I've got some of the data from Marina Alexander's electronics," he said. His name was Tom, and he was tall and thin and had skin the color of coal. He also looked as if he were just out of high school, but Gabe knew that wasn't the case—a fact which made him feel very old. "Do you want it now?"

"Yes," said Helen before Gabe could respond.

Gabe tensed automatically, and managed to keep his expression blank when Helen glanced at him. He had a bad feeling about this—either whatever was on that phone was going to connect Marina tightly to the Skaladeskas, completely obliterating any trust he left in her and very possibly putting her on a terrorist list, or it was going to be unpleasant or embarrassing in another way.

He had no idea if Marina was seeing anyone else, or whether she'd kept a few suggestive texts they'd shared a few months ago, or whatever. At least they'd not taken any pictures.

At least, *he* hadn't.

"I've got it here," said Tom, fairly bouncing into the office. "Here's a list of calls she's made and received in the last week, and also whatever emails she downloaded to her phone. She doesn't have as many texts, but they're here. We're still working on the laptop, but I thought you'd want to review this first."

Gabe snatched up the paper and scanned it rapidly. When he didn't see anything suspicious—no calls to anyone that didn't make sense, nothing he couldn't explain—he felt his insides loosen slightly. "Do you have her actual phone with you? Maybe I'll find something you didn't realize was pertinent." He felt Helen's eyes on him as he took the phone from Tom, but ignored it and passed her the list of calls and texts.

He felt his tension deplete, replaced by something more like discomfort, as he scrolled through her texts, calls, and even email. Nothing that bothered him, except for the invasion of privacy.

He set the phone on Helen's desk. "Mind if we keep it for a while, just in case someone tries to contact her?"

"That's fine," Helen said, still scanning the list of communications Tom had provided. "Thanks, Tom. Let me know what you find on the laptop."

"I'm going to call Inez to see if she's made any progress in connecting our list of targets to any events," Gabe said.

"In the meantime," Helen said, "I was thinking…there's nothing to indicate the deaths from the cuprobeus bacteria were intentional. One was a Skaladeska himself, who likely got infected accidentally while setting up the power outage. The timing's exactly right. The other is a guy who bought a pinball machine infested with the bugs, and then his emergency physician was exposed and died. No relation to the Skaladeskas, not a target of them as far as we can tell…"

Gabe's eyes went wide, because he saw where she was going. "But where did the pinball machine come from?"

She smiled with satisfaction. "That's right. *That*, MacNeil, is going to be our lucky break."

"Roman has just notified me—Mariska has arrived, along with this Dr. Sanchez," said Lev's grainy face on the tablet screen.

Varden had no reason to hide his relief. "They will be treated for the bacteria, then. They've arrived in time." In excellent time, in fact. By his calculations, it was hardly more than fifteen hours since he'd arrived at Marina's empty hotel room to lie in wait for MacNeil. Now he was in his own ratty hotel room, trying for a few moments of reprieve before he was on his way to meet Dannen Fridkov just outside of Chicago.

He grimaced. That should be a pleasant meeting.

"I have not yet seen Mariska nor her companion, but Roman is optimistic. He says though Sanchez is weak and disoriented, covered with the hives, she is displaying no symptoms."

No symptoms? Bloody hell. Varden sank onto the bed, gritting his teeth. She'd lied. She wasn't infected at all.

"But Roman says she will be treated regardless. We will take no chances with the Heir of Gaia."

Of course not. Mariska Aleksandrov must be protected at all costs. Brought into the Skaladeska fold, tempted and groomed and prepared for the inevitable. To carry on the Skaladeska legacy.

Damn it to *hell*. Now she was there, in the compound, and would surely never be allowed to leave.

Or want to leave.

"I am going to see her now," said Lev. "But before we disconnect, you must tell me the whole of it. What happened to Marcko?"

"He was infected by the bacteria shortly after he left St. Louis. Several of the beetles were in his vehicle."

"And you weren't able to treat him?"

"I was not in possession of the antibiotic at the time," Varden told him. "He didn't believe me, and there was an altercation."

Lev's lips pursed. "Marcko was always a bad-tempered and suspicious one. I warned Roman about those shortcomings, but he has always trusted him."

Varden kept his face blank. Only one of Roman's many shortcomings. The man was driven, intelligent, and clever, but he shared Marcko's impatience and arrogance. "Marcko made certain I was also infected with the bacteria."

Lev's expression darkened. "He would do that? Why? What was subject of your altercation?"

"He likely assumed I was lying about not having the antibiotic, and believed if I were infected, I would have to produce it."

"And you did not have it to produce." Even through the tablet screen, Lev's eyes were sharp. They held Varden's for a long moment. "And the reason for your altercation with Marcko, Rue?"

"I attempted to keep him from leaving the room where he was staying. He intended to spread the infection as publicly as possible. Beginning with me."

"I see."

"I saw no reason to advertise our presence, to draw attention to us and our initiatives."

"And to kill innocent people."

"It wasn't part of the plan," Varden replied coolly.

"No. It wasn't." Lev held his gaze, and though they were a thousand miles apart, connected only by pixels, Varden felt the energy and strength emanating from the old man. Dangerous, very perceptive, and incredibly wise. One would be a fool to underestimate him, or to write him off as having outlived his abilities.

"And so now Marcko is dead, having been identified in an American hospital by his mark," continued Lev.

"Very possibly, though I don't have confirmation of that. The authorities are fumbling about, trying to put pieces together that they cannot make fit. I have done what I can to obstruct that without drawing attention to myself or Fridkov. However, because of our altercation, Marcko was physically injured. I'm not certain whether he died from his injuries or the bacterial infection. It would, of course, be in the Skaladeskas' best interest if it were the former."

"Agreed." Still Lev's gaze held his.

Varden was never one to mince words. "If you don't trust me, then call me home."

The old man's eyes narrowed. "There are times, Rue, when I cannot be certain whether that is what you truly want or not."

"You intend for me to be Roman's successor—but only if I'm worthy of the position. If you believe me loyal. It's not my decision but yours."

"There is no doubt of your worthiness. I have never doubted your worthiness or your loyalty—to Gaia and to me, at any rate." His lips twisted. "But to Roman…?"

"His ways are not my ways."

"And now you quote the Christian Bible to me."

Varden couldn't keep his lips from twitching into a smile. "And, not surprising, you recognize it."

"So you have seen Fridkov?" Lev asked, obviously ready to change the subject.

"Yes, of course," Varden replied. "Fridkov and I are scheduled to meet in three hours. As far as he is concerned, Roman's plan should remain intact at this point. He will deliver the package. I will report back on the results immediately. The schedule remains unchanged? October 1 is still the date?"

"Yes."

Varden nodded. "Very well. Do give Marina my best," he added with a cool smile.

"Of course I will." Lev signed off, and Varden flipped the protective case over his tablet with more force than necessary.

Feck, his head hurt. Still throbbed like a bloody bitch from where Marcko had taken that swing at him with a metal rod. The man always had been short-tempered and untrustworthy—hence the reason Varden carried a weapon when meeting with him.

The stitch job Marina had done was better than average, but it didn't take away the blasted pain. And couldn't account for the loss of blood.

But it was lucky for him she'd arrived in time to doctor him up—and before he'd become contagious. He couldn't have gone into the lab bleeding all over without attracting a lot of attention… and if he hadn't gone into the lab, he too would be dead from the cuprobeus infection, thanks to Marcko.

It was too bad Marcko had been infected by the bacteria, but in the end it had worked out all right on many fronts—he wasn't around to tell tales about about Varden, and Rue didn't have to have the man's death on his conscience.

Bloody damn hell. He was exhausted. He looked down at his hands. His fingers were shaking.

Couldn't remember the last time he'd slept more than an hour. Too much shit going on, too damn many balls in the air, too many lies to keep straight. And now Marina Alexander was doing exactly what she shouldn't be doing, and there wasn't a bloody damned thing he could do to stop her without risking everything he'd worked for for a decade.

He wanted to be there, in Chacahoya with Lev and Roman and Marina...but he was also, more urgently, needed here.

Damn, the bed felt good. He needed to close his eyes. He sank back, tried to relax.

He'd been going without pause since the ill-fated meeting with Marcko, traveling from Chicago to Ann Arbor, and back again, and other places in between. But there was too much at stake to let his guard down. He could get news at any moment. The plans could be altered, someone could interfere, Roman could adjust the schedule like he had done before...

Varden still couldn't believe MacNeil had let him walk. He'd been prepared to force the issue if the man hadn't, but it hadn't been necessary. Surprisingly.

His eyes shot wide open.

He sat bolt upright, and swore when the head rush had his wound throbbing like a baller, radiating pain all around his skull. Even his eyes hurt, but Varden ignored the discomfort as he dug in each of his pockets.

Then—sonofabitch. There it was.

He pulled out the tiny electronic node that had been tucked deep down inside his back pocket. *Slick, MacNeil.*

Varden looked at it, holding it in the palm of his hand. Then a cold, wry smile broke through the nagging exhaustion.

He could work with this.

TWENTY-EIGHT

Your grandfather has arrived. He wishes to see you." Nora gestured behind her.

Marina turned. There was a glass barrier between the tiny clinic where she and Eli were being treated and the chamber where Roman waited. Lev was there, watching her through the partition.

Something inside her thudded and thumped when their eyes met. He looked so old and frail, so harmless…yet she knew better. She knew he was the mastermind behind all of the Skaladeska efforts to save Gaia.

And yet something drew her to him. Genes? Heritage?

"Go on," Nora said when Marina made no move to leave. "You will be able to see everything through the glass and watch over your friend. The only thing we can do for him now is to wait and allow him to rest. Lev cannot take the chance of becoming exposed, so he will not come in here."

She looked over at Eli, who seemed to be breathing much more steadily and slowly now. His vitals were being monitored by familiar-looking medical equipment, and one of the techs sat in a chair next to him as if to keep watch.

Marina nodded and left the room, hoping she wasn't making the wrong decision.

The door to the other chamber opened immediately for her, and she stepped in, heart pounding, palms damp, insides in turmoil. Her father and her grandfather. Her blood, her family. Terrorists.

Roman appeared less commanding when in his father's presence, although he loomed over his parent. In both demeanor and action, he deferred to his father.

Lev was hardly taller than five feet, being stooped with age. He seemed frailer than the last time she'd seen him, yet there was still an aura of energy emanating from him. His skin was wrinkled and very nearly translucent, showing blue veins and the rope and texture of every tendon and muscle in his forearms and bare feet. He had thin wisps of stark white hair that gathered like a soft cloud above his skull, and that covering was thin enough to reveal age spots of brown and beige.

"Mariska," Lev said, reaching to touch her.

She didn't move away, and his soft, gnarled hand curled around hers. A shock of something bolted through her—energy, recognition, connection; she couldn't quite define it—and, startled, she looked at him with wide eyes.

His sharp gaze caught hers and held as firmly as his fingers. His blue-gray eyes were steady and delving, penetrating, and yet…kind. He exuded kindness. Affection. And truth. The word popped into her head from nowhere.

Truth.

How could that be?

Marina withdrew her hand, feeling a little unsteady. She collected her thoughts. "Where is Cora Allegan?"

If Roman was surprised at her knowledge, he didn't show it. "She is no longer here. We have released her."

"Released her? Why would you do that?"

"She has been released into the arms of Gaia. It will be Gaia's decision, Her judgment, as to whether Her tormentor will live."

"Do you mean to say you set her loose in the jungle?"

"Precisely. If Gaia means to forgive her for what she's done, then the woman shall live. And perhaps, one hopes, with a deeper respect and conscientiousness for our Mother."

"That's a certain death sentence. For all intents and purposes, you've murdered the woman."

Roman shrugged. "But no, I wouldn't say that. After all, there are countless people who live in the jungle, who have survived in the rainforest. It is more than possible, more than reasonable that she could survive. It truly is up to Ms. Allegan herself, and whether she shows respect and care for her environment. Gaia is forgiving. She will provide for those who care for her. She always has. Therefore, there is an excellent chance Ms. Allegan will survive this little game of roulette. And if not…then Gaia has spoken."

Marina stared at him for a moment. "You had no right to bring this—this judgment upon her. Or anyone."

Roman shook his head. "It is not only my right, but my duty. Someone must speak for Gaia."

Marina hardly knew what to say. Her father was a murderer—no, she'd known that for five years. But he was also delusional. She recovered. "Then I must thank you for treating Dr. Sanchez and myself, instead of allowing Gaia to make her own judgment on our worthiness."

Lev made a sharp noise, but he smothered it when Roman glanced at him. "You knew we would take no chances on your well-being," Roman told her. "You were safe coming here."

"You will always be safe coming here," said Lev. "Mariska, I am so pleased you have returned to us."

"You can't possibly think I'm going to stay here." She quelled a stab of apprehension and kept her expression cool. This conversation had been inevitable. It was the outcome that she feared.

The two men exchanged looks, but it was Roman who spoke. "Your heritage, our family—our legacy and responsibility—demands a member of the direct bloodline of Gaia lead this tribe. You are the last, Mariska. You are the last of the blood, and you must do your duty."

"While I want nothing more than to protect and save our earth, and while I am utterly sympathetic to your goals, I will have nothing to do with a terrorist organization. You know that.

You'll have to destroy me before I'd join you. I told you this five years ago. Nothing has changed. Not even"—she turned to look at Lev—"the temptation of a career-making discovery."

"You speak of the library," said her grandfather with a mild smile. "It is your rightful heritage, Mariska. But not only that—those writings are merely one aspect of our legacy. But above all, it is allegiance to Gaia that supersedes everything. You must accept it."

"Not at the price of human lives. Never at that."

She was shocked when his expression turned dark with fury. Anger rolled from him, palpable enough that she felt heat and energy stirring the room. "You would deny our Earth what she so desperately needs? Our Gaia is *dying*. Do you not see what they are doing to her? How the Out-Worlders violate and molest and torture her? She is changing before our eyes, weakening, and yet *they continue on*. They don't listen, they don't change.

"It has long been a universal truth—one that Gaia Herself embodies, and one that even our race has come to accept—that the sacrifice of a few to protect the greater number is imperative. Even heroic. That the weak and the destructive must be annihilated for the greater good. It is right, it is *natural*. It is survival of the fittest. It is Gaia's law." His eyes flashed, and though he had not raised his voice, the words reverberated through her, filling her like an ice-cold bath, submerging her in truth.

Truth.

There was that word again.

Marina felt a little dizzy. His words were truth. She sank into a chair, lightheaded and suddenly weak.

Lev continued in a powerful voice, one that filled her ears and resonated through her—as if he were making a proclamation, and she were somehow absorbing it. "I am born of Gaia. I am her Son, brought to save Her. I am one with Her. And thus someday so will your uncle be, and so would have been your father. And so you will be, Mariska. You are not like the others in the Out-World. You cannot turn away. You cannot ignore your legacy."

She shook her head; his words had meaning, but they were absurd. Yet they settled inside her like truth. "What do you mean, you are born of Gaia? Brought to save her? What makes you special? Is it because you are a Shaman? But there are many Shaman, and they don't claim to be one with Gaia."

Lev stiffened, and his anger abated slightly. "Roman..." he breathed, as if shocked. "She does not know."

Her father looked at her, but there was no surprise in his face. "No, apparently she does not." He turned to Marina, and once again she had the sense he wished to move closer to her, to touch her as Lev had done. Did he know he was her father? "Are you aware of what is known as the Tunguska Event?"

"Vaguely. In the early 1900s, there was a—something—that happened in Siberia, in Tunguska. Scientists believe a meteor struck the earth, but there was never any real evidence of the metal that would have been left behind. Is that right?"

"Yes, so far as the rest of the world knows. But there is much more to it than that." Roman steepled his hands and continued. "The Skaladeska tribe had long lived in the mountains and forests of the Tunguska area. It was a small group that existed off the land, utilizing caves for shelter, living simple lives close to Gaia, worshipping her. They were highly attuned to her moods and her seasons—as are your grandfather and I. And as you will be when you allow it.

"Upon each Skaladeska child's birth, he or she was marked with the symbol with which you are familiar. It most often was placed on the sole of the foot, but sometimes on the arm or even the back of the calf.

"In the mid-sixteenth century, as I believe you are aware, Ivan the Fourth secretly sent his Byzantine library down the Moscow River with its guardians. The group was led by Leonid Aleksandrov, who was a beloved cousin of Anastasia Romanovna—Ivan's wife. He was charged to protect the writings, and to study them as needed.

"The Romanovna party eventually found the Skaladeskas and they merged, so to speak, and began to live and procreate together, becoming one entity that lived in the harsh wilderness of Taymyria. But in 1908, a most curious and frightening thing happened. The sky turned red and the ground burned, and explosions happened. The elk and owls and hares and all the rest of the living creatures ran to hiding, for the earth was moving and shaking, burning and glowing.

"The Skaladeskas were no different, fleeing the area, but many of them couldn't get away quickly enough. They tried, but many members of the small tribe disappeared—presumed dead—after the smoke cleared, so to speak. But after the smoke cleared," he said, the rhythm of his voice lulling Marina into the story, "a miracle occurred. An infant was discovered, in the midst of the devastated area—lying on the ground, surrounded by blackened trees and scorched grass and burned ground. The child was untouched, unclothed, unmarked…except for the mark of the Skaladeskas on his foot."

Marina was entranced by the tale, and at last she understood. "That babe was you." She looked at Lev, stunned, disbelieving, and yet…wishful. If that were true…if it were actually true… He hadn't told her this story before.

Her grandfather nodded. "It was I. Gaia protected me, took me into her arms and held me while the world was destroyed around me…and she released me back to do her bidding. And so, you see, I must listen to her. I must help you."

"But then there was yet another miracle," Roman continued in his mellow storyteller voice. "The miracle of Irina. Your grandmother, my mother."

"She was a fighter pilot," Marina said. Lev had told her that story, at least, when she was in Siberia. "During the Second World War. She got lost in the mountains of Siberia, long separated from her group."

"That's correct. She was out of fuel and had to jump from her plane in the dead of night, in an unfamiliar terrain. Very brave, very heroic. Like her granddaughter." Lev's eyes glittered with emotion. "You have her eyes."

"And so you've told me."

"The miracle," Roman said, picking up the story once more, "is that she conducted her jump safely, and was rescued by the Skaladeskas. She was brought in to live with them and never left."

"By her own choice?" Marina asked. "Was she held captive—as you would do to me?"

Lev's expression flashed anger again, but Roman spoke. "My father fell in love with her immediately, and yes, as the tale is told, she did need some convincing to remain. She had a lover and family, and wanted to return to Moscow. But it was nearly impossible to travel out of the area, particularly in the winter—as it was when she arrived. And once she got to know Lev, and know us she did, in the end she willingly decided to remain. Not long after she came to live among the tribe, they discovered a most miraculous thing. Irina Yusovsky was an Aleksandrov; or, more specifically, her mother was—a member of the very same family that had been charged to protect Czar Ivan's library. A library that we know holds secrets and truths that will not only fill in the holes of history, but will also help us to carry out our tasks. There are ancient words there, from those who have lived on this earth much longer than we have. From those who lived during a time when our race existed close to the land, to the earth…who communed with our Mother…who *listened* to her and protected her."

There was silence for a moment, and then Lev spoke in a low, sober voice. "And thus you see how neatly Gaia has provided for us, for our legacy, and for her health and safety. She delivered to me—from out of the sky—the only woman worthy of being my partner. The only woman worthy of carrying on Her line."

Marina was torn between utter disbelief and entranced fascination. She couldn't speak, for though she wanted to ignore it—all of it—she could not deny her own connection to the earth, her own sense of the oneness of the planet and her entire ecosystem. She'd always been drawn to caves, to going deep into the bowels of the earth, being surrounded by the planet.

"Mariska," said Lev after a long moment. "Will you come with me? I would like you to see your heritage."

An ugly sense of trepidation and mistrust took hold of her…
and yet she wanted to see that library again. She craved it.

Was that not, after all, why she had risked coming here?

That was *her* truth.

TWENTY-NINE

The library was furnished just as Marina remembered it, but the space it inhabited was larger than the one in the Siberian mountains.

Dimly lit, the room boasted shallow, table-sized display cases arranged in the center of the space. There were eight of them, in two rows, lined up neatly.

There was a single entrance to the rectangular room. Nudged against two walls were stacks of drawers, each one just as shallow as the display cases, but arranged atop each other. They were large, meant to hold papyruses, scrolls, parchments, and even slabs of rock and metal of various sizes.

Two chairs fashioned of animal hide, horns, and wood graced one of the narrow walls. They appeared comfortable and inviting, a remnant of Lev's century of life in Siberia. His Shamanic drum hung between the seats, and when Marina was drawn closer, she saw a thick rug of fur on the floor. It was large enough to be from a bear. Crystals sat in a shallow dish on the round table between the chairs. A stack of bowls of various sizes stood on a small table that also held jars, utensils, and a mortar and pestle.

Roman had accompanied them, but, as before, he stood silently, watching. Waiting.

Marina couldn't control the prickling of excitement and energy as she paused in front of one of the glassed tabletop display cases. She folded her hands behind her back and curled her fingers together like a small child told to look but not touch—and fearful her fingers might do so under their own volition.

Of course, she couldn't read every language—and certainly not very many ancient languages—though she was rudimentary in several, and expert in a few. But when faced with a sample, such as now, she could usually identify the type and culture. However, this sample, this particular one… She couldn't control a soft gasp of recognition.

It was part of the same piece she'd been sent in the Pandora's box from Lev. The one that matched the writing in Matt Granger's cave.

It could not be a coincidence.

Marina looked up to find Roman's gaze on her. She caught him by surprise, and he was unable to hide the desperation in his eyes. Then it disappeared, so quickly she could question whether she'd actually recognized that emotion, and was replaced with a knowing look.

"I see you recognize that piece." He came to stand next to her, and Marina found herself flanked by her father and grandfather, looking down at the protected sample.

"Of course. You sent it to me."

"But you've seen it elsewhere as well, have you not?"

She pulled back from the display to look at him. "What do you mean?" But she was beginning to understand.

Matt Granger had been told about the cave by a stranger they met, hiking through the area. There had been that paper wrapping and a recent receipt from Zingerman's, an Ann Arbor landmark, in the ruins of her father's—no, Victor's—home in Northern Michigan.

Roman smiled complacently. All trace of weakness—of desperation, if that was what she'd seen—was gone. "I see you're beginning to comprehend just how carefully this was all planned. I have to admit, I didn't expect you to come to us because you'd been infected by the cuprobeus bacteria, but that just moved the timeline along a little more quickly. You might have dithered about it for weeks, or even months. But I knew that eventually you'd need to come. To see this." He gestured to the library.

Marina shook her head, trying to make sense of it all. "Do you mean you purposely set it up so Matt Granger would find that cave—how? *How* could you know I'd be there, and have to rescue him, and…how did you even know the cave was *there*?" It couldn't be. There were too many variables.

And yet…it was too coincidental not to have been purposely arranged.

"Viktor found the cave, and the writings. It took him some time, of course—it was a project of many years, and it began long before you even knew we existed, I'm certain. In fact, his determination to find the location mentioned in these writings was originally for no other purpose than the mere discovery of it, and confirmation that it existed. You see, the information is written here," Roman said, gesturing to the piece of stone in the case. "And with some study, Viktor was actually able to locate the cave a year or more before he came back to us. It's a burial site, I understand. Many of the visiting white people—the Phoenicians, I believe they are?—died one harsh winter, and so they buried them with their stones. The rest of them left to go south."

Roman patted her hand, the first time he'd touched her. "I see you are in shock. Did you not realize we haven't been simply the caretakers of this library, but also its scholars? Despite the fact that the depths of this collection have hardly begun to be plumbed, Lev has long studied some of the pieces, as have others of our tribe. This is a rather important piece of writing, Mariska. Or so I've been told." Roman gestured to his father. "I can't read it myself."

"But…*I* only found the cave by accident."

Her father folded his hands over his chest. "No, you found the cave because you were led there. You were in the area, and so we gave you the opportunity to find the cave. It's a shame the young man was killed—but he shouldn't have been taking a risk like that. Everyone knows not to go into a cave without certain preparations."

She could do nothing but stare at him. "Someone told Matt Granger the cave existed, hoping he would find it and then be trapped in it so I would have to extract him?"

"To be sure, Granger wasn't the only person to whom the information was fed. We weren't taking any chances with you in such close proximity. But since a great number of people are foolish when it comes to exploring caves, the probability was high you would need to intervene.

"And even if a search and rescue mission hadn't been necessary, surely you would have heard about the find while you were in the area and been compelled to see it. And then the rest would have fallen into place." He spread his hands nonchalantly. "You already had the sample of writing, you would surely have at least made some initial study of it, and it would have been simple for you to make the connection…and then wonder about the rest of it. And then it would have fallen into place, Mariska—for surely you've heard about the White Cloud People of Peru. The Chachapoya people, who died out in the 1500s."

Marina felt numb. "Of course I've heard of them—the fair-skinned, blond-haired tribe whose origins are a mystery."

"Or were. Until now." The temptation dangled, reflected in his eyes and the knowing smile.

She shook her head, but he was correct about her assessment, and the steps she'd taken. She'd been played, to some extent. "I'm not staying," she told them once more. "I will never be a part of your terrorist attacks."

Lev made a soft noise, something like a cross between negation and pain. She looked at him, and was caught by his gaze. It seemed to delve deeply inside her mind, almost as if he were attempting hypnosis.

"Stop that," she snapped, and tore her gaze away.

Lev merely blinked, and his expression returned to normal. "There are times, Mariska, when the decision to act is painful, and it isn't a clear path, and it is frightening. You belong with us. Someday, you will understand."

THIRTY

Marina opened her eyes.

It took a moment before she remembered where she was, and what had happened.

Eli.

She sat up, realizing she was on a comfortable bed. The room was dark, lit only by a soft glow that came from a tiny light in the corner. She was back in the clinic room.

The last thing she remembered was demanding from Lev and Roman that she be brought here from the library so she could stay with Eli. "I'm not letting you take him away like you did to Gabe MacNeil."

Marina scrambled off the bed and swayed a little before she caught her balance. *Did they drug me?*

How long had she been out? Where was Eli?

If they'd done anything to him...killed him, taken him away—

She became aware that she wasn't alone. Someone else was in the room. Soft breathing, the rustling of fabric—blankets or sheets?

There was another bed; now that her eyes were adjusting to the dim light, she could make out its shape. Someone was on it. Hope rushed through her as she crept carefully over to the prone figure.

She touched the other bed first, then worked her way lightly over until she found skin. Warm. Smooth. An arm, face up. His pulse pounded in his wrist, and suddenly his fingers closed around her hand.

"Dr. Alexander?"

Marina's knees nearly buckled in her relief. "Dr. Sanchez. Thank God." He was alive, at least. And his forearm—the one that had been rough with rash and hives—felt smooth. A normal temperature. "How do you feel?"

"Not bad at all." He hadn't released her hand, and he tugged gently as he pulled himself to a seated position. "You?"

"I'm fine. I can't believe it," she whispered. She was lightheaded with relief. "They really did cure you. I was certain they would—"

"And without all that torture you were talking about." There was a lift of humor in his voice. "Thank you. You saved my life."

"Well, so far, anyway," she said. "You're not out of here yet."

"All at great risk to yourself. Don't think I don't realize what you've done, Dr. Alexander. They don't care about me. It's you they want."

"I'll be able to get you out of here. If they wanted you dead, you'd already be—dead."

"And no torture either. I'm beginning to be a little envious of MacNeil. Apparently he got it all—a bullet, death threats, *and* torture."

"But I promised you a beetle. I'm certain I can get you a beetle too." She couldn't hold back a soft laugh.

"Don't forget, MacNeil got the girl too."

"*Girl?*"

His laugh was deep and rich in the darkness. "It just sounded better that way."

"Right." She couldn't help a smile herself. He was damned charming.

"Let's get one thing clear, Dr. Alexander. I'm not leaving without you. Beetle or no beetle."

"That might not be possible. As long as I'm here, I'm a bargaining chip for your safety."

"Bargain away. But like I said…I'm not leaving you behind." He slid off the bed and stood next to her. Their bodies were very close in the small space, and Marina's breath caught as she realized he was reaching for her. She stepped nearer, her fingers brushing his arm, and tipped up her face.

His mouth was full and soft and warm, covering hers with confidence, yet without demand. One hand came up to curl around the back of her neck, just enough to steady her, his fingers weaving into her hair. She sank into him a little, enjoying a kiss that could only be described as thoughtful, thorough, and sensual.

When he pulled away, still touching her, Marina smiled. "Well, Dr. Sanchez," she managed to say. "That was a surprise."

"Definitely not going to leave you behind," he murmured. Then his voice turned brisk, but still held a note of levity. "I think we can dispense with the formality at this point, Dr. Alexander. Besides, your name is too much of a mouthful, and if I need to get your attention quickly, I may not have time to speak six syllables." He gave her a quick kiss on the mouth, then stepped back.

"All right then, Dr. Sanchez. Let's see if we can get out of here and find your beetles. But first…let's see if they left any of that antidote in here. Do you remember anything of what they did to you?"

"Some, but I was pretty out of it by then. I remember them taking my vitals, and maybe putting some topical cream on…and definitely I was the recipient of a shot. That I remember. Any idea how long we've been here?"

"No. I was—gone for a while, and when they brought me back it felt as if it were near evening. I ate…" She frowned. "Let's look around."

Marina fumbled in her cargo shorts—the same ones she'd been wearing yesterday (it had been yesterday, hadn't it?) in Helen Darrow's office. Deep in one of the cargo pockets was a small squeeze flashlight, no bigger than a large cherry—small enough it hadn't been noticed by their traveling escorts, or they hadn't cared.

She flashed it around and confirmed they were in the same room they'd been in when their treatments had been administered. The room next door, visible through the glass partition, was empty and dark. The door to the medical room also had a glass panel, and beyond, the area was unlit, leading Marina to believe it was night and everyone had gone to sleep. She turned back to the counter where the medical technicians had been working and, though her fingers were becoming tired from pinching on the light, she and Eli began to search through drawers and shelves.

There were more cannulas and some small unmarked vials. Though she wasn't certain they were the antibiotic, she knew the medication Nora had administered to her was the color of Cabernet. She took two vials of dark red liquid and shoved them in her pockets, along with a couple of syringes. Eli filched a few as well, along with a small tube of gel.

"I think they put this on me," he said, replacing the cap. "I remember the scent. Not pretty."

Marina's fingers gave out and the light winked into darkness as she rested her grip. They moved to the door without speaking and peered out the glass. The space beyond was filled with shadows of all shades of black and gray, along with tiny random lights that appeared to be from a computer or something else electronic. They blinked red, green, yellow, and orange

"There's probably an alarm on the door," she said. "Or it's locked."

Eli reached for the knob and turned. Nothing happened— neither an alarm nor the delightful sound of the door opening. "Shine that here."

Marina obliged, training her tiny light on the knob. No keyhole on this side, no way to unlock it. "Got any other ideas?"

Eli had moved to the glass partition and peered through it. He knocked softly on the glass, then returned to the door and tapped on that glass. "Let's break it."

"The sound would bring everyone running."

"Right. But…" He turned back to the cabinets and drawers and began to dig through one of them. Marina brought over her light without being asked, shining it for him while she considered other options. "Maybe there's something in here we could use to cut it," he muttered. "A scalpel? A diamond-headed cutter?"

"Or this!" She snatched up a roll of bandage tape in the drawer next to his.

They looked at each other and grinned. "That'll do."

Working quickly and efficiently, they tore strips of tape and crisscrossed them over the lower left quadrant of the door window.

"Ready?" Eli asked, holding a pair of heavy scissors. With a sharp movement, he slammed it into the center of the crisscrossed section. The glass crunched silently, held in place by the tape except for one shard that tinkled to the floor. Marina picked away enough of the pieces to make a hole through which her arm would fit.

After taking care of the jagged glass, she reached out and down and found the door handle. It moved, and the door unlocked audibly.

"Ready?" she whispered. "If an alarm sounds, head to those stairs there, and when you get to the top, look for the door right there. That'll lead to the outside. I'm pretty sure we could find our way back to where they landed the plane."

"Or…maybe we don't want to be in the jungle at night without any protection," he said, putting his hand over hers to keep her from turning the knob. "Maybe we hide somewhere in here— where they wouldn't expect to find us; they'll expect us to fly the coop, right?—until we can get our bearings and some provisions. I know better than to be out in the jungle without a plan—even if we could find the plane. I assume you'd be the one flying it? And I'd like to find those beetles. If I can get a specimen—a live one— and bring it back, it'll help with the development of a treatment."

Marina nodded. "I'm willing to take that risk if you are."

"Damn straight."

She turned the knob and pushed on the door…and it didn't move.

"Bolt lock," Eli said, stepping up close behind her. He reached his own arm out and around at an awkward angle, trapping her gently against the door. Marina heard the dull clunk of the bolt being thrown open. He withdrew his hand, brushing his fingers over her cheek in a light caress. "All right, Doc. Let's go."

Marina held her breath, turned the knob, and pushed the door slowly open. A low, moaning creak that seemed to shatter the silence had the hair at the back of her neck standing on end, but the rest of the world remained still. Eli's hand curled around her wrist as they slipped out of the room and into the dimly lit laboratory area.

The only sound was the soft scuff of her sandal and the low hum of the computer equipment on the other side of the lab. A soft blue-white glow from the perimeter of the room gave just enough illumination for them to navigate through the worktables and electronics stations.

She tugged him with her as she made her way to the computers. If there was an Internet connection and she could figure out how to access it, she could send some information to Gabe: that they had been treated for the bacteria, and, more importantly, that she'd left him a clue…and their general location could maybe be traced through her email.

She shifted a mouse, and the monitor rumbled awake with a soft buzz, casting a familiar circle of light into the area. Eli moved to the station next to hers and did the same. After a quick glance to make sure no one had appeared, Marina turned her attention to the screen. Her palm was slick and the mouse didn't want to cooperate at first, but she got it working and began to fumble around the desktop—which wasn't familiar to her, but she found something that looked like the Internet.

"Any luck?" Eli murmured, clicking and shuffling his mouse.

"Yes…I think…*yes*." She'd gotten online, and quickly typed in her webmail address. "And the date—it's already the 29th. We've been here more than a day."

Her stomach was in knots as she logged in, and, without checking any of her messages, immediately created a new one. To Gabe. "As soon as we're done here, let's look for the beetles," she said as she typed: *Treated. Learned infection can be spread by touch!! Check my phone*, she typed. *Listen—*

"So you want to see the beetles, do you?"

Marina's heart dumped to her feet as she and Eli whirled around.

A man stood there, silhouetted by the soft light behind him. In his hand was the unmistakable shape of a firearm.

THIRTY-ONE

Marina swallowed back her heart, and swiftly clicked SEND as Eli bolted to his feet, putting himself between her and the newcomer.

"I was under the understanding Roman didn't allow firearms in his workhouse," Marina said, stepping out from behind Eli. Her heart was thudding crazily, and she hoped the email had gone.

The man laughed softly. "What Roman doesn't know won't hurt him. Or perhaps it will. Move away from there now."

"Who are you?"

"My name is Hedron. And of course I am well aware of your identity, Mariska Aleksandrov. Welcome back to the fold." The definite sneer in his tone belied the words. "Step away from there, if you please. I won't ask again." He gestured with the gun. "Unlike your uncle, I am not afraid to employ this sort of weapon. Now, come this way...slowly. No sudden moves, no sounds—or, I promise you, the treatment they gave you for the bacteria will have been wasted. I have no qualms about ridding the world of the Aleksandrov progeny."

Marina and Eli did as he ordered, and as they drew nearer, Hedron moved quickly and neatly. The next thing Marina knew, he had her by the arm, and yanked her toward him. The barrel of the gun was jammed into her neck.

"Excellent," he said, pushing it none too gently into the soft part of her throat as Eli froze, holding his hands up in surrender.

"Now, sir, if you would lead the way—you did say you wanted to see the beetles, did you not? Down the corridor to the right."

Even in the dim light, Eli was able to catch Marina's eye before doing as ordered. She was relieved his expression was one of determination and not fear.

Hedron relaxed his grip only slightly as they made their way down the hall he'd indicated. Her best guess was they were moving toward what had appeared to be the back left side of the compound when they'd arrived.

"You made this very convenient for me," Hedron said, gesturing for Eli to turn left at the end of a hall. "I thought I'd have to manufacture your escape, but you beat me to it. And rather quickly, too. Thank you for that. Now, do you see the door with the metal frame? Good. You will open it, and once we've stepped through, you'll close it behind us. And remember, I'll put a bullet in her neck the instant you step out of line."

Eli complied, taking his time, clearly trying to think his way out of the situation. Once they stepped through the door, and it closed behind them, light flooded the place.

Marina blinked at the shock of illumination and heard the clunk of a lock, then, blessedly, Hedron released her with a rough shove. She stumbled, still half blind, and knocked into the wall. Eli pulled her to her feet.

For the first time, she could see their captor.

Hedron was younger than Roman, she guessed. Just sixty or so. He had a full head of stark white hair in a flattop buzz cut that was short over the ears. Clean-shaven, with olive skin and a pair of cold gray eyes, he presented a formidable picture. Dressed in the familiar garb of the Skaladeskas, he also wore a pair of gloves.

Having taken in the details of their captor, Marina looked around the room. There were no windows, and only two doors: the one through which they'd entered, and another one on the far wall. The space held the faint scent of rotten eggs, and it seemed to be coming from several canisters with hoses—they looked like rectangular fire extinguishers—lined up along the floor near her. There were no furnishings, and the rest of the space was empty except for an array of suits hanging along the fourth wall. They were made of white material, unlike the normal clothing worn by the Skaladeskas. Above each suit was a hood shaped like a helmet, and a pair of boots sat below.

Marina's first impression was they were hazmat suits. And the fire extinguishers…

None of this was a good sign.

"Your uncle is a fool, leaving you unattended," said Hedron. "But his folly will clearly be to my benefit." He gestured to the opposite door, a heavy metal one that looked as if it led to a safe. "Through that door. Both of you."

Marina and Eli looked at each other, but the gun was pointed directly in her face, and close enough Hedron couldn't miss if he pulled the trigger. And she had no doubt he would. Whoever this man was, he had no respect or care for the Heir to Gaia, or whatever they were calling Marina.

Eli turned reluctantly and stumbled. A sudden loud clanging and clattering filled the air, and Eli glanced up guiltily as he righted one of several canisters he'd overturned. "Sorry. I tripped."

"Be careful," Hedron snapped, glancing at Eli, but with the firearm still pointed much too close to Marina.

"I didn't mean to knock those over; good thing they didn't break," Eli said in a loud, nervous voice as he stooped to pick up the other canisters. "Whew. They smell awf—"

"Stop talking and open that door." Hedron was clearly losing his patience, and Marina began to get a little nervous.

Eli must have caught on, for he kept himself focused on the door without turning back. He slid open the three bolts that held the door closed, then, with an apologetic look over his shoulder at Marina, pulled it open.

"Go on." Hedron gestured sharply with his weapon.

Eli took her by the hand and yanked her through the opening so quickly she nearly tripped herself. No sooner had they stepped through than the door clanged shut behind them.

Marina whirled to see that Hedron had not followed, and then heard the dull clunk of a bolt being thrown.

"What the hell?" said Eli. He sounded more disappointed than confused, and that was when Marina noticed he was holding one of the canisters. "I was going swing around and brain him with this," he explained, letting the can slide to the floor. "Damn."

"Good thinking," she said, impressed. "And nice sleight of hand, picking it up."

"What do you think this place is? And what's he up to? I bet he's going to release some of the beetles in here. Did you see all those hazmat suits?"

Unfortunately, Marina was inclined to agree. "There's no way out, I'm guessing."

They were in a much smaller chamber now—hardly bigger than a closet. The light in here was dim and frosty green, filtering from the periphery of the ceiling and shining down in a doubtful glow. The rest of the chamber was completely empty, except for one wall cloaked in a heavy, dark curtain.

Eli appeared eerie and ghostlike in the strange color, and he gestured to the drapery. "I have a feeling I know what's behind the curtain. And it isn't the Wizard of Oz."

When he tugged the covering aside, Marina was prepared for anything—but the moment was anticlimactic. Behind the swag was a door, and next to it was a large window. And on the other side of the window was the same eerie green light, and—

"There she is," Eli said in a hushed voice. He stepped up to the glass as if drawn by a rope, planting his fingers on the glass as he peered through. "There they *all* are."

Marina joined him, stunned and fascinated by the sight revealed through the glass. "It looks like a...like an underground temple," she murmured. Her breath fogged the window, and she stepped aside to a clear spot. For the moment, she forgot about Hedron locking them in, about being trapped, and possibly being exposed to the beetles...

Because what she saw was incredible.

Whatever they were looking at was certainly man-made, and ancient. It was built into the earth; a cave, perhaps, that had been formed into a rectangular room with a tall ceiling, underground.

Through the dim green light filtering through the window and in the temple itself, she could see the edges of rock and natural formations between the room where she was, and where the underground chamber's walls and floors ended.

The cavern had smooth walls, floor, and ceiling of an iridescent, foamy-green hue. A dais was situated in the center, and on it was a pedestal. Other than that, the space was empty. The metal of the walls glinted dully in the light, and seemed to glitter like the bottom of a fountain filled with pennies. Rusty glints, shimmering with movement, filtering over the walls and floor.

"Copper," she whispered. "It's all copper. The walls, the ceiling, the floor…"

"And it's crawling with my beetles," Eli murmured like a lover. "Look at those beauties." He caressed the glass where several of the coppery insects crawled, safely on the other side.

"It's amazing," she breathed, then jumped when the door opened behind them.

"I see you've discovered our little secret." Hedron still held his weapon, but he'd taken the time to don one of the white suits, boots, and helmet. He closed the door quickly behind himself, but not before a shaft of bright light blazed into the chamber for a moment. On the other side of the glass, the beetles caught in the sudden illumination suddenly took flight in a startled, crazy swarm.

Eli made a sound of fascination and went back to staring through the glass. "They don't like the light."

"No, hence our convenient little antechamber." Hedron gestured to include the space. "White or bright light sends them into a frenzy. Not a surprise, for those bugs have been living and breeding there in the dark for millennia—if your grandfather is to be believed." This last was, of course, directed at Marina. "Would you like to take a closer look?" He laughed unpleasantly.

"Did you build this place? This building?"

"No," replied Hedron. "Not precisely. We renovated it, shall we say. In fact, it was my sons who managed the project, to Lev and Roman's specifications. You met them several years ago, in fact." She couldn't see his face behind the helmet, of course, but Marina could tell he wasn't pleased. "It was because of you my son Bran died in a Canadian prison."

Now it all made sense. Bran and George were the two men who'd abducted Marina and Gabe from Northern Michigan and taken them into Canada. Marina and Gabe escaped, and their captors were taken into custody in Canada, with the intention of being turned over to the American authorities. She knew one of them had escaped during a transfer, but... "I wasn't aware Bran was dead."

"Such a cloistered young woman you are," Hedron replied bitterly. Then, abruptly, he returned to his guided tour. "The original building here, the one in which you entered earlier today, was the hideaway of an Ecuadorean drug lord a decade or more ago. The way I understand it, he heard the legend about a sacred place in the rainforest where electronics didn't work properly, and there was supposedly an energy source—blah, blah, blah. Something like that. Apparently Rico—that was his name—built the house in this area, camouflaging it into the jungle, so he'd have a safe place to live and raise his family.

"He had no idea the reason electronics and radar didn't work in this area was because of this massive quantity of copper, built into the ground in an underground sanctuary or temple. He had no idea until his workers came upon it one day while trying to dig into the side of the rocky mountain abutting the compound. No one realized the mountain was man-made, and they certainly didn't realize our lovely cuprobeus bugs were living in there...

"You can imagine the rest of the story, I'm certain. The drug lord died—not from a gunshot wound or in jail, but from a little copper bug. And so did the rest of his crew. And that left this real estate available for us to take over back in the late nineties."

"It's amazing," Marina said. "It's a major archeological find."

Hedron still held the gun, but it wasn't exactly pointed at her anymore. He'd become more relaxed as he told his story, and his grip loosened a bit. "That might be the case, but it's also the key to our work. The Skaladeskas long ago learned that Gaia always provides."

"Provides?" asked Eli, who'd at last turned from the window. He began to edge toward the canister on the ground.

"Oh, yes. She provides the means—the weapons, the tools, the opportunity—for us to carry out Her will. To protect and save Her. And what an elegant weapon She's given us here. Your uncle is infatuated with these little six-legged beasts, and for once, I cannot disagree with him."

"What are you going to do with them?" Marina shifted so Hedron would turn slightly, giving Eli the opportunity to get near the metal can. Keeping her attention averted from her companion, she continued, "You've already caused a blackout—or wasn't that intentional? Was it a test?"

"The blackout was a test—an unnecessary one, but my blasted nephew Varden convinced Roman it was the best way to move forward. He wanted to make certain the insects could be brought into the country and used in the manner we believed. A test run. I argued against it, but the Naslegi is blind and fawns over your uncle. They believe he can do no wrong. Now we've done nothing but alerted the authorities to our tactics. Surely they're expecting another threat, and—"

Clanggg!

It happened so fast Marina didn't even see Eli move until he swung up sharply. The canister smashed up and into Hedron just behind the ear. His gun went flying, and she dove for the firearm as it clattered to the ground.

But her speed wasn't necessary, for Hedron, caught fully unawares and in the tender side of the head, had dropped to the ground like a stone.

"Nice job," she crowed, surging into Eli's arms for a victory hug. That was followed by a quick kiss that could easily have turned into something more if there hadn't been other things on her mind.

"You kept him talking," he said, giving the man a nudge with his toe. Hedron didn't stir. "He's out."

"Great. Let's get out of here," she said—then stopped. "You should put on that suit and get your specimen while we're here. Then we can fly."

"I like the way you think, Dr. Alexander. Among other things." His smile confirmed he meant exactly what she thought he meant.

Marina shook her head, laughing a little as she began to tug a boot from Hedron's inert foot. "You must wreak havoc on the hearts of all those co-eds at U of I. I can only imagine the waiting lists for your classes."

Eli gave a snort as he yanked the helmet from Hedron and let the man's head clunk to the ground with a satisfying thud. "They're terrified of me, and that's the way I like it. They're much too young. I prefer to avoid drama and immaturity as much as possible, so I cultivate a terrifying persona."

"I can't say I find you all that terrifying."

"Well, I'm glad to hear that, at least." He laughed as she helped him into the suit.

"Ready?" she asked.

"Ready." He showed her the small jar he'd either swiped from the clinic or brought with him, and then nodded toward the entrance through which Hedron had come. "You should go. I'm not sure what's going to happen when I go through that door."

Marina looked down. "Guess I'd better take him too." She went to the door, then stopped in front of it. Her heart began to thud, and she scrambled to pull her tiny light from the pocket of her shorts. "I don't see any way to open this..." she murmured.

She stared at it, shining the light all over the smooth metal door, along its edges and around, only to find there was no hardware except three deep-set hinges. There had to be a way out. Of course there was a way to open the door...

There it was, embedded in the wall next to the entrance. A small door, no larger than the size of a garage door keypad. Trepidation settled over her as she fumbled it open to find exactly what she expected.

"I'm guessing you don't know the code."

She shook her head, staring at the keypad numbers as if they would somehow present themselves to her in the order in which they must be pushed. "I haven't any idea. And I don't think... well, how many chances would it give us before sending up an alarm—or worse?"

"An alarm might not be a bad idea—they'd come and let us out of here, right? You're some sort of royalty, aren't you?" There was a little teasing in his voice.

"Probably. But maybe not. I know Roman wouldn't hurt me, but obviously Hedron would. There might be others who would be threats as well." She hesitated, reached to touch one of the buttons, then dropped her hand. "Get your specimens. I'll think about this while you're doing that. Just don't let any of those beetles in here when you open the door."

He hadn't donned the helmet yet, and his face looked serious. "I don't know if I should take that chance. What if they all swarm in here when I open the door?"

Marina patted her pocket. "Well, I have the antibiotic. I think."

Eli shook his head, his face grim. "Not sure that's a good idea. We don't even know for sure if that's what it is. But...let me look at this first." He went over to the door that led into the underground temple. There was also a window in it. "Looks like there's a curtain on the other side of the door. That's probably what they do—go through the door, close it, then step out from behind the curtain so the insects don't see the light and fly through. Okay?"

"Sure. Go for it. I'll...see what I can think of while you're in there."

Eli pulled on the helmet, and she made certain not a centimeter of skin showed from beneath the suit. Then, standing in the farthest corner, she watched as he opened the door—apparently this one didn't need a lock—and quickly stepped through. The door closed behind him, and through the window, she saw the flutter of the black curtain.

And then he was there, on the other side of the window, in the white suit.

THIRTY-TWO

When Eli slipped back into the chamber where Marina was waiting, even though he was cloaked in the white suit, she could tell he was ready to burst.

"We have *got* to get out of here. *Stat!*" he said, whipping off the protective helmet.

Her heart lurched. "What happened? What did you find?"

"It's amazing. They're amazing! My paper isn't going to just be in an ESA journal—*Nature*'s going to want it—maybe *Science* too." His eyes were dancing; *he* was practically dancing. "Those darlings are amazing! They're clearly social—there's obviously a reproductive caste, and I identified a specimen from a defensive caste too—which isn't terribly common with coleops, you know. The mandibles on the defensives are fascinating—of course, I couldn't see very well in that light in there, but I saw enough."

Marina exhaled with relief. "I thought you'd found something wrong."

"Wrong? There's not one thing wrong! This is definitely not only a new suborder, but it's going to be beyond anything I'd imagined. Everyone's going to want to see them, pathogenic bacteria aside. And once I get to observing their social behavior—even in the few moments I had in there, I could see clearly they have social, possibly even eusocial characteristics—yes, you heard me right, *eusocial*—it's going to be a bombshell. It's going to change the way we look at coleops! I'll probably be featured in

National Geographic—" He stopped, looked around, and came back to earth. A sheepish grin spread over his face. "Whoa. Sorry. I guess we've got other things to think about. Like getting out of here safely."

She shook her head, unable to keep from smiling. "I felt the same way when I saw the library."

"Library?"

Marina exhaled a long breath, then shook her head. "I'll explain later. Let me just say, I feel your pain—such as it is."

"All right." He seemed much calmer now, more focused. "No luck with the keypad?"

"No. I didn't want to try too many times, because I was afraid of setting off an alarm—although, like you said, I'm not certain that would be such a bad thing. I did try my grandfather's birthday as a code, thinking that might be it—but no go. And he"—she gestured at Hedron with a toe—"hasn't moved. I checked his pulse—he's alive, but it's weak."

"So we can wait until someone comes to let us out or until he wakes up." Eli's attention slid toward the window, where the beetles still shuttled over the glass. "If he does."

"I think those are our only choices." Marina looked out into the copper temple as well. She'd really like to take a look on the other side of the window too. "Can I borrow that suit? I want to look around. There might be an entomological anomaly in there, but I suspect it's also a major archeological find."

Eli peeled off his gloves. "Hey. Did you happen to check him for a cell phone?" he said suddenly.

With an irritated huff, Marina dove toward Hedron's inert body. "Don't know why I didn't think of that." The man's tunic was long and plain, but she rifled through the pockets of his loose trousers, and with a crow of triumph, produced a sleek, state-of-the-art smartphone. "The question will be…does it work down here."

Eli, who by now had stepped out of the protective suit, helped her to her feet and watched as she tapped the phone's touchscreen.

"And the answer would be...no. Damn. Not one bar. But the battery is completely charged, so we'll keep it." She shoved the phone in her cargo shorts pocket and Velcroed the flap closed. "So how about I put on that suit, since it doesn't look as if we're going anywhere soon."

"You know," he said as he handed her the white garment, "I'm pretty covered up—wearing pants and shoes. Only my arms would be exposed if I went in there without the suit on."

"And face, and neck, and head, and hands," she said, giving him an are-you-nuts look. "I don't think you should chance it."

"Well, I just got dosed with an antibiotic—or some sort of antidote. Maybe I've got immunity for a while." He flashed that hopeful grin and she shook her head.

"For a renowned coleopterist, you sure are crazy. It's not worth the risk. I won't be long. If he begins to wake up, knock on the glass and I'll come right back in," Marina said, yanking on the gloves. "I promise not to step on any of your darling beetles."

Eli gave a little laugh, but the last thing she saw when she slipped through the door into the curtained alcove was him looking wistfully through the window.

Inside the temple, as she had begun to think of it but actually hadn't confirmed, Marina found herself enclosed in a hazy green light that filtered up from the corners of the chamber. The air was damp and moist, and smelled of earth and metal, and something else she couldn't define.

What if the bacteria was also airborne...and one could breathe it in through the nose? She shivered. Yet another reason it wouldn't be smart for Eli to come in here without protective covering.

The ceiling was eight feet above the ground, and it too glowed dull sea-foam green. There were four electrical lights spaced out along two of the walls, casting an olive glow from the floor up and into the space. Now that she was inside, Marina could tell the temple wasn't simply a large rectangle, but in the shape of a T. She was entering from one of the crossbars, and could see straight along across the top of the T. But the dais where the small altar had been constructed was in the center, where the crossbar and leg met. There didn't seem to be any lights other than in this immediate area.

There were beetles on every surface, but there weren't so many she found it impossible to avoid stepping on them. They crawled along the walls and in areas of the floor, but as she walked through, they scuttled out of her path. She had her small squeeze light, but hesitated to use it unless she found it necessary. Even enclosed in the safe white suit, she saw no reason to send the little beasts into a frenzy. Besides, Eli would probably go through the glass window if he saw his little "darlings" get stirred up like that.

She picked her way carefully to one of the foam-green walls and, avoiding rushing beetles, brushed her hand over the smooth, oxidized metal. It would have been gorgeous when it was first constructed: all gleaming copper, shining in the dim light like a new penny. Not surprising, the wall was mottled with black residue, and when she pulled her hand away, the glove was streaked with what could only be the deadly bacteria.

Marina grimaced and wiped her hand on a pant leg. She refrained from touching the surface again, but instead leaned close to the wall near one of the greenish lights to see if she could tell how the wall was constructed (blocks, slabs of metal, tiles, or something else), and whether there were any sorts of drawings, text, or other designs on the copper.

It was too dark to tell, and after a moment of hesitation, Marina pulled out her squeeze light. Cupping one hand around it to keep the illumination to a minimum, she activated it. A small circle of white light burst into the chamber, focused on the wall directly in front of her. Beetles erupted into action, scattering like a cloud of disrupted bats and swirling around her. They thudded into her arms and helmet, seemingly incensed by the simple addition of white light.

After glancing guiltily toward the glass window, where Eli was surely watching her terrorize the insects, Marina scanned the wall in front of her before letting the light go out.

She noticed two things before doing so: only the beetles touched by the white light, or near the edge of it, flew into a frenzy, and the wall seemed devoid of markings or design.

That didn't mean this wasn't a find. This whole man-made space would be fascinating to any archaeologist or historian.

Marina shot a look toward the window, and Eli gave her a thumbs-up. Apparently he hadn't seen the cyclone of beetles, Hedron was still out cold, and she had more time.

Great. She'd take it.

She picked her way over to the small dais and its altar. They were nothing more than a two-meter square for the base, and a tall, slender rectangle topped by a wider, thick one. If there had ever been anything on the surface—offerings, vessels, or statues—it was long gone. But here could be a place with writings or images too—or some sort of decorative design that might help identify the peoples who'd built the copper temple.

Marina crouched next to it, and turned on the squeeze light once more. The beetles spun into a ferocious maelstrom around her again, and she ignored the angry thuds as they ricocheted into her protected head, arms, and back. Instead, she peered at the weathered altar, tracing the edge with her light.

Working her way around the dais, she examined the base as closely as possible, glancing back regularly to make certain Eli wasn't trying to catch her attention. Her knees and ankles were protesting when she finally stood, having been unable to find any sort of markings in the copper on this first perusal. That didn't mean there weren't any—again, there was black residue streaking the damp, oxidized copper, and the light was faulty.

Now she was facing the vertical leg of the T, and it stretched away, long and dark. No one had installed lights down that leg of the chamber, so of course Marina wanted to explore there. Maybe it led to another way out of the temple, and she and Eli could escape that way.

Although how would they both make their way through without two protective suits?

Still, she inched her way along carefully, using the green glow from the four lights to supplement her small white one. Hands cupped around it to keep the beetle disruption to a minimum, she took her time—especially when she felt a distinct *crunch* beneath one foot.

Marina winced. Eli wouldn't be pleased if he knew she'd just murdered one of his darlings. Not that there weren't plenty to go around…

By now she was ignoring the frantic insects that zipped around like mad fleas, and moved along at a more comfortable pace. Her light indicated another T-intersection, and when she reached the juncture, Marina paused. Which way?

She looked right, and then left, and then—

Her heart gave a little bump. Was the area a more charcoal gray than ink black down toward the left? Marina hesitated just for a moment, then started down in that direction.

Now that she was out of sight of Eli and any signal he might give her, she moved more quickly. The sooner to return…

The end of the passage was definitely gray. Not black.

Dressed as she was in the protective clothing, Marina couldn't feel any change in the air, but she hurried along quickly, taking less care to keep the squeeze light cupped. The pelting insects were simply part of the environment, and she had this sense of urgency that propelled her on. Whether it was because she wanted to get back to Eli, or because of what she might discover, she didn't know.

Suddenly, she saw it. On the floor, bathed in a wedge of dark gray.

Something that didn't belong there—a crumpled heap, a lumpy shadow…

A body.

A human body.

Marina hesitated for half a second, then moved toward the prone figure. It was obvious even at first glance that the woman— she was dressed in something pink—wasn't merely sleeping or resting.

Yes, it was a woman. And she was wearing track pants, and a tank top…Marina shone the light over the still body, her heart pounding.

Cora Allegan.

The squeeze light clearly identified the missing CEO, even though her face and décolletage were red and blotchy with frightening-looking hives. Marina had seen enough photos of the woman, thanks to Gabe, and she had no doubt of the identification. Allegan was wearing the same clothing she'd had on when abducted.

Still cloaked in her protective gear, Marina put her light on the ground and stepped on it with her toe so she had two hands with which to work.

"Cora?" she said, feeling for a pulse. Even through her gloves, she felt the heat of the woman's skin burning through the stretchy material. No pulse…or else it was very weak.

Placing a hand on Cora's chest, Marina waited to see if it would rise and fall…and after a long, tense moment, it did.

She was still alive. But not for long; it was clear she was well into the late stages of the bacterial infection from the beetles.

"Cora? Can you hear me?" she said. "I'm here to help you."

Then Marina scrambled to her feet. *The antibiotics.* She had the antibiotic on her—or what she and Eli believed was the treatment—deep in the pockets of her cargo pants. Beneath the protective covering of her suit.

Damn.

If Cora went into sudden cardiac arrest, there'd be no help for her. It might yet be too late for the antibiotic, but she had to at least try.

Marina looked around hastily. Cora must have come in here somehow…hadn't she? If there was another way out, Marina could—no, *wait.*

I'll run back to Eli, tell him what's going on, and get the antibiotic prepared in the safe room.

She wouldn't tell him how many beetles she trounced on the way to and from, however.

No. There wasn't time. She would take off the suit right here, pull out the antibiotic, and give it to Cora now. *No time to waste.*

She began to unfasten the suit, her fingers quick and brisk... then paused. *Don't want to contaminate the treatment.* Who knew what was in the air, or what might happen—insects were still buzzing around.

She'd just have to be careful. But her gloves were tinged with the bacteria too...if she took them off, she'd be exposed, and if she left them on, she'd likely infect herself as well as corrupt the medication.

Marina was hardly ever this indecisive. She waffled, then decided five more minutes wouldn't likely make a difference to Cora—but could keep her and the antidote from being contaminated.

"I'll be right back," she said to Cora—who thus far had given no indication of awareness. "Five minutes. With a treatment."

Hoping she'd made the right decision, Marina bolted away from the prone woman, dashing down the corridor, squeeze light bobbing in her hands. The insects were infuriated by the wild light, small as it was, and they swarmed and whirled in an angry maelstrom that attacked her as she ran.

When she got in sight of the window, she didn't see Eli.

Marina's heart surged into her throat as she dashed to the glass and peered through.

The chamber was empty. Hedron and Eli were gone.

And when she rushed to try the door leading back into the room...

It was locked.

THIRTY-THREE

September 30

"Any news from Inez?" Helen asked as Gabe walked into her office without knocking. It was five in the morning and still dark outside. He'd gone back to the hotel at midnight and she'd dozed on a sofa in the break room, waiting for an update from Tech. Not that she'd slept much, and from the looks of it, he hadn't either.

And here he was, barging in without warning—what if she'd been changing her blouse (as she often did after a night on the break room couch), or on a personal call?—and without the very necessary accessory of a cup of some sort of caffeine.

"That's exactly why I'm here," he said, settling himself on the corner of her desk—another habit of his that she found irritating.

It was good to remind herself of Gabe's imperfections, in light of spending hours working this closely with him again. It would be so easy to fall back into—well, whatever it was she had felt for him when they were together. So why couldn't the guy sit on a freaking chair? Why did he have to perch right on the edge of her desk, too close and sort of looming over her?

He looked exhausted. And he'd done a hasty job shaving this morning, with a patch of missed stubble in front of his left ear lobe. He smelled good, though, which didn't help the situation, along with the fact that his hair was disheveled so he looked like a tousled little boy—or like he'd just had sex.

She pushed away the distractions and gave him—or more accurately, his information—her full attention. "All right, then let's hear it."

"Inez sent a preliminary list of upcoming events in the US that could be considered to support industries that have poor environmental records. There might be ones internationally, but since the Skalas started here with the blackout, we're working under the assumption they're going to stay here."

"I agree."

"There's one particular candidate that looks promising—it's an event in Vegas on the first. After that, there's really nothing that pings until after the first of the year. A few smaller, regional events, but nothing this big."

"October first? That's *tomorrow*. Damn, that's tight." Her brain began to buzz with thoughts, probabilities, plans. She sipped her chai, noticing Gabe's eyes following the cup. Apparently he'd forgotten to get his own. Probably breakfast too. He always had been ravenous in the morning. She strictly turned her thoughts back on track. "All right. Tell me more."

"It's a big convention of food conglomerates—you know, the ones who have the factory farms, and the chicken and cattle ranches. If you can call them ranches," he added ruefully. "The cows are packed in, the chickens stuck in their carrels, and let's not talk about what they do for veal. Plus we all know what effect these industries have on the environment. The Skaladeskas probably wouldn't be happy about that. We're looking at almost two thousand attendees."

"There was that agribusiness meeting in St. Louis that was canceled because of the blackout," Helen said. "The Skalas could be targeting food producers this time, instead of automobile manufacturers."

"That's why I zoned in on the one in Vegas. Like I said, there are other possibilities, but that one seemed most likely. Biggest bang for the buck. Inez, the goddess, is already cross-checking the attendees and corporations with the list from the flash drive," Gabe said.

"If Varden is on his way west, that would be a good sign."

"Right. But he's not. He's in Michigan. At least, according to the tracker."

"Which could be on a semi."

"Yep."

Helen's eyes narrowed. "They couldn't be targeting something in Detroit again, could they?"

"Well, if so, at least you'll be familiar with the area." His lips stretched in a wry smile. "But that's a good thought. I'll look more closely at the list and let Inez know to watch especially for pings in Michigan."

"All right. But how else can we narrow this down?" she said.

They looked at each other. After a moment, she broke contact and shook her head. "Not even sure what we should be looking for. Beetles? It's not like they're big equipment or explosives. It'd be nearly impossible to find them. How many do they need? How big of a box or crate would they have to put them in?"

"Can't imagine they'd need a large crew for this either— releasing a box of insects is a one-man job."

"Probably." She wanted to sink her head into her hands and rub her temples in hopes of making her brain work better... or at least slow down. But the words kept coming as fast as her mouth could form them. "Unless they've got something more involved planned. Insects can be unpredictable, so maybe they're going to release them in a closed room, to make sure they hit whatever target they want? Or into the ventilation system? Would the bacteria get into the ventilation system and spread that way? What about into the food?"

"But would they do something as simple as exposing a group of people to the bacteria, and then wait for three days for them to die? That just doesn't seem...flashy enough."

"No. Not after fake earthquakes. Still...in a creepy sort of way, it makes sense. The Skaladeskas are all about Mother Earth, and maybe their choice of weapon or tool is always going to be something from the earth. You know, as if she's giving them the tools. Using only natural things. The insects are 'hers,' if you will."

"Earthquakes are natural," he said, nodding. "Last time they manufactured earthquakes."

"I sure as hell hope they don't ever figure out how to create tsunamis," she said grimly.

"You don't look like you've been getting much sleep." Gabe slid off the corner of her desk and wandered over to stare at her whiteboard.

"Goes with the territory."

"Yeah." He picked up a marker and under her neatly printed *Possible Targets* heading, he scrawled, *October 1, Vegas, Int'l Beef, Poultry & Dairy Producers Convention.* Then he added: *Detroit (?)* and looked at the board. "I should go to Vegas. Just see if there's anything that pings. Maybe you want to check out Detroit?"

"Not a bad idea. And Bergstrom will authorize you to go to Vegas?"

"Hell yeah. He wants to nail these guys as much as I do. Though I haven't told him I know about Nora and Roman Aleksandrov."

"Probably better if you don't for now. I have a feeling he'd be mortified if he knew we knew. It's…well, it's a challenge keeping our personal life from influencing our professional decisions."

She swore the back of his neck, only visible from the side because his hair was long enough to brush his collar, turned pink. "I know you think I'm blinded by love for Marina Alexander, and it's influencing my decisions," Gabe said, still facing the whiteboard. "But I'm not."

Suddenly, she didn't want to continue this conversation. "Look, MacNeil, I didn't mean anything by that comment except as a review of my own actions. When I pulled Jerome Blankenship in here for questioning about Allegan's disappearance, I already hated—well, intensely disliked—the man because I knew he'd been cheating on his wife. I'd sort of been in her shoes; not that I was a wife or anything, but I—well, anyway, my feelings came out in my handling of Blankenship as a witness. I was impolite, cold, and gave it to him a lot harder than I needed to."

Gabe's shoulders relaxed a little. "I'm sorry. Is that why you aren't seeing Geoff Garrett anymore? Or was it someone else?"

Helen was shocked he'd even known about Geoff, let alone that he knew they weren't together any longer. "Yes."

"Idiot."

"I had a few stronger words than that for the guy," she muttered, then picked up her tablet. Time to move on from the personal topics back to more pressing ones. She held up her tablet and its information like a little electronic shield. "So you want to go to Vegas." That wouldn't be a bad thing—at least he wouldn't be in her office every day. And Detroit was less than an hour flight for her…

He turned from the whiteboard. "We don't have anything else to go on. I'm at a loss. I—" There was a soft chime from the vicinity of his coat pocket. "Finally." He pulled out his smartphone. "I've been trying to download my email all morning, and the damned Wi-Fi was acting up or something."

Helen, who'd had no such trouble, returned to her tablet and scrolled through the notes she'd already reviewed multiple times, including a new report from Tom from Tech. There'd been nothing on Marina Alexander's laptop that was questionable or raised any concerns, and—

A noise from Gabe snatched her attention.

"An email from Marina," he said, stabbing at the phone. "Damn," he muttered, stabbing again, more violently, as if the touchscreen wasn't responding.

Another reason Helen was lukewarm about technology.

He fidgeted, swearing under his breath as he stared at the device, clearly waiting for the email to load. Helen could tell when it did, for he stilled, his eyes moving rapidly over it—twice—then he looked up at her. "She's alive. Been treated—presumably Sanchez too, though she doesn't say specifically. And—this is not good news—she says 'learned bacterial infection can spread by touch.' Since we already know it comes from the bugs, does that mean from person to person?"

"That would not be good." Helen's chest tightened. "If they release beetles in a room, and people are infected and then they leave and touch anyone else before they realize what it is…it'll be an epidemic before we can even stop it." She looked grimly at him. "Is that flashy enough for you?"

Gabe muttered a word Helen didn't usually use, but in this case, she wholeheartedly agreed. "I don't know. Marina was obviously interrupted while sending this, because she didn't finish typing it." His knuckles were white where he gripped the device. "I don't believe the Skalas would hurt her. And if I know Marina, she'll do everything she can to protect Sanchez."

"I agree with you. When did she send the message? Is there a time stamp? We can get Tech on it and trace the ISP and maybe the location—but you already know that. Did it say anything else?"

"Yes. And I'm not sure what she means. She says, 'Check my phone. Listen,' and that's it."

Helen dug Marina's phone out of her desk drawer, and handed it—still in its plastic bag—to Gabe. "We listened to all her voice mails—current, deleted, and even recovered ones."

"I know. What else would we listen to?" He unfastened the plastic bag and pulled out the device. Helen had kept it on and charged so they would have instant knowledge of any incoming texts or calls that could assist. "The ring tone? Music?"

"Wait! Check her voice memos." Helen almost snatched the phone out of his hand in her excitement. "She recorded something she wants us to hear. Maybe when the Skaladeskas were taking them."

Gabe started to scroll through the phone, then stopped. "No, wait—not the voice memos." His voice was almost as excited as Helen's. "The camera. You know how easy it is to get to the camera and video setting on these phones—one button, pushed unobtrusively, and the phone is recording."

She crowded next to him, leaning over his shoulder this time, as he found it. "Yes. Here it is—two days ago. The last thing on her phone."

They both held their breaths as he pushed the button.

Immediately, there were scuffling noises, the sounds of people moving, low, indistinct voices speaking, shuffling, rustling. The screen remained dark and shadowed, as if the phone had been placed on a surface. But they could hear...

Hardly more than snatches.

Helen sensed Gabe's frustration, and without thinking too hard about it, she closed her fingers around his bicep in a steadying grip and moved in closer. Still they listened, their breathing falling into a synchronized rhythm. Straining, listening...

A few phrases—a command here and there, Marina's clear alto voice responding flatly to a few baritone and bass tones—but hardly anything discernible, until...they must have moved closer to the phone.

"...won't be in touch, but you..."

"Roman...on...as planned."

"...on the first..."

"Let's go."

Then the noises changed, and there was the sound of a door opening, then the distinct noise of it clanging shut. Then silence.

Helen stepped back, removing her hand. "There's more."

"It must have continued to record after they left." Gabe stared at it, his frustration obvious. "And then stopped on its own. It was dead when I found it." He stopped the video.

"I'm sure Tech can get more out of that conversation."

Helen nodded. "But at least we have something."

The first.

On the first.

If that wasn't a clue, what was?

THIRTY-FOUR

University of Michigan
Biochemistry Lab 24D
Ann Arbor

Quinn Suszko stifled a yawn and jammed the key into the lock of the laboratory door. That had been a *late* night last night, but she and Jessie had gotten into a *Friends* binge-watch on Netflix, and once you got the episodes flowing…well, it was hard to look away. *Just one more*, they kept saying.

But she'd told Dr. Milani she'd be into the lab by seven o'clock today to finish up the grant—it had to be submitted by midnight—and even though she and Jessie had turned off "The One With All the Thanksgivings" at four o'clock in the freaking a.m., Quinn was here. Right on time.

Well, almost. It was seven-oh-five…but no one else was—*hey.*

"Hello?" she called, setting her almost-empty Sweetwaters to-go cup on the table. Either an early riser was here in the chem lab, or someone—not her, thank goodness, because Milani would have a cow—had left a light on in the other room.

"Back here," called a voice, and Quinn heard a soft clink and some other noises that might have been definable if she didn't have a little bit of a headache from a couple too many Sam Adamses and an overdose of Netflix.

She picked up her coffee cup again, drained it, and tossed it into the recycle bin, then wandered back to see who in the hell had beaten her into the lab on a Sunday morning. Probably Ahlahna Brown, the overachiever. Why the hell hadn't Milani asked *her* to come in on Sunday at the crack of dawn to finish the grant?

But Quinn knew why—because she, not Ahlahna, was the best writer in the lab, and she had already done four grants this year. They were tedious, but she knew what she was doing, and she was damn good at them.

When Quinn poked around into the back room of the lab, she stopped short. There was an unfamiliar man at one of the stations, muttering to himself as he worked.

Well, well…how you *doin'?*

Blond, broad-shouldered, rangy of build, and—*whoa.* Those green eyes had to be contacts, right?

"Hi," she said, making the word more of a question than a mere greeting. "Um…can I help you?"

"Good morning," said the man who exuded some major raw sexuality. He returned to his work, which included a heat plate with a flask and several bottles scattered around. "Can you grab me that acetone there?"

"Um…sure…?" Quinn did as requested, for by now she'd seen his University of Michigan ID badge clipped to the white lab coat he wore. The pic looked like him, but she couldn't read his name because of the way the badge hung, nestled behind his arm. "Are you a friend of Doc Milani's?" She set the acetone next to him and tried to figure out what he was doing.

There was a prescription bottle of…she squinted at the small letters…ciprofloxacn? And a bottle of methyl ethyl ketone.

"Got to methylate the c3 position on the second phenyl group," he muttered…and she wasn't certain whether he was talking to her or himself.

"Um…" she said again, feeling very uncertain. The guy had a badge, he clearly belonged here and knew what he was doing, but…

Suddenly he looked up. Those green eyes fastened on her, and Quinn felt a little weak in the knees. And it wasn't because she was hung over and tired. Dang. He was *hot*. "Sorry," he said. "I'll be done here in a minute. Didn't think anyone would be here so early on a Sunday."

He had a little bit of an accent she couldn't place—but half the students, faculty, and staff at U of M did. If she had to guess, she'd put him as British or something like that, but he looked Scandinavian or maybe Slavic.

"Don't let me keep you," he said, returning to his work. "I'm sure you're here so early because you have things to do."

"Right. I...what was your name again?" Quinn said, wondering if she should call Milani. But on a Sunday? At seven? She shuddered. If the guy was a friend of the doc's, he would *not* be pleased.

He mumbled something—presumably his name—but she couldn't understand him, and thought it would be rude to press. After all, it wasn't as if he was doing anything dangerous—like making an explosive or anything.

In fact, he was working with an antibiotic. Almost as if he were trying to morph it into something else, like a different strain of an antibiotic or something like that. She frowned. That did make sense—*methylate the c3 on the*—what had he said? The third phenyl? No, second. That would effectively alter an antibiotic into something else...possibly useful.

Quinn backed from the room and pulled out her phone. Should she call Milani or not? She hesitated, then stuck it back in her pocket. Then pulled it back out.

She had it in her hands, ready to press Send, when the guy appeared. He strode from the back room like a man on a mission, and crossed the lab before Quinn could speak. He was holding a small bottle filled with dark red liquid.

"Thanks. Have a great day," he said, tucking the bottle into his lab coat. Then he walked out the door without a hitch in his step.

She blinked, then slipped the phone back in her pocket, staring after him.

Quinn locked the door (though what good that would do, since he'd obviously gotten in somehow anyway) and went into the back room.

What the—?

He'd left everything out and unwashed. A big mess.

Damn. Wasn't that just like a guy?

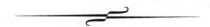

Marina stared at the locked door where she'd left Eli, then tried it a second time. When it didn't open, she spun around and began to rush, willy-nilly, back to where she'd found Cora Allegan.

Eli.

Now she had to figure out how to save him *and* Allegan.

Hedron must have awakened and surprised Eli from behind— while he was watching his amazing beetles.

One thing at a time, she reminded herself. *Allegan first.*

Then what? How was she going to drag the ill woman back… and where to? If there was another exit from the temple, maybe she could find her way to the main compound…but how would that help?

Maybe Roman had lied and they hadn't released Cora Allegan into the jungle, but had just shoved her into the copper temple with the beetles, knowing she'd die—at the hands of Gaia.

Marina's mind whirled with possibilities and worries.

One thing at a time.

Allegan hadn't moved from where she left her, and Marina knelt next to her once more to determine whether the woman was still breathing and had a pulse. She had to figure out a way to prepare the antibiotic without contaminating it. The woman's condition hadn't changed—her pulse was very weak, and her breathing shallow but steady.

Marina stood, shining her tiny light around. The pelting insects no longer bothered her; it was like being in a hailstorm.

The light fell on Cora Allegan's shoes, and Marina stepped closer to examine them.

Mud. Green streaks. A stalk of grass clung to the treads, glued there by the mud.

There was no mud in the temple. The floor was made from copper. Cora Allegan had to have come from the outside.

Marina bolted to her feet, shining the light onto the walls and ceiling. The insects didn't like this, but she ignored them when she saw the wedge of gray in a corner.

It was an opening. Hardly large enough for an arm to fit through…how had Cora Allegan come through there?

Marina's fingers were becoming sore from pinching the light for so long. She let it go out and tucked it into her pocket. The insects calmed. She curled her fingers on what seemed to be the edge of the opening, and pulled.

It moved…slid wider, then, when she released it, the heavy—wall? door?—eased back nearly closed. But she'd seen enough: there was light beyond. Pale, faint, but definite light.

Marina pulled at the wall again, her feet solid against the floor in their boots, and it eased open once more. She slid herself around the edge of it and pushed…*pushed*…and then it was wide enough for her to slip through.

A delicate gray light filtered down from above, making a small circle in the center of the floor. And on the far wall, there was a tall, slender rectangle of darker gray.

Suddenly, a flash of light filled the space, and Marina jolted in shock…but it was followed by the familiar rumble of thunder, and she realized it was going to storm. That was why the light was dark and gray.

But that told her: there was a way out. She was there.

And…there seemed to be no beetles here in this small antechamber.

Marina yanked off the helmet and drew in a gulp of cool, fresh, damp air. Conscious of the ill woman left on the floor behind her, she hurried toward what was clearly an opening to the outside world. A heavy stone door, plated with oxidized copper, stood slightly ajar...and beyond it was the jungle: dim, wet, still but for the thrashing by pounding, whipping rain. It was quite a storm.

Another flash of light caught her by surprise, illuminating the shuddering trees, bushes, and grass that rose beyond the opening. Only a moment later, the thunder rumbled, loud and threatening. It echoed eerily in this ancient, tomblike chamber where a woman lay dying.

Marina made a quick decision. She replaced her helmet and went back to the sliding wall. It had rolled back into place, leaving Cora Allegan on the other side of a too-small opening. Her best option would be to try and move the woman out of the beetle-ridden chamber to where she could attempt to treat her without fear of contaminating either of them further—or the medicine.

Once again, Marina muscled it open, positioning herself between the edge of the moving wall and the side of the cave and using the full weight of her body to push it. But as soon as she slipped back inside, it slid back into place. *Damn.* How was she going to get Allegan out of here?

At the same time, the knowledge that Eli was in the hands of the Skaladeskas—who had no reason to keep him alive now that Marina was gone, and every reason to silence a man who knew too many of their secrets—filled her with anxiety and fear.

If only she hadn't left him...if only she hadn't gone out of sight...

But Marina knew better than to allow herself to become paralyzed with regrets and anxiety. She ruthlessly put the thoughts away and bent once more to check her patient.

"Cora? Can you hear me? I'm here to—"

Marina's words strangled off as two booted feet came into view. Startled, she looked up at the hazmat-suited figure looming over her.

THIRTY-FIVE

Marina stared up at the suited figure. The white clothing seemed to draw what little illumination there was, making the fabric appear to glow in the dark. But she couldn't see the face behind the black plastic plate of the helmet.

"Marina?"

"Eli!" She surged to her feet, and he caught her by the arm to help steady her. "What happened?"

"Who's this?" he asked at the same time.

"This is Cora Allegan," she replied. "She's still alive. I want to give her the antibiotic—I don't know if it's too late or not—"

"That's a way out?" he said, just as a flash of lightning surged beyond the small opening, sending a shaft of illumination into the chamber beyond. Some of the beetles swirled into a frenzy once again, but Marina ignored them.

"Yes, a way out—once the storm ends." She was still buzzing with relief that he was alive, free, and wearing a suit. She could get the details as to how later. "The opening isn't wide enough to get her through—help me," she said. The thunder answered, loud and overhead. The noise made the chamber shudder, as if Gaia herself was in agreement.

Or not.

Marina shoved away the unpleasant thought.

Together, she and Eli found it an easy task to move Cora Allegan through the opening. He lifted the woman and carried her, while Marina held the sliding wall ajar. Just as they made their way through, it began to rain. Water streamed down through the opening in the ceiling, but because of the rainforest's canopy of trees, the brunt of the pounding rain was interrupted.

Nevertheless, this left only a small area where Cora could lie without getting wet or splashed. Once they settled her off to the side away from the growing damp, Marina removed her helmet. After a brief hesitation, Eli did the same. She looked up at him, about to explain her plan, but he grabbed her by the shoulders and pulled her to him for a hard, fast kiss.

"More to come," he said, looking down at her in the dim light, "but that'll do for now. I thought you were—well, I didn't know where you were, and—what the hell happened?"

"I should ask you the same question," she said, taking off her gloves carefully. Then she began unfastening her suit. "I came back to tell you what I found, but you and Hedron were gone." She fumbled one of the small vials of red liquid from her cargo pocket. "I want to give this to her. Don't know if it's too late, but I have to try. Can you hold the light?" She stepped on it gently so he could see it.

"Yep. And I have the gel they put on me too. You can dig it out of my pocket." He picked up the squeeze light—which she'd been holding with contaminated gloves, so couldn't touch with her bare hands—and held it in place as Marina gave her attention to the syringe and antibiotic.

"What happened?" she asked as she slid the cannula into Cora Allegan's arm and slowly pushed the plunger.

"You disappeared, and you didn't come back…I didn't know what happened. I was getting very worried, and I didn't know what else to do, so I started—er—waking up Hedron. I might have gotten a little…well, insistent—but I was pretty worried. Finally he came around, and I had the gun on him. I used it as an incentive for him to give me the door code, then I bonked him on the head again. Left him in the room we were in—you couldn't have seen him, because he was right under the window. I grabbed a suit and then I came after you."

"I thought he'd come awake and they'd taken you off somewhere," she said, sitting back on her haunches. Cora Allegan hadn't moved or made any indication of awareness as she gave her the injection. "I hope that works. Where's that gel?"

"Left side pocket," said Eli, unfastening his suit and holding it away so she could slip her ungloved hand down inside without touching the outside.

She tried not to think about the intimacy of the situation, though several "or are you just happy to see me?" jokes taunted her. He might have been feeling the same way, for when she stepped away with the tube in hand, she saw his mouth was quirked in a half-smile.

"Such a tease," was all he said, shaking his head.

Lightning flashed, and the thunder boomed so loudly they both looked toward the dark gray opening.

"I don't think we're going anywhere soon," he said. His words were light, but his face was sober.

"Whatever we do, we have to take her with us."

"And somehow find our way out of here—to the airstrip where we landed." He released a long breath and stared out at the storm. "That's going to be interesting."

Marina stood and went to the entrance. It was getting a little lighter outside. The shadows had more definition, and even through the steady downpour—which would have been much stronger if there hadn't been so many tall, thick trees—she saw the shapes of their trunks and surrounding bushes. A flash of lightning blinded her and illuminated the inside of the chamber, sending the beetles into their frenzy.

But this time, she was standing near the entrance and saw some of the insects buzz through the opening. All of a sudden there were small pops of light outside, like fireflies glowing then being immediately squelched.

"Sanchez," she said. "Look at this!"

He came to the opening, and a moment later the lightning flashed again. More beetles whipped into a frenzy, careening out of the doorway and into the electrically charged air.

"Holy Mother of God," he whispered, watching the copper coleops combust: flaring with light then exploding into nothing with a soft sizzle. "They're *frying*. Right in mid-flight. I can't believe this…" He stared in wonder, apparently not all that broken up about the sudden deaths of numerous of his little darlings. "All the electricity in the air from the storm…it's just…incredible…" They stared out in wonder at the storm and the havoc it wreaked on the beetles.

Marina heard a strange sound behind her and turned. With a shout, she lunged toward Cora Allegan, who was shuddering and writhing on the ground. The woman wasn't conscious, and this was just what Marina had feared.

"CPR," she muttered, ready to dive forward—but Eli caught her.

"She's contaminated," he said, pulling Marina back. He slapped gloves into her hands. "Put these on."

Thankful for his quick thinking, she yanked on the coverings, but he'd already begun the chest compressions with his gloved hands. Marina watched anxiously, knowing it was extremely unlikely they could save Cora Allegan without a defibrillator. And giving mouth-to-mouth was not only risky for contamination, it was secondary to keeping the chest compressions steady and without pause.

Nevertheless, she considered trying it with her headgear on… but when she picked up her helmet, Eli looked at her. "No. Don't risk it," he said between compressions. "You know this is a long shot anyway."

She muttered, but realized he was right. After all, if something happened to her, Eli would have little to no chance of escaping the Skaladeskas—unless he knew how to fly a plane or could talk himself out of Roman's custody. Neither of which she thought was likely.

"My turn," she said after a few minutes. But their patient had subsided into stillness, and she knew their chances were even lower now. Even so, she and Eli switched places just as lightning flashed from the outside once more. A few of the beetles popped and sizzled near the top of the chamber. This time, Marina felt a little jolt of electricity herself, in this small space.

Both of them looked up, then stared at each other.

"Is there any way"—*compress*—"we could use that?" she huffed in time with her compressions. "Channel that"—*compress*—"energy?"

"Like a defibrillator." He bolted to his feet, looking around as if trying to figure out how to build one… "Maybe with a metal rod, we could…I don't know, attract the lightning somehow… and channel it into her heart?" He shook his head, as if knowing how ridiculous it sounded.

But… "What about a bunch of dead…beetles?" Marina said, still compressing. Cora Allegan had given no sign of response thus far. Marina paused and put her ear to the woman's chest, careful not to touch her skin directly.

"My turn," said Eli.

Her arms were tired, so Marina moved back and let him take over, looking around for something to use that might help. But she had no better idea than Eli how to use the beetles to create a defibrillator.

Then she saw something glinting on the floor near the entrance, just inside the door. "She must have dropped this," Marina said, picking up a water bottle (still full), a knife, and a *gun*. "Whoa."

A flash of lightning lit Eli's face as he looked up at her. "That might come"—*compress*—"in handy."

"I'll say."

The crash of thunder was so close and loud Marina jolted, and she felt the earth move beneath her feet.

Gaia is angry.

The thought popped into her mind and she automatically took a step away from the entrance. What an odd thing to think. She frowned, looking around, and tried to dismiss the odd, unsettling sensation.

Yet when she came to sit back on the ground near Eli and Cora, Marina placed her hand on the ground next to her…as if to feel for Gaia's own heartbeat.

"My turn," she said, catching Eli's eye.

He sat back and let her take over, but surely he knew as well as she did that it was a lost cause. There was no saving Cora Allegan…and that meant yet another death was to be put at the feet of Roman Aleksandrov, Lev, and the other Skaladeskas.

All in the name of Gaia.

THIRTY-SIX

By the time the Marina and Eli gave up on working on Cora Allegan, the storm had stopped. Light filtered through the soaking leaves and brush, and when Marina pulled out Hedron's cell phone—which still had no bars—she saw the time was almost nine in the morning.

"If the Skaladeskas haven't figured out we're missing yet, they will soon," she said, giving one last look at Cora Allegan.

They would have to leave her body here, but Marina and Eli covered the woman with their protective suits—which they wouldn't need as long as they weren't in the temple—and left her in a corner away from the entrance.

"With any luck it'll take them a while to find Hedron and realize we've come out this way," said Eli. They'd already decided to close the outside door to the temple when they left. That would protect Cora's body from wild animals until—if—they could somehow come back for it.

"If they even know there is a way out through the temple," Marina said. "I think Cora stumbled on it by accident. Look at how overgrown and hidden the entrance is. Those vines look as if they were just recently torn away—they're still green and fresh, just wilting. And she obviously came from the outside—look at her shoes."

By now they stood in the thick, dim jungle. Rain dripped randomly from leaves and lianas, and the air was heavy with moisture. Sunlight dappled the ground, fighting its way through the heavy overbrush to mottle the area with illumination.

Marina drew in a deep breath, suddenly acutely aware of the beauty, the depth, the lushness of Gaia's world. She felt a shiver of sensation flutter through her as she closed her eyes and simply... felt.

Whether Eli sensed her preoccupation or not, she wasn't certain, but he didn't speak. She didn't know how long she stood there, one hand planted on the rough, stony exterior of the temple's cavern, and the other touching a rain-spotted leaf. She felt the energy, the life, buzzing through her.

At last, she opened her eyes. Eli was watching her, but silent. There was no judgment or surprise in his expression. He seemed, somehow, to understand.

Nevertheless, Marina felt unusually self-conscious about her lapse of attention. She spoke brusquely. "Let's try to find our way to the airstrip where the plane landed. I can fly us out of here if we can get there."

"And if the plane is still there," Eli reminded her with a grim smile.

"That would help."

Their situation was dire, but not as dire as Cora Allegan's had been. Both Eli and Marina had spent time in the Amazon and knew more than basic survival skills. Still...if they got lost, the longer they spent in the jungle, the less likely they'd live to tell the tale.

"I want to draw a map of the temple and how we came out of the building," he said, "so we can orient ourselves."

"Good plan. If we can navigate our way back to where we came in to the compound, we should be able to follow the trail back to the airstrip."

Eli was able to use the tip of Cora Allegan's knife to scratch a makeshift map in the soft copper floor of the temple's antechamber. The soft spill of light through the opening helped illuminate his drawing.

"No, we turned left there," said Marina.

"You're right. And then came out here," he said, correcting his sketch.

"Exactly. And if we go nor—"

They both froze, looking up. Marina felt a rush of unease prickling her shoulders, and they bolted to their feet at the same time.

Neither of them needed to speak. They'd heard the same thing: voices.

Voices coming from deep inside the temple.

Still without words, they slipped from the antechamber and tried to muscle the door back into place. Rain from the leaves and vines pattered down on them as they struggled with the heavy stone door.

"How did she get this open by herself?" Marina muttered.

"Don't know," Eli said. "Maybe some sort of lever we can't find?"

But the voices were close now—distinct, echoing in the copper-plated corridor.

Marina and Eli had no choice. They had to run, and the open exit and discarded suits would clearly indicate their path.

Armed only with a single bottle of water, a knife, and the gun with one bullet, as well as Hedron's non-working cell phone, Marina and Eli hurried off into the jungle, following the route they believed would take them back to the main compound entrance.

They were still in earshot of the temple when she heard the voice calling after them: "Mariska! You cannot survive out there. Return, and we will release your companion."

"Right," she muttered to Eli as they stepped over a fallen log, pushing through the wet leaves and bushes. "Notice he doesn't say what they'll do for me." She stopped. "But they won't hurt *me*. And I can make certain they'll release you." She turned, ready to go back, but Eli grabbed her arm. "I told you, they'll negotiate with me—"

"I don't think so," he said. "I'll take my chances with you out here, rather than trusting them to let me go. Look what happened to Cora Allegan when they set her free."

She gave him a brief smile, and looked up at the sky. The path to the sun was blocked by the tall trees, and it was difficult to tell where it was and what direction they were going. *North.*

"And if you think I'd actually leave you here with them, not only are you crazy, but you insult me. Let's go," he said. "This way."

Marina followed, still glancing up at the sky. She thought he was right.

She *hoped* he was right.

I hope to hell I'm doing the best thing.

I hope we figure out where we are before nightfall.

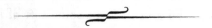

The sun was high overhead, filtering through the canopy, when Marina grabbed Eli's arm and pointed. "There. That's got to be part of the compound wall. See that through the trees?"

"And so it is."

They looked at each other. They'd found it…now all they needed to do was make their way around to the entrance of the compound without being seen…then follow the dubious path to the airstrip.

It sounded simple.

The jungle was filled with sounds—but all of Gaia's making. No voices or human noises filled the air. Birds sang, chirped, and warned. A breeze riffled through the trees above. The call from some mammal reverberated in the distance. Invisible creatures rustled in the grasses. A snake wound itself around a sapling. Heavy floral scents wafted through the humid air, and the smaller leaves were nearly dry by now. Insects buzzed and whirred.

They'd been hiking, slowly and carefully, for more than two hours. Earlier there'd been plenty of water collected in large leaves from which to drink. They saved the water bottle. And Eli had snagged a few dried berries and shared them with her when they stopped to listen for their pursuers.

Marina still wore the boots from her protective suit—better for hiking than the sandals she'd had on. But her arms were bare in the short-sleeved tee, and she was scratched and cut in a variety of places. She was more than a little hungry, and beginning to tire.

Yet the voices were long behind them. They may not have even followed them into the jungle.

But now, as they drew near the front of the compound, the risk they'd be seen became greater. But perhaps…perhaps that wouldn't be the worst thing. At least in the compound, they'd have food, plenty of water, and shelter.

And the library.

Marina paused. "Eli…"

"What happened to all the formality of 'Dr. Sanchez'?" he asked, then immediately shook his head. "Don't even suggest it. I don't trust them. I trust you—and me. Together. We made it this far."

"And if the plane isn't there?"

"We'll cross that bridge when we come to it."

She nodded, and they set off once more, sticking as close to the compound wall as possible.

"I see it," he said.

"The entrance?"

"No, the trail we walked. From the airstrip. There. I might have been in a fog, but I remember that banyan with the large red bromeliad. See how it's cupped by that large root—like a hand?"

Gaia's hand. "Yes. Let's go."

They ducked beneath a group of low-hanging lianas, watching the ground for dangerous reptiles and insects as they made their way more quickly and confidently.

The trail was fairly well marked, and Marina's pulse began to race as they hurried along. They kept just off the pathway, skirting palms and bushes, fallen trunks, and crossing small ditches. She avoided a snake, and nearly grabbed a small, bright-colored frog once when she reached out to steady herself. She thought it was a flower…

When they caught sight of the metal hangar—hangar being an optimistic word for the decrepit metal structure that would hardly be large enough to hold the plane—Marina drew in a deep, slow breath. Disappointment and something like fear settled over her.

The airstrip was nothing to write home about—only a long, narrow patch of short grass with a few iffy tire tracks—but it would work. The entire area was silent and still, but, to her dismay, the RV-5 was nowhere in sight. If she didn't know better, hadn't landed there two days ago, Marina wouldn't have believed it.

"Maybe the plane's inside," she whispered, uncertain why she felt the urge to keep her voice low.

They stepped out from the cover of the brush and began to skirt their way along the edge of the clearing. At the very least, they could find shelter in the hangar.

Just as they approached, the large door in the building rolled open.

"I thought you'd come here," said Roman, stepping out into the clearing. Two others flanked him.

Marina spun, but Eli grabbed her arm—and she saw.

They were holding guns.

Well, that was new.

THIRTY-SEVEN

We're leaving," Marina said, holding her father's gaze from across the clearing. "Cora Allegan is dead, thanks to you. I want nothing to do with you and your Skaladeskas—or your library."

Roman shook his head and stepped out of the hangar. His companions followed, still holding their weapons. "Gaia makes Her judgments. We merely facilitate delivering the offenders to Her."

Marina didn't bother to disguise her sneer. "That's not the way I work. This is new." She gestured to the firearms, irony in her movement and tone. For the first time, she noticed one of the people flanking him was Nora. The man was someone she didn't recognize.

Roman shrugged. "One must adjust one's tactics and strategy as necessary. What did you think you were going to do, Mariska? Fly away? Did you truly think we'd allow you to leave?"

By now he was very near, and Marina could see the glint in his eyes. In apparent deference, his two companions held back.

"And what about Dr. Sanchez?"

There was a flare of hope, perhaps, in Roman's expression. "If you stay, I will personally see to it that he is safely delivered to a neutral location. A *safe* neutral location."

"You will guarantee his safety. You'll provide me proof of it. *If* I remain."

"You must remain. But to prove we wish you and your companion no harm, as I say, I will ensure his safe departure and return. With proof."

"Why should I believe that? You and I both know the moment Dr. Sanchez is free, he'll contact the authorities with information about where you are and how to find you. I know you dare not risk that. So, I'd take my chances in the arms of Gaia rather than in your presence. After all I am her Heir, am I not—Father Mine?"

Roman blanched and his breath caught. But he recovered immediately. "How long have you known?"

"Since Victor died, five years ago. On a river in Siberia, in my presence. Those were his dying words. The more pertinent question, however, is whether my grandfather knows the truth."

His expression told her everything.

Marina lifted her chin. "I can only imagine why you and Victor would have kept such a secret."

"It no longer matters, if what you say is true—that my brother is dead. I suspected he was gone, but didn't know for certain." Roman regained his composure. "Now, if you please, let us return to the compound. There is no escape for you here, and you will not survive in the jungle—Heir to Gaia or no. Of course I was not so foolish as to leave you a mode of transport. But I will make the arrangements for Dr. Sanchez's safe return. And never fear, Mariska darling—he'll never be able to accurately describe this location to anyone. Thanks to the great accumulation of copper in our Gaia's belly here, electronics, radar, and any other tracking devices, we are—what do you say?—off the grid."

Marina had purposely avoided looking at Eli during the negotiation—for she was certain he'd never go for it. But she'd come to the conclusion, made the proper decision, that this time there would be no going back for anyone...that in order to save him, she would have to send him away.

She'd be the one left behind.

She would speak with Lev, make certain Eli was released safely, as Roman had promised. And perhaps she'd even use the knowledge of her father's lies about her paternity as leverage to ensure Dr. Sanchez's safety.

Eli, for his part, had made no sound or movement during the entire conversation. Now, she flickered a glance over him and was surprised to see him staring off to the side. There was an arrested expression on his face.

"Don't...move," he murmured from between stiff lips.

Marina froze.

"What is it?" Roman demanded—but he too became still.

"Over there," muttered Eli. "Behind—dammit, *don't move*!"

It wasn't Marina who'd turned to look, but Roman and his companions. They stopped.

"I don't see anything," said Roman. "There's nothing there."

Eli reached for Marina's arm, carefully, his eyes still trained just beyond Roman's head. "You're looking in the wrong place. The hive of a vasilijech coleopteron, a rare species of the regilorum suborder. It's above you—just above your head—*don't* move. My God, I've never seen—but we don't want to...disturb...it. *Jee-sus*...Marina, whatever you do—don't move. But...I really need to—"

"What the hell are you talking about? There's nothing there," Roman said. Yet tension strained his voice.

"Dr. Sanchez is a renowned entomologist," Marina said, her own heart racing. "He knows what he's talking about."

"The most deadly coleop in the Amazon," Eli said, edging away as if drawn by the sight. "And the most rare. One sting... Holy Mother of God...I'd really like to take a look," he said, moving a little more. "But they're very—"

"Are you *insane*?" Marina said.

"No," said Eli, still staring. "Just dedicated. Could you imagine? Two papers in one year..."

Marina looked in the direction he was staring. She saw nothing. Wait...was that a hive? Up high—yes, oh, yes, he was right. She grabbed his wrist. "Is that it?"

"What in the hell is going on?" Roman said, and was no longer able to keep from looking up and over his shoulder.

Eli moved quickly. He spun Marina by the arm, sending her whipping toward Nora as he body-slammed the man holding the gun. All three of the Skaladeskas tumbled roughly into each other, but Eli kept hold of Marina to keep her from joining them.

Then, just as he spun out of the melee, he raised Cora Allegan's gun and fired up above them.

"*Yes*," Eli muttered as something hurtled down from above.

Marina didn't see what it was, for he yanked her by the arm and bolted into the jungle as Roman and the others were scrambling to their feet. But she heard a dull thud, then the sounds of shouts, then terrified cries.

And then, the distinct sound of furious buzzing.

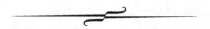

Eli released Marina as soon as they got into the thick part of the jungle. She was right on his heels as he tore through a patch of underbrush.

A bullet whizzed through the air and thudded into a tree. She could hear the sounds of their pursuers—beetles or bees or whatever had been in that hive notwithstanding—and Marina realized they couldn't continue to evade them.

Not without food, water, and rest—all of which they were sorely lacking. Not to mention the fact that they didn't know the area well, and presumably the Skalas had a better orientation. And that they had no more bullets.

Still, she kept up with Eli, wondering if he had any further plans. And wondering how much of what he'd said about the beetles in the hive—did that even make sense? did beetles have hives?—was true.

When he tripped over a hidden root and took a hard spill, she just missed tumbling into him herself. But she quickly pulled upright and turned to see Eli, pain wrenching his face.

"I twisted it—maybe even sprained it," he said, scrambling to his feet with the help of a dangling liana. "Damn." He tried to put some weight on his right foot, but Marina saw immediately how painful it was.

The voices and thrashing in the bushes were coming closer. Her heart thudded. How willing would Roman be to negotiate now? Would he be furious? They had guns…

"We need a place to hide." She spun around, looking, hoping for something to present itself in this patchy jungle. There were areas of thick overgrowth, and other areas of openness—like a lacy patchwork of texture. But what they needed was another temple, a cave, a *something*. Some hollow, some protective shelter. A hidden embrace from Gaia.

Gaia.

Without thinking too hard about what she was doing, Marina crouched, placing her hands directly on the ground. She closed her eyes and thought the name like a mantra, and felt a sizzle through her…as if something was surging up from the earth through her body. An awareness, a sense of life, consciousness, energy.

She felt the upheaval from the Mother, she felt her pain and confusion and sadness, and the churning heat of her burning magma…and she felt warmth and knowledge. She became as one with her…rooted. Connected.

When she opened her eyes, Marina was breathing hard, lightheaded, dizzy. Eli was staring at her, pain lancing his face, his right foot gingerly placed on the ground.

She blinked, shook off the strange moment, and looked around desperately, aware she'd wasted time going off into a— whatever that had been.

But—there was a massive banyan tree. *There.*

Conscious of the sounds of their pursuers—who, oddly, seemed farther away, or separated from them by some sort of barrier—Marina curved her arm around Eli's waist. "This way."

They maneuvered toward the large tree, with Marina looking beyond it for shelter—and there was nothing. The land was flat. The brush was thin. She searched in the opposite directions, making a small, hasty circuit fueled by fear and anxiety, searching for whatever had drawn her in this direction…

"Perfect," said Eli, still gritting his teeth. He pulled from her embrace, one hand braced against the massive tree trunk. As she turned, he bent awkwardly to pick up a large stick, and that was when Marina saw the opening beneath the banyan. The roots erupted from the ground, forming a covering shingled with moss and vines. Hidden. Safe.

An embrace.

Eli shoved the branch up inside the opening, thrusting it all along the inside to ensure there were no critters living inside. A few beetles and some other insects she couldn't identify skittered out, followed by some sort of rodent, and then nothing.

The shouts came closer, becoming distinct once more, and Eli dove inside, pulling Marina along with him. She heard his smothered groan of pain as he used his injured foot to lever himself down into the base of the massive tree.

The trunk itself was hollow, and the root system merely the covered entrance to an amazingly empty and roomy space. Dirt and roots formed the sides, and the hollow tree rose above them. Light filtered in from one side, giving enough illumination so they could see there were no other creatures to disturb.

She looked at Eli, whose heavy breathing indicated the level of pain he'd inflicted on himself. His face was tight, his teeth clearly gritted as he settled himself into place. They were each able to sit upright, backs against a wall of roots threading through earth. He was required to slouch a little, being taller, and they folded their legs into a modified lotus position, knees touching as they sat perpendicular to each other.

"I'm not going to ask how you knew this was here," Eli whispered after he caught his breath.

"I didn't," she said, then hushed when the sounds of rustling and crashing were upon them. Literally.

She and Eli stared out into the jungle from behind and beneath the thick canopy of leaves, vines, and moss, watching for shoes or boots to appear, shouts to announce their presence, gunshots to be fired…

But after a moment, the human sounds that had been just above them faded.

And then there was silence, but for the warning of a bird who'd been disturbed, and the beginning of a sprinkle of rain.

"We need to bind your ankle," she said, looking at Eli. The pain had eased from his face.

"I have a sock. That might work."

She helped him remove it in the cramped space, then bound his right foot as tightly as possible. It was already swelling; his shoe would no longer fit. The best treatment would be ice and elevation—but neither were an option right now.

"Thanks," he said, settling back against his side of the space. "Can't believe I did that." His mouth twisted with disgust.

"Even so, nice going on the distraction, Dr. Sanchez," she said. "Was that really a—whatever you called it? I didn't catch all the Latin words."

His dark eyes glinted with humor. "No wonder—I was just making up names. Wanted it to sound good. That hive contained nothing more than a common Ecuadorean honeybee."

She laughed. "Well, you convinced me. Nice shot, by the way."

"Yeah. I even surprised myself. But it was a fairly big target." He shrugged.

Their eyes met. "Well," she began, suddenly acutely aware of their plight. "I'm not sure what our next move should be. We could go back—I'm sure Roman would be happy to see me."

"So he's your father."

She pursed her lips and nodded. "Yes."

"And what's all this about a library? Might as well tell me—we aren't going anywhere for a while."

She did. Without a lot of detail, but enough that he got the picture.

"So you weren't kidding when you said you understood why I'd take the risk to see those beetles. You could make your career with those writings."

"If I wanted to be one of them—a Skaladeska. That's the lure they're dangling for me." She sighed. "I don't want to go back, but I don't think there's any choice. You're not going to make it far, and I have no idea what distance we'd have to travel to find civilization—or at least someone who could help us."

"Maybe we should check the hangar just to be sure there's no plane in there."

He sounded hopeful, and Marina didn't have the heart to tell him there was no way that RV-5 would have fit inside. "We can do that. Later, when we're sure they aren't around."

If that ever happened. Surely they'd be watching the hangar…

Marina tipped her head back against the earthen wall and closed her eyes. Her thoughts spun. They were safe—for now. But what was the plan? How were they going to get out of here, escape not only the Skalas, but the jungle itself?

Especially now that Eli was handicapped…

Despite their predicament, she forced herself to relax for the first time since she'd awakened last night in the clinic room with Eli. They'd been on the go, running and evading and exploring ever since then. Her fingers shook a little and her head was light from lack of food, but they still had the water and, now, a place to rest.

Her mind emptied and she let herself float, safe and protected within the earth. Rain pattered down beyond their hideaway, and she heard and felt the sounds, the sensations of life. She felt embraced. Content.

The ground thudded softly beneath her, like a heartbeat: strong and steady. Yet she sensed the pain and anger the earth felt. It was as if the magma far below her surged and churned with anger and desperation… And the rain was like weeping: soft, hopeless, steady.

She felt light, floating…then heavy, sinking…then light blazed behind her closed eyes. Arms encircled her. Warmth enveloped her.

And then, in the silence, entombed as she was, far from any distraction or man-made noise, she felt *Her.*

The presence of life.

Marina's eyes bolted open.

The light was dim. Everything was still.

Eli was there, dozing against his own side of the small cave.

They were alone…except for Gaia herself.

The question was: would Gaia release them, or would she hold them?

THIRTY-EIGHT

Marina wasn't certain what time it was. The light was low—as if it were dusk—but it had been raining for a while. She wasn't certain how close it was to night, or whether clouds lingered. When she thought about the amount of time they'd hiked, hid, rested, and even slept, she thought it might even be the next day, which would make it the 30th. Had they really left Chicago almost three days ago?

She went to pull Hedron's cell phone out of her pocket to check the time, she realized it wasn't there. Great. Must have fallen out during their mad dash, or when Eli flung her into Nora. She gritted her teeth. Marina hated to admit how much she'd hoped the phone would eventually work, that it would eventually have been their saving grace—a connection, a GPS map, *something*.

But now they didn't even have that.

"Ready to go?"

Marina looked at Eli. "Go?"

"Back to the airstrip. Who knows what's in that hangar. Maybe there's a jeep."

"They'll be watching for us. And you've got a bum ankle."

He nodded. "I do. But we can't stay in here forever. I'll be all right. I once played an entire round of golf on a strained ankle. And we didn't use carts."

"Another example of your dedication?"

He grinned. "Or stupidity. Take your pick. I was off my feet for two weeks after."

Despite his confidence, Eli couldn't quite smother a groan of discomfort as he crawled out of their hiding spot. After they stood up—for the first time in hours—and stretched, he immediately found a walking stick.

"This way?"

Marina nodded, and used Cora's knife to hack off the end of a vine. Water poured from its hollow tube and she drank. When she was finished, she cut off another one for Eli. "I think we should approach the landing strip from the back this time."

"Agreed. So." Eli squinted, looking up at the sky. "We go west from here. Sun's there."

Off they went. Marina was impressed at the speed and agility with which her companion moved—he hobbled, winced occasionally, but kept a fair pace using his walking stick and her to assist. He had to be in great pain, but she couldn't tell.

It took much longer to make their way back to the airstrip than it had to leave, of course, but they managed without encountering any problems more serious than a trail of fire ants—which, of course, Eli saw in plenty of time to avoid.

They were nearly to the clearing, approaching, as planned, from the far, rear side of the hangar, when Marina lifted an arm to silently halt her companion. This was the test.

Silently, slowly, they began to draw in toward the area—this time listening for any human sound, any warning from the wildlife in the area. From the rear, the metal building seemed even more decrepit and rundown, and Marina had little hope they'd find the plane inside.

Eli grabbed her arm and pointed. Marina caught her breath. Guards. Two men, each at opposite corners of the hangar.

They were either guarding something inside, or watching for her, or both. The men patrolled each side of the hangar, sometimes within sight of the other—sometimes without.

Eli pulled something from his pocket and Marina saw the gun they'd taken from Cora Allegan. Fat lot of good it would do them without any ammunition. He seemed to read her mind, but shrugged and quirked a hopeful smile, making a hitting motion with it.

A few gestures and he made his intention clear: he'd creep up behind the nearer guard, so Marina—who was more physically agile—could try to sneak into the hangar. There was a door on this side, hanging awkwardly from its moorings. She might be able to slip through the wedge-shaped opening without having to move the metal door.

Marina eased away from Eli and watched with her heart in her throat as he moved unevenly through the bushes whenever the near guard wasn't looking in their direction. She did the same, and both she and Eli reached the edge of the clearing at the same time—spread apart by more than the length of the hangar. The guard turned the corner away from them and Marina dashed toward the building.

Out of the corner of her eye, she saw Eli lope forward and duck behind a small bush just beyond the edge of the jungle.

The narrow triangular opening beckoned, and Marina bolted toward it. If the other guard came around the corner before she made it through—

But he didn't, and she did, diving through the lower, wider part of the opening. She slid across the gritty dirt floor on her palms and knees, suddenly in the shadowy interior.

She looked up and around.

The space was larger than she thought.

And there was a plane.

Surging to her feet, Marina dashed across the room, already realizing the aircraft was not the same RV-5 they'd flown in on… but an older model. A much older, abandoned, likely-not-working Cessna.

A sound had her spinning around, her heels digging into the dusty floor. She turned in time to see Eli duck through the opening.

She waited, but, miracle of miracles—he was alone. And she could read the excitement and relief in his movements as he made his way over to her.

"What'd you do?" she asked, smoothing a hand over the aircraft's wing. Rust spots.

"Didn't have to do anything. They stopped to talk on the front side of the building, and I took the opportunity to slip in here and join you. No one saw me. Look at this," he said, delight in his voice. "Can you fly it?"

"If it runs, I can fly it," she said, opening the plane's door very slowly in case it squeaked or squealed. "But whether it'll start up is the big question. And whether it has fuel, and…"

Long shots. Every single question was a long shot.

"All right. Let me poke around and see what else is in here." He was looking at a long counter with a jumble of boxes on and around it. The whole place looked like someone's abandoned, disorganized garage.

Marina climbed inside and sat in the pilot's seat. Something skittered away beneath her feet, and there were plenty of cobwebs to be brushed away. At least no snakes…

How long had this plane been here?

She didn't dare try and start it, did she? While the guards were just outside? And the door would have to be opened…

The controls were familiar, and everything seemed to be in working order—at least from the cockpit's standpoint. The engine and its fuel were another situation entirely.

Marina climbed out and began to go through her normal engine check. Dust and dirt coated the engine, but there was fuel. Not enough to get far, but enough to get away. The prop was in good shape; the wings too.

The only question, it seemed, was whether the engine would start. And she didn't want to try that until they were ready to go.

"Here," said Eli, appearing at her elbow. He thrust a wrapped granola bar at her. "Found a whole case of these. Hope you aren't allergic to nuts."

She took it gratefully. "Anything else?"

They kept their voices low, aware of the other voices belonging to the guards just beyond the metal wall of the hangar.

"Case of bottled water, some beef jerky, and some cans of soup. Those big canisters—fuel, maybe?"

Marina looked over. "Yes. Oh, that's great."

The voices outside became more distinct, and Marina and Eli exchanged looks. A soft metal clang, followed by a scraping noise, heralded the opening of the main hangar door—the one large enough for the plane to move through, the one through which Roman had walked.

Without speaking, Marina and Eli separated. She ducked behind the far side of the plane. She didn't see where he went; her attention was on the single figure walking through the door.

The new arrival didn't appear to be looking for them; he went directly to the counter where Eli had been exploring the boxes. Maybe the guy was thirsty?

Suddenly, Eli slipped from the shadows and, still clearly favoring his right leg, surged up behind the man and swung the gun at the back of his head.

The man dropped like a stone, hitting his face on the counter as he fell. The clatter was audible, and someone—the other guard—called from outside. Anticipating his move, Marina dashed quickly to the other end of the hangar. She grabbed a metal pipe from the ground, and when the second man came inside, she waited until he moved away from the door toward his friend.

She bolted out of her hiding place and cracked him at the back of the head like she was returning a tennis serve.

"Nice work," said Eli, who was already using something to tie up the first intruder. Electrical tape. That was handy.

Together they tied the two unconscious guards and arranged them in a corner out of the way.

"Don't know when their shifts change or how soon anyone's going to be looking for them," Marina said, unnecessarily. "We need to work fast. I won't know if the plane will start until I try it, but it definitely needs fuel added."

She showed him how to do that, then climbed into the cockpit. "If it starts, stand back—there'll be dust and dirt and wind going everywhere—and open the door wide. If not…" She didn't bother to finish the sentence.

Drawing a deep breath, she set the controls, readied herself, and pushed the ignition button.

Nothing happened.

Swearing, she tried again, pushing harder—as if that would make a difference.

This time, there was a soft moan, a faint cranking sound.

Then nothing.

THIRTY-NINE

"The magneto isn't working—no electrical current to start the ignition," Marina said. "It's dead as a doornail."

"Maybe there's something we can use over here." Eli limped over to the scramble of things along the counter on one side of the hangar, casting a brief glance at the two guards still slumped in the corner.

"Unless there's a battery, I don't know what would help. We need an electrical charge. Too bad there's no storm tonight." Marina didn't try to hide her frustration and anxiety.

She had the feeling they were going to end up back in the hands of the Skaladeskas sooner rather than later.

And would that be such a bad thing?

They would let Eli go—she would make certain of it. No one would die in the jungle.

And she'd have an excuse to study the contents of the library. The decision would be made for her—she'd done everything possible, everything she could do to *not* have to agree, to *not* take the temptation offered her.

Was it worth the risk of dying, of Eli dying somewhere in the wilds of the Amazon?

Maybe it *was* her calling. Maybe it *was* her legacy. The very thought of poring over numerous scrolls, scripts, papyruses, and books made her lightheaded and her fingers tingle. What secrets would she find? What secrets had Lev already found? What information could she discern, and bring to the world, and use to answer questions, to share knowledge and history?

A sudden rush of energy flushed through her, overwhelming her with the hot, prickling sensation. It was similar to how she'd felt huddled in the embrace of the banyan tree, curled up in Gaia's palm, close to the source of life.

It was as if Gaia agreed.

As if Gaia wanted her here.

The flood of emotion made her nauseated and lightheaded, and she reached out to touch the body of the plane to steady herself.

"I have an idea." Suddenly Eli was there in front of her, and his words jolted Marina from her reverie. "Are you all right?"

"Yes, sorry. I was just—"

"Contemplating going back? Giving in? Setting aside your moral convictions in order to save my life?" His grin was wry, his eyes held her steadily. "I don't know where you stand on the moral scale, but in my mind, there's nothing worth more than a life. Not a treasure, not a book, not even a sexy, rare, electrically charged coleop." He was holding a can of Campbell's Chicken Noodle soup and a bottle of water. "If you go back to the Skaladeskas, you might save our lives, but you'd be joining a clan responsible for taking those of others."

Marina nodded. "I know. And—understand this, Eli—I wouldn't join them. Even if I went back, it would be only temporary. Until I could find a way to escape." Surely Varden would help her.

"So we're back to 'Eli,' are we? That's good." His gaze flashed warm. "I'm looking forward to getting out of here and somewhere with a good glass of red, a big, fat steak, and—most important of all—a comfortable bed. So let's make it happen."

"You have an idea?" she said, mortified at the heat that flushed her cheeks at his plain speaking. And that she was just as eager for that outcome as he was—and not just for the steak.

"It's crazy. But I think it could work." He set the can of soup and the bottle of water on the plane wing and began to dig in one of his bulky side pockets. "We've got a source of electrical charge right here."

When he pulled out a dark plastic bottle, at first Marina was confused. Then she gave a short laugh. "You want to use the beetles?"

Eli grinned. "Why not? We know they have an electrical charge—that's why they were sizzling and popping in the air during the thunderstorm. Obviously each one doesn't have much of a charge on its own, but if we were to harness the power from, say, ten or more of them…"

She was shaking her head and laughing, yet amazed. "Well, hell, if a cluster of them took down the power plant in St. Louis, why not? But what's up with the Campbell's?"

"You ever watch *MacGyver*?" he said, using the pull-top ring to open the soup can. He held up the lid. "This is going to be our plunger. And the collector of the charge. And this," he said, twisting off the cap of the water bottle, "is going to be our bug container."

"You're going to sacrifice a bunch of your little darlings?" Marina said as he drained the bottle of water in several big gulps.

"Survival of the fittest," Eli said, swiping his mouth. "Besides. I have more." He patted another pocket, also weighted down and bulky.

Marina helped him rig up the MacGyver-like battery. They used the knife to cut the bottom off the water bottle. The soup can top barely fit inside at an angle, but Eli nodded with satisfaction. "The idea is to push all the beetles together so the charge is collected in one small area and is strong enough to do what we need."

Then he ran the red wire from the ignition through the pull-top ring of the soup can and twisted it tightly around it. "If this works—and why wouldn't it?—the charge will be collected by the metal circle and travel along the wire to the ignition. And *boom*— it jumps it and we're in business."

"Don't we need something to ground it?" Marina asked.

"Yep. That's why I'm cutting off this other end of the bottle—so we can set it right on something metal…let's see. Right here's good." He gestured to a piece of the plane's metal frame. "Probably should scrape some of that paint off, though, just to make sure…"

Marina did that while he worked on the only other problem: how to transfer the beetles from his opaque carrying bottle into the clear plastic water bottle without them swarming into a frenzy. Though the light was dim, it would be enough to set them off. But then she saw him wrapping the plastic bottle in a rag and knew he had it all figured out.

"I'll dump them into the plastic bottle, then fit the soup can top in place again. Then when we're ready, I'll pull away the rag and shine your squeeze light on them," Eli said. "Get 'em all worked up."

"And I'll be pushing the ignition switch. Ready to go." Marina nodded. *This could actually work.*

This could work.

A soft metal clang startled her, and both Marina and Eli spun to look. The small rear doorway was shivering—as if someone had just passed hastily through it.

Yes. One of the guards was gone. The other remained slumped in the corner—but that didn't matter. One was gone. They would be discovered.

"Now. This has to work *now,*" snapped Eli. "They'll be here in minutes. Let's go."

Marina had already given him her light, and she scrambled into the cockpit. "Ready when you are."

Shouts reached their ears. "So soon? They must have sent off a signal of some sort!" Eli's voice was tense. "Push it."

She pushed the ignition switch and watched as he whipped the rag from the plastic bottle and used the cut-off part of it to push the metal disk down into the bottle. The squeeze light flashed and Marina heard a *pop* and *the engine rolled over.*

And caught.

"Hurry!" she cried, then bolted from her seat to grab Eli's arm and drag him up and into the plane.

He tumbled face-first into the seat next to hers, but she couldn't wait to help him. The shouts were there, the roar of the engine drowning out everything, and she crossed her fingers.

Fly, baby, fly!

When the wheels began to turn, and the aircraft began to move, Marina blocked out everything else: the shouts, the hangar door—which wasn't open!

Eli flung himself from the plane before she could speak, and fell when he landed on his bad ankle. Marina gasped, but he pulled himself up and dashed unsteadily to the door. As he rolled it open, barely wide enough for the plane to clear, she saw dark figures running across the airstrip toward them.

Marina shot the plane forward, forcing it to pick up speed. She left the controls and lunged from her seat to reach over and down. Eli was there…right there, but the figures were coming closer. Then the sound of gunshots—*gunshots!*

"Here!" she cried as the plane careened wildly through the doorway. He flung himself toward the aircraft and she caught him by the arm, gave a good, hard yank, and then tumbled back into her seat.

Something pinged into the side of the plane, another *ping* on the glass shield in front, and Eli jolted and muffled a cry as Marina pulled on the wheel and the plane's nose lifted.

One hand on the wheel, another grappling him into the seat next to her with the door still open, surrounded by shots and shouts, and the jungle looming just in front of her—too close, too tall, the air was too humid for them to get high enough…

Marina closed her eyes, pulled back steadily on the wheel, accelerated…and prayed.

October 1, 9 a.m.
Detroit, Michigan

Helen Darrow was just climbing into her rental car—the administrative work fast-tracked because she was a Fed, thank goodness—when her phone rang. She recognized the number as the Tech department back in Chicago, and shoved the key into the vehicle ignition, then answered the call.

"Agent Darrow, I've got something that might be relevant." It was Tom's young, eager voice. She smiled because he still called her Agent Darrow, which bespoke of his newly minted condition and awe for the Bureau itself.

"Good, because I'm still not sure what the hell I'm doing here in the Motor City." But she and Gabe had decided it was a good idea to have her on the ground in Detroit while he went to Vegas, since they seemed to be the only two locations that pinged either of their so-called radar. Nevertheless, her plans were wishy-washy—something that made Helen very uncomfortable.

Since Rue Varden's tracker had stopped moving yesterday in Ann Arbor, her first plan was to go there and check out the last location he (or it) had been—in a building on campus at the University of Michigan. After that...she wasn't certain.

"We were able to get a little more from that recorded conversation in the room before Dr. Alexander and Dr. Sanchez were abducted," Tom said. "And they mentioned New York."

"They? Who? Could you tell who was speaking?" She sat in the car, her fingers still grasping the ignition key...but she hadn't turned it yet.

"It wasn't Dr. Alexander. It was one of the others in the room. It was part of the same conversation about the first. The actual transcript reads: 'Traveling to New York as planned.' Then something still indiscernible. And then, 'the first as scheduled. No changes. I'll report to...' And then indiscernible."

New York.

"New York City? Or just upstate New York?" she mused aloud. Now what? Everything seemed to indicate east rather than west, but Gabe should be landing in Vegas in a couple hours. "Thank you, Tom. This is very helpful. If you get anything else, please let me know immediately. I'm on the ground now and available by cell."

"I will, Agent Darrow. Thank you," he said just as she disconnected the call.

New York. She looked down at her phone, then, sighing, dragged out the iPad from her briefcase. Better call someone in NYC to give them a heads-up. Not that she knew what to warn them about...

Her voice mail dinged and she saw that a call had come in and gone to voice mail—likely while she was on the plane. But by the time she'd finished listening to the message, Helen was pulling out of the rental car parking lot, heading to Ann Arbor.

The message had been from local law enforcement in Michigan who'd checked on the location of Rue Varden's tracker at the request of the Feds. "He was in a biochem lab, mixing up something to do with an antibiotic. I've got a witness who saw him. She's here and happy to talk to you."

An antibiotic. Curious.

According to the GPS, Ann Arbor was thirty minutes away. Helen intended to make it in twenty. Her fingers were tingling like crazy—which told her she was onto something important.

But she was just pulling into a parking structure after driving around for ten minutes looking for an empty spot when her phone rang again.

The area code was 212. *New York.*

She slammed on the brakes in the middle of the structure (good thing no one was behind her) and fumbled the phone to her ear. "Agent Darrow," she said, inching the car along once more.

"Agent Helen Darrow? This is Dr. Westfall, hospital administrator at Mount Sinai Hospital in New York," said a businesslike female voice. "We've had a patient here whose symptoms pinged a notification you filed with the CDC, and your name came up as an urgent law enforcement contact. Her name is Melissa Addington, aged twenty-eight, and she expired two hours ago from sudden cardiac arrest."

"Did she present with a severe rash?" Helen was asking before the woman even stopped speaking. "If so, it's extremely contagious—"

"Yes, we saw the notice and have taken the necessary precautions. Local law enforcement is on their way here as we speak."

"Put them in touch with me when they arrive. I'll be in New York as soon as I can get there." Helen looked around at the rows of parking places filled with cars. "Screw it." She could interview the research assistant by phone, for clearly Rue Varden was no longer here in Ann Arbor.

Time to head to New York. Her fingers were really tingling now.

Las Vegas
October 1
10:00 a.m., PST

Gabe fished the cell phone out of his suit pocket as the plane taxied to the terminal. He powered it on and waited for any texts, voice mails, and emails to settle in and download.

Ding. Ding. Ding.

The soft alerts went on for more than a minute; not a big surprise, for he'd been on the plane for almost three hours. Normally he would have paid for Wi-Fi while in the air (business expense), but as his luck with electronics had continued to be shitty, there was something wrong with the service on this flight, so he'd been off-grid for far too long.

He tensed when he saw that several of the alerts were from Helen Darrow, and one from Colin Bergstrom. Another from Inez.

Damn.

That probably wasn't good.

He paged through the texts as the plane edged up to the terminal bridge and stopped.

It's NYC.

Helen's text was terse and to the point.

Not Vegas.

Gabe swore, looked at the time stamp, and swore again. He glanced up when the elderly woman next to him huffed, but even her shocked blue eyes didn't make him feel guilty.

He was already on the phone to Helen by the time it was his turn to deplane.

"Where are you?" he demanded as soon as she answered.

"Getting off the plane in New York," she said, her voice jerky with motion. "From Detroit."

"I'll get there as soon as I can," he said, furious with himself, with the whole situation. "What else? How do you know it's there?"

"I sent you an email. Details there. We got more info from the recording on Marina's phone."

He could tell she was getting ready to hang up. "Wait!" He was rushing through the terminal now, threading between the other deplaning passengers, heading for a ticket desk—any ticket desk. *Four hours to NYC at least. That'll put me there after six o'clock. Damn.*

"What?" Helen barked through the phone. "The deets are in your email. Short version: the bugs have killed someone in New York. Gotta go—"

"Helen," he said. "I'm sorry. I was wrong about Vegas! I shouldn't have—"

"It's all right. We did the best we could—I have to go; getting a call from my local contact."

"Helen!" he said loudly, his fingers tightening on the phone.

"What? Gabe, I have to take—"

"Please, Helen—please be careful."

"I will." The phone went dead, and Gabe took off at a run.

He was getting to New York by six if he had to fly there himself.

FORTY

5 p.m., EST
New York
The apartment of Missy Addington

"A gent Darrow, take a look at this."

"Excuse me for a moment, Miss Crutcheon," Helen said to Delia Crutcheon, Missy Addington's roommate, whom she'd been interviewing. The young woman wore the stunned look of someone who'd just had the shocking news of a friend's death.

She walked over to the cluttered desk where NYPD Officer Valliencourt had been combing through folders and papers and three inboxes. The papers the officer gave Helen were a stack of purchase orders, contracts, and menus for La Beau-Joux Catering. A glance showed Missy Addington's signature on all of them. She was the owner of the company, which Delia had already informed her. The caterer did medium and small jobs for school PTOs, baby showers, business meetings. Run-of-the-mill sorts of events; nothing that jumped out at her.

Yet her fingers were really prickling now. *There has to be something here.* She watched over her shoulder as the NYPD officer shuffled through more papers, and then something caught her eye.

An invoice for today's date: October 1. Helen snatched it up, along with its attached menu and contract. Invoice to: *The*

Alliance. Location: Pembel-Rose Building. Date: October 1. Time of event: 6 p.m. New York. Helen looked at the clock, her pulse shooting through the roof. It was after five.

She scanned the contract, and saw that it was a very different sort of event than Le Beau-Joux Catering usually handled. Larger, and from the looks of the menu—and the price per head!—Miss Addington's company had hit the big time. She flipped to the last page to see who'd signed the contract. Susan Gottlieb. No company name.

Helen pulled out her trusty iPad and searched for The Alliance, Pembel-Rose Building, and today's date. Nothing popped.

Nothing.

She frowned.

The date of the event was October 1. Missy Addington had died today, after being exposed to the beetles within the last forty-eight hours at the most. Something was going to happen today. It had to be related.

Still mulling, Helen searched Susan Gottlieb, and *that* produced pages of information. CEO of Macrohl Chemical. Adrenaline shot through her when she saw one of the headlines from the list of results—an article from *Time* magazine: Worst Environmental Defenders of the Year. Macrohl Chemical Corporation was listed as one of them.

Now Helen's mind was racing and her fingers were alive with energy.

"Everyone! I think we've found something. Look around for anything else related to this event"—she showed them the papers, read the info—"in the trash, on her cell, laptop, anything you can find."

Helen turned back to the roommate, who hadn't moved from the tiny efficiency kitchen. "Do you know anything about this event?" she asked.

"A little," Delia said. She still looked as if she had seen a ghost. "Missy was very excited about this gig because it was the biggest, most prestigious one she'd ever landed. It came about because the regular caterer had to cancel at the last minute, and someone called her to fill in. She was in a tizzy yesterday because she'd just gotten a last-minute change to the menu—one of the attendees had ordered some special wine or something, and then he added something else to it. She kept complaining about these last-minute changes, but she loved it—she was so excited about it."

Helen was shaking her head. There had to be more. The beetles had to figure in somehow, didn't they? And what if she was on the wrong track…what if it wasn't—

"Agent Darrow, check this out."

She took the paper, which was crumpled and had been found in the trash. Special delicacies? Mr. Wen-Ho… She picked up the iPad to search, then froze when she saw the name of the company hired to deliver the "special delicacies."

Gaia, Inc.

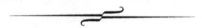

New York City
October 1
6:00 p.m., EST

The members of The Alliance filed into the conference room, conversing loudly. By all accounts, their two-day summit had been a success, and whatever business this group of a dozen ladies and gentlemen had conducted had been happily finished.

Despite the fact that their business had concluded and they'd clearly moved on to informal socializing, LaTrelle didn't have the luxury of relaxing just yet. Not until dessert was served would he be able to draw a deep breath. The reputation of Le Beau-Joux Events rode on everything going smoothly.

He wasn't going to think about the fact that his boss, Missy, hadn't been in contact at all. Last he'd heard, she'd gone to the hospital with that severe allergic reaction—but that was really early this morning. She should be home by now. Very unlike her not to be checking in with him—especially with an event of this magnitude happening.

Instead of worrying about it, though, he watched his staff with an eagle eye as they served the first course flawlessly. Not one drop of wine spilled, not one clatter of flatware or clink of dish. When it was time to peel away from Le Beau-Joux, he'd definitely poach Yoyo to go with him. Maybe BeckyAnn too.

And so it went on, course served, course removed, glasses refilled, replaced, and filled, and another course served.

LaTrelle pulled out his cell to check the time and peek at his texts and realized it had been on silent for hours. But he'd been busy, tending to things here, so it didn't matter. There were quite a few messages, but none from Missy.

He shook his head. That wasn't like her, not to be breathing down his neck. She must really be sick.

Slipping into the back room, where the prepped food had been finished, plated, and now was being put away, LaTrelle scanned his messages.

He stopped at one, and the hair on the back of his neck rose. *I must have read that wrong.*

He looked at it again, his heart pounding. *Is this some kind of joke?*

The message was from Missy's roommate—whom he hardly knew, but had gone out with once or twice a few years ago. Delia had written: *Missy died at hospital 2day. Sudden cardiac arrest! Police are here! Call me when u get this! I can't believe it!*

LaTrelle stared at the text. It had to be a joke. What sort of allergic reaction had Missy *had*? And why were the police involved?

Confused, distracted, and stunned, he shoved the phone into his pocket. It was time for dessert—no, wait, those special delicacies that guy had brought in. He'd forgotten about them.

That wouldn't have been good. Mr. Wen-Ho wouldn't be pleased if his gesture had been ignored.

"And now for the special delicacy," said LaTrelle. He was so upset about the text from Delia his voice trembled, and so did the box in his hands.

The diners looked over in curiosity—and well so, for normally the caterer was seen and not heard, flitting about silently and efficiently. But LaTrelle was shaken up, and he wasn't thinking clearly.

He thought perhaps Mr. Wen-Ho would appreciate the attention being drawn to his special gift. LaTrelle broke the seals and pulled the silver ribbons from the box.

"I present to you, the special delicacies—courtesy of Mr. Wen-Ho!" LaTrelle lifted the lid, suddenly aware that Mr. Wen-Ho was protesting in confusion and surprise.

But whatever Mr. Wen-Ho was saying was drowned out as a swarm of bees—or something—erupted into the room, pouring from the open box. They were furious, whizzing about, flying, buzzing, swirling in a cyclone of fury.

Everyone in the room reacted—rising from their chairs, batting ineffectually at the insects, shrieking and exclaiming in shock and fear.

LaTrelle stumbled back from the box, stunned by the vast number of bugs that had burst forth, and the fury with which they raged about the room. People, windows, walls, table—all were pelted by the creatures, which left black stains on the skin, walls, windows…

"What is happening? What is going on in here?" the voices, in a variety of accents and languages, demanded.

LaTrelle tried to replace the lid on the box, but it was too late. The box was empty, and its whizzing contents had filled the room.

People were batting at the insects, slapping at them with napkins, coats, hands, and even plates.

"Let's get out of here!" someone cried.

LaTrelle lunged for the door.

FORTY-ONE

Helen Darrow stabbed the door-close button in the service elevator in the Pembel-Rose Building. The conference room where the dinner was being served by Le Beau-Joux Catering was on the fifteenth floor, and the regular elevators were taking forever.

She'd coordinated with the NYPD and they'd sent a team up the stairs, and another through a different bank of elevators, but Helen had elected to take the service elevator—for where else would a caterer go? She didn't exactly know what was going to happen, but she knew it involved the beetles. She chafed as the elevator rumbled and rolled, taking its sweet time moving from four to five.

The delay, the sort of pause in the midst of adrenaline rush and physical activity, forced her to be patient. And allowed her mind to go where she had resolutely kept it from going.

Helen…please be careful.

Gabe's words, rushed and heartfelt, echoed in her mind as she watched the lights flash on the elevator. Much too slowly. Six.

Please be careful.

She needn't read anything more into that except for one colleague's warning to another. An old friend wishing another well.

I know you think I'm blinded by love for Marina Alexander, and it's influencing my decisions. But I'm not.

The lights on the elevator blinked *so* slowly. Nine... *Get me out of here. Get me doing something other than waiting and thinking about things that are irrelevant right now.*

People's lives were at stake.

"But I'm not," he'd said.

Did that mean he wasn't blinded by love, or that he wasn't *in* love? He'd said, "I'm not." He hadn't said, "It isn't"—meaning his love wasn't influencing his decisions. Helen groaned aloud, forcing her thoughts back to the matter at hand. *Hurry up, elevator!*

Ten.

Good grief, can't this damned thing go any faster?

Helen had her weapon in hand, but what that was going to do to a swarm of beetles was ineffectual. What would kill copper-infused insects? She highly suspected Raid or its ilk wouldn't.

Eleven.

Thank God. Almost there. And she'd managed to put Gabe out of her mind for two floors.

Twelve.

Helen held her breath, tightened her hands on her weapon, and eased to the side of the doors...just in case.

Finally, at fifteen, the elevator rolled to a stop. The doors slid open, revealing the service hall for the building. Listening, fingers prickling, firearm in hand, Helen arced around the area as she stepped quickly and carefully from the elevator.

No sign of anyone; everything was still. But from somewhere, she could hear shouts and exclamations.

The conference room.

Helen hurried through the service room toward the sounds. Instincts on high alert, watching and waiting, blood rushing through her, heart pumping, fingers tight, thumb on the safety.

The sounds of chaos drew closer as she moved down the hall, along with shouts and thuds. Sounded like someone trying to break down a door.

Cries of "Let us out!" and "Help!" became more clear as she rushed quickly and carefully down the service hall, then out into the main corridor. She'd taken only a few steps toward her goal when a figure appeared, emerging from one of the alcoves halfway between her and the conference room.

Helen halted, holding her weapon at the ready, taking a strong stance. "FBI. Identify yourself."

But by then, she'd recognized the man who stood in the hall, hands slightly removed from his rangy body in the most halfhearted of surrender poses. In one of them, his fingers curled around a vial.

"Agent Darrow. It's a pleasure to meet you, and very convenient you should be the one to arrive first on the scene." He smiled pleasantly, calm and easy despite being covered by a gun. "This saves me from an awkward situation."

The photos she'd seen hadn't been able to capture the intensity of his green eyes, nor the confidence exuding from him. "Dr. Rue Varden. We meet at last," she said, inching closer. "Keep your hands where I can see them—"

"I have something you need." He gestured slightly with the hand holding the vial and jerked his chin in the general vicinity of the conference room, where a door shuddered and rocked in its hinges. "If you want it, you're going to need to put that weapon back in its holster and allow me to go on my way."

Helen didn't move. "Unlike my colleague MacNeil, I don't bargain with terrorists."

Varden quirked a brow. "As you like." He removed the top from the vial and his intention became clear. "I made certain the conference room doors were locked so the insects and contaminate can be contained, but if you prefer to do this on your own, then by all means...I'm sure you have plenty of time to develop an antibiotic." His smile was cool and pleasant as he began to tip the vial. The dark red liquid inside crept to the edge of the opening.

"We tracked you to Ann Arbor. I know the lab where you made that," she said, stepping closer, gun steady.

He nodded briefly. "Yes, of course you did—so you know that what I have here is what you need to save those people. Don't be a fool, Agent Darrow. You can't save them any other way. You have no time to develop something like this. I've done you a favor. But you can't have it both ways. You get the antibiotic, or you get me."

The conference room door shuddered again, and the cries of its occupants—shouts, exclamations, but not really terror, for they didn't understand what the threat was—grew louder and more intense.

"The minutes are ticking by," Varden said. His voice was smooth and precise, as if he'd learned English as a second language. "When your colleagues arrive—and I can hear the rumble of the elevators; they're nearly here—they'll open the door to the conference room and all those insects will pour out. The people inside are already infected, and will soon contaminate everyone they touch... You really have no choice, Agent Darrow. And believe it or not, I am here to help." He offered the vial again. "Put your weapon down. Slide it away from both of us—I have no need or desire to grab it. And I'll give you what you need."

Helen gritted her teeth. Damn. Now she understood Gabe's situation. She slowly lowered the gun, then set it on the ground. With a sharp shove, she kicked it away from both of them.

"Believe me when I say 'thank you.'" Varden put the top back on the vial and walked toward her, reaching into his pocket. Helen tensed, suddenly afraid she'd completely miscalculated—but when he pulled out his hand, he had a second vial. He offered them to her. "Five mils per person. Should be enough for everyone."

She took the vials, resisting the urge to grab him and try to stop the terrorist...but he gave her a brief smile, those green eyes meeting hers boldly. "It's been a pleasure to meet you at last, Agent Darrow. Until we meet again. And...here come your colleagues."

And then he was gone, and she was running to the conference room door.

FORTY-TWO

October 2
Quito, Ecuador

It had been a harrowing moment, during their takeoff. Though she'd closed her eyes, Marina had to open them as the plane lifted, and she eased on the yoke with numb fingers as they rose…and rose…and *rose.*

They just cleared the trees, giving the tallest one a trim as they roared over. Eli had indeed been shot as he climbed into the craft, but it wasn't until a short time later she learned it was from the rubber bullets Roman favored—which also indicated to Marina how serious her father was about her safety.

They flew through the dusk, with Marina simply searching for another airstrip or clearing on which she could land. She didn't know how far they could make it, nor did she trust the ratty plane…but it was two hours before she found a place to land in the middle of nowhere.

Fifteen hours later, with some help from non-English-speaking locals, they'd arrived in Quito.

She called Gabe—who was beside himself with worry—and told him about Cora Allegan. She learned from him what had happened in New York, and was stunned to discover that Helen Darrow had somehow obtained the antibiotic needed to treat those contaminated.

"How did she do that?" Marina asked.

"Helen's not saying much," Gabe replied, his voice odd. "But we did track Varden back to Ann Arbor before he ditched the GPS bug...and someone in a chem lab reported a strange incident with a man who gained access, and who wore a University of Michigan badge."

Interesting.

"How is Helen?" Marina asked.

There was a pause. "She's fine. By the time I got to New York, she already had things under control."

"I'm not surprised."

"When will you be back? I'm sure we have things to discuss."

"Eli—Dr. Sanchez—and I will be back tomorrow."

After Marina hung up the phone, she made her way to the restaurant connected to the hotel where she and Eli had booked rooms.

Now, she settled back into her chair. The eatery was decorated in traditional style. It was also cozy, dim, and, she had quickly discovered, had a most excellent Cabernet. Not to mention what smelled like a most perfect buffalo steak. She'd ordered it grilled to a gorgeous medium rare. Fried plantains and a chopped avocado salad with pineapple completed her meal.

She looked up as Eli sank into the seat opposite her. "Everything good?" she asked, sipping from the wine.

He laughed. "Typical of my mother—she didn't even realize I was gone. Said I travel so much and to too many crazy places she can't keep track of me." He picked up his own wine and tasted it, nodding in affirmation. Then he lifted the glass. "To one hell of a getaway, Captain Alexander."

"So now it's *captain*?" She looked at him from over the edge of her glass. "I'll take it, *doctor.*"

"Now," he said, pausing to check on the status of his own steak. "Excellent," he muttered, then looked up again. His eyes settled on her, and there was a definite glint of heat therein as they lingered. "All right then, before we move on to what I'm beginning to believe is the inevitable conclusion to this adventure," Eli said, sobering, "I'd like to know a little more about the situation with you and MacNeil. Are you or are you not together, or is he with Agent Darrow—or what?"

She smiled. "Gabe and Helen were together years ago. There's probably more than a spark still between them, though. As for Gabe and me…like I said before, we're friends, we respect each other and enjoy each other's company—but there's no commitment, no expectation. We're just too busy."

Eli settled back into his chair. The corners of his eyes crinkled. "I'm very glad to hear that. I didn't want to get on the bad side of Homeland Security."

"Now it's my turn," she said, easing back into her seat as well, enjoying this sort of foreplay as much as any other. "What precisely is it that you do to terrify all those undergrads and keep them away from you? Because…other than your love for six-legged creatures, and your unerring aim with the butt of a gun, I'm not finding a lot about you that's terrifying. Oh, wait—I forgot about your driving. *That* was terrifying."

He laughed again and finished his wine. "First few days of class every year, I sit in the ento lunchroom and open up my lunch…which always consists of a lot of beetles, grubs, and worms. They're pretty crunchy, too, you know. I'm always willing to share, but for some reason…no one ever wants to. Especially the females."

"As a lover of mopanē worms myself, I can't imagine why not."

Eli shook his head, his eyes light with pleasant surprise. "Damn it, doc. You just continue to surprise me. Well, if you like mopanēs, you ought to try my deep-fried grubs in ginger sauce."

"Anytime."

Their eyes met and held.

Still smiling, Eli lifted his glass. "To dining on grubs. With you."

EPILOGUE

Lev shuddered deep inside, felt the white light and pleasant heat surrounding him. He had the sensation of weightlessness, yet that of being anchored, connected…rooted to the earth.

Gaia, he thought deep in his heart. *I am here. I am listening to Your council. I await Your guidance.*

Lush green surrounded him…cold, sharp ice and snow…the cool, salty embrace of the sea…the rough, hard stone…it was all there, like a kaleidoscope of nature.

Of Gaia.

Then he heard Her speak to him. He felt it, deep inside, like his own breath, his own thoughts. He knew it.

She will return. Your flesh and blood, my Heir…she will return. You were right to release her, but her work is not yet finished. She knows this.

Mariska will return.

FROM THE AUTHOR

Thank you for reading *Amazon Roulette*. This book was more than five years in the making, and I hope you enjoyed the sequel to *Siberian Treasure*. I sincerely hope (and intend) for it not to be another five years before the third Marina Alexander Adventure is published.

I get many questions from readers about what part of my stories are fact, and which parts are fiction, so I'd like to clear a few things up in case you're wondering.

The lost library of Ivan the Terrible is real. It hasn't been seen since shortly after his death, but it did exist. There are many rumors about what happened to it—it may have been destroyed, it may still be in a vault somewhere in Moscow.

The Tunguska Event of 1908 actually happened, and although many scientists believe the cause was related to an asteroid or piece of an asteroid hitting the earth, there is still some question. There is still mystery surrounding this event and its cause, as no one survived to tell about it.

In regards to the so-called missing copper from Northern Michigan: most geologists argue that it's not really missing, and that if there were pre-historic European traders that came for the copper, it wasn't in such great amounts. But there is some compelling evidence that suggests otherwise, including the fact that Nez Perce Indian Chief Joseph did, in fact, carry a piece of cuneiform text on a stone fragment in his medicine bag. This text has been dated to 2042 BC. Chief Joseph claimed it was from his ancestors. And then there are the round white stones found in Rock Lake in Wisconsin—I borrowed them for the cave discovered by Matt Granger, but many people believe those white stones, arranged so perfectly in large pyramids, suggest that there were, indeed, Europeans in North America long before is generally acknowledged.

In fact, the White Cloud People of Peru—a now-extinct white-skinned, blonde-haired tribe that died out in the 16th century—is certainly a possible explanation for the early European influence (as I have presented via Marina) in this book.

Additionally, scuba divers recently pulled two large ceramic jars from a 120-foot depth in Castine Bay in Maine. They appear to be ancient olive jars from the Iberian peninsula, potentially connects even further the Iberian Celts, the Phoenicians, and the Europeans of the Bronze Age.

Clearly, it's possible Marina's theory is correct.

And finally, regarding Eli Sanchez's little darlings—the beetles. They, unfortunately, are of my own creation, although I am confident that, given the environment I created for them—in the damp copper temple created millennia ago—they could have evolved as they did in *Amazon Roulette*.

Thank you again for reading, and I hope you will stick with Marina, Gabe, Helen, and the rest for their next adventure!

— **C. M. Gleason, March 2015**

ACKNOWLEDGMENTS

I could never have written this book without the help from a number of people.

Thanks, first and foremost, to Dr. Gary March—who not only asked me "how about those copper bugs?" every time he saw me (and over the last four years, it was countless)—but also helped me with all the medical and Emergency Room details—including Varden's crazy, blood-pumping injury and the tales from the Emergency Room scene shared between Brenda Hatcher and her colleague.

I owe a depth of gratitude to Drs. Patricia and Jeff Denke, both PhD entomologists, who helped me immensely with not only the laboratory details for Eli's workspace, but also helped steer me in the right direction when it came to dealing with those deadly coleopterans.

Mike Wiley, the erstwhile and tragic pinball machine restorer, is an old friend of mine who really does rebuild and fix pinball machines for a living—and is one of the best in the country. He gladly allowed me to send him to an ugly, painful death, and also gave me all the information I needed about old, rare pinball machines. And he waited patiently for this book's release to learn about his own demise.

Dr. Scott Swanson's vast knowledge about everything assisted Varden when he needed to create the antibiotic at the University of Michigan lab, and he was the one who gave me an idea of how it could possibly be done.

Bob Henderson and David Sullivan were my pilot consultants, and helped me figure out what sorts of planes the Skaladeskas could use—and still stay off the grid, so to speak.

Brian Geise used his mechanical knowhow to help Eli and Marina figure out how to jumpstart the aircraft for their escape, and without him, I think they'd still be stuck in the Amazon jungle.

Also, big thanks to Dennis Galloway and Steve Schulte, as well as MaryAlice Galloway, Erin Wolfe, and Joyce Doele for being constant sounding boards, pre-readers and beta-readers, and generally all around letting me bug them (ha!) with theories about this book for literally *years*.

I am grateful and appreciative for all the expertise the above people have provided me, and please note that any mistakes are mine alone.

C.M. Gleason is the pen name of the award-winning, *New York Times* and *USA Today* best-selling author Colleen Gleason, who has written more than thirty novels in a variety of genres. Her international bestselling series, the Gardella Vampire Hunters, is an historical urban fantasy about a female vampire hunter who lives during the time of Jane Austen.

Most recently, her Stoker & Holmes series for teens and adults has received wide acclaim from *The New York Times, Library Journal,* and is a YALSA (Young Adult Library Services Association) pick.

She has published more than thirty novels with New American Library, MIRA Books, Chronicle Books, and HarperCollins.

Her books have been translated into more than seven languages and are available worldwide.

Visit Colleen at:

colleengleason.com

facebook.com/colleen.gleason.author

Or sign up for new book release information from

Colleen Gleason at colleengleason.com/contact/

CPSIA information can be obtained
at www.ICGtesting.com
Printed in the USA
LVHW021946280920
667305LV00005B/1175